The Eye of the

Beholder

Thomas Murray

Table of Contents

Introductory Notes

This is a work of fiction. Names, characters, businesses, places, events, and incidents are either the products of the author's imagination or used in a fictitious manner. Any resemblance to actual events and persons, living or dead, is purely coincidental.

The characters (and their fans) use the measurement systems of their national locations. A conversion table is below:

1 degree Celsius = 1.8 degrees Fahrenheit
1 kilometer =0.62 miles
1 meter = 39 inches
1 centimeter = 0.39 inches
1 millimeter = 0.039 inches
1 milliliter = 0.03 ounces
1 kilogram = 2.2 pounds
750 milliliters = 0.79 quarts (a bottle of wine or vodka)

1 degree Fahrenheit = 0.55 degrees Celsius
1 mile = 1.6 kilometers
1 inch = 2.54 centimeters
1 inch = 25.4 millimeters
1 pound = 0.45 kilograms
1 ounce = 29.57 milliliters

PROLOGUE

"We have updated the top story of the hour with more details that we have since learned about the tragedy in Malibu. Mr. and Mrs. Robertson were found murdered in their Malibu home early this morning after a call to 911 at 4:12 AM by the main suspect, a young woman, who only identified herself as 'Gwendolyn' and confessed to the crime.

"According to the 911 transcript, the suspect claimed that she was a guest of the Robertsons staying at their Malibu home. Mr. Robertson came into her room and sexually assaulted her around one o'clock. His wife came in and a fight ensued. During the confusion, the suspect pulled her handgun out of her purse.

"Mr. Robertson tried to grab her arm, causing the gun to misfire and kill Mrs. Robertson. That stopped Mr. Robertson long enough for the suspect to shoot him. The suspect claims she acted in self-defense and it was Mr. Robertson who caused his wife to be shot.

"For more, we are joined at the scene with our journalist, Samantha Rodriguez. Hello, Samantha, what's the latest?"

"We're waiting for Captain Slarpniak, the Head of the LA Robbery Homicide Division, to make a statement of what they know so far. Oh, he's about to start."

"Good morning, everyone. This is what we know so far. We

estimate the time of death at around 0100 this morning for both victims. The cause of death for both was a shot to the head with a 10 mm handgun. A suspect made a call to 911 at 0412 this morning and confessed, saying it was in self-defense to a sexual assault. We have found a blood sample of the suspect that will identify her DNA. We have not found the weapon.

"Because the security system was down from about 2200, we have no idea who came or left from that time onwards. The security video does show that the last person who arrived was the suspect. And it showed that the last person to leave was the Robertsons' driver, who dropped her off by car and then left on a motorcycle a bit after 1300. The suspect has not turned herself in. We are locating all the domestic help for questioning.

"My message to the suspect who called 911 earlier this morning is this. Please come into any police station for questioning. If what you say is true, we can clear all of this up quickly. Otherwise, we'll have to find you and we will. The longer you wait, the harder it'll be for you. That's all for now. We will make more announcements as the situation develops."

"That is basically all we know now. Back to you, Anita."

CHAPTER ONE

"In an unjust society, to be wealthy and honored is a shame." Gwendolyn quoted Confucius to herself, as the yellow cab approached the front of the Malibu manor house of Ferdinand and Isabella Robertson.

He was a wealthy philandering philanthropist, who speculated in the government protected world of oil drilling with some dabbling in real estate. Most of his wealth came from his inheritances and marrying well.

Ferdinand's grandfather certainly showed imagination when he built this magnificent estate. Gwendolyn immediately recognized that his architect was inspired by the Medici's old villa at Cafaggiolo near Florence, the villa where most evenings, Michelangelo, Leonardo de Vinci, and other luminaries of Florence in the mid-1400's shared dinner with Lorenzo Medici, the great benefactor of the arts and all things humanist.

This marvel was on a side road off Anacapa View Drive in Malibu, one of the finer beach villages of southern California. The taxi had to twist and turn, rising high above the town below. About 200 yards in from the front gate, an enormous marble fountain with bronze mermaids and other sea creatures riding in the wake of Poseidon's chariot, drawn by fierce dwellers of the deep, split the driveway in two.

The driveway then disappeared into a grove of mature oak trees. Once past that, an impressive expanse of manicured Tuscan gardens and large ponds introduced the great manor itself.

That evening, Ferdinand and his darling wife, Isabella, were having a money-raising soirée to help the barefoot children of Bolivia. Gwendolyn held tightly her engraved invitation card when the taxi stopped in front of the sweeping stairway.

The waiting uniformed doorman opened Gwendolyn's door. She stepped out of the taxi, straightened her dress, and breathed in the cool air of the early evening. Her cat-green eyes attractively countered her natural Irish setter red hair. Many would describe her face as interesting - a face with many stories, both good and bad.

Her most unusual attribute was her pouting full lips. They verily cried out to be kissed. She had learned early in life the power of a timely pout from these special 'kiss me' lips.

Her slender but womanly body at 5' 9" filled out her black 'Chanel' dress nicely. The dress plus some classy heels made up her outfit, which showed what a young woman could do on less than $100 at Ross's.

But then there were her outstanding earrings and pearl necklace. They were the genuine thing; the earrings were emerald and sapphire Art Nouveau antiques that were worth well into six figures. Thirty-six natural saltwater pearls from Fiji made up her necklace. If anyone asked, she would say they were gifts from her dearly departed grandmother (on her mother's side).

Gwendolyn could easily be mistaken for a somewhat naïve aspiring girl in her very early 20's. But something in her eyes, for those who really looked carefully, told a different story. In short, she was rather mysterious, an attractive characteristic to many.

She had another talent: understanding what older wealthy men liked to hear and what attracted their attention. Gwendolyn also understood how to give deserved attention and respect to their very influential but neglected wives. If one were astute, one would gather

4

that her rather too large handbag meant that Gwendolyn intended not to leave her hosts' home that evening.

The doorman motioned to the open front doors and prepared to meet the next guest in the car behind. Gwendolyn sauntered up the stairs and entered. Another well-dressed man with white gloves asked for her invitation card. She handed him the gold-engraved card. He peered at her for a moment with a doubtful look. He examined the invitation card carefully and shrugged his shoulders. Crossing off her name, he motioned her to enter.

Inside was old-money class. A brilliant yellow glow shone in from the back veranda, which faced directly to the western sun, slowly setting into the Pacific. The floors' dark Brazilian cherry planks coordinated well with the lighter oak-paneled walls. Great antique tapestries interspersed with original oil paintings hung from the walls. The furniture was Art Nouveau.

Everyone gathered in small groups of four or five. They were the 'beautiful people' of Los Angeles. Gwendolyn recognized quite a few A-listed actors and some of the other type interspersed with power brokers from a wide stratum of the wealthy. Waiters weaved their way around with trays of dainties and excellent wines. Rather than the typical modern jazz quintet, in the corner was a chamber music group on loan from the LA Philharmonic. They were playing the joyous music of Vivaldi.

However, Gwendolyn was not there for fine wine and listening to Vivaldi's The Four Seasons. She scanned the main room for Ferdinand Robertson and found him being schmoozed by the Mayor of Los Angeles. From the sound of it, there must be an election coming up.

Since Mr. Robertson was obviously bored, she considered how to gain his attention. Fortunately, hanging on the wall in front of him was a Cezanne painting. She recognized it as The Boy in a Red Vest. She walked over to the painting and started studying it intently.

It worked. Just as Gwendolyn felt his presence, she said out loud, "He's the father of us all!"

"Yes, both Matisse and Picasso said that about Cezanne. My name is Ferdinand, the owner of this fine painting. What's your name?"

"Gwendolyn. I must compliment your wonderful taste in art. It's so rare in this part of the world."

"Well, thank you. I was born and raised, surrounded by fine art. In fact, there is a lot of excellent taste in southern California. Norton Simon, J. Paul Getty, Armand Hammer, the Timken family in San Diego, the Irvine family in Orange County, just to name a few. But I'll take any compliment from a beautiful young woman. So, what can you tell me about this painting?"

"What I like about Cezanne is that he is the bridge from the Impressionists to abstract modern art. For example, do you see how he has moved away from the strict rules of perspective? The angles make little sense from a geometric point of view. But they work in his paintings."

She was starting to get excited. "For example, look at this angle behind the boy. I mean, what is that anyway? It looks like it goes right through the wall, coming in from behind the boy's head. And look how you can already start to notice the beginning of a Cubist way of seeing things.

"Now look at the boy's eyes. You can see how the one closest to us seems realistic, but look at his left eye, further from us. That looks like something Picasso would have done."

As Gwendolyn was working up to a proper art lecture, Ferdinand interrupted, gently pulled her away. "You are a very impressive young woman! You know more about art than I do. I just like collecting them. Let's have a glass of wine and watch the sun set, shall we?"

She allowed him to lead her away. Her intention was only to intrigue him. He beckoned over a wine waiter. He picked up two glasses, giving her one of them. "Now tell me about yourself."

As she was about to start, a handsome actor who played Batman in one of those never-ending series of movies came up to them and wanted to introduce an up-and-coming director to Ferdinand. Ferdinand and Batman evidently knew each other well, so he stopped to shake hands.

Gwendolyn took this unexpected opportunity to escape. She really did not want to spend any more time with him. She had a new mission in mind: to find Isabella.

Eventually, Gwendolyn found Isabella in the garden behind the house, but not before catching the eye of Ferdinand and exchanging smiles. Gwendolyn had to make her way past the crowd admiring the sunset on the grand balcony and down the stairway to the French garden below. She noticed the stables large enough to house a polo team to the left and an eight lane Olympic-sized swimming pool to the right.

There must have been at least 200 guests gathered to help the poor little Bolivian dears. The results of the silent auction for donated artworks that evening would raise $7.3 million. It would cost the IRS at least ten times that in tax deductions. Each donated item had its own story of why it would change hands that night.

She approached the group of a dozen well-dressed pretty movie studio boy-men surrounding Isabella. They were discussing with her movie genres, hoping to understand what kind of movie ideas might interest her to invest.

Gwendolyn mingled into the group. They were bandying about basic plots, like a terrorist attack on a New York subway, a car-jacking gang in LA, astronauts lost in space, an animated comedy about a cute gong-fu fighting zombie, etc. Isabella was becoming bored and was about to move on to the next group, when she noticed Gwendolyn.

"Love your earrings, dearie. If I had to guess, I'd say they are a René Lalique design. Are they?" Isabella asked, cutting right through the movie plot nonsense like a hot knife through butter.

"You do know your Art Nouveau jewelry. He made them for my great grandmother when they met in Paris in the 1920's. I think they were lovers for a while." Gwendolyn lied.

She had bought them from a Cartier designer's private collection after her adventures in Nice for $225,000. But they were inspired by a design Lalique did for Cartier in the late 1890's. Isabella seemed quite pleased for being so astute, herself being decked out in Bulgari.

"What a wonderful history they have! Now tell me, if you had $3 million to invest in a movie idea, what would it be?"

Gwendolyn reflected a moment before answering her, "I think something totally outrageous like the adventures of a young woman art forger who runs afoul of the Russian mafia. It could be something like a Pink Panther series or in an opposite direction something like James Bond. I don't know. I'm not in the movie business."

"Now that would be a marvelous story. Right. You boys have something to think about. Now, I would like to spend some time with this charming girl. Let's start with your name."

As the circle of boy-men melted away, the two women walked toward the edge of the lawn to have a better view of the setting sun. "Gwendolyn."

"Well, Gwendolyn is such a special pretty name. Anglo-Saxon, I believe. What brings you to LA?"

"I just finished my MFA on the east coast and decided to move out to LA for something different."

"Really? My daughter, Gabriella, received her MFA in London at Goldsmiths College four years ago. She had plans to live in New York, Berlin, or Paris after she graduated. But for some reason, which I just can't understand, she moved to Asia - Thailand actually - to do some kind of charity work repairing the heads of destroyed Buddhas, as if we could not set her up with an excellent charity right here in Los Angeles. She specialized in sculpture and architecture, which I guess she is putting to some use. But Thailand? I don't even know where that is.

"Her father and I are patiently waiting for her to come to her senses. What else can we do? Too bad you two couldn't meet tonight. Maybe you could have talked some sense into her. Where did you do your studies?"

"I went to Yale where I majored in painting and minored in sculpture. I would love to meet Gabriella. How did she end up in Thailand?"

"Yale? Well, well, well. You chose well. Well, to start, she received a grant to work with local sculptors in Asia. With the additional help from western volunteers, they started to replace the heads and other body parts on the Buddha statues that trophy hunters hacked off or been destroyed by war. I say the idol worshipers got what Our Heavenly Father meant for them.

"I thought she might have returned when the grant money ran out, but now she's surviving on contributions. I suppose I should be proud of her, with her own NGO. Anyway, she is a good girl. I miss her so much." Isabella's voice broke and almost started to cry.

Pausing to look out upon her beautiful garden, Isabella continued speaking fondly about her only child, "Gabriella could never get warm enough, living like we do by the ocean, yet she would flit about the garden with barely anything on in the middle of the night. It just made no sense to me.

"During these nocturnal waltzes, she would never walk out the door, but had to climb out her window. She is such a free spirit. Free thinking in a way I never could be. In some ways, you remind me of her."

Gwendolyn allowed a period of silence to follow such emotion before continuing, "Oh, Mrs. Robertson, where I grew up, we never had such a beautiful garden. I had to show my free spirit in other ways, like... art." She caught herself before going into too much detail.

"Were you always interested in art?"

"Yes. I found it kept me out of trouble for the most part and brought calm to my restless spirit."

"Come now, what kind of trouble could a well-raised and educated young woman like yourself have ever been in?"

"Just silly teenage girl things. I went through my phases."

"Well, we all have, my dear." Isabella patted Gwendolyn on her shoulder. "What kind of art did you start doing?"

"I guess I started doodling in class as soon as I could hold a pencil, usually complex and realistic drawings. It's a wonder I ever learned to read and write. I did all the usual silly art class things, but just much better than the teacher expected. Later, as a teenager, I made money for myself in the summers at the county fairs and other summer events where I would do portraits for people.

"I never did the quick and silly cartoonish caricatures. No, I did authentic portraits that people would be proud of. I had to keep each one down to thirty minutes, because I always had long lines of people. When the lines caused the event organizers to complain, I had to have people make private appointments. I was terribly busy with that long after the event was over."

"I never see them spend more than five minutes on a portrait," Mrs. Robertson commented.

"Yes, but being only fourteen, I had no business sense. I made myself way too busy. My grandfather suggested I stop charging only $5 per portrait, and charge $50, instead. This in no way shortened the waiting list. Eventually, I charged $100 and then even $500 per portrait and allowed myself a full hour to do them. That finally shortened the waiting list.

"After some years, doing portraits bored me and I started hated doing them, even though my family needed the money. But I understood that art could be at least some kind of career I could use to support myself. That's why I decided on the path of an MFA."

"What an interesting story!" Isabella repaid Gwendolyn with a period of respectful silence before changing the subject. "Tell me, where are you staying in LA?"

"I just arrived yesterday. I'm staying at the Holiday Inn in Santa Monica until I find an apartment."

"You don't mean the one on Santa Monica Boulevard?"

"Yes, that's the one."

"That's not in Santa Monica. That's still West LA. The horrid place! I think someone was shot there a few months ago. Oh no, you cannot stay there. With those earrings? No, you simply cannot! I will talk this over with my husband right now. We have plenty of space here. You can even stay in Gabriella's room. You wait right here."

With that, Isabella walked gracefully but purposely off to the house to find her husband in the crowd, still cutting a fine figure of a woman, even at age 57. Gwendolyn thought she could be a highly successful cougar if she ever felt the need for some passion, or to embarrass her husband if he ever overstepped his bounds.

Gwendolyn figured it would take some time for Isabella to tear her husband away from the circle of starlet wanna-be's surrounding him. During this break, Gwendolyn pondered the strange daughter of the Robertsons. She tried to imagine Gabriella "flitting" around the gardens at night with little or nothing on under the full moon, maybe she imagined she was dancing nude with the Devil under the pale moonlight. Gwendolyn decided that she would indeed like to meet Gabriella, who was probably much more interesting than her parents could imagine.

Gwendolyn snatched a glass of Zinfandel from a passing waiter. The evening was turning out nicely. The sun had already set, and guests were considering their last bids for the silent auction. The cool California evening air was settling in. While putting on her wrap, she heard Isabella's approaching voice carry through the air, remonstrating with her husband about allowing a starlet-to-be get so close to him.

Ferdinand always took it in good nature, as he never stopped loving her. His love was just never meant to be exclusive. Many men love their women the same way. Isabella, like many women, knew this but could never understand it; nonetheless, she knew how to work this trait to her advantage.

"Come, come, my child. I want you to meet my husband, Ferdinand." Her voice sounded like the little bells hanging from the eaves of Chinese temples. *If I was a man of a certain age, I would love her exclusively*, thought Gwendolyn.

"All right, let's meet this wonderful young artiste," Ferdinand nearly shouted. He approached Gwendolyn and stopped a bit too close to her, being more than a bit tipsy. But he still had enough of his wits about him to pretend he had never met her.

"Dear husband, let me introduce you to Gabriella, our new artist friend, trying to settle in our majestic city of Los Angeles."

Ferdinand looked at Gwendolyn a bit startled, "Did you say your name is Gabriella?"

"No, I never said so. My name is Gwendolyn. And you must be Ferdinand." Gwendolyn blurted, taking attention away from Isabella's Freudian mistake. The growing darkness hid Isabella's embarrassment.

"That's me, but my close friends call me Ferdi. But we're not that yet. Call me what you want. My wife has been telling me about you. Love your hair. Oh, and those earrings! Now that's class. Well, what can I do for you?"

"The pleasure of meeting you is all mine, Mr. Robertson," she replied with a slow bat of her eyelashes, continuing the charade. "Since I'm not asking for anything, I'm not sure what you can do for me. Except that I must thank you for your wonderful soirée."

Mr. Robertson, even in his state, somehow had the notion that he probably should be offended in some way, but he decided not to be. Gwendolyn seemed to both vex and intrigue him in equal measure. Isabella rushed to the rescue.

"Now, remember, dear, what we discussed inside? Gwendolyn is a newly minted MFA trying to start her life in LA, just like our Gabriella will do someday when she leaves the horrid jungles of Asia. God knows why she loathes this city.

"Anyway, I was thinking that Gwendolyn here could stay in Gabriella's room for a few weeks, until she gets her feet on solid ground. We can't let her stay at any of those dangerous hotels around here. I wouldn't even let her stay at the Beverly Hills Hotel. They let just anyone come off the street and wander around there. Imagine our Gabriella staying in a hotel!" She exclaimed.

"No, we would not want that, would we, my dear?" Fernando

replied. "But still... I just don't like opening our doors to strangers."

He was about to turn and leave when he noticed a near-pout forming on Gwendolyn's lips. He froze for a few seconds. Regaining his composure with a shake of his head, he said with some irritation directed at himself, "Oh all right. But no more than two weeks."

"We're doing the right thing, my dear." Isabella said loudly to his departing back. Turning to Gwendolyn, she continued, "Now, let's discuss practical details. Our driver will take you now to pick up your things at the hotel. You must not even return there on your own, especially after dark."

"Oh, let's not fret about it, Mrs. Robertson. We can go pick up my things tomorrow during the day. I have all the essentials to get me through one night in my purse. Besides, it would be more discreet that way. Your guests might wonder who I am walking in with all my suitcases at such a late hour. We mustn't let tongues wag and get the Robertsons mentioned in the Tattler Magazine for anything but the outstanding works you do."

"Well, you modern girls prepare for anything. You are right about wagging tongues. You're so much wiser than your age. If you're fine with it, then let's go pick up everything tomorrow. From now on, just call me "Bella" like my daughter does. She usually calls me "Bella Luna", but "Bella" is fine. Come, let's enjoy the rest of this party."

Isabella took Gwendolyn's hand, and they walked back to the house. Isabella chattering away about all manner of things. Gwendolyn marveled at how easy it had been. Her meticulous preparation and acting skills had paid off. The first and most important step in her plan was successful: she was a welcome guest of the Robertsons, surrounded by their fine art.

CHAPTER TWO

Gwendolyn awoke late the next morning to the sounds of seagulls outside the window. She did not feel rested, despite the late hour. She blamed too much of the previous night's wine. Before she completely awoke, she pondered her vaguely remembered bizarre dreams that still lurked like shadows at dusk in the recesses of her mind.

The earliest dream was of Ferdinand brushing his lips with hers and whispering, "my sweet Gabriella, so glad you are home" while he stroked her breasts gently. His breath reeked alternatively of cigars and alcohol. She dismissed the dream with a quick shake of her head, admitting that Ferdinand did have his charms, but was still basically a bore.

Later there was another dream of the same thing, except it was Isabella taking the place of Ferdinand and instead of smelling of cigars and booze, she smelled of Chanel, the same perfume she had on the evening before.

Gwendolyn suppressed the urge to wake up and tried to understand it from the semi-conscious state where dreams can still make sense. She could not remember Isabella being anything but maternal toward her during the party. She dismissed it, too, with a quick shake of her head. But the third dream really confused her.

It was the same dream yet again, except this time it was Gabriella herself and she whispered: "my sweet Gwendolyn, so glad you are home." The same brushing of the lips and light pressure on her breasts. But at the end, Gabriella started sobbing into Gwendolyn's hair, "Please don't take my place!" This greatly disturbed Gwendolyn. She tried to go back to sleep to fix her dream. She tried to reach out to Gabriella and hold her, consoling her that she had no intention of doing that at all, but Gabriella was not there.

Her eyes now wide open, she laid on her back looking up at the rich tapestry that made up the canopy of the large solid four post bed. She wondered how she even knew it was Gabriella, a woman she never met. But then she noticed on a side table a photo in an antique baroque frame of the three of them staring at her, all three with beguiling smiles taken years before in happier days. At this, Gwendolyn decided she had to start her day and get straight to work.

Gwendolyn headed to the large attached bathroom to take the shower she would normally take in the evening. She had been in no state for showers the night before, not even remembering getting into bed completely nude.

She was not in the shower more than a minute when Ferdinand's chipper voice called to her from the bathroom's open doorway: "Sleepy head has finally risen!"

He must have been listening at the closed bedroom door for when she got out of bed. Gwendolyn shouted back for him to get out and give her some privacy. She heard Isabella echoing her request in the hallway outside her bedroom door, but in a surprisingly lighthearted way for him to do the same. *God! What have I gotten myself into?* Gwendolyn thought. Ferdinand left her alone.

When she arrived in the kitchen looking for some coffee, Isabella was there, offering her some breakfast. Ferdinand had disappeared into his office down the hall. Since it was nearly noon, Gwendolyn politely refused. She just wanted some coffee and maybe some orange juice to perk herself up.

After Gwendolyn sipped some of the fine Guatemalan coffee,

Isabella asked her, "Are you feeling better now? You don't look well rested. Did you not sleep well?"

"I had some strange dreams, Isabella. I mean, Bella. That's all. I guess I'm not used to the bed yet, or something. Your wonderful wine did not help my sleep either. I only have myself to blame."

"Ah, you remembered. You cannot imagine how good it makes me feel when you use the nickname my precious daughter gave me." Isabella paused with her eyes closed. "Well, now. What would you like to do today, my dear?"

"If it's not too much trouble, I would like to gather my things from the motel and start looking for a place to rent. I don't want to trouble you anymore than I have to."

"Our driver will take you. I would take you myself, but I loathe leaving my paradise here. Driving here is dreadful. I only go to LA if I absolutely must. The next time I must go is for the BAFTA (British Annual Film and Theater Awards) events coming up in about two weeks, but I so enjoy those."

"Our driver is completely at your disposal. I will tell him to use the Bentley convertible. The only way for a beauty like you to travel in southern California is in a convertible with your beautiful hair blowing in the wind. Do you have sunglasses?"

"Yes, thank you. That is truly kind of you, but I can just call a taxi."

"What are you talking about? The things you say! A taxi? You have no idea who has sat in that seat before you. No, I'll not hear of it!"

"No, really, I don't mind taking taxis at all. In New York, it's the only way to get around." Oh, how she wanted to escape them for a while, and it was only the first day.

"Not another word! Daphne? Tell Lorenzo to get the Bentley ready."

Gwendolyn resigned herself to having her hair blown into a mess in the Bentley. "Well, all right, Bella. Thank you again. I guess I'm ready to go now." Gwendolyn noticed the profound effect of calling her "Bella."

Isabella walked her to the car waiting outside the front door. Lorenzo, the driver, wore an absurd black leather driver's uniform that looked more like what motorcycle racers wear, except for the black leather cap. That reminded her of certain bars in West Hollywood and certain pride parades.

"What do you think about his chauffeur's uniform?" Isabella asked Gwendolyn. She had a strange quizzical look that meant it was not a rhetorical question.

"Very imaginative. I feel somehow that I should be getting into a sidecar."

"He designed it himself. I always thought it silly, but he looks good in it."

That he does, my dear Isabella. That he does.

Lorenzo was indeed a good-looking man in his early 30's with long jet-black hair tied up in the back. He was quite proud of his wonderful moustache. When he spoke with his deep Italian accent, Gwendolyn thought it was no wonder that rich women ended up in bed with their drivers and grooms like Lady Chatterley's Lover and her Sir John.

"Where to, Madame?"

"Take her to this address, pick up her things, and generally go wherever she asks. There is no rush as Mr. Robertson and I will be going nowhere today. Take the top down and let our pale guest enjoy our California sunshine. Just make sure she is back for Sherry Hour."

Lorenzo did so and opened the rear door with a flourish that showed he really enjoyed his job. Gwendolyn almost blurted out, "Oh, let me sit up front with you." But no, she was doing so well with Isabella. A stupid mistake like that would have been unprofessional. Flirting with her benefactor's boy toy would be the quickest way to be thrown out.

Off they drove. As the gate closed behind them and the sun was at its finest, Gwendolyn could feel a great weight lift off her shoulders. She surprised herself with a great sigh. She closed her eyes to relax and speed her recovery from the night before.

Being the sensitive kind, she noticed that something really was not quite right with Lorenzo. Something was bothering him. Had he been crying? Maybe she would find out later. And then maybe not. Besides, the sound of the wind as the car raced down the hills toward the ocean below forbade any kind of talk.

Gwendolyn had a most deep dreamless nap. She only awoke to the traffic noises as they approached Santa Monica where the Pacific Coast Highway turns into Ocean Avenue. She felt much better and would have loved to change places with those playing Frisbee in the park overlooking the beach below.

The shady trees, the deep green grass, and the ocean breeze all beckoned her to leave her current craziness for the more down-to-earth craziness of southern California beach life. She unconsciously already had her hand on the door handle. The ringing of Lorenzo's cell phone interrupted her confused thoughts.

"Please, Signorina, may I take this call?" Lorenzo asked almost mournfully.

"Well, of course." she stammered, being nonplused by such an unexpected question.

Starting to tear up as he raised the phone to his ear, Lorenzo cried out, "Where were you last night?"

The reply on the other line made him shudder.

"No! All right, I won't ask. But please come back!"

He almost drove through a red light. "Why not just pull over, Lorenzo?" Gwendolyn asked.

He made a quick wag of the head and drove slowly. She had to listen to Lorenzo plead with his mate for the next half hour. *God! She's such a bitch!* she thought. *Give him a chance.* She hated to see (or hear) a man grovel to a woman. Trying to ignore the histrionics from her driver, Gwendolyn watched the craziness of Santa Monica, instead.

"I just don't understand what you see in him! All right, all right, you can still see him sometimes, but you must come back to me! No! Please don't say such things! You're breaking my heart!"

This continued until they almost reached the hotel.

Lorenzo finished the call, "Oh thank you, Jonathan! You know I love you so much! I'll see you there as soon as I can."

She turned and stared at him with her mouth open in astonishment. *Oh, God! Why didn't I see that coming?* she asked herself. *Why are the gorgeous guys usually gay? I doubt Isabella knows about this. Would a devote Catholic not fire him for his perverted fornicating ways?*

Lorenzo hung up when they pulled up to the front door of the hotel. Gwendolyn ran in, retrieved her things, and checked out. He put her bags in the trunk. Noticing how upset he still was, she told him, "Look, Lorenzo, I know you have to go now to... uhhh, Jonathan. Drop me off at the LACMA (Los Angeles County Museum of Art). Meet me in front of the museum in four hours."

Lorenzo was so relieved that he almost hugged her. But stopped himself and drove off with an enormous smile. Pulling up to the museum entrance, Gwendolyn was already out of the car before the car stopped.

"See you later." she yelled, as she darted up the front stairs. But he was already half a block away. She ran into the museum courtyard and hurried out the back. She made for a little one-bedroom apartment about a block north. The key was already in her hand when she arrived at the stone entrance and let herself in. This was where she had already set up shop for her current artistic project.

Gwendolyn had chosen this apartment not because of its elegant classy building, though that was nice. She had chosen it because it was just behind the art museum and very quiet on Metropolitan Plaza, deep within a complex of stately apartment buildings from a bygone era just north of West 6th Street's Hancock Park. She needed both to complete her task.

The living room had a balcony facing south over the park-like grounds of the complex. A large white leather sectional sofa filled a third of the room. A large black lamb skin nearly covered it. Her easel and art supplies occupied most of the dining area. She had a desk, but no television, which she never watched anyway.

A queen bed filled up her bedroom, though she never planned to sleep there. The kitchen was empty of food, for the same reason that she would never eat there. She did make sure there were two excellent wine glasses, specially designed for complex reds. She could not imagine why she would need a second one, but it was always best to be prepared.

The first thing Gwendolyn did after entering her apartment was to open the double doors that led out to the balcony, letting in the warm southern California air. Then, knowing she did not have much time, she pulled her cell phone out and quickly connected it to her top-of-the-line graphics design computer. She uploaded the photos from the previous evening.

When anyone saw her with her phone at the party the night before, they thought she was checking text messages. But in fact, she had been taking various photos of the soothing The Woods Near Chateau Marneux painted by Camille Pissarro in 1870.

Pissarro was one of her favorite artists. It was ironic that this very famous French artist was actually born on St. Thomas, one of the US Virgin Islands (when it was still a part of Denmark), which should make him an 'American' artist, or even 'Danish.' Gwendolyn remembered with a smile when her literary friend, Tomas, pointed that out to her during her college days. Always ready with a retort, she reminded him that his favorite (Polish) author, Joseph Conrad, was born in Russian territory at the time, in what is today Ukraine. Did that make him Russian or Ukrainian? She missed the banter of her college days. The conversations might have been silly, but they never were banal.

She had a state-of-the-art color analysis program that could dissect the colors of the beautiful The Woods Near Chateau Marneux to their exact pixel detail. It was so good at what it did, that even cell phone photos were fine. She began the process of color dissection for each photo, which would take three hours to complete.

Gwendolyn sat on her balcony overlooking the quiet wooded streets below, closed her eyes and imagined herself walking in the woods near Chateau Marneux. She loved the painting and marveled that it was one of the 1500 paintings that disappeared during the German occupation of Pissarro's studio north of Paris during the Franco-Prussian War between 1870 and 1871.

It reminded her of growing up in southeastern Pennsylvania. Her father had taken her and her brothers for hikes on the Horseshoe Trail, a network of trails that fed into the Appalachian Trail. In mid-to-late October the leaves would turn into a symphony of magnificent reds and yellows.

The forest would be so thick that the trees would form a canopy, a leafy tunnel, above the trails. Fallen leaves would create a carpet below that would produce a slight crunchy sound as one walked upon them.

But ever with an artist's eye, Gwendolyn reminded herself that Pissarro's autumn forests tended more to the yellow spectrum rather than to the reds of Pennsylvania. The complete mapping of the spectrogram would solve this problem. To be successful, she would have to recreate not just the look, but also the feel of the painting.

She was a master of her peculiar art. Her work had fooled the eyes of curators from the most famous museums in the world. Giles would provide the paints and canvases of the period and the pedigree to explain their existence in the art market. She would recreate the masterpiece that Giles' hired her to do. He would take care of the rest.

She remembered how she first met Giles. As a young art student, she would practice painting by recreating as close as possible the work of the masters at the New York Metropolitan Art Museum, a practice that so many art students have done in art museums since the Renaissance.

Once when she was painting a Vermeer, a strange, well-dressed middle-aged man watched her paint for hours, standing right behind her. After about a week, she had completed it. The man still present, as he had been every day she was there, told her to sign it with Vermeer's signature. That challenged her artistic ability, so she reproduced that exactly, too.

As they both stood back admiring her work, he sighed and offered to buy it from her. At first, she declined, especially since she had signed Vermeer's signature and not her own, as she normally would have done. But then he offered her $100,000, a sum that could pay her entire tuition for her MFA and her living expenses for the program's two years. It was too tempting for a girl who had grown up only knowing money problems, not to mention one who chose a career that probably would not change things much for her financially.

"I can't sell you something that is a copy of someone else's work." Gwendolyn replied. "This is not a forgery, but a study. Especially since I signed his name and not mine. It just would not be right."

"Oh, I know it could never pass as the genuine thing." He assured her in his English boarding school accent. "I would never even pretend it's a real Vermeer. You have used modern paints and canvas. It would be discovered immediately. Besides, the real one is right there, hanging on the wall, as seen by millions every year."

"Then, why are you offering me such an enormous amount to buy it?" Her tone of voice revealed her annoyance with English accents. They sounded to her so arrogant with their pathetic dysfunctional royal family.

"I'm not buying your painting. Oh no, no, not at all!" he answered. "Think of it as an investment in your career."

He noticed her disdain for his accent and added, "Don't let my accent fool you. I grew up a Royal Air Force brat and, by putting me in a series of British boarding schools, this accent is the only thing my parents gave me. It turns out it's worth something. But everything I am today came from my own hard work, just like with you."

She rolled her eyes and said, "If one must speak with a British accent, then at least speak with a Scottish, Irish, or even a Cockney accent. At least that would be more endearing. I have ancestors buried in old churchyards across the Hudson, who died killing redcoats during the Revolution."

"Well, now if you want to get personal about it, then perhaps we should end our conversation and forget about the whole thing. It would be a shame, since I genuinely believe you are well worth the investment. But we must get along, too. In case you're wondering, I have no interest in you other than professionally. My preference is for young Asian men if you must know."

Gwendolyn apologized with a quick smile that hid her fear that she had poked him a bit too hard with her last comment, "Well, that's all right. We can't decide our upbringing. I speak with a Philadelphian accent. Don't ask me how I pronounce the word w-a-t-e-r."

He smiled in return, "Nor ask me why I pronounce the a's differently when I say the words 'potato' and 'tomato'."

"Fine, fair enough. Just what do you mean by 'investing' in my career?"

"You have a wonderful talent that with continued hard work you could develop into a highly successful career. There are only a few artists with your skill and eye. You can capture the look and feel of a painting exactly. Believe me, I know. It is my job to know who the best are."

"Just what is your 'job' anyway?" she asked.

"The less you know, the better. Over the coming months, I will give you, shall we say, assignments. I will pay you well if I cannot distinguish your paintings from the originals. They will be well-known paintings, hanging in the world's best galleries. I would never try to pass them off as the originals. They're just for practice."

"For practice?"

"Yes, they will represent a wide range of genres and periods. I need to know what you're good at."

"Fine, I guess I can give it a try."

"Great. One more thing: you are to keep our connection secret from everyone and do my assignments discreetly. This can only work if you can promise me this."

"Sure, no problem."

Gwendolyn lived in a small studio in New Haven, near Yale, where she also did her artistic work. She had no time for boyfriends and the studio was too small to entertain friends. They always met at the many coffee houses instead.

Giles wrote a check for her right there in the museum and they exchanged contact information. The check cleared in her bank and she completed the degree she always feared she could never finish. His assignments arrived about every three months. They were always famous paintings in galleries around the world. He paid her travel expenses, always first class and five stars. The least he ever paid her for these "assignments" was $50,000 for a Kandinsky work on paper that took her about four hours to do. Upon graduation, she started working for Giles St. John, nearly 6 years ago.

Since then, they would meet clandestinely in a public place about once every few months. He would give her projects that were in private collections in the homes of the wealthy. To complete the jobs successfully, she had to study the paintings closely and in person. It would take her about two weeks to complete his projects. Giles would provide the period-correct materials and the entrance into their homes, like an invitation to a private function. The rest was up to her.

After Gwendolyn completed her painting came the part she disliked the most. She had to replace the original painting with her forgery. Giles would sell the original to unscrupulous art collectors. The hapless owners were not art experts and would not notice the forgery.

Giles had other experts who could reproduce the frame exactly with wood and paint from the same time as the painting's material. If the original owners ever did notice years later, the insurance company would pay the painting's insured value and she would be long gone.

Giles paid her from $250,000 to over a million, depending on the value of the painting. He would sell them to emirs, potentates, and oligarchs for far more. She enjoyed the artistic challenge and the money if not the actual thieving part. She had quickly learned to appreciate the good life. Living like a starving bohemian artist lost its charm.

The sound of her software completing its analysis brought her back to the present. She looked at her watch and saw that she only had about an hour to meet Lorenzo at the front door of LACMA. She wanted to study a few paintings at the museum before then.

The canvas was already stretched on a frame made from wood and nails from the late 1860's. Gwendolyn had all the required brushes, and most importantly, the oil paint from the same period. It always amazed her how Giles could find old inventories from paint companies defunct for sometimes several hundred years.

Gwendolyn visited LACMA to review Pissarro's brushwork from the painting The Path to Les Pouilleux, Pontoise. She studied closely the painting's brush strokes, the value and tone of the colors. But it was the order of the brush strokes that most interested her. This would form the strategy of how she would paint her re-creation.

Pissarro did not start at one end of the canvas and work toward the other; rather he painted across the whole canvas at once. It seemed like he was trying to get down as much of the basic forms and motifs of the subject as soon as possible, then fill in the details later. She would have to paint it the same way.

After examining the painting, even with a magnifying glass, Gwendolyn was sure what the correct strategy would be. She would return there often over the next two weeks. She did not have the luxury of crumpling up the canvas and throwing it away if she made a mistake. It had to be perfect the first time.

She walked out the front of the museum and stood on Wilshire Boulevard at the scheduled time. Lorenzo pulled up right away.

Before he could jump out to open the door for her, she was already in the backseat.

"Where to, Signorina?" He asked brightly with the most cheerful of smiles.

"First, tell me. Did everything go well with Jonathan?"

"Oh yes. Everything is fine now," he replied, almost blushing.

Oh, dear God! With a blush like that, it would endear him to the Pope himself, thought Gwendolyn. "Glad to hear that." She said. "Your secret is safe with me. Look, we must get our story straight every time we go out looking for apartments. I have my reasons for not wanting them to know where I'm looking and you certainly have your reasons for not wanting them to know where you go, right?"

Lorenzo went pale at the thought of Isabella finding out. "Yes, of course, Signorina. What will it be for today? Think of something!"

"All right, fine. Let's say today, after picking up my things, I went looking around Venice Beach. You waited a few hours and then we came back. How does that sound?"

"Venice Beach? That's one of my favorite places. Sure, let's make it Venice Beach." he agreed.

"Then we're all set."

"Andiamo!" He yelled to the wind with a smile. He accelerated down Wilshire Boulevard, throwing her back against the plush leather seat.

CHAPTER THREE

"So, how was your search, my dear?" asked Isabella.

"Oh, it was fine, but it's too early to say for sure, Bella. I'll tell you all about it at dinner." Gwendolyn replied.

"Dinner will be served at eight. Our dinners are a bit formal for southern California. We dress up somewhat for them. I am sure you have something nice to wear?"

"Yes, I do."

"I sure hope Lorenzo drove carefully."

"He is an excellent driver and knows LA very well."

"We will meet on the balcony for some sherry and cheese in about an hour to watch the sun set."

"Oh, that would be great. That leaves me time for a quick swim in your lovely pool if that's all right."

"Please do! That wonderful pool hasn't had a beautiful young woman in it since Gabriella left home. It's perfect for doing laps. Perhaps I will come sit by the pool and join you."

"I'll see you there." There had to be some perks to her job. Doing laps in the late afternoon California sun above the Pacific was surely one of them.

The water was a bit too cool, but she just dove in. She would have preferred to swim in the nude as God intended and as our great ancestors once did, but things were already getting weird. No need to hurry them along that path. Isabella sat down on one of the divans and watched her.

"My, you're a fit and fine example of a young woman!" Isabella exclaimed when Gwendolyn emerged from the pool. "You and Gabriella have so much in common. She was her high school's swimming champion for the last three years before she graduated. Would you like to lay awhile in the sun?"

"No, thanks, Bella. I never enjoyed sunbathing. I think I'll take a shower and get ready for some of your fine sherry," she said as she walked toward the house.

"Sensible girl. Will see you in about twenty minutes on the back terrace!" Isabella called out after her.

Sensible girl? Wish my parents could've heard that. Gwendolyn thought to herself. *High school swimming champion? My high school only had a fishing pond where we could only swim for a few weeks out of the school year.*

She took a quick shower and dressed in the best she could pull together in fifteen minutes. She did not know these people and did not want to be late. Who knew how they might react? The upper classes were always so strange to her.

She strode confidently onto the balcony with a minute to spare. The Robertsons were already on their second drink. A barman stood behind their elegant bar to the right of the French doors that opened onto the expansive balcony. There was a large spread of light yellow Iberian almonds, Greek Kalamata olives, dried Turkish figs, dried California apricots, and cheeses from across Europe. The view was just as magnificent as the previous evening.

"Ah, here is our resident artiste!" Ferdinand called out when he saw her.

"Good evening to you both, kind benefactors," Gwendolyn replied.

"Pierre, pour our guest the best you have on offer," Ferdinand said to the bartender.

28

"Already on the way, sir," he replied walking over to Gwendolyn with a sherry glass full of the beautiful amber liquid.

She thanked him and took a sip. Sherry can be great when it is aged exactly right. This Amontillado was sailing close to being a wonderfully aged tawny port. It reminded her of her undergraduate days when she was assigned to eat in the law school's cafeteria.

The law students always had a Sherry Hour before everyone would retire for dinner in the adjacent great stone dining hall with high wood buttressed ceilings. Her friend would play jazz piano in the corner while everyone would unwind. She was all of eighteen then and quickly learning the wonders of being an adult.

"I suggest you sip it with a Turkish fig," Ferdinand offered.

"Oh, you're so right. Taste is nurtured with experience, as is anything else in life."

"Let me guess... Dylan Thomas?"

"No."

"Then, it must be Walt Whitman or Thoreau?"

"No. It was me. I just said it," Gwendolyn realized she could never take him seriously.

"If you say so, dear Gwendolyn. Come over here and enjoy the view. The sun still has eighteen minutes before he sinks into the realms below the waves, which have risen up to receive him as they have since the day our great Benefactor created the earth." He motioned behind him toward the incredible sunset.

Like Ferdinand, Gwendolyn took a somewhat odd interest in knowing at what minute the sun set and rose, when the tides were at their lowest and highest, and at what phase would the moon be each night. She had her own names for all the phases of the moon. For example, she named the crescent moon already rising in the evening sky: a "Cheshire Cat" moon. She imagined it was the great Cat in the sky smiling down upon humanity.

Ferdinand raised his glass to the setting sun, "Let's toast the earth spinning on its axis!"

They all stood silently, watching the great orange orb disappear into the distant watery horizon. Ferdinand broke the silence. "So, our young artiste, how was your day exploring the mean streets of LA?"

"I'll tell you all about it at dinner."

"Dinner is not for chatting, my dear. That's what Sherry Hour is for." Isabella admonished.

"Um, ah ... OK." Gwendolyn would have to create a story quicker than expected. "Lorenzo took me to the hotel where I picked up my things. Then, I thought it'd be interesting to see what the beach towns had to offer. Wouldn't it be nice to have a little studio with a balcony above the beach? Of course, everything I saw was way beyond my budget. But I'll keep looking."

She took a long sip of sherry to gather her thoughts and continued. "Wherever I end up will be fine. I did enjoy walking down the boardwalk of Venice Beach. You meet the craziest people there. For example, a young man gathered quite a crowd by hammering long nails into his nostrils. They were real nails, about four or five inches long. I checked them out afterwards." She waited for the expected response to that one. She really had seen that on a visit there a few years before.

"He did what?" exploded Isabella. "You see, Ferdinand? This is why I hate leaving our beautiful home. There is just too much craziness out there." She said waving her arm in an arc in the general direction of the magnificent city laying to the east.

"Go on, dear friend," Ferdinand encouraged Gwendolyn. He clearly took delight in seeing his wife shocked.

"Well, there were mimes and people posing as statues and mannequins. The body builders had their section on the beach. There was also a row of pot clinics with touts outside trying to persuade everyone that they needed to sign up right then to get their prescription filled there and not at the clinic next door. Some of them were quite aggressive. They probably needed a prescription themselves."

"Really?" Isabella asked. "Have you ever tried it? What does it do? I'm curious."

"Hmm, I really don't know, Bella," lied Gwendolyn, knowing full well that within ten miles of where they were standing grew the world's best pot. She had to give it up as it was just too powerful. One puff would send her into a semi-comatose state for hours.

Her parents told her that back in the 1970's they had to first spend quite some time picking out all the seeds and then smoke for several hours before achieving any high worthy of the name. And if they missed a seed, it would pop when the flame reached it, much to everyone's amusement. She never could tell if her parents were just kidding.

"Now, my dearest, if you are curious, with all of your ailments, I'm sure we can easily arrange a prescription for you to try," offered Ferdinand.

"My God, Ferdinand, the crazy things you say!"

The sherry clearly was having its effect. Gwendolyn understood booze and could (usually) control herself better with it compared to anything else. She was also determined not to overdo it, not wanting anymore bizarre dreams like the night before. This time, if she felt a hand on her breast while asleep, she would break it. Oh no, she corrected herself. Breaking hands would immediately end her 'project'. Even so, she decided to control her consumption that evening.

"But seriously, did you see any place you liked?" Ferdinand asked.

"I saw a few studios, er… one-bedrooms not too far from the beach. But I'm not sure I want to be near the craziness of the place. It may be distracting."

"As you may know, I am quite familiar with the LA real estate market, granted on a different level than one-bedroom Venice Beach apartments. However, I do know a few agents excellent at finding the kind of place you would like. Remind me to find their cards after dinner."

"Well, um… that would be immensely helpful. Thank you very

much," Gwendolyn lied. The last thing she wanted was to waste more time shaking off Ferdinand's lackeys. She hoped he would forget.

They bantered about silly things until the hour ended. The butler announced that dinner would be served in the dining room in fifteen minutes. The Robertsons left to freshen up. She spent that time alone on the balcony, admiring her Cheshire Cat smiling down on her from on high.

Dinner was indeed a formal affair. Isabella wore a Valentino dress and Ferdinand dressed in a finely tailored dinner jacket with a well-tied ascot, a deep blue and gold tartan. He sat at one end of the thirty plus foot long dining table and Isabella at the other. Gwendolyn sat between them on the side where she could see her Pissarro on the wall in the hallway, visible through the open dining room door.

They were right. Dinner was not for chatting. The closest person to her was fifteen feet away. She imagined there must be a lot of conversation when the table sat its full complement of twenty plus guests. She admired the enormous chandelier above the table and the candelabras placed all around.

When she told her hosts that the dinner was a five-star experience, they corrected her. Their chef 'only' had two Michelin stars, so it was only a two-star experience. Not one star more.

Though the portions were not large, the sheer number of dishes made up for it. That was how the Robertsons ate every night, yet neither one was fat. In fact, they looked good for any age.

Gwendolyn thought it very odd to not talk at dinner. The courses were spread out so that one could relate an entire day's adventure before the next course. She spent the interminable silences studying her beloved Pissarro, studying the essence of the color and style that she needed to perfect quickly.

When they finished the last glass of finely matured port, it was already past nine thirty. Ferdinand invited her to the study for a nightcap of exceptionally fine cognac. Isabella had already announced she was going to bed.

Gwendolyn did not think she could handle any more of him that evening, so she went for a walk alone around their gardens. "ALONE" she emphasized trying to hide her exasperation with him when he offered to show her a special night flower that bloomed only under the moon light.

"Well, then maybe tomorrow evening?" he asked hopefully.

"Yes, maybe. That would be nice." She became a little friendlier, realizing he had totally forgotten about the real estate agents.

Gwendolyn needed to walk in the cool Californian night air to clear her head from the booze that had slowly crept up on her after a dinner with her hosts. Two glasses of sherry during Sherry Hour, three very generous pours of excellent Cabernet at dinner, and two wonderful glasses of port added up to well over a bottle of wine just for her. Isabella had about twice that, and Ferdinand three times more. It was a normal weekday dinner in Malibu.

Of course, no one worked in that household. If people like the Robertsons were awake before noon, the next day was not all wasted. Gwendolyn later understood that after four decades of practice, Ferdinand always appeared as if the booze had little effect on him. Incredibly every morning at 0600 he swam a mile in their lap pool, no matter what time he went to sleep or how much booze he had the night before. He probably took a nap later, but still, it impressed her. Ah, the life of the idle rich!

After dinner, Gwendolyn enjoyed an hour wandering around their maze of flowers and topiaries, communing with her favorite feline moon god. He was still grinning down at her, though he had gotten up and moved to the other side of the ornate tapestry that made up the night sky.

She considered the crazy life she had chosen for herself. Few people were paid as much as she was to do her life's passion. Still, she sometimes wondered if there was a better way, like developing her own art. She shook her head. *Banish the thought! It's not fun being a starving artist. Been there; done that.*

She understood the art world all too well. She had proved it dozens of times that a contemporary artist can create a painting that would rival a Picasso, a Pollock, or even a Pissarro, but without a recognized name painted in the lower right corner, it would probably not sell for more than $1000 at a small struggling gallery. If artists sold most everything they created, they would have to make do on an annual income of about $25,000. If they were lucky, they could double that by teaching art classes at a local college.

Gwendolyn sold her work for ten or more times that. Yet, it irritated her to no end that if she reproduced one of the famous paintings exactly, the difference between $10,000 and $10 million was the artist's signature. Most art buyers could not distinguish the artistic value between graffiti by a troubled teen, a painting by a chimpanzee or a horse, and a Jackson Pollock.

They would need a renowned art critic to tell them which one was trendier to have over their fireplace and thus be able to brag to their fellows. There were times when each of them was in vogue. It was certainly a bizarre world she worked in.

Gwendolyn spent most of the rest of the hour putting together a plan of attack for the canvas sitting in her apartment. She had one chance to get it right. The Robertsons had to go somewhere the next morning. She would spend that time studying minutely Pissarro's wonderful painting. Only a week and a half of time remained.

Her support team needed her to get a tiny sample of the frame and its paint, so they could reproduce the frame exactly. She had a gadget that could extract a small bit of wood with its paint from the frame at the push of a button.

Gwendolyn also had an app that precisely measured the dimensions of an object her cell phone camera captured. She would pass the frame sample and a flash drive with the frame's photo and dimensions to a young colleague of Giles the next morning at LACMA. She guessed his name Ralfred was a combination of Ralf and Alfred.

She only hoped to keep it together while dealing with the crazy

Robertsons. Gwendolyn had to continue flawlessly playing the grateful struggling naïve artist, a young damsel in a distressed situation.

She had learned to play so many roles in her young life that this one was not a challenge. She had thought years before that if being a struggling artist did not work out, she could easily switch to being a struggling actress.

When Gwendolyn went to sleep, she propped a chair up against the door. She needed her sleep that night. She awoke once when someone tried to open the door about an hour later. The door remained closed. She turned over and fell back to sleep with a smile and a sigh.

CHAPTER FOUR

Gwendolyn awoke to the sun streaming in through the curtains and the birds merrily chirping outside her windows. She had been dreaming the whole night about her painting. This was the day she would start and, except for late afternoons returning to the manor house - would not want to miss Sherry Hour! – she would finish within eleven days.

The Robertsons did not often leave their wonderful wonderland overlooking the Pacific. But when they did, it usually was for an important social function, a "soirée" as Isabella would call them. They had one such event that would take most of the next Friday and probably late into the evening: the BAFTA awards. This would happen in twelve days' time. It would be the best chance for her colleagues to make the switch.

She threw the covers off and leapt from bed like a child on Christmas morning. She started feeling the buzz she got when she would soon put paint to canvas. Even after the previous night's wonderful dinner, she was very hungry from her mind working all night.

In the kitchen was the chef of the same inspired dinner from the evening before. She accepted his offer to make her a proper breakfast, knowing she would not stop painting until late afternoon when she had to return.

Gwendolyn wandered through the garden, waiting impatiently for nearly forty-five minutes before her Michelin starred breakfast was served at the kitchen table. She felt bad for finishing it in less than fifteen minutes. As she was sipping her espresso, she noted that except for the Pacific morning breeze, the house was silent as if it were empty. Gwendolyn used to always fill the void of silence with music, but with some age, she learned to appreciate the sounds of nature that most call "silence."

Isabella had insisted that she feel free to use Lorenzo's services whenever she wanted, for as long as she wanted. If they had to use a car for anything that came up suddenly, they could always drive "that old" Ferrari in the garage (a 1965 Ferrari 275 GTB/C in mint condition). Gwendolyn had noticed it and several other museum quality classic cars when she had walked past the garage.

She had already told Lorenzo the day before to be ready early in the morning for a long day of house searching and time spent viewing the art at LACMA. She was excited to embark on her spiritual journey with Pissarro.

Lorenzo dropped her off at LACMA's front door. She told him not to return until 4 PM, which would allow them to escape rush hour and Gwendolyn to not miss Sherry Hour. As usual, she passed through the Expressionists' galleries on her way to her studio. She was startled to find Giles sitting on a bench taking in the beauty of Pissarro's Effet de Pluie.

He always wore a disguise. Usually it would be a beard and sunglasses. But whenever she met him, they were always in different styles. For example, his hair could be shaved, bald, long-haired, blond, grey, white, etc. Gwendolyn believed that the first time they met he was his true self, but she was never sure of it. Today he had thinning grey hair, with wrap around shades.

She sat down next to him and whispered, "What are you doing here?"

"Isn't it sardonic?" he replied, referring to the painting and ignoring her question. "Usually, his paintings are full of light, using all the colors of his palette. And yet with this one, it seems he only used a black ink pen. Nonetheless, the artist managed to portray a rainy day exactly, relying more on the energy and motion of the rain than on any color arrangement."

She should have known better. Giles never answered anything directly without first meandering through some unfinished thought. "Yes, of course. It is not the first time I have studied this painting. Forgive my impatience. I am anxious to get started." She started to get up.

His hand held her arm firmly. She sat down again. "My dear Gwendolyn, I am here to mention that your next project has a narrow window of opportunity. I have recently learned that the owners of our desire will be leaving the country soon for an extended stay abroad. You only have five weeks to complete it counting from now, not the six months we originally thought."

"Have you ever considered simple burglary?" she asked with exasperation.

"Dearest," came the patient answer. "I'll pretend I didn't hear that. After all, we are not criminals! I will meet you in about a week from today to give you the details. Be prepared to deliver our current desire during the BAFTA awards next Friday evening and to check out of LA at the same time. I know that takes away the 'down time' you had planned to visit Machu Picchu. Sorry about that, but at least you will not be doing a Kandinsky. I have something more challenging in mind."

He raised one eyebrow and added: "I'm confident that you can pull it off with time for the paint to dry. I will organize the pickup on the evening of next Friday."

Barely hiding her disappointment, Gwendolyn nodded her head in agreement.

"By the way, we have gained unwanted attention. So, be careful. I have been followed recently by some Russian competitors I've had the misfortune of meeting before. They're now following you. See the older well-dressed man in the corner by the Van Gogh? He has been following you since you entered the museum. I bet you'll find him walking his dog or, God knows, maybe even a cat over near your studio, trying to figure out your schedule and where your studio is."

Her disappointment turned into alarm as she discretely turned her head to look at him.

"No matter how discreet I've always been, the longer one stays in this business, sooner or later one becomes known anyway. There's nothing to be done about it. We simply must play smarter and stay one step ahead. I can't guess how much they know about what we're doing, but we must be careful and complete our project before they learn anymore.

"But let's not become distracted. Be prepared to join the event the Petersons are planning in two and a half weeks in La Jolla. I warn you that Mr. Peterson is a connoisseur of incredibly old rum and well-seasoned cigars."

Regaining her composure, "Great! I love them both. Sounds like you're jealous you weren't invited."

"Who says I wasn't invited? Now get to work," he said as he lifted her up by the arm and gave her a slight nudge toward the exit. "By the way, I still think it extremely unseemly for a young woman to smoke cigars."

"Don't worry," she replied starting to walk away. "When I was a little girl, my mother smoked a pipe. And besides, remember what Freud said: 'sometimes a cigar is just a cigar.'"

His words, "Oh, give me a break!" trailed behind her. She also noticed that the Russian gentleman, dressed in a luxurious tweed double-breasted suit with an ornate walking stick, followed her as well. He obviously was an Anglophile, dressing in a stereotype that only the Russians could create. It was easy to lose him. She went to the women's room on the ground floor, opened a window, and climbed outside.

Gwendolyn returned to her studio and spent the first hour

meditating on the great works of Pissarro, getting into the spirit of his creative genius. It was paramount that she grasped this on a subconscious level. She had learned the technique when she had studied Chinese art in Taiwan from a Chan Buddhist who perfected his art by forging Tibetan tantric mandalas.

After Gwendolyn was sure she was ready, she rose and started her work. First, she mixed the specially prepared antique oil paint, according to the color map her computer created. She only used the computer to get the colors precisely right. The computer could even map out the colors by exact location on a canvas, creating a paint by numbers sort of painting. But that would so miss the feeling of the painting, the most important aspect that goes beyond color and motion, that it would be a laughable caricature.

Two hours later, Gwendolyn stood before the canvas with her brush in hand and paint ready. She paused for about five minutes, eyes closed, and paint brush hovering. She did not believe in any nonsense of trying to channel the spirit of the artist. She only said a little prayer requesting his inspiration so she could honor him and the beauty he had given the world, not unlike a Catholic requesting the notice of a particular patron saint before starting an important activity.

Then, with a long exhale, she started painting. As with Pissarro, she was a frenzy of action as her brush placed paint on canvas at all places, seemingly at once. Just like the Impressionists painted, she built layer upon layer of colors that created not the photo image of the subject, but something more important, capturing the mind's impression of the subject.

What made the Impressionists' art so great was that they were not capturing their mind's impression of something - but the mind of Mankind's impression of something. Otherwise, as in Abstract painting, the artist could simply paint a red dot on a blue canvas and call it Red Coated Fisherman. No one else would know what the red dot was except for the title.

Monet painted lilies floating on a French countryside pond in the summer so that he could inspire the beauty of all lilies floating on all ponds in all summers for all people. Pissarro did the same for the Fall foliage in a French forest for all Fall foliage in all forests for all people lucky to be able to witness such a sight.

This is what Gwendolyn was capturing on the canvas before her. About once an hour, she stepped back to examine her work. She mixed some more paint and then again stepped up to the canvas. She dabbed ochre in a corner for a little while, then dabbed light yellow near the center for a few minutes. Nothing would have made sense to anyone looking at it, except a very gifted artist. It would have appeared to any non-artist as a strange abstract painting of warm colors.

She could have stopped after the first day and sold it for $15,000 calling it Autumn in Bucks County. But she yearned for something more, not just the money, but the sense of accomplishment to recreate something of universal beauty that would surpass all time and cultures. In short, she intended to step into the shoes of one of the greatest artists that Mankind had ever produced and feel like a goddess of the Spirit of Man, even for just one day.

In the early afternoon, Gwendolyn set another canvas on an easel next to the main one. She spent an hour recreating her reproduction but in a much less careful way. She would leave this one out in case any curious burglars came to visit after she left. She would hide her reproduction in a harness hanging snugly under the bed.

Gwendolyn stopped working on the decoy about a quarter of the way through. She did not want anyone to recognize what she was really working on. As she left it, it could have looked like anything with some warm color schemes blotched across the canvas. Of course, she would not waste an antique canvas and rare period oil paint on it. It would not matter if the competition broke in before it was complete. They would wait, as an unfinished copy was not worth anything.

There were many competing gangs of art thieves feeding the demand of rich African tyrants and well-connected Russian oligarchs. She already had drawn the attention of one or more of these gangs. They were more urbane and sophisticated than your average criminal.

The reason was simple. To be an art thief, one needed to have a real appreciation and an excellent understanding of art. That would mean, if not an MFA, at least several years of serious art study. Not many criminals were cut out for that. Of course, Giles' clients made an LA street gang look like a group of cub scouts. But they fortunately were a step or two away from her. Giles had to deal with them.

Around 3:30 Gwendolyn prepared to leave. She went down the back fire escape and through the main pathways winding through the grounds of the complex. Sure enough, the same man who had followed her in the museum was there, walking a bulldog of all things. She smiled even at that bit of an Anglo touch.

Instead of trying to avoid him, she decided to have some fun. She walked up to him and said in Russian, "Dubri deen, Gaspodeen [Good day, Gentleman]."

With an eyebrow raised, he replied in slightly accented English, "Don't call me 'gaspodeen'. All the gaspodeen live in Paris now."

"Ah, Dog's Heart," she replied. "You like Bulgakov, too. I love his work. Surely, you have read Master and Margherita?"

"How can you make so many plans for the future, when you cannot even control the next fifteen minutes of your life?" he quoted from that masterpiece.

"What a great line. You're dressed exactly like the Devil in the book."

"Even the Devil is a gentleman. You are obviously a well-educated young woman. Shall we continue our conversation on Russian literature at a nice Russian tea house only a few blocks from here?"

"You can't follow me if I'm not moving. Maybe another time, when this is all over, we can discuss one of my favorite Russian novels, Dostoevsky's Brothers Karamazov over good Georgian

Saperavi wine? I know where we can buy some in LA."

"I accept your kind offer, young lady, but let's change the beverage to Armenian Mount Ararat Five Star brandy. We don't like the Georgians much anymore. Now tell me. When will 'this' be over, so I can plan accordingly?"

"It depends on my degree of inspiration. We can't rush that can we?" She then left him behind wondering what had just happened. He played it well, she had to admit.

Gwendolyn ducked behind a tree and texted Lorenzo to meet her at the furthest free parking spot on the south side of the third level of the museum's parking garage. While walking in, she noticed two suspicious men smoking in a large black Mercedes waiting at the exit of the garage. They were not tourists and certainly not locals. No one in southern California smokes in their car.

Since she needed the exercise, Gwendolyn decided to take the stairs. She opened the heavy steel door and started walking up. When she arrived at the third floor, there were two boys in their late teens talking. One was standing in front of the closed door to the third level and another one was a few steps up the stairs toward the fourth floor. She could see a clear bottleneck sticking up from a paper bag on the steps. Bored teens and booze are never a good combination.

"Excuse me," Gwendolyn said while reaching for the door to push it open.

"Where ya' goin' sweet thaang?" the boy blocking the door asked flirtatiously without moving out of her way.

"Just going to my car," she said calmly.

"Hey, what's the rush? Let's hangout. We can have some drinks, listen to some tunes, maybe hook up. You know, an afternoon in LA."

"Don't have time for that." Gwendolyn had no interest in conversing with a pair of drunken teenage thugs in a quiet stairwell. She was in a dangerous situation and was getting nervous. There was a thug in front of her and one behind her. She was too close to

43

the one in front to turn and run. He could just grab her as she was turning. Each of them was at least twice her size. She had to think and react fast to whatever happened next.

"No time for that? Tell ya' what. I'll give you a choice. A choice, right? You decide. Either you decide to hook up with both of us right now right here or you give us a gift, a kind of memento, like that pretty pearl necklace you're wearing. Now, you understand that we could have it both ways, but I respect women too much to not let them decide which way it'll be. We've been drinking some hooch and I'm in a good mood. What'll it be?"

"How about you just let me through the door?" she said bravely. "That's my choice. Whatever you're offering just doesn't work for me. I'm not in the mood. You know how girls can be.

"As for my pearl necklace, my grandmother who raised me gave it to me. I can't part with it. It has too much sentimental value for me to give it away to some stranger. You must have something that means a lot to you that you wouldn't part with. So, as I see it, the only other choice we have here is to let me through that door."

"Oh, now you're starting to irritate me. We're not having a debate about it. You only have two choices. If you don't take either of them, then we're back to my original idea that we take both you and the necklace. I'll count to three. Ready? Maybe this will help concentrate your mind." He sneered at her as he pulled out a large knife.

"You're starting to irritate me. Put your knife away and let me pass before someone gets hurt." Her mind was now razor sharp.

He extended the knife to her throat. "Well now, we don't want anyone to get hurt, do we? I'll give you one more chance. Will it be the necklace?" He lifted the pearl necklace a few inches from her throat with the knife point. "Or will it be a bit of fun, instead?" He placed the knife blade on her cleavage and scraped the top edge of her blouse. "Or should we have it both ways?" His partner started to step down the stairs behind her.

As he brought the knife back up to her throat, she blurted, "Damn it! I don't have time for this crap. I warned you!"

She quickly swung ninety degrees to his right side. With her right hand, she grabbed the wrist of his hand holding the knife and pulled him forward and off balance. At the same time, her left hand hit his extended right elbow, breaking it, and causing him to drop the knife. A second later, still holding his right wrist, she leaned slightly away from him and with her right foot hit him hard at the side of his knee, breaking that, too. With this, he dropped to the ground screaming in pain.

To drive the point home that he needed to respect women better, she pulled out her knife without the blade extended. She always had her secret weapon strapped snuggly inside her left forearm, hidden under a loose long sleeve shirt exactly for such occasions. She put the end next to his right temple.

"You know what this is? It's a five-inch-long spring-loaded stiletto. All I need to do is press the trigger and five inches of steel will slice into your brain. Now, I'll give you two choices and only two and you better decide before I finish talking. I'm not counting to give you a chance to think about it. Are you ready? First choice is to have your friend get you to a hospital. I hope he has a car nearby because you're not walking there.

"Second choice is for me to release the trigger and your last thought will be 'Damn, what was I thinking?' as your brain is cut in two. I see your friend is already running away. All right, time's up. It's your move."

The boy crumpled before her was crying, "No! No-o-o-o-! Let me go."

"What do you say to someone whom you've seriously offended?"

"Sorry! S-s-s-o-r-r-y! I'm so sorry! I promise to be nicer to women. Oh God, please let me go!"

"Will you start respecting women now? Don't you have a mother and sisters? How would you like someone to treat them the same way? Damn it. I should just put you out of your misery. Would be doing you and the world a favor. Are you ready for the final journey?"

"No, no-o-o-o-o! I'm not ready! Please, I beg you, let me go!"

"You don't have to beg. Just ask politely. If I let you go, will I ever see you again?"

"No, no! You'll never see me again. I'll run away if I even see you in the distance. Please, ma'am. Please let me go."

"Well, trust me. You'll never run again. But I'll accept that you'll hobble away, if you ever see me."

"Oh, please!" He whimpered in his pain and fear.

"Fine. Better use your cell phone and call your friend back to get you out of the stairwell." She stood up and put her knife away. Opening the door, she turned to him, smiled, and said, "Have a nice day!"

The whole encounter lasted less than two minutes. The intense martial arts training she did for the few years she lived in Taiwan had been useful. Men just do not understand what women put up with daily. She straightened out her skirt and walked calmly over to hide behind the car parked next to the location where she had told Lorenzo to meet her.

As soon as Lorenzo arrived, she slipped into the back seat before he came to a complete stop. As they drove out the exit she slid down in her seat. The black Mercedes did not see her, and another day of work was done.

To Lorenzo's quizzical look, Gwendolyn explained: "There was a creepy old dude following me around and I had to give him the slip."

"Oh, no problem. I understand. It happens to me all the time," he replied.

After a nice swim to clear her mind, Gwendolyn showed up at Sherry Hour on time. But she was not really in the mood to deal with the Robertsons. Her encounter with the strange Russian and the street punks had stressed her. She hated complications and even more hated her plans being changed.

She had really looked forward to some free time in Peru.

However, there was something particularly important she had to do. She had to plant the reason for her nearing sudden departure.

After all three of them safely had a sherry glass in hand and fine nibbles within reach, Ferdinand started: "How was your search today? Did you meet any strange craziness in your travels?"

"No, not really. Not much to report," she replied.

"You spent all day in LA and met with no craziness? How is that possible?" Isabella wanted to know.

"Nothing out of the ordinary. Really," Gwendolyn replied rather glumly.

"Is something bothering you, my lass? I feel there is," Ferdinand asked with real feeling.

"Well, to tell you the truth, my old grandmother who basically raised me has gone into the hospital for pneumonia. They tell me it's nothing serious, but at ninety-two everything is serious. If it does get worse, I'll have to fly back east and see her."

She had used this excuse for sudden departures many times. Her dearly departed grandmother of many years would not mind Gwendolyn using her as an excuse to further her dearest granddaughter's position in the tough man-dominated world.

"Oh no, my dear!" Isabella replied, rather upset. "I'm so sorry to hear that. Well, no wonder you're a bit glum. We'll not speak another word about it, but rest assured I will pray to the Blessed Virgin for your grandmother's health during my evening prayers.

"When my grandmother was in the hospital for the last time, I flew back to Buenos Aires to be by her side. Oh, I'm sorry! We're still talking about it. Ok, not another word until you tell us she has recovered and returned home. Where does she live?"

"She lives in a small town outside of Philadelphia."

"Well, may she return quickly to health and to her nice home."

"How's the apartment search going, Gwendolyn?" Ferdinand asked with some slight impatience, which she guessed was impatience of finding her bedroom door barred at night. She was sure the reason he had no locks on any door in his home was to allow

47

free access to anywhere, anytime.

This stupid poorly timed question brought a strong reaction from Isabella: "Don't you answer that, dear! How can you be so crass, Ferdinand? The girl obviously is in pain over her dear grandmother. What is the matter with you?"

"Sorry, dearest. You're right. Please forgive my lack of manners, Gwendolyn. I don't know what came over me," was the penitent Ferdinand's response.

"Sure, don't worry about it. It's nothing," Gwendolyn mumbled with eyes lowered.

That sharp exchange between them stopped all conversation for the rest of the evening. Ferdinand and Isabella did not have a lot to talk about at the best of times. Their guest was being quiet, too, pretending to be in part offended and in part distressed, though in her heart she was very pleased by how it all was going.

CHAPTER FIVE

A good night's sleep ended with the sound of Ferdinand's 6 AM dive into the pool. Gwendolyn turned over and noticed she had her eight hours of sleep already. She would not leave for her studio until after 9 AM to escape LA's terrible rush hour. She had plenty of time, but she was tired of sleeping.

Gwendolyn laid back and recalled the strange events with the Russians and the local thugs the day before. She did not know if she should even take them seriously. The lot yesterday was so buffoon-like and the Anglophile gaspodeen was completely silly. But something about it all put her at great unease. For just a moment, her blood turned cold, but then she shook it off with a little laugh, remembering that poor bulldog being dragged into all of this.

Even so, the whole thing spooked her. She remembered there was a coldness in the gaspodeen's eyes. They were certainly not the sensitive eyes of a rogue MFA. When they met, he spoke of literature and not painting. What MFA would have done that? They only care about their particular fine art and ignore everything else.

Her thoughts continued to ponder what it all meant. Two things stood out. First, she would never forget the gaspodeen's face or voice, nor what they talked about. Second, she knew that under no circumstances was she to allow them to find her real work or lead them back to the Robertsons. She had to tread with the utmost care for a bit more than another week. In the meantime, she had to distract herself, so she checked her email on her cell phone.

Her electronic ramblings took her to the time of her morning ablutions and then to breakfast where Gwendolyn met Ferdinand.

"Good morning, artiste friend. Did you sleep well?"

"Very fine, Ferdinand. Thanks for asking."

"Off to continue your search now?"

"Yes, after breakfast. I think I'm close to finding something."

"Oh, well, please don't rush. I really am sorry for what I said yesterday. I don't know what came over me."

"Well, you're right in wondering how long this stranger will continue pushing the limits of your hospitality."

"My hospitality to you has no limits. In fact, I think I would rather like to show you a very nice apartment I know of right on Hermosa Beach," He said this last part in a near whisper, revealing the true nature of the "very nice" apartment.

As she was wondering how to answer this, Isabella called to him from the other room: "Ferdinand, don't forget you have to do the final fitting of your new shoes this morning. We want them ready before next week's BAFTA events."

"Actually, dearest, I was thinking of showing… Oh, never mind. I'll do it before lunch." He realized there was nothing he could do to get out of that. Besides, so many of the sweet young starlets of today, the very ones who would be at the BAFTA rewards ceremony, judge a man by the shoes he wears. He would have to offer to help her later.

Gwendolyn was relieved, not knowing how to reject Ferdinand's offer of 'help' or how to fend him off later. He was plainly becoming impatient and wanted the whole thing to come to a head, one way or the other.

In any case, the word "BAFTA" sent a small chill of fear down her spine, reminding her that everything would have to be complete in about a week, a work which had taken Pissarro almost three months to complete. There could be no delay now. Wasting a day with Ferdinand would have destroyed the whole timetable.

The Michelin chef made beautiful scones, complete with strawberries and clotted cream with freshly picked mint leaves on top for breakfast. A scone should be light and airy, and these did not disappoint. The bit of mint was pure genius. He set beside her scones and a cappuccino that was just as she remembered them in Tuscany.

Around 9 AM she went outside, where she found Lorenzo and the Bentley waiting. As she felt the car door close by Lorenzo's gentle touch, she decided to be extremely careful. There were only a few days left with no room for error. She somehow had drawn the attention of a strange bunch of weirdos. Just how weird they were, she could not guess, but she could not let down her guard.

"To the art museum, as usual, Signorina?"

"No, Lorenzo. I'm craving those golden raisins that Trader Joe's sells. Drop me off at the one on West 3rd and South Fairfax. But do me a favor and take the 2 to West Hollywood and turn right on North Fairfax. I'd like to see if West Hollywood has become any tamer."

The truth was Gwendolyn did not want him to try to turn left into the Trader Joe's parking lot. That would take too much time. A quick right would let her quickly disappear into the store. She still did not know if the Russians could recognize the Bentley yet.

"Well, cara amie, "tamer" is a relative word. Besides, it's still quite early in the day."

"If that creepy old man is still around, I'll text you where to pick me up." She did not know how the day would play out.

As soon as he turned into the parking lot and stopped in front of the entrance, she was out and in the store before anyone could notice. She wandered through the store, sampling the daily offering and had a small cup of their coffee. Slipping out the back, she walked around Gilmore Station and crossed the street into the LA Farmer's Market.

The LA Farmers Market is much more than a normal farmers market in a normal town. This one is full of the wonderful craziness that LA is famous for. But most important, it is always very crowded.

The first thing Gwendolyn did was buy an umbrella cap from a vendor just inside the entrance. She guessed that there would be lookouts on every corner around her block, waiting for her to appear. The LA Farmer's Market happened to be across the northwest corner. She figured she would have to attract her followers' attention and then lose them in the crowd.

She casually stepped into and out of the stalls with her colorful umbrella hat indicating her exact location. Sure enough, she noticed two heavy set men with a look of being somewhat hungover -the hallmark of middle-aged Russian men - wearing off-the-rack suits while pretending to be shopping, but all the time with their eyes on her umbrella hat.

Oh, come on. Haven't you guys ever been to a farmers market? Who wears suits while shopping for organic arugula? she asked herself. Now that the wolves had been discovered, it was time for the doe to start her evasion.

Walking slowly, she drew them deeper into the crowds. They kept a distance of about three stalls. She wondered if they would chase her if she started to run, crashing through the stalls like they do in the movies. They would never catch her, but it would ruin the day for the vendors. So, she decided to lose them the old-fashioned way.

Gwendolyn noticed a surfer chick with multicolored hair, the same colors of her umbrella hat, around a corner that would make her invisible to her followers for a brief moment. Quickly walking up to her, she said, "Well, hey dude. You need to wear this. It matches your hair," and placed the umbrella hat on her head.

"Hey man. Far out! Thanks!"

Gwendolyn chuckled to herself about how young women in southern California call each other by male monikers like "dude" and "man." She then quickly ducked into the changing space in the back corner of a nearby stall selling incense and long hippy dresses.

From there she could watch.

As the umbrella cap drew her followers past her, she could hear them speaking Russian, confirming their nationality. She took off her black pull-over and changed into a white lace blouse that she pulled from her little handbag. The pull-over took its place in her handbag and she disappeared into the crowd, going in the opposite direction.

She hurried to the exit of the farmers market at South Gilmore, walked into Nordstrom's, crossed West 3rd into South Ogden. From there it was a quick trot down the block into her studio's complex while those two dullards were still following the wrong woman. She climbed up the fire escape confident that no one saw her.

It was this kind of evasion that she had to do for the entire next week. She played this cat and mouse game, going to and from her studio. Then, she had to play another kind of cat and mouse game with Ferdinand when she returned. The whole thing was exceedingly draining. No one could say Gwendolyn did not work hard for her money.

But one morning, a week after her rainbow bonnet evasion, when her painting was almost complete, it turned out her evasions had been a waste of time. Entering her apartment, she noticed that clearly someone discovered her studio anyway. All her clothes were emptied from her suitcase and dumped on the bed. They had been looking for something, but what?

The computer was there but turned on. They had not been able to figure out how to get past her computer's security system that Yuri, her Ukrainian ex-boyfriend and professional hacker, had installed. He had given her many uniquely useful little programs that could fit on a thumb drive.

Her unfinished decoy painting was sitting on its easel. The real painting was still in its hiding place, safely nestled under her bed. She checked that all her belongings were there.

Gwendolyn checked the bathroom, and nothing seemed amiss there. She started wondering if they were not just small-time burglars. Even so. she could not understand why they did not steal her computer, the only object worth anything to a simple thief. But then she noticed something that froze her heart. The sanitary pads she had left in the trash can the day before were gone. She forgot to empty the trash before leaving.

She sank down on the edge of the bathtub to try to make sense of it. She would contact Giles about it on the way back to Malibu. She tried to form a scenario in her head of what had happened and why.

After about five minutes she decided that her trackers had found her studio, despite her best efforts, and broke in to steal her completed painting. They saw the decoy, noticing it was not even close to being finished, and one of them, being some kind of pervert, took her sanitary pads. Then, with the mystery solved, she banished the whole episode from her mind to concentrate on her nearly finished painting.

Gwendolyn repacked everything, took a deep breath, and went back to work. She only needed about another hour to finish the painting, the final few touches that would stand the test of the experts. The painting had to be dry when Giles and his team would make the exchange the following evening. She had been using linseed oil with the paint and kept the studio well heated. She was also keeping the air very dry with a small but powerful dehumidifier and had been putting a little bit of a drying agent into the paint that could not be detected when dried.

When Gwendolyn put the last dab of paint on, she sat back and studied the painting carefully. Not detecting any difference in the two paintings with her eye, she took a digital photo of her painting and compared it with the photo of the original on her computer. She blew them both up and compared them minutely. Even blown up way past the ability of the eye to detect, they were identical. Sighing loudly, she sat done, very satisfied with another job well done.

She texted Lorenzo to meet her at 3 PM at Molly Malone's, the Irish pub a block up from Wilshire on Fairfax and behind Gwendolyn's apartment complex. Once he confirmed, she took a nap for about an hour. After carefully putting her painting in its hiding place, she left out the back fire escape and hid in the trees across the street from the pub. When Lorenzo arrived, she ran across the street, and jumped into the back seat. It was time to text Giles what had happened and get his opinion.

Someone's been in my studio. Big mess. Painting OK. Nothing missing, except used sanitary pads in trashcan. What do you make of it? Painting finished. What next?

About ten minutes later came the reply: **What was missing?!?**

No typos. Exactly as written.

Another five minutes passed, then: **No idea. Need to think about it. Stay away from studio. Will take it from here. Meet me tomorrow at 10:30 by Vexed Man at Getty Center. Do you know him?**

Of course. In the west wing. See you there.

Gwendolyn felt vexed with Giles. Sculpture being her second specialty, how could she not know Messerschmidt's masterpiece of vexation?

She was unnerved by the events of the day. Her activity had clearly drawn the attention of several strange characters. They found her studio and broke in, despite her best efforts. They knew she was up to something. But how much did they know exactly? Should she call the whole thing off?

With her mind starting to slip, she got a grip on herself. She only had one more night at the Robertsons and Giles would take care of everything. All she needed to do was act normal until they went to the BAFTA ceremonies the next afternoon. Giles would explain it all to her the next morning and everything would be fine. She asked herself, *what's the worst that could happen?* And then, she answered her question.

The burglars could break in again, find her real painting under the bed, and steal it. But why steal a copy? They could inform the Robertsons before the switch and at worst, Mr. Robertson would throw her out. They could inform the Robertsons after they switched the paintings. But by the time experts could prove the painting was a copy, she would have disappeared with the original. What would they gain from doing either? She concluded that the upside was much greater than the downside and decided to relax.

Back in time for Sherry Hour, Gwendolyn really was not in the mood to engage with Ferdinand's rapier wit. The day's events had already mentally exhausted her. Isabella asked her about her sick grandmother, which gave her the much-needed opening to explain why she might suddenly have to leave.

She explained to Isabella that the doctor should tell her the news sometime Friday. If bad news, Gwendolyn would have to take the next plane to Philadelphia. But no one expected that. So, she would continue with her apartment search, which was coming along well. She should settle on a place by the middle of the next week, probably at one of the beach communities on the way to Orange County. That was the extent of Gwendolyn's conversation for the evening.

Dinner was unusually quick, about forty-five minutes. Gwendolyn drank little and ate less. She was glad to be in bed early. From this point onward, Giles and his team would do everything else.

Since the next project was planned for La Jolla, she would drive to San Diego and stay at one of the motels on Nimitz Boulevard. Gwendolyn knew a few great seafood restaurants overlooking the city skyline across the bay and looked forward to some time there. She would watch the glorious sun set on the Point Loma hills during Happy Hour at Mr. A's just below Balboa Park. She hoped Giles would leave her alone for a few days in one of her favorite American cities.

Spending some time in San Diego would calm her. Otherwise, it would have been almost impossible to sleep that night. She looked forward to meeting Giles the next morning. He always could shed light on perplexing things. Finally, Gwendolyn fell asleep, smiling at the thought of having breakfast on Pacific Beach.

CHAPTER SIX

The next morning, Gwendolyn again awoke to Ferdinand's 6 AM dive. It was as good as an alarm clock. But with a late night ahead of her, she decided to roll over and sleep for a few more hours. She did not have to leave until 09:30 to meet Giles at the Getty by 10:30. As she drifted off to sleep again, she thought of Gabriella, wondering what kind of daughter the Robertsons could have produced.

Gabriella was clearly a beautiful girl of about Gwendolyn's age. She, too, had found her way from a strange upbringing to the creative life of an artist. Fortunately for her, she did not have to struggle like Gwendolyn had. Gwendolyn's hatred of poverty while growing up put her on her current path of 'special projects' that she so excelled at.

Gwendolyn remembered as a little girl standing at the supermarket check-out line while her mother figured out what she needed to put back because she did not have enough money to pay for it all. It happened every time.

She was a teenager before she ate in a restaurant. Gwendolyn simply wanted to never have to worry about not having enough money to buy something she wanted or eat where she wanted.

Because money had never been an issue with Gabriella, she was clearly not driven in the same way. The Robertson's only child merely needed to find a path and it would open for her with little effort. Instead of seeking personal fame or fortune, Gabriella had chosen to do something good in the world with her art, by creating a foundation that repaired the many nearly destroyed Buddha statues around Asia.

From the many Sherry Hours, Gwendolyn learned much about Gabriella. Based in Thailand, she led the volunteer artists from around the world, idealists like her. They carved from local stone the arms and heads to make whole again the thousands of representations of the Compassionate One throughout the jungles and caves of Asia, from India and Indonesia to China and the remote mountain temples of Japan.

Gwendolyn marveled at the knowledge needed to recreate all those different styles from so many different eras. And even more incredible was the skill and talent to pull it off. In her own way, Gabriella was equally as talented as Gwendolyn, but actually doing good. It was at this point when she was entering the dangerous ground of questioning everything she was doing in life that she drifted off to sleep.

About thirty minutes later, she awoke. She still had a lot of time, so she packed up her things that she did not immediately need. The Robertsons would be gone from the early afternoon until late that night. First, there was a high tea sponsored by BAFTA for young film makers who hoped to meet possible backers of their films. Then, there would be a pre-event party that would fill the gap to dinner with the ceremony that followed.

The post-event parties would go on as long as the attendees could last into the wee hours. In any case, they would not return home until well after midnight.

The Robertsons would be busy most of the morning getting their hair done, tailored shoes picked up, etc. Gwendolyn timed emerging from the bedroom to breakfast in the kitchen so that she would not meet them. All the hired help had the day off, except for Lorenzo, who was on call to take her on her apartment search. He would be the only one of the Robertson's household that she would see before she left that evening.

After her second cup of excellent coffee, Gwendolyn decided she was ready to receive whatever news Giles had for her. She hoped there would be no change in plan. Her painting was truly a great work of art. All her effort would be worthless if he cancelled the whole thing. But if he did, there would certainly be a valid reason, like avoiding jail or worse.

She walked out to the ready Bentley. Lorenzo was in an especially cheery mood as he had the whole weekend to look forward to. He told her that his weekend plan was to visit Santa Barbara wineries with Jonathan. Things seemed to be much improved with them.

"To LACMA, as usual, Signorina?"

"No, Lorenzo, we are going to the Getty Museum this time for an hour or so. There is a statue there I really love. After that, I'll tell you."

"Which statue is that?"

"It's the Vexed Man. Have you seen it?"

"I have. It's impossible to forget. I once dated a professor of art at UCLA who specialized in African masks. He thought that was one of the best examples of what a western mask would be if there were a ritual dance to rid Europeans of angst and anxiety. I prefer getting high to doing an energetic African dance myself. Did you know that UCLA has one of the best African Art programs in the world?"

"You're talking to an MFA, Lorenzo. Of course, I know that. I even took a course on African masks from Professor Williams there."

"Yes, Signorina, I know him well. How did you guess?"

"I didn't guess. Just a coincidence, I suppose."

"His private collection of masks from all over the world is incredible. Too bad he would never remove his own mask with me,"

Lorenzo said with a slight sigh.

"Sometimes, Lorenzo, it is better to stay unattached. Like me."

"I wish I could!" he said in exasperation. "But I am such the romantic. I believe in love. I just can't help it. It's out there somewhere for everyone, even you, sweety."

They bantered on that subject for a bit more, until Gwendolyn saw that the traffic would make her late. "We're not making good time, Lorenzo. Why don't you take Barrington to Sunset and then take Sepulveda in the backway? That way, we can avoid the 405."

"How do you know LA so well?"

"I've visited the Getty many times during my studies. I just hate wasting time in traffic jams."

"Well, you picked the wrong city for that."

Following her directions, they arrived still early enough for her to meet Giles on time. She told Lorenzo to wait in the parking garage for her. She took the monorail from the parking garage to the hilltop museum where no cars are allowed, and one can see the Pacific on one side and LA's downtown on the other. The view alone is worth the trip.

Giles was already there, minutely examining the vexed statue's left eye with a magnifying glass.

"Are you looking for the mote in his eye?" She asked.

"Good morning, Gwendolyn. No, just examining a slight imperfection. Imperfections in art do not detract from their beauty. In fact, they add to it, showing the true imperfections that are in all of us. It's what makes us human."

"Should I be taking notes?"

"No. You already know all this. Your amazing talent is to not only identify these imperfections, but also to recreate them exactly. As I remember, you did a fine womanly version of the same. What ever happened to that sculpture you did? The last I saw it was at a Manhattan art opening on 19th Street, in Chelsea. Never mind. Come, let's sit and talk."

They sat down on the nearest bench. After a pause, Giles

continued.

"Here's what I think. Regarding the missing item from your bathroom trashcan, I think we can assume a pervert did that. Since you are sure that those following you never found your studio, the pervert was a common burglar who took that thing for his amusement."

"All right, fine. What else?"

"I'd not worry much about them. I've run into our Anglo-Ruskie gentleman before. His name is Ivanov Ivanovich Ilyich. He'll steal anything of ascetic value that he can resell for a profit. I think he specializes in old manuscripts like first printings which the author has signed. About five years ago, he tried to sell me a first edition of Walden with Thoreau's signature on the cover page for $50,000.

"I told him I already had one and countered with an offer to sell a mint first edition of 1001 Nights, translated by Sir Richard Burton for $250,000. That really made him interested. He wanted to see it and asked all sorts of questions. Of course, he did not blush at the price, because he had every intention of stealing it. I was just having fun with him. I would never part with it. Anyway, it was enough for me to understand him somewhat. He is no comparison with what we do. But I am curious who is sponsoring him and what role he is supposed to play exactly."

"What's your take on it all?"

"From what I can tell, someone who knows something about what we're doing must have hired him. His task is simply to find whatever you're copying and steal it. Our client's particularly good about these things and wouldn't leak our project to anyone.

"So, that leads me to another possible conclusion, which is that our literary friend is following you with his own little team to steal whatever you're working on. Steal it to sell to another customer that he's found. Many of the manuscripts he tries to sell as originals are really reproductions.

"He or his little gang broke into your apartment and saw that your painting, the decoy, was nowhere near ready and left to wait until you've finished the painting. Now, if they were true professionals like us, they would have broken in, found the painting not finished, and left without leaving any trace they were there. The fact they made a mess of it, makes me think they were common burglars."

"But what about my computer? They didn't take that."

"Probably because you had secured it to your desk like I taught you and they didn't have the tools to cut it free."

"But what if you're wrong?" Gwendolyn asked worriedly.

"Even if it is Ivanov, I don't believe he has the know-how or experience to be anything but an annoyance. We either must accept him as part of the equation and up our game by keeping your movements secret or we must remove him from the equation altogether. He has many enemies in Russia who would gladly remove him with the proper incentive or even with no incentive at all. Let's see how this plays out and I will decide without involving you in the slightest."

"Fine. What about tonight?"

"Are you sure no one will be there this evening?"

"Yes. After Lorenzo takes me back, I will let him start his weekend early. It'll just be me there the rest of the day."

"Great. We'll be waiting a five-minute drive away in a silent electric minivan with the words "Toblerone Delivery" on the sides. At exactly 8 PM, text us if the coast is clear. I'll text you when we approach the gate, which will be your signal to turn off the security system. After doing so, confirm back and in we'll go. Any questions?"

"None so far. It's just like we discussed before."

"As usual, I prepared the postcard and envelope with your message to the Robertsons on it. It's the same message you always use: thanking them and explaining that you had to take an evening flight back to Philadelphia to visit you grandmother in the hospital.

"Things have evidently taken a turn for the worse. When you have nothing else to do this afternoon, you can sketch something artistic and original for once to show your thanks for their great hospitality.

"About ten minutes after we leave, and you have turned the security system back on, a taxi, driven by a close friend of mine, will take you to LAX. Then, --"

"Wait a minute, I thought --"

He interrupted her, "I know, but we have to have you on the security camera as a record that you did leave for the airport with a time stamp." Once you have arrived at the airport and there is a record that your taxi did go to LAX, he will drive you to San Diego and you'll continue as planned. During the ten minutes you're waiting for the taxi, you'll make sure there's no trace of our ever having been there. Is everything clear?"

"Yeah, I suppose. Just don't like plans changing, that's all."

"We have to be flexible. Are we OK here?"

"Sure, no problem. Just another job, nearly done."

"That's right. Will see you this evening."

She got up and left. When she was outdoors, she stopped to admire the view of the ocean. She sighed to herself: *Yet another beautiful day in California.* After a few moments, she took the monorail back to the parking garage, where she found Lorenzo dusting the car with a feather duster.

"Let's go, Lorenzo."

"I know you can't search for housing up here. Where to today?"

"Just take me back to the Robertsons. I am waiting for a call from my grandmother's hospital later. If the news is bad, I will take the next plane back east. I'm not in the mood for anything else right now. I thought the museum would cheer me up, but I was wrong."

"Sorry to hear that, Signorina. I'll wait for the phone call and take you to the airport if the news is bad."

"Oh, no, no, Lorenzo, thanks anyway. I'll take a taxi. I want you to start your nice weekend plans earlier. That would make me feel better."

"But you'll be there all alone."

"I'll be fine with a swim and some reading. Do me a favor and take Sunset Boulevard back."

"Fine, and thank you, my dear."

They returned just after noon. No one was there, as expected. It was the first time Gwendolyn had to use the key they had given her to get in. She watched through the window and about ten minutes later, he started up his motorcycle with a weekend bag across his back and sped out the front gate.

The first thing was to see what she could scrounge up for lunch in the kitchen. Scrounging would be quite easy in such a well-stocked kitchen. Gwendolyn found and ate the leftovers from the previous dinner, sitting at the grand dining table.

She washed it down with some Vinho Verde, a light, cold and lightly sparkling wine from Portugal. Still at the dining table, she took out the farewell and thank you card that Giles had prepared for her. Retrieving the set of colored pencils she always had in her suitcase, she did a colorful rendition of their house complete with the gatão ['large kitty' in Portuguese] with a green collar just like the one on the wine bottle's label, sitting in their garden. She then placed the card in an obvious spot they could not miss when they returned later that night.

Next, Gwendolyn walked through the entire house, all the exterior buildings, and the grounds looking for anyone at all. She was alone. The walk took over forty-five minutes, just enough time for the Vinho Verde to wear off. She passed a few hours reading Proust's A la Recherche du le Temps Perdu [In Search for Time Lost] in the garden.

His very glacial pace describing his childhood was just what she needed to relax. When she could not take it anymore, she went for a swim. She took a shower then a nap and awoke toward the end of the afternoon.

As for the security system, she already had mapped out where all the cameras were and found the security system itself in Ferdinand's study. Yuri had given her a nifty little program that could erase a recorded segment of a security system and make it appear as one continuous recording. She went over everything to make sure that when the painting arrived, there would be no snafus.

For a light dinner, Gwendolyn finished off the octopus salad from the night before. Gwendolyn placed her packed bags by the door, did a final walk-through ensuring everything was ready and no one else was there.

She whiled away the remaining time by sitting down on the back veranda watching the sun set. At 8 PM, she texted Giles that everything was ready. Four minutes later, he texted back that they were approaching the front gate, signaling her to turn off the security cameras. After activating her nifty Ukrainian security program, she texted back two minutes later that they were free to enter the gates.

Gwendolyn opened the door, and Giles entered the foyer with his two helpers. He was in disguise as usual, but this time he had beach-blonde hair and a four-day stubble that he definitely did not have that morning. The two helpers were carrying Gwendolyn's beautiful painting. They carefully replaced Pissarro's masterpiece with Gwendolyn's.

They returned and just as carefully placed Gwendolyn's work in its place. No one spoke a word or even made a sound. Giles stopped and whispered in Gwendolyn's ear, "The taxi will be here in ten minutes. I'll call you tomorrow morning at 09:45 on your hotel phone. The driver knows where to take you. I have already taken care of the hotel. Brilliant work!"

In a little over a minute the electric minivan disappeared into the darkness as silently as it had arrived. Exactly at the start of the second minute, Gwendolyn turned back on the security system. She walked about the living room, the dining room, and the hallway, looking at her painting.

It indeed looked exactly like the original. She made sure her thank you note was sitting in an obvious place. She did not mind replacing one of the family's heirlooms with her creation, but she hated the thought of being rude about it. She checked again for any evidence that her three colleagues ever were there. Everything was fine.

The taxi arrived on time. The driver put her bags into the trunk, while she got into the back. They drove off. Gwendolyn noted that the security cameras caught the taxi exactly right. She settled into the back seat with a sigh of relief. Everything had gone well, and she was rid of the strange Robertsons. She looked forward to a few days in San Diego.

On the way to LAX, Gwendolyn thought the trip was a bit pointless. So, she took a taxi to the airport, but then what? There would be no record of her flying anywhere. Then, she played out a little scenario in her over-active mind that went like this:

Gwendolyn would buy a ticket to Philadelphia, go through security, and arrive at the gate. The taxi driver would park in the garage and wait for her. She would meet a woman accomplice at the gate who had a ticket on a different flight. They would exchange boarding passes and the alternate Gwendolyn would be on the flight to Philadelphia, and the real Gwendolyn would walk out to the waiting taxi to continue to San Diego, as planned, giving her a perfect alibi.

But a perfect alibi for what? The security cameras clearly noted that she did not leave with a large painting. It all seemed rather moot.

Leaving LAX, they headed south to San Diego. During the three hour drive, they talked across a wide range of topics, including art, poetry, literature. Clearly Al was not a typical taxi driver. It was nearly midnight when he took the San Diego airport exit off the I-5 and proceeded almost to the end where Harbor meets Rosecrans.

"Everything is taken care of. If anyone asks where I am, just say Daddy-o went fishing and you're my friend waiting for me. Should be no problem. I know the manager. You must be tired, so I'll get out of your hair. It was a real pleasure getting to know you. I hope we can meet again."

"I hope so, too."

CHAPTER SEVEN

A little after 8 AM, the old clunky bedside phone rang right by Gwendolyn's head for a good fifteen seconds before its ring burrowed into her consciousness and woke her.

"What? Hnh…"

"It's me."

"Giles? Why are you calling me so early!"

"Listen! Turn on your TV to Channel 7. There's something you must see after the commercial break. Go wash your face. Make sure you're fully awake. I'll wait on the phone."

She turned the TV on to Channel 7. She went to the sink and threw cold water on her face. Returning, she sat on the bed in front of the TV with the phone back in her hand.

"Giles! What's this all about? Just tell me."

"First, listen. Then, we'll talk. Here it is."

"We have updated the top story of the hour with more details that we have since learned about the tragedy in Malibu. Mr. and Mrs. Robertson were found murdered in their Malibu home early this morning after a call to 911 at 4:12 AM by the main suspect, a young woman, who only identified herself as 'Gwendolyn' and confessed to the crime.

"According to the 911 transcript, the suspect claimed that she was a guest of the Robertsons staying at their Malibu home. Mr. Robertson came into her room and sexually assaulted her around one o'clock. His wife came in and a fight ensued. During the confusion, the suspect pulled her handgun out of her purse.

"Mr. Robertson tried to grab her arm, causing the gun to misfire and kill Mrs. Robertson. That stopped Mr. Robertson long enough for the suspect to shoot him. The suspect claims she acted in self-defense and it was Mr. Robertson who caused his wife to be shot.

"For more, we are joined at the scene with our journalist, Samantha Rodriguez. Hello, Samantha, what's the latest?"

"We're waiting for Captain Slarpniak, the Head of the LA Robbery Homicide Division, to make a statement of what they know so far. Oh, he's about to start."

"Good morning, everyone. This is what we know at the current time. We estimate the time of death at around 0100 this morning for both victims. The cause of death for both was a shot to the head with a 10 mm handgun. A suspect made a call to 911 at 0412 this morning and confessed, saying it was in self-defense to a sexual assault. We have found a blood sample of the suspect that will identify her DNA. We have not found the weapon.

"Because the security system was down from about 2200, we have no idea who came or left from that time onwards. The security video does show that the last person who arrived was the suspect. And it showed that the last person to leave was the Robertsons' driver, who dropped her off by car and later left on a motorcycle a bit after 1300. The suspect has not turned herself in. We are locating all the domestic help for questioning.

"My message to the suspect who called 911 earlier this morning is this. Please come into any police station for questioning. If what you say is true, we can clear all of this up quickly. Otherwise, we'll have to find you and we will. The longer you wait, the harder it'll be for you. That's all for the present. We will make more announcements as the situation develops."

"That is basically all we know now. Back to you, Anita."

"Thank you, Samantha. Next up: a local Ocean Beach dog dove into the San Diego River to save a cat. It was all caught on video…"

"Holy Sh*t! Giles! What the hell? What the… what is going on?"

"Now, we must stay calm."

"Stay calm? Stay calm?! Obviously, I must go to the police and clear this all up!"

"Gwendolyn, may I speak now?"

"All right, Giles! For God's sake, what is it?"

"You cannot go to the police for several reasons. First, you were not even there when it happened. How can you clear anything up? Second, that is exactly what the real murderers want. They are in complete control of the situation. As soon as you turn yourself in for questioning, they can manipulate things to appear that you did it with malice. Then you are trapped and finished for twenty or more years. I need you out of prison. Third, I also need you to find out who did it. Only then will you be able to clear your name. Do you understand?"

"How can I find the murderers? Where would I even start? I'm an artist, not a detective! Most importantly, why would anyone want to do this to me?"

"Before we go there, let's review what we do know. Someone entered the place around ten o'clock last night and not only turned off the security system but also erased the part of you leaving in a taxi much earlier and the point when they entered, committed the crime and left. Now we understand why they took your used sanitary pads. They probably kept it in a humidifier until they spread it on the sheets last night. The police have your DNA, your face on the security system, and even your first name."

"Damn it, Giles! They practically have me already! Wait a minute, what about Al? He can be my alibi."

"He could except for a few things. LAX and the motel will have on security cameras images of the arrival and departure of his taxi. Unfortunately, the police will discover at once that his is not a real taxi. Now your alibi is a suspect himself.

Besides, the motel's security cameras will have a record of him leaving at about 10:45. From that point on, you have no alibi of any kind. It's possible that you snuck out with him. From about 11:00 to 1:30, you would have had plenty of time to fly back to LA to commit the crime and fly back here by small plane.

"You see, Gwendolyn, the problem is how can you prove you're innocent when you've already confessed to the crime? All you can do now is either try to explain that it was self-defense and hope for the best or find the real murderers and clear it all up with no loose ends.

"We need to do only two things right now: First, we need to get you to a safe place and second, we must find the culprits with enough proof to clear your name. I cannot help you much. But I can put you in touch with the one person who can. That's our Russian client. Someone is probably trying to destroy his reputation. In his world, losing that is worse than losing his life. Only he would know who would want to do that."

"But what about the note I left?"

"They would have taken that with them as soon as they saw it."

"How could they even find the Robertsons? I made sure we were never followed."

"No one needs to follow you. All they need to do is have a friendly chat with your driver, who would suspect nothing."

"Damn it! I knew I should have had a double fly to Philadelphia using my boarding pass. I thought of that on the way to LAX in the taxi. Then, I'd have a rock-solid alibi. Why didn't we think of that before and prepare for it?"

"Calm yourself, my friend. This is something neither of us could have expected."

"Fine, Giles. Now, get me out of this mess!"

"First thing's first. Your money has already been transferred to your Cayman Islands account."

"Thanks, but that's not the most important thing now." she muttered, knowing that Giles was always meticulous about business.

"Actually, it is. Next, we must do the two things I said before. First, get you to a safe place. Al will pick you up at 6:30 this evening. He will take you to an airstrip where you'll travel by small plane to a private air strip at a large ranch about ten miles south of Mexicali.

"The owner of the ranch will meet you and fly you to Mexico City where you will take a late-night flight to Moscow. That will be your safe haven. First problem solved. Al will give you a Mexican passport. I think the photo came out well. How's your Spanish? Never mind, just pretend you're a deaf mute if anyone speaks Spanish to you."

"My Spanish is good enough to get around. I'll tell them I'm from an isolated rogue Mormon commune near Acapulco. We all spoke English there. They'll believe that."

"Good! Your sense of humor has returned. Now, for the second problem. Al will give you information on how to contact our client there. I'll let him know you'll be looking for him. He should be able to help you find the murderers, if the murderers are Russians, which everything points to that they are."

"God, this sounds very farfetched. At least, I'll have you to guide me."

"Now, that is the bad news. After I hang up, we cannot have any direct communication until you've cleared your name. I can't be connected to this in any way. I have, I mean we have too much at stake, too much to lose if I become incriminated in anyway. We would never find another client who would trust us again. I hope you understand. Besides, I fully expect you to clear this whole thing up before our La Jolla friends go on vacation."

"Are you frickin' out of your mind? What do you mean you're breaking off all contact with me? I need guidance; someone to tell me what to do and how am I supposed to do it?"

"You're a resourceful and very smart girl. Take it as a fresh challenge to be overcome, as you have overcome so many before. I will at least have you safely away in Russia. Even if you can't clear your name, you will be away from the long arm of US law. Besides, the Russians really love the arts of all kinds, like no one else. You'll do fine as an artist there, if you must stay there for some time. Al will have more answers by the time he meets you this evening."

"Why, you…. Giles, damn you! You can't leave me alone with this!"

"It really pains me to do this, but I've no other choice. I'll be watching your progress from afar. If I can think of anything else, I'll let Al tell you this evening. In the meantime, stay out of sight. They probably downloaded your picture from the security cameras. Al left you some breakfast in the refrigerator yesterday before driving to LA to pick you up. He'll stop by early afternoon with some lunch. We have a lot to do now. Don't let the cleaning ladies in, either."

"Giles! If I ever get out of this …"

"You'll thank me because I'll have a lot more work for you. Save your anger for when you meet the real murderers. You'll need it then and add to it all the anger from all the wrongs and frustrations of your entire life. Trust me. It'll be great, cathartic really. You'll feel like a new woman as you take out a lifetime of anger onto the poor son of a bitch. Just don't kill him until you get the proof you need."

"Giles! I am stepping into the dark world of violent Russian gangsters!"

"You'll know what to do when the time comes. Besides, you've studied martial arts for many years. That's prepared your mind."

"Oh, bullsh*t! What's that supposed to mean? That's not the same thing at all. I have nothing more to say to you."

"Well, great then. I guess I'll let you rest from all the shock. And Gwendolyn, take care. You're the daughter I never had. If I can help you along the way, I'll do so, but only indirectly. I've made a lot of friends in my work, and a lot of enemies. After this saga is all over, maybe we can climb to Machu Picchu together and I'll tell you some stories from my past. Bye for now." And the phone clicked silent.

Gwendolyn looked at the TV for another twenty minutes, not registering a single sound except the panic surging within her. Finally, she pulled back to the here and now. She turned it off and suddenly felt completely exhausted, like she had not slept in three days, though she had just woken up not thirty minutes before.

She crawled back into bed and curled into a fetal position, thinking that she had been skating close to the edge for many years already, trusting that the ice would always hold. Now, the ice had broken, and she was sinking into the icy depths miles from dry land. The deathly darkness closed in as she sunk further from the disappearing hole in the ice above. And then, she fell asleep.

About mid-afternoon, there was a knock on the door. The knock grew louder and more impatient. It gently pulled Gwendolyn back into consciousness. When she finally awoke, her whole body reacted like a jolt of electricity flowed through her and she fell out of bed with a thump. There was nowhere to run. *If they've found me already, then so be it*, she thought while heading for the door. She peered through the peephole and saw a worried Al looking back at her.

She opened the door. He was relieved to see her.

"Al! Come in!"

He quickly did and closed the door.

"Thank God you're here. I thought you'd wandered off and I wouldn't be able to find you. We have a lot to do."

"Al! What the hell is going on? What have I gotten myself into?"

"Giles has told you most of what we know. Have you been following the news on TV?"

"No, I sort of collapsed into a deep sleep after we talked. Wow! Looking at the clock, I've been sleeping for almost 6 hours. I guess I'm hoping I'll wake up from this nightmare and it'll all go away. Listening to you, I guess it hasn't."

"No, it hasn't, and it's worse. Since this morning, the cops found all the staff and questioned them. They have identified you in the security camera recordings of your comings and goings. A rather poor photo of you is being televised everywhere. People are on the lookout. It'd be impossible for you to travel anywhere on public transportation.

"At least one person in the Robertson's household is adamant of your innocence. That's the driver. He was so shocked they had to send him to the hospital. Once he woke up, he claimed he was the murderer. Fortunately for him, he has a rock-solid alibi. He was an 'exotic' dancer at a gay bar in Santa Barbara when it happened. I think that's what I heard them call it. He was pole dancing, or lap dancing, or something. Anyway, there are over fifty patrons who were there at the time."

"Poor Lorenzo! He was the best one in that whole place."

"Yeah, well, whatever. We have more things to worry about. First, I brought you a late lunch." Looking in the refrigerator, he continued, "I see you haven't eaten anything all day. You'll need your strength for another long night, even longer than the last, I'm sorry to say."

"Now that you mention it, I'm starving. What did you bring me?"

"Giles told me you like sushi. I brought you a selection of the best this town has to offer. It comes from the fish market across the street. It's so fresh, it's still squirming. I also brought you a bottle of New Zealand Sauvignon Blanc. He told me you like that, too. But you'll need to share that with me. I need you alert for the rest of the day."

"Thanks, Al. I will gladly share with you. Thanks for providing breakfast. Never got around to exploring the fridge. What was it?"

"Oh, breakfast burritos. It's my favorite breakfast anyway. They are a wonderful union of California and Mexico."

"Maybe I can take them with me?"

"No. Where you're going this evening, they'll laugh at you for bringing something so nasty. You might get the real thing there before you must fly on. Mexican food is one of the world's great cuisines."

Gwendolyn started spreading the food out on the desk. She opened the wine and hesitated a moment before pouring out two glasses in the terrible thin plastic cups common in cheap motels. Passing a cup to Al, she said:

"Here, Al. Salud. Talk to me about what's happening next, while I eat. Help yourself to any of this."

"I'll take some of that Caterpillar Roll. You know, whenever I order one of these, I always ask the same thing to the one taking my order: 'Is the caterpillar fresh?' Sometimes they get it; sometimes they don't. No matter. I do, and I chuckle every time. My jokes never get stale with me."

Al continued, "Any young friend of Giles is like a son or daughter to me. Never had my own, so I don't mind going the extra mile for anyone Giles wants me to help. Just trying to while away some time before your next adventure. It's only silly banter. Hope I'm not bothering you."

"We can banter away in any direction you want. You're at least occupying my mind with something else besides dark thoughts and worries."

Al paused a bit and then changed the subject. "Let's check the news to see what the hunters know. We have to start thinking about our next move."

He turned on the TV.

"... Yes, Janet, here is what we know and don't know about the Robertson case. We have the first name of the suspect, but not the last name. We have a decent picture of the suspect from the security cameras. [A grainy, unclear photo of Gwendolyn was shown on the screen.] We have the 911 transcript of the suspect and her voice sample. We have a DNA sample of her, too. But so far none of that has produced any leads. The murder weapon has not been found yet, either.

"The best we can hope for currently is that between playing the 911 recording and showing her picture often on all media, someone may identify the suspect. She must come up for air sometime. Of course, the other alternative is that she will heed the advice of the authorities and turn herself in."

"Thank you, Jack. Now, we move on to the story of the mother cat who in addition to nursing her kittens has taken in a new family member. A baby rat is the new adopted sibling. Take a look."

"Damn it, Al! Turn that crap off! The nonsense they call news these days. That is quite an awful picture of me, and the voice analysts can analyze all they want. Seems to me that as long as I don't show myself to anyone, I should be fine. Well, that certainly limits things. What if I give myself up and prove that the 911 caller was not me?"

"Gwendolyn, the 911 call is the only thing that is preventing this from being an act of cold-blooded murder. You disprove that and you're facing a capital crime charge. The only reason that 911 call exists is to trick you into giving yourself up. Forget about it!"

"You're right, of course. They know my name. I'll change it to Gwennie. That way, it could be short either for Gwendolyn or Guinevere. I'll die my hair blonde. I'll make myself fat."

"Yeah, and Holly came from Miami, FLA. Hitchhiked her way across the USA. Plucked her eyebrows on the way. Shaved her legs and then he was a she. We don't want you to walk on Lou Reed's wild side, 'Gwennie'. We have better plans for you. In fact, it's getting awfully close to setting them in motion. Let's get going."

"Luckily, I haven't had time to settle in. I'm still packed. Giles told me the plan to get me out of here. I'm taking a small plane to a ranch near Mexicali, owned by one of Giles' contacts, right?"

"Ah, so he already told you. Good. This backpack has your Mexican passport, boarding pass, and cash. It's a little heavy, because it also has a SIG-Sauer P226 12mm pistol with ammunition, a silencer, and whatever else a very well-armed girl may need.

"Your hotel reservations have been made for a young Mexican woman enjoying her long holiday in Moscow. There is also quite a bit of cash - dollars, euros, and rubles. Quite a bit.

"Here, let me show you how to use this thing. Giles wants me to tell you to use it not with anger, but with love in your heart, the kind of love used when putting down a critically ill pet. You will be much more effective that way. Besides violent thugs are not much more than animals."

"Please, Al. Don't offend animals."

Al smiled and took out the P226, showed her where the safety catch was, and how to load and unload it, making sure there were no rounds in the chamber. He made certain she was sure how to handle it.

He continued: "Señor Garcia will teach you how to fire it before he flies you to Mexico City. Giles wanted to make sure you had enough fire power. He didn't want you to have some pathetic 9 or 10 mm popgun.

"Now, Gwendolyn, one more thing. Don't be angry with Giles. He had no idea this would happen. We have entered a twilight zone. He will help you when he can, behind the scenes."

She paused and then sighed: "Oh, Al, how can I be angry with him? He could have just thrown me to the dogs and found another aspiring art criminal. I can see from all this in the backpack, all these arrangements, and your help that he does care. Screw it. Let's go."

"Well, all right then. Let's get you and your things into the car without anyone noticing."

Al had already backed up his car to the motel room door. He went out and made sure no one was around. He put her things in the trunk and opened the back door. Gwendolyn darted in with her new backpack.

"Al, what happened to your taxi?"

"This is my taxi. It's just missing the taxi skin I had on it yesterday. Sit back as low as you can. We don't want any attention from passersby's."

"You've been very busy since we last met."

"It was all Giles. I'm only the errand boy. In your backpack, you will also find the contact information for the client in Moscow. All we know, on our end, is what Giles told you about the strange Russian man you met in LA. He is strange enough that our client probably knows him, or at least knows of him. That should be enough to find him. Also, follow the money. It would be important to know who paid them, the one who ordered the crime done, so we can stop something like this from happening again."

"Al, I just want to find the perps and clear my name. I must think what kind of evidence I need to do that. A full confession clearly recorded would probably do it. Might have to beat it out of them. Now, there's a joke."

"Might not need to do any beating. Just putting the fear of God into them should be enough. Maybe our client can help. He's well connected. If he is just like all the other gangster thugs over there, he may even do most of the heavy lifting for you and think it fun."

Gwendolyn went silent as she mulled this over in her mind. Until then, she had only been thinking about her immediate future. Giles had taken care of all that. But after arriving in Moscow, she would need to do the rest. How she would do that was a great mystery to her. She figured a plan would present itself when the time came.

Half an hour later, they arrived at a small airstrip where there was a propeller plane waiting at the end, ready to take off. Al put her things in the back seat.

"Well, Gwendolyn," he said, "it's been a real pleasure to get to know you during the short time we had together. Giles and I will be with you in spirit and will do whatever we can to help you from the shadows. We're completely confident you will be successful." He held out his hand to shake hers.

"Oh, come on, Al. We're in southern California." And she gave him a hug with three kisses on Al's alternate cheeks. "Thanks for everything. Hope to meet you again soon."

"Wow! Three. Thanks. Take care of yourself and return soon in triumph." He helped her up into her seat next to the pilot and closed the door behind her.

The pilot smiled and shook her hand. He was a Korean American in his early 30's. "Welcome aboard! The name is Charles Kim. You can call me Captain Kim, or even Captain Kid, if you prefer. The flying time will be about thirty minutes."

"Aye, aye, Captain!"

The plane accelerated down the runway and took off.

CHAPTER EIGHT

Captain Kim flew across the US-Mexican border, over Mexicali, and landed on Señor Garcia's nicely laid-out landing strip a few minutes later.

"Good job flying us here, Captain Kim." She could see he loved being called "Captain."

"My pleasure."

Gwendolyn opened the door and eased down to the ground with her backpack in hand. Señor Garcia and three armed bodyguards walked up to the plane. Señor Garcia was well into his fifties and developing a paunch, despite living a very physical life of running a large ranch and an even larger crime empire.

Yet, his Mexican compatriots would consider him to be in excellent shape. Apparently, he had rebelled against the never-satisfied god of vanity and was comfortable that his once-black thick hair was balding and copious moustache was now greying.

"Welcome, welcome, Señorita. I should call you by your family name, not your given one. We consider that very impolite here."

"Thank you, Señor Garcia, but the less you know about me the better. What's the plan?"

"Oh my, Señorita, we don't rush things here. First, I must offer you some traditional Mexican hospitality."

"Thanks, but I am in a bit of a rush. I have a plane to catch, Señor, and it takes at least three hours to fly there. The flight leaves at 1:30 AM."

"Don't worry. I can assure you the plane will not leave without you. Now, if you would be so kind as to accompany me for dinner." He offered her his arm. She took it, and he led her to the well-designed private airport building.

"You see, Señorita, I used to greet guests in tents, but that's not very hospitable. So, I had this built in the manner of Frank Lloyd Wright, a Prairie-style house with a control tower. If you replace the tumble weed blowing about around here with long grass, you might think you were on a prairie."

"It's beautiful, Señor Garcia. I've never been to an airport like this before."

Inside, it was surprisingly a tastefully appointed hunting lodge, complete with a fire in the stone fireplace. The river rock piled all the way to the soaring twenty-foot ceiling. Much to Gwendolyn's horror, the walls were covered with the trophy heads of the poor murdered big game animals from mostly the northern parts of the US and Canada. She always hated to see the heads of animals staring down at her with their black glass eyes, wondering how they had wronged the men who brought them down in their prime.

"Señorita Gwendolyn, it's time for dinner." He led her out onto the veranda, indicating a chair at the dining table, "Please, sit here."

There was a dining table placed out on the deck. It had an uninterrupted view of the distant hills and the setting sun across the Sonoran Desert. Many gas heaters around the table kept the cool evening air at bay. There was quite a feast laid out and nine men standing behind their chairs, waiting for her to take her seat. Looking at all the fine dishes spread out in front of her, she was glad she had left the breakfast burritos behind.

Once everyone was seated, including Captain Kim at the far end, Señor Garcia explained, "Now, my honored guest, you can see we eat well here. Not like the crap they serve in so-called "Mexican" restaurants in your country. It is a great shame to even call them "Mexican". The Chinese and Italians living in your land must feel the same way. Don't you agree, Kim? How is Korean food in US restaurants?"

Kim winced at the idea.

"Rest assured, Señorita, I have instructed our guests to keep their conversations clean and fit to share with a refined cultured young lady. They won't say anything that will cause you to blush."

"Oh, I doubt you could make me blush, Señor." Gwendolyn interrupted; her confidence regained.

"Really? Well, we don't have time for that today. Perhaps you'll give me the honor of trying to make you blush at a future date? Hm?"

"Let's just stay on task, Señor Garcia."

"As you wish, but the next time I order a work of art from Giles, I will require you to present it to me personally. After all, he owes me a few favors. While you are helping yourself, let me introduce my comrades who have honored us with their presence."

He proceeded to introduce each one around the table with their full five or more-word names. One of them had eight words to his name. They were all members of his large extended family, all of whom had an important role to play in his empire. They were ranchers, bankers, mayors, police chiefs, judges, businessmen of various interests, and in short, a good crosscut of the influential of the State he lived in.

"My apologies, Señorita, I never could stomach the womanly dishes of salads and soups. We are meat eaters here. And ordinarily, we would have our meal with Tequila, the tears of the gods, but our after-dinner amusement this evening is to teach you how to fire the firearm you have in that sack of yours. We never mix alcohol and firearms. Also, I must fly you to the next step of your journey. Let's have a fine meal and talk about art."

And so, the meal proceeded happily for over an hour. Indeed, there were no soups or salads. Besides various grilled meats and stews, there were a variety of dishes with excellent moles [savory chocolate-based sauces]. After they finished their spicy coffees, Señor Garcia announced it was time to leave the table for cigars and shooting.

Instead of going out into the surrounding desert to fire at targets in the bush, they went downstairs into a basement that had a movie theater, a bar on one side and a fully set up firing range on the other. About half of the party went into the bar area to have their fine tequila and cigars.

The other half filed into the shooting range, donning the ear protection that hung by pegs on the wall. Gwendolyn looked for the gun lockers and was surprised when each of the guests simply pulled their side arms from under their dinner jackets.

"Now, Señorita Gwendolyn, follow me into my personal firing room. I want you to be able to hear what I tell you while they're firing."

She followed him through a heavy door into a wood paneled firing range with moving targets that could pop up at unexpected places.

"Now, be careful and take out that fine piece that Giles gave you."

Gwendolyn slowly pulled it out of her backpack, making sure it was always pointing at the ground. She remembered what she had learned in her high school rifle club. She had earned the Marksman grade and was even the team's captain for the last two years. But they had only used .22 rifles. That is close to 6 mm. She had to learn to fire a bullet twice that size with a handgun, no less.

"I see you understand safe handling. We only have an hour to get this right." And proceeded to explain how to use it.

Gwendolyn paid very close attention and held the P226 in both hands, looking down the sight, ready for the unexpected targets to pop up. At first, she was wildly off target. Then, she remembered from her years of meditating that it is all about controlling the mind. After an hour, she was not doing too badly. Señor Garcia was helping her throughout, by fixing her posture, adjusting her stance, and basically getting her trained as best he could within the time allotted.

"Well, I must say, you have a talent for this, Señorita. When you're in Moscow, find a firing range and keep practicing. Take the rest of the magazines here. The clips are not light, but make sure you have at least five of them with you. If you ever find yourself in a situation when you are using more than two of them, it's better to make a hasty retreat. I can't train you here in dealing with a fire fight. I think we better get going. You need to catch a plane."

"That was really exhilarating! Thanks. I still don't think we'll make the flight on time."

"I already told you to relax about that. One of my brother-in-law's is the top brass in the Mexican Airforce. He will shut down the airspace over Mexico City until you are comfortably seated and on your second Tequila drink. Besides, my little jet flies fast and true."

"You're well connected. That helps."

"Indeed, I am. I come from an extensive family even by Mexican standards and my family has married well. Your bags are already on the plane. Since I will be flying, we can't talk, but you can either watch movies, sleep, have some nice refreshment. Whatever you like. You can even have a shower. My flight attendant will attend to you properly."

They talked while they walked to the jet already on the tarmac.

"I've a question before we get going, Señor Garcia. How will I check my bags?"

"You will take them on board."

"But I will have a pistol with me. How will I get it through inspections?"

"You will have none on this end. No guest of mine ever suffers the indignity. Giles has arranged for you to be a VIP on the Russian side. Have you ever been an arriving VIP before?"

"I haven't rated being a VIP, ever."

"Oh, you'll like it. You are met on the other end by a welcoming committee. They will take you and your things to a special lounge while your passport is being stamped. Usually, it only takes the time to drink a coffee. Then, they put you into a classy luxury car and drive you to your hotel. No lines, no waiting, no hassles at all."

"I like the way you travel, Señor Garcia."

"I do, too, and so could you, if you remember my offer to make you blush."

"Señor Garcia, I respect you too much to even give that a response."

"Nicely spoken, Señorita. Now, find a nice seat and we'll be off."

Gwendolyn settled into a seat, and within five minutes they were airborne. The flight attendant offered her some wine and cheese. She was too wired from her shooting practice to sleep. After they were at their stable flying altitude, she took a shower and changed her clothes. The day had given her a bit to sweat about. She watched *The Good, the Bad, and the Ugly,* and soon after that they started their descent into Mexico City.

A Jaguar XJ drove up to the just-parked plane. Señor Garcia took her bags and got into the back seat with her.

"I'll ride with you to the plane. Want to make sure there are no problems. I prefer the classic Jaguar designs before they became like Sebrings and suburban station wagons. This one may be old in years, but it has almost no miles on it. It only drives from the hangar to my jet and back to the hangar about once a week. That's about 25 miles a year."

"I must say, Señor Garcia, you have class."

"The next time you come for a visit; I will show you my nice little car collection. This is a working car. I own many who have never done a day of work in their lives. They're like Arabian racing stallions, which reminds of something else I need to show you next time."

"I get the idea, Señor. I appreciate nice things, but they don't impress. I'd never judge someone by the car they drive."

"Oh, believe me, Señorita. If I wanted to impress you, it would not be about cars and horses. But this conversation must wait until next time. We're here already."

The car stopped by a stairway leading up to the front of the plane. Señor Garcia gave her bags and boarding pass to a waiting flight attendant.

"Here, Señorita Gwendolyn, keep your backpack with you." He motioned to the driver, who stepped up and offered Gwendolyn two large boxes and a bag. "Unfortunately, you are going to Moscow in the depths of winter. I'm sure you had no time to prepare. You'll need these. My wife picked everything out for you, according to Giles' sense of your size. She told me the coat is sable and is all the rage in Moscow this year.

"The hat and mittens match each other, but she could only find them in mink. Hope you don't mind. We didn't receive much warning of your arrival and after all, we don't have a Rodeo Drive in Mexicali. After our conversation, I'm confident you won't mind beautiful animals protecting you from the icy winds.

"Whatever you may think, I'm quite certain they would love to wrap themselves around you. If you wear an extra pair of socks, the boots should fit, too. The high for tomorrow is -8 degrees."

Gwendolyn, caught up in the events of the day, had completely forgotten that the rest of the world is not like southern California in February.

"Oh, my God, Señor Garcia, thank you so much! You're right! I'd completely forgotten about the weather there. I'd never make it without you and Giles. As for my new winter furry friends, I'm sure they were all farm-raised." She said, raising her eyebrows.

"Yes, my wife assures me they were. I am quite certain that the cow that gave itself to the glory of protecting your feet from the ice and snow was ranch-raised. Well, Gwendolyn, it's been a real honor to get to know you in the little time we had. I have already placed an order with Giles for a Monet. I'll let him choose which one. I fully expect you'll have it done in a few months and we'll meet soon.

Until then, bon voyage!"

"Thanks for everything, Señor Garcia. You have given me confidence to face something that had me in a panic just a few hours ago. I look forward to presenting you with an example of my best work. And who knows? Maybe you can make me blush. You have me intrigued, and that means I must do what I need to do in Russia and return quickly. You know what they say about curiosity and cats."

"And the satisfaction that brings them back. Until next time, Señorita" He said with a deep bow.

They exchanged cheek-to-cheek farewells and Gwendolyn climbed into the plane. She was led to her seat in first class. She settled in and was well relaxed when they started general boarding fifteen minutes later.

"Is everything fine, Señorita Garcia? …Señorita Garcia?"

"A-a-a-h, Garcia? You mean me? Oh, yes, everything is fine. Thank you."

Gwendolyn had not looked at the name on her boarding pass. It had to be the same on her Mexican passport, too. It read Margarita Garcia. This was Giles' idea of a joke - a joke on many levels, the best kind of all. He always urged Gwendolyn to have more fun in life.

Apparently, he thought she might have some fun with a member of Mexico's upper-class underworld. She had to admit that Señor Garcia had a certain charm and nobility, despite being a gangster. Then, she reminded herself that she was part of a gang, too - the gang of Giles and his strange cohorts.

After all the announcements, the captain apologized to the passengers for the flight delay due to Mexico's Air Force closing the airspace for drills. That made Gwendolyn chuckle. About thirty minutes after take-off, Gwendolyn put the seat all the way back and finally started to relax.

She settled in for the fifteen-hour flight and sighed to herself. *Jeez, Giles, whatever will you think of next? It's been a very long time since a man made me blush. I wonder how the intriguing Señor thinks he could do it?* A slow smile formed on her lips as she drifted into sleep.

CHAPTER NINE

It was nearly midnight when the flight approached Sheremetyevo Airport. Gwendolyn had slept most of the way quite soundly. The events of the previous day had taken a toll on her energy. Still bleary-eyed, she blankly took in the majestic city sprawling below her, home to many of her clients.

While the plane was taxiing, Gwendolyn opened her new gifts. She had to admit Señor Garcia's wife had great taste. She put on her boots. They were a quite tasteful English riding boot style. She put away her nice but flimsy California shoes. Opening the box with her new hat and mittens, she noticed a shoulder holster in with them. She put the holster in with her shoes. When the plane door opened, she rose and put on her luxurious sable coat. She smiled when she remembered that her first car was a very used Mercury Sable.

The flight attendants had her bigger bags waiting for her as she entered the jetway. She pulled them both after her with her backpack on her shoulder. She imagined how silly she must look in such an expensive and elegant coat and hat carrying a backpack.

She perched her backpack on top of one of her larger bags and pulled them all behind her. So far, she had gotten away without speaking much Spanish. Now, in Russia she would not have to concern herself with it. She was not prepared for the VIP welcoming committee.

At the bottom of the heated jet way before entering the terminal itself, stood three young women looking in earnest at the passengers deplaning. One held a large sign welcoming Margarita Garcia – her new name - another held an enormous bouquet of flowers, and another a large box of Swiss chocolate. They were all wearing rather splendid hotel uniforms.

Gwendolyn walked up to them and introduced herself in her best Spanish. They gushed in their excitement. They rushed her with her presents, which Gwendolyn had no hands to hold. She moved the whole show to the side, so they were not blocking everyone else. Since they spoke much better Spanish than her, moving to the side would give her more time to consider how to respond.

Figuring that she spoke passable French and because the hotel chose these girls for their ability to greet their esteemed Mexican guest in her native language, she changed languages. It should buy her some breathing room to at least get her to the hotel. But no, after a few seconds of confusion, they did not skip a beat and spoke excellent French, too.

After deciding that the girl holding the sign would pull Gwendolyn's bags and the other two would continue holding her welcome gifts, leaving Gwendolyn with her backpack, they all piled into a waiting electric cart. The cart whizzed past everyone else and a few minutes later stopped in front of what appeared to be a First-Class airline lounge. It was the VIP lounge that Señor Garcia had told her about.

One of the lounge staff led them into a private salon. The girls motioned Gwendolyn to sit on a plush leather divan and asked if she would like some champagne.

"I'll have a quadruple expresso," she replied in English. Gwendolyn figured they were way too bubbly already. They most likely had a bottle or two of champagne in the VIP room while waiting for her flight. As usual, it took a bit to explain what a quadruple expresso meant. NO! Not four cups of espresso, but one cup with four shots of espresso in it. This caused some wonderment with the hotel girls.

Their attention soon turned to much more important matters. What would they order? They murmured among themselves and it was decided they would have cappuccinos with strawberry scones and side glasses of the most expensive Cognac on the menu. They could only enjoy the VIP treatment when special guests arrived, and they meant to enjoy it the best they could in the short time they had.

"I see you speak English. Would you prefer that?" asked the prettiest of the three. After Gwendolyn nodded, she continued, "Tell us about Mexico. What is your favorite telenovela?"

"I don't have one. I never watch TV," Gwendolyn replied rather glumly. Her answer produced gasps.

"Never watch TV? How's that even possible? Ah, I see you're joking." And they all giggled at the idea.

"Sorry, not joking. TV bores me." This caused about a minute of silent shock. Gwendolyn enjoyed the respite.

"Um, well then tell us about your favorite places to go shopping in Mexico City. You obviously have fine taste. We love your coat."

The shorter, fatter one reached out and felt it. "Sable! The real thing. Looks like the fur was hunted and not farmed. That's the best quality. Hard to find these days and VERY expensive. Ooh, we like you!"

"No, it was definitely farmed raised!" Gwendolyn was starting to really dislike these girls. They had nothing in common with her. She yearned to get to her hotel room as soon as possible.

"Fine, if you say so. But why did you come to Moscow in February?"

"Had some free time. So, I decided to take a holiday in Moscow. Heard so much about it. Never been. Will be busy in a few weeks, so I chose to come now."

"But your hotel reservation is for two months."

"Well, I never know. My plans change all the time."

"Wow! What a life. Anyway, we can take you to the best

boutiques in our city. We have everything here. We can start tomorrow. What will it be? Jewelry? Shoes?"

"Look, can we just stop talking? It was a long flight and I'm not in the mood for conversation. Thank you."

The three of them looked at each other, murmuring in Russian.

"Forgive us, Miss Garcia," one of them finally said, "We're just trying to be friendly. That is how the hotel trained us. Please don't take offense. Please, please do not complain about us to the hotel manager."

"Don't worry. But trust me, we have nothing to talk about."

The situation was saved when the waiter appeared with Gwendolyn's four-shot espresso (she determined to use that expression in the future; 'quadruple' has too many syllables). Two uniformed immigration inspectors walked over with her passport, duly stamped, and approved. About ten minutes later the waiter brought their order. By then, Gwendolyn had finished her coffee and was ready to go. She decided to give the little girls five minutes to finish. If not, she would find a taxi and go to the hotel herself. The VIP experience was turning into a drag.

Gwendolyn looked at the time on her cell phone. Five minutes later, she noticed they were not intending to leave anytime soon. She was extremely annoyed.

"Time to go," Gwendolyn said as she rose.

"But we're not finished yet," came the plaintive reply.

"Not my problem. You're supposed to meet me and take me to the hotel, not to enjoy yourselves at the hotel's expense." This produced the desired reaction.

"Yes, yes, you're right. But it would be a shame to waste such good cognac. The bartender would end up drinking them. Come on girls, let's show her how we drink in Russia."

They all three stood up with their so far untouched glasses in one hand and their scones in the other. They held their glasses out in front of their faces with their elbows at a right angle parallel to the floor and solemnly finished off the Cognac in one gulp, followed by immediately taking a big bite of their scones to act as a chaser. They grabbed their things and started off to the exit. Gwendolyn felt sorry for the very expensive Cognac being treated like a cheap tequila.

They left the VIP lounge and piled back into the waiting electric cart. Gwendolyn was glad to see her luggage still in the back. They cruised past Customs. Evidently, a VIP's luggage did not need to be checked. They went out a side door to the waiting hotel limousine, escaping all the hustle and bustle of the main exit.

The frigid wind was bracing. She knew what winter in Chicago was like and this was worse. Luckily, the driver had the heat on and the engine running when they arrived. The driver opened the back door and Gwendolyn jumped in. The three girls entered the car any way they could.

During the hour drive from the airport, Gwendolyn peered out the window and took in the sights of a new city, including the snow that lay deep all around her. Turning on to Leningradskaya, she could see how the city's personality changed as the road changed its name to the prestigious Tverskaya that ended at Red Square.

The car stopped in front of the entrance of the Ritz-Carlton. *Giles has come through again*, she thought as the doorman opened her door. She rushed inside.

The girls escorted her to a chair in front of a desk where she sat down. Before they left, the tall more confident girl asked Gwendolyn if everything was fine with their welcome at the airport. Gwendolyn confirmed that it was. They were relieved and wandered off. A sharply dressed man started the check-in process. He looked at her passport and started speaking to her in excellent Spanish.

Gwendolyn stopped him. "English, please!"

"Oh, certainly, Miss. Sorry about my poor Spanish. It must be hard on your ears. Welcome to the Ritz-Carlton Moscow. I see you are staying for sixty nights. Since you are such an important guest for us, we have upgraded you to the Club Suite with access to the Business Lounge. It has a great view of the Kremlin and St. Basil in Red Square.

"A deposit has already been made to cover our requirements, so we do not need your credit card. Here are your keys. The bellboy will take you and your luggage to your room now. The concierge is available twenty-four hours a day to help with your every whim. Have a great stay!"

Gwendolyn was relieved to not need to explain why the names on her credit card and her passport did not match. Giles thought of everything.

Gwendolyn wondered what he meant by her "every whim." What whim could she have at three in the morning? She pondered that over as she followed the bellboy with her luggage to the elevator. He took her key and led her to the place she would call home until straightening out the mess she found herself in. If she could not straighten it out, she might die trying.

The door opened to a richly tasteful rich one-bedroom apartment that had the floor space of a small house. She could see the lights of Red Square through the wide glass windows of the living room. There was even a fire burning in a fireplace. No wonder the check-in man had not asked about her choice of a smoking room. An enormous vase of flowers sat prominently on a table behind the sofas with a bottle of fine champagne in an ice bucket sitting next to it. A large chess board with pieces at the ready laid open on a coffee table between the sofas.

Her thoughts of being impressed were temporarily interrupted by the question; why would anyone want to drink something sitting in ice when it was twenty below outside? If she were a man, there probably would have been a bottle of high-end vodka instead. In any case, she decided that the Ritz-Carlton Moscow was a fine place to base herself.

The bellboy took her bags into the bedroom. When she followed him in a few moments later, she noticed that he was unpacking her suitcase and starting to hang her clothes in the closet. She quickly stopped him. He placed her key on a side table and left.

Gwendolyn brought her thoughts back to more practical matters.

Not normally a bath person, the bathtub nonetheless was extremely inviting. While the water was filling up, she bolted the door and emptied the contents of her mysterious backpack onto the dining table. There were stacks of cash in US Dollars, Euros, and Rubles - about $50,000 worth of each and each currency separated neatly with rubber bands. There was also a letter from Giles.

"Wish I could be there to help you through this, but as I explained, I can't. Besides, I think you are better mentally equipped to deal with something like this than I am. You might have noticed that I have spared no expense or effort to at least get you started.

I called in a few past and future favors, too. And no, I did not deduct any of this from your payment. I consider it an investment in my favorite asset. I want you back and working as soon as possible.

I trust Señor Garcia delivered you to the plane on time and provided you with some winter clothes. I also hope he helped you become more comfortable using the heavy armament I provided. It is a serious weapon for serious jobs. Please be careful with that thing and use it only as a last resort.

If you can find a shooting range in Moscow that would be helpful. I have a friend who is one of the managers at your hotel. He will keep an eye on you and let me know how you are doing. Other than that, I cannot really help you much more.

Let me know when you are ready to return and have everything neatly tied up with ironclad evidence. Our Russian client's contact information is below. I cannot tell you exactly what evidence we will need, but just remember you will probably not be able to convince anyone to return with you to confess to the crime. So, your evidence must be written, recorded, and otherwise a physical thing. It must be proof that can stand up in a court of law.

Good luck, my dear, and come back soon!

Dimitri Fomavich Kandinsky (when you see him, ask him if

he is related to the famous artist.)

Remember to call him Dimitri Fomavich and not just Dimitri! You are not lovers or family. (What happens after you two meet may change that. Always thinking of your best interests.)

who?me?3@au.ru

495 221-86-66 (will only go to voicemail)

Gwendolyn sighed. *Can't do anything about it now*, she thought. *Might as well soak in a proper bubble bath.* She brought the champagne bucket over to the side of the bath, opened it, poured herself a glass, and sank beneath the slightly too hot bubbly water. *Bubbly with bubbles. How nice,* she thought.

She pondered on the events of the last day. She woke up in San Diego by Giles' bad news phone call. She had been to a strange airstrip somewhere near Mexicali, learned how to shoot a heavy pistol, flew to Mexico City on a private jet, overnight to Moscow, and now here she was soaking in a wonderful bathtub in the heart of the city rather than spending a few days in San Diego before the new project in La Jolla.

Bulgakov's words from *Master and Margarita* rang in her mind: *How can you make such long-term plans when you cannot even control the next fifteen minutes of your life?* Truer words were never written.

Those were the exact words spoken by the murderous anglophile in LA outside her studio just a few days before. She decided that after her bath, the first thing to do was write down every detail she could remember about him. He was her target, and she had to find him fast.

Having finished the champagne, she ended her bath. She dried herself and put on the most luxurious bathrobes she had ever worn. Sitting by the fire, she started writing down every detail she could recall about the murderous gaspodeen. Any detail might be the one that might undo him: his shoes, his hair, his glasses, a ring, a lapel pin, anything.

The desk looked out over the lights of Red Square. City centers are the soul of a city and this one was more impressive than most. St. Basil and the Kremlin were all lit up - no expense was spared to impress. Gwendolyn wrote a quick email, telling her would-be benefactor that she had arrived at the Ritz, and needed to meet him right away. She even gave him her cell phone number, something she would normally never do, but these were desperate times.

After sending the email, she realized she was starving. It was nearly 3 AM. She ordered room service - black caviar (finally, the real thing!) and smoked salmon. It all came within ten minutes, complete with candles.

Gwendolyn was faced with the problem international travelers have often: how to go to sleep for at least another seven hours, three or four hours after they had just woken up. Her answer was to drink wine and take Valerian. It was a mild relaxant in use since before the time of the ancient Greeks.

The Soviets prescribed it for all ailments. They even had a liquid form. It had a very pungent, somewhat unpleasant smell, but it worked for her: four or five capsules and wine helped her sleep through most of a night. She always travelled with a bottle of it. Her ex, Yuri, introduced it to her.

Sometime around 3:30 AM, Gwendolyn climbed into bed. The Valerian and champagne were having their desired effect. The bed was so comfortable it practically sang a lullaby. She figured if she was awake before noon the next day, she should be fine.

Hopefully, Dimitri would have answered her email by then. While she waited for his reply, she would visit some of the sights and blast away at targets in a shooting range. She drifted off to sleep, open to whatever the universe would throw her way.

CHAPTER TEN

Gwendolyn opened her eyes and saw a ray of sunlight slipping through where the thick black-out curtains did not quite close tightly. She gathered her thoughts, starting from determining where she was exactly. Despite the wonderfully comfortable bed and the crackling fire in the next room, she had been tossing and turning the whole night, maybe only getting about five hours of actual sleep.

She turned to the clock on the side table. It was already 11:20. Time to get up. She had a rule she lived by - no matter what happened the night before, she would always be out of bed before noon. A second rule was to never go to sleep with her shoes on.

After finishing her morning ablutions, she checked her email, being particularly curious if the mysterious who?me?3 had answered her. Sure enough, he had. It was short and to the point.

Our mutual friend has told me everything. My deepest apologies for the disgraceful actions of my countrymen. The gift I ordered will arrive this afternoon. Maybe we can admire it over dinner this evening? Wait for my email later in the afternoon.

Fine, Gwendolyn thought. That would give her time to see Red Square and find a shooting range. She went to the executive lounge to get something to eat. Besides being in the same taste as her suite, it had an even more exhilarating view of Red Square, front and center. The famous landmark was only two blocks away. The food on offer was a smaller version of the lunch buffet in the main hotel restaurant.

She was not in the mood for eating, but she knew she had to eat something. She started with her quadruple espresso, then had perfectly cooked scrambled eggs (just a bit wet) with bacon. She finished with freshly squeezed grapefruit juice.

After admiring the view for some minutes, Gwendolyn went to the desk at the entrance of the lounge and asked the young woman there about shooting ranges.

"Oh, you Americans (meaning anyone from the Americas) and your guns! You can't even go on a vacation without shooting them. We have many guests from countries like the US, Mexico, Venezuela, Columbia, and Honduras, who have asked about this. We have a list of the closest ones here."

She pulled out a laminated list. "This one is the closest and seems to be popular with our guests. I will write down the name for you to give to the taxi driver. Also, take one of our cards, so you can tell the taxi driver how to bring you back."

"Do you know the first thing Russian immigrants do when they arrive in the US? They buy the most powerful automatic weapon they can legally buy. They all do," Gwendolyn replied.

"Of course, they would. I would too, with all the violence there. I see it on the news every night."

Gwendolyn decided not to reply. She was shocked that there would be a hotel employee in such a place that would make guests angry. Unfortunately, Gwendolyn had to admit that what she said was basically true. Later, she would have many such conversations with Russians whose only understanding of the world came from their TV news, which was not much more than pro-Russian nationalist propaganda.

It was a bit after noon when Gwendolyn returned to her room. Putting on the holster, she adjusted it nice and tight under her left arm. She put on her winter clothes, grabbed her backpack, and left. Exiting the hotel, she started walking the short distance to Red Square. She was hit full in the face with a strong Siberian wind.

The weather report said that the high of the day would be -12, even with the sun shining. She had walked half a block and already decided that it was not a good idea. She understood why the doorman could not believe she would turn down a taxi even for only two blocks.

Nonetheless, Gwendolyn pushed on to the way-over-the-top St. Basil's Cathedral with its mushroom domes in unique colors and spirals. It is truly one of the world's iconic constructions. She was glad to get inside and out of the wind. The interior was covered in intricate designs and icons - icons everywhere.

Russian Orthodox churches do not have pews, so she could not sit for a while and contemplate the higher truths. Instead she would have to stand, craning her neck to see the impressive ceiling above.

Back into the freezing wind, she made her way to the Kremlin across the street. The Kremlin complex being so huge, she only had time to choose one of the museums. She chose the Patriarch's Palace. It would be hard to see another church right after St. Basil's. Wandering through the palace fit for a tsar but used by the head of the Church, Gwendolyn wondered how far from God a 'man of God' must have fallen to live in such regal wealth.

Walking back to the hotel, she felt good that at least she was not a wanted woman in Moscow and could walk about freely. She was getting impatient to meet Dimitri; the one string left to grasp and pull her life back together. She had no clue how to even start without his help.

After returning to the hotel, Gwendolyn decided to stand in front of the hotel lobby fireplace and warm up before going back outside. She checked her email on her cell phone, no messages. It was only a bit after 3 PM anyway. She showed the doorman the firing range address, and he called a taxi over.

The drive was only twenty minutes. The firing range was in the basement of a small college sitting in a complex of buildings surrounded by walls with a great iron fence. Walking down the dark cold stairs inside one of the secondary buildings that the taxi driver had pointed out to her, she heard muffled shots and knew he was correct.

Down the cold corridor lit by twenty- watt light bulbs hanging from the ceiling, she found the door from where the sounds were coming. She opened the door and approached the desk where a young man was studying his cell phone.

Using the Russian she had learned from her Ukrainian friend, she spoke to him. "Good day. Want to shoot."

"Shoot what? Let's speak English."

"Oh, let's do. I want to practice firing my PS226 with moving targets. Do you have rounds for it?"

"Yes, we have a moving target range and PS226 clips. Did you say "my" PS226? If you brought your own, I will need to see your permit. Since it is illegal to carry firearms without a permit, I hope you have one. If you don't, I must inform the police. Since you are obviously a foreign tourist and not a member of the Russian security forces, I guess I should call them now."

"No, no, no! I meant I want to rent a PS226. I don't have one. See?" she quickly blurted out while opening her backpack to show there was no PS226 in there. It was in her shoulder holster deep inside her fur coat.

He gave her a quick side glance and said, "Don't worry. I was only joking. It's called Russian humor. Go down that hall and the last door on the left is the women's locker room. When you're ready, you will return here with your payment. It is $100 an hour, including everything. If you want to pay in Euros, we can do that as well."

"How about paying in rubles?"

"You can, but with the exchange rate we use, it works out to be about $120."

"If this is a college, how can students pay so much?"

"Russian students in private colleges are quite rich. Those who aren't must take jobs like this. Why do you choose to practice with a PS226? That is a big pistol for a small woman."

"Just make sure it has a recoil dampener. My father gave me one for Christmas and I want to learn how to use it when I return home." She proceeded down the hall and into the women's locker room.

In Russia, shooting was even more of a man's world than in the US. The locker room was quite small. It only had four wooden closets with their own locks with keys.

She took off her coat and holster, glad that she was alone in the locker room. She placed her pistol in her backpack, opened a locker, and put everything in. She took out a $100 bill and locked the wooden door.

Returning to the young man at the desk, she gave him the money, and he gave her a written receipt. He directed her down another hall to another door. Following his directions, she stepped into a small room with a man behind a cage with various firearms and hearing protection in racks behind him. The cage had a small opening where she shoved through the receipt. He returned with everything and motioned her to walk through another side door.

After about an hour of practice, Gwendolyn was ready to quit. She returned everything and walked back to the locker room. As she was putting her things on, she suddenly panicked. She had to sit down. Doubts started hurling themselves against her normally impenetrable self-confidence.

What if she could never find the perpetrators? What would she do then? Where would she go? She also fretted about when her Mexican passport expired - if she could not renew it, then what? She checked her cell phone and there was still no message from Dimitri, even though it was already well after 4 PM. That did not help her state of mind.

Whenever she found herself in such a state, she would do the breathing exercises she had learned from her Buddhist studies in Taiwan. Slowly breathing through her nose, feeling the air enter and leave, she emptied her mind and slowed her heartbeat.

After a few minutes of calm, an idea presented itself. Since Gwendolyn was in a college, they must have an English department. If she met with the head of the department, perhaps he could help her find an unforgettable eccentric middle-aged Anglophilic Russian.

This electrified her. At last, she had found an action to take. If this English Department had no idea, there were many others she could investigate in Moscow. She no longer felt so helpless.

Quickly back in front of the check-in desk, she asked the student if the college had an English Literature Department. Of course, they did. She then pleaded for him to take her there.

But how could he leave his desk? She offered him $10. He agreed. He grabbed his coat and hat and led her outside, across the snow-covered courtyard, into a better appointed and better heated building.

He explained as they walked up the carpet covered stairway that the English Department was better funded than the utility building where they had put the rifle club of which, as it turned out, he was the club captain. He was also on the Russian sharpshooting team for the next Olympics.

He needed to let her know that he was not just a flunkey with no prospects. In Soviet times, he added, he would have been treated like royalty, with no need to worry about money.

That was all very impressive, but Gwendolyn had more important things on her mind. She interrupted him, "You understand, I want the English Literature Department and not just the English Language Department, where Russians learn how to speak English?"

"Yes, I know. I understood you the first time you asked. Our English Literature Department is quite small with only two professors," he replied sounding somewhat annoyed by her changing the subject from him back to her, a common problem of young men worldwide.

They reached the third floor, walked about halfway down the

hall, and stopped at a heavy wooden door. He knocked, and a voice answered. He led her inside. There were two desks facing each other.

Behind one sat an older man with a grey beard. Across from him sat a middle-aged woman who had dyed her hair a crimson red. Bookshelves filled with books in all states of overuse, surrounded them in their small office. There were two wooden classroom-type chairs at the side of each desk for student interviews.

"Ahh, it is young Igor. Have you decided to return to the great and inspiring world of English literature?" Asked the old professor in Russian-accented English. "I remember you particularly enjoyed O. Henry."

"No, Doctor Teneyov. I have brought an American who is interested in meeting the professors of our English Literature Department. I have to get back to work at the firing range." And made a quick escape.

Both sets of eyes looked at Gwendolyn with curiosity.

Doctor Teneyov smiled and gestured to the chair by his desk. "Please girl, hang your coat on the coat rack and have a seat. What brings you to our esteemed college?"

As Gwendolyn hung up her coat, she was pleased to have had the foresight to put her pistol back into her backpack. She sat down and had to think about how to even start. She had to make a convincing pitch but not let on too much. Fortunately, quick thinking was her forte.

"Sorry for the intrusion. My name is Clio, Doctor Teneyov." She looked at the woman professor. "I'm sorry, we have not been introduced."

"Her name is Professor Korsakova."

"Thank you, Professor Teneyov. I'm quite capable of answering such a question myself. So, what brings you here, Clio?"

"I'm visiting Moscow on business. Since I have some extra time and I'm looking for someone you may know. His name is Ivanov Ivanovich Ilyich."

"That name does not ring a bell, as you say. You'll have to tell us more, including details about your connection to this Mr. Ilyich," Professor Korsakova said, trying to regain the initiative from her colleague.

"We met at a Russian tea house in Los Angeles. We had a remarkably interesting conversation about English and, most especially, Russian literature, which is his specialty. In fact, he collects rare books that are signed by their famous authors.

"He told me he had a first edition of *Walden*, signed by Thoreau himself, and that if I was ever in Moscow, to look him up. He would show me his collection. He wrote down on a napkin all his contact information, but I've lost it. I can't find it anywhere! So, that's why I'm here, on the off-chance you might know him."

They paused a while, as they considered what they had just heard. Doctor Teneyov broke the silence. "We may know people who do that. But you need to tell us more - at least a description."

"Well, he dresses very unusually. He dresses like a character out of Dickens or maybe even out of a Sherlock Holmes story. He has a great mutton chop beard with a well-trained moustache. His hair is perfectly trimmed. He's mostly grey, being I suppose around fifty or perhaps a bit more.

"He has a monocle, which hangs from his neck. He wears a vest with a pocket watch and its gold chain looped across the front. He likes to wear tweed suits tailored in London with a monogrammed kerchief in his suit's breast pocket. His shoes match the London tailored look. His cologne is traditional and expensive, maybe a Burberry. And he has a pet bulldog.

"He speaks with an Oxford English accent. Despite all his Anglophile getup, we ended up mostly discussing Bulgakov and Chekov. He presents himself as a very cultured and educated person. He also claims he has one of the original scripts of *The Seagull* with notes and a signature by Chekov himself. Does that remind you of anyone?"

"A bulldog, did you say?" asked Doctor Teneyov. "That is very interesting. I would say, very signature, indeed. Was he smoking cigars and drinking whiskey, too?"

"No, he smoked Sobranies, and we drank Armenian brandy."

"Armenian brandy? Which one did you drink?" Doctor Teneyov was testing.

"It was Ararat Five Star." Gwendolyn continued with as many details as she could remember from her imaginary meeting with the gaspodeen at the Russian teahouse in LA.

"Now, at least we can be sure he was a product of the Soviet Union," Doctor Teneyov said approvingly.

Professor Korsakova piped in: "A young woman like you and a man of his age, there must be more to this quest than what you have told us. He probably is a married man. What other possibility could there be?"

Gwendolyn shifted a bit in her seat, wondering if she should encourage or discourage the professor's insinuation. "He told me he was a widower. And we did nothing untoward. As interesting as he is, my interest is only in Thoreau and Chekov."

This brought on another moment of silence, broken by a heated discussion in Russian across their cluttered desks. Gwendolyn sat there praying that they would turn to her and hand over her prey on a silver platter. She would break him in half like a matchstick and be on the next plane to Los Angeles.

After a few minutes of discussion, Doctor Teneyov turned to her and said, "We can't say we are familiar with such a person. You might try the English Literature Association of Moscow. They meet the last Wednesday of the month for dinner at the Petroff Palace Hotel. However, we can make a few enquiries on our own and if we do find this Ilyich, we will let him know you are looking for him. What contact information should we give him?"

That was not the reply Gwendolyn hoped to hear. She blurted out, "NO! No, no, no … um… I mean, no. I want to surprise him. I have found a first edition of *1001 Nights*, the one that was translated by Sir Richard Burton. My edition was signed by him. It was Mr.

Ilyich's grand dream to own a copy. He will want to buy it from me, and I would happily give you 10% of the price he pays to me. That could easily be $60,000. But if you find him, you absolutely must not tell him I am looking for him. I so want this to be a surprise. Please! Can you promise me this?"

They looked at each other, eyes wide open. Then, they immediately turned to her and both asked, "Did you say $60,000?"

"That's what I said. Of course, I will try for more. I expect he will try to negotiate, but I won't let him go below that. He has money from the trade in these kinds of books."

"All right, fine. If we find such an Ivanov Ivanovich Ilyich, how should we contact you?" Professor Korsakova asked.

"Here is my email address." Just then, her cell phone vibrated, informing her that an email had arrived. "Thank you for your help. I must go now. It was good meeting you. Please remember not to tell him I'm here in Moscow looking for him. That is critical. Would you be so kind as to call a taxi for me?"

"Don't worry, my dear, we will abide by the terms of our arrangement and keep your search secret. Here is my card. In case you've found him, let us know. Professor Korsakova, give her one of yours, too. Of course, we will call a taxi for you. Where are you going?"

"Thank you for your cards. Ah-h-h, the Four Seasons. And if I do find him at the English Literature Association, I will still give you 5% for your help. Thank you again."

Gwendolyn waited while Professor Korsakova called the taxi. "There will be one outside our gate in five minutes," she told Gwendolyn. "Doctor Teneyov, please pretend to be an English gentleman. Walk our new friend Clio to the gate and wait there with her."

"Oh no, please don't. I can find my way to the gate on my own. There is no reason for anyone but me to be cold. I have a wonderfully warm coat, so I'll be fine."

With that, Gwendolyn grabbed her coat and hurried out the door before anyone could insist. Back in the empty corridor, she quickly hitched up her holster and pistol before putting on her coat.

Walking along the snow-covered pathway to the main gate, Gwendolyn's hope and excitement turned into panic and an icy fear that matched the freezing air blowing in her face. *What did I do? Why didn't I just wait to talk to Dimitri first? What if they do find him and tell him anyway? Then, he'll be hunting me! Damn it! Sometimes I am just too smart for my own good.* She continued cussing herself out, while standing by the gate. But then, a ray of light entered her mind. At least she had received the significant lead of the English Literature Association's dinner at the Petroff Palace. That was indeed something.

Suddenly, she remembered about her cell phone vibrating. She checked her email and saw that Dimitri's email had arrived. It read: **Be at the east end of the entrance to Red Square at 1815. Stand by the side of the road where the traffic is going south. Keep your face uncovered, so we can see who you are.**

Gwendolyn glanced at the time and saw that the meeting was only forty minutes away. She had to go there directly. Just then, a taxi honked, making her look up. "Is your name Clio, going to the Four Seasons?" the driver asked. She got in the front seat next to the driver.

"Yes, I am Clio, but no, we are not going to the Four Seasons. Go to the east side of the entrance to Red Square. Quickly, please. Bistro pasholsta!"

The driver nodded, activated the meter, and sped away. Gwendolyn hoped he understood. She started looking up words on her cell phone's Google translate.

The driver looked over at her cell phone and said: "Hey, no problem, Miss. I understood what you said."

Relieved, she put away her cell phone and tried to relax in another stifling hot Moscow taxi. She marveled at how fast her magnificent idea had turned into a terrible one. If she had contacted every English Literature Department in Moscow in the same way, there would be dozens of people out looking for her prey and the odds were that at least one of them would have let slipped that she was searching for him.

After kicking herself for such a stupid idea, she was somewhat relieved that she had stopped after only letting two people know about it. She would discuss it all with Dimitri and let him decide what to do.

The taxi dropped her off at the east end of Red Square with less than ten minutes to spare. She stood facing the rush-hour traffic going in the correct direction with her face exposed to the wind.

Taxis were constantly swerving over to her, offering her a ride. A few minutes after the appointed time, a black Mercedes stopped in front of her and the front passenger window rolled down.

"Margarita, I presume?"

"Are you the Master?"

"No, he's back at the house waiting for you. Get in the back seat."

CHAPTER ELEVEN

Gwendolyn was startled by a man sitting in the backseat next to her. He took up two-thirds of the seat and was a perfect rectangle. Luckily, she could fit in the remaining space. After about 20 minutes of heavy traffic, they drove into the underground parking of an art deco apartment building.

Except for the driver, who stayed with the car, the three of them took an elevator straight to the 16th floor penthouse. The elevator doors opened directly onto a living room. The furniture and décor looked like what she had seen at the Archbishop's Palace earlier that day. It was certainly tasteful and special, though not her style. The wide windows had a beautiful view of Red Square in the distance.

Her two companions stood by the elevator. The English-speaking one told her to sit on the sofa. Off to the side in the dimly lit room she noticed a large easel had been set up and on it was a very familiar painting. It was the Pissarro! It arrived safely.

After a few minutes, Dimitri entered. He was in his early fifties, clean-shaven, looking quite fit and sharp. He was about six feet tall and had an air of command. His double-breasted navy-blue smoking jacket looked like something a man would wear while smoking a Cohiba Churchill and sipping an old single malt after a fine meal.

"Ah, Margarita, you have arrived!" Dimitri said walking over to her with a smile and his hand extended. "What a journey, and totally unexpected. How are you holding up? Giles has told me all about your tribulations, my sad put-upon lass."

Rising from the sofa, forgetting she still had her coat on with her holstered side arm underneath, she took his hand in both of hers. His hand might as well have been a life preserver thrown to her while she was floundering in rough deep seas. After holding his hand for a bit too long, she dropped it with some embarrassment.

"Yes, I can understand why you are so happy to see me. I am the one friend you have here and as a friend, I must help you out of your predicament."

He called out: "Anna! Come and take our guest's coat and things. Be careful with the big pistol in her shoulder holster."

Turning to Gwendolyn, he said: "Don't worry. She understands how to handle firearms. Just to point out, by the way your left arm sticks out further than your right one, it's obvious your arm is resting on something rather large and it certainly isn't a large babushka breast.

"You would need another fifty years and fifty kilograms for that. Even your beautiful coat cannot hide that to an experienced eye, and my eye by necessity is extremely experienced. The coat is sable, I believe. Beautiful! I doubt you bought this for yourself. Whoever gave it to you must care for you a lot. No one buys such a thing of beauty for themselves."

Gwendolyn handed everything over to the attractive young woman standing by her side who was dressed in a French maid's uniform. Gwendolyn had only ever seen such uniforms on mannequins in erotic toy stores. She almost laughed.

"Yes, I am glad to see you," she said. "And yes, I will need your help. Well, how should I wear my holster so that it's not so obvious?"

"We'll have to adjust it, so it hangs tightly by your side lower down." Admiring the PS226 he pulled from her holster, he said: "Giles certainly prepared you well. It's a thing of beauty."

"It's not a beautiful thing at all, Dimitri Fomavich. That painting over there is a thing of beauty." She at once regretted saying it. It was not time for her opinions. In fact, it was time to be as agreeable as possible.

Luckily, Dimitri had a sense of humor. He also greatly respected her artistic ability. Something he could never aspire to, but any Russian could appreciate. "Yes, you are quite correct, my young Margarita. But if you had to rely on these things for your very life for as long as I have, you would start looking at them in a greatly different light.

"Talk to me about the other thing of beauty here: your beautiful coat. Of course, you don't need to tell me about the admirer who gave it to you, though he has already made me jealous."

"Now, Dimitri Fomavich, you're being silly! It was bought for me by the wife of Giles' friend in Mexico, who helped me get on the flight to Moscow."

"His wife, did you say? He bought it himself. He's clearly a man of taste and experience, buying nice things for women he admires or at least wants to impress."

"OK, if you say so, Dimitri Fomavich."

"My apologies. Most of Giles' business acquaintances are older men with too much money and time. We probably all have something in common. We enjoy flirting with sweet young women like you. We really aren't good for much else.

"But enough of this silliness, as you rightfully call it. Let's sit and admire this wonderful gift I bought myself from a certain exclusive mail order company we both are very familiar with. What would you prefer to start with? Wine? A liqueur? Vodka? A cocktail? I have almost anything at my bar." He motioned with his hand to the full bar he had against the wall near the windows.

"Red wine, please. It is too cold to drink anything chilled."

"Even red wine should be served at 17 C to 18 C, my dear. Do you want to change your mind?"

"Dimitri Fomavich, I'm not a yahoo! Of course, I know that.

What I meant is nothing that requires ice."

"You have the temper of a Ukrainian! Oh, I like your passion. Forgive me. We Europeans naturally assume Americans understand nothing about the finer things in life. But I am in the presence of an internationally renowned artist. From what I understand from Giles, you have dozens of secret admirers all around the world. I am one of the few who has the honor and pleasure to meet you in person.

"It would be my greatest honor to help you with your small problem. But first, let's admire this wonderful work of art before our very eyes. Anna, bring us a bottle of one of Margarita's favorite wines, a Gevrey-Chambertin."

Turning to Gwendolyn, "Giles has told me a great deal about you and your tastes."

As two full glasses were placed beside them, Dimitri sat back and looked at the Pissarro for a time in silent contemplation before he broke the silence:

"Beautiful! We must take a stroll through the Tretyakov Gallery together before you leave. Perhaps I will order from Giles one of the Russian Masters from off the museum wall. If you can never return to the US, I can give Giles enough business for you to live exceedingly well right here." It was obvious he was not joking.

Gwendolyn's heart sank at the idea of remaining in Russia.

Trying to sound upbeat, she said: "You know, what really irritates me about the Tretyakov is that whenever they send a traveling exhibit to other countries, they never include any of the great Russian art, only their collection of foreign art.

"That just forces us to make the long trip here to see the art of the likes of Shishkin, Levitan, Repin, Peredvizhniki, etc. No one can paint the sea like Aivazovsky. The list goes on.

"Classical Russian culture is one of the greatest and least understood by Western countries. If you think about it, much of the world's greatest literature, music, art, poetry, even many of the greatest movies came from here. Tarkovsky's *Stalker* and *Solaris* are superb examples.

"Only Americans and the Russians can write great science fiction. I mean, the Strugatski Brothers' *Monday Starts on Friday*! And comedy! Again, something that Americans and Russians excel at." Gwendolyn was clearly getting excited.

"Well, that's settled," he interrupted her lecture: "Tomorrow we'll enjoy the Russian Masters, as you call them. Indeed, as the world should call them! As for your other comments about our culture, I must dial it back a bit, as you Americans say. Arthur C Clarke's *2001* is just as good as *Solaris*, if not better, and he was British. Stanislaw Lem, who wrote the novel *Solaris*, was Polish. But anyway, I'll accept any praise and appreciation of our culture by a Westerner.

"I think we could become best friends quite quickly and I mean that with the most respect that someone like me can muster for another person. Contemporary Russian culture disgusts me. It is a caricature of the greatness we once gave to the world. But enough of this idle chitchat. Will you give me the honor of dining with me tonight? It's all prepared in the next room."

"I would love to, Dimitri Fomavich. But as for going to museums and the like, I have a small matter I must discuss with you first."

"No, not another word about it. First, we eat, then we'll talk about serious affairs. How can we discuss anything serious on an empty stomach?"

The pretty pert 'French' maid led them into the next room where a dining table for eight was laden with enough food for eighteen. But instead of eight or even ten at the table, there were only two men a few years younger than Dimitri standing by their chairs.

Dimitri introduced them, one as a younger brother and the other as an army buddy from the war in Afghanistan. He elaborated that they both held responsible positions in his business - his right and left hands, really. Dimitri invited everyone to sit. The maid remained standing, serving as needed.

"Before we start, will you join us for some vodka?" Dimitri asked Gwendolyn.

"No, I'll stick with this fine wine."

"I guessed as much. Traditionally, a bottle of vodka is best drunk by three," he said as he opened a bottle sitting at his place at the head of the table and threw the cap over his left shoulder.

"On one hand, we should not drink so much before discussing important matters. On the other hand, important matters should never be discussed without some vodka under our belts. It helps the thinking process."

"Let's see," Gwendolyn calculated. "A third of a bottle of vodka is 250 milliliters. There are on average about 40 milliliters in a shot. That would be about six shots of vodka. Are you sure we shouldn't meet for breakfast? We need to discuss extremely important matters, matters of life and death."

"One should never even think important thoughts before lunch, not to mention discuss them. My dear devotchka [young woman], just relax. Everything will be fine."

Gwendolyn tried to relax, but anxiety was simmering in her heart. Since she had no other choice and her brief attempt at finding her own solution seemed like a disaster in the making, she decided to settle back in her chair and enjoy dinner.

In front of them was a large array of salad-like dishes made from smoked fish, beetroots, mushrooms, red cabbage, and many things Gwendolyn could not identify, but enjoyed them greatly. Just when she thought she could not eat anything more, the hot dishes started to arrive.

First was beef tongue, one of her favorite dishes, then fish, pork loin, goose, etc. all grilled, roasted, stewed, and otherwise prepared in the most delicious ways imaginable. She decided that she liked Russian food.

She noticed something strange. "Dimitri Fomavich, why are there no knives at the table?"

"It's a tradition of ours. Maybe because in the old days, there were too many knife fights after dinner from drinking too much vodka."

Noticing Gwendolyn's expression, he quickly added: "Don't worry, we never drink that much, at least at my table, well, at least not with a young lady as our guest.

Every time someone wanted to drink, they would toast each other or some noble concept or something quite banal with a very formal long eloquence of at least a few minutes. They would hold their crystal shot glasses in front of them with arm and elbow parallel to the floor and in the other hand they would hold something pickled like a cucumber, onion, or mushroom that they would take from one of the small dishes before them.

When the one toasting was finished, they would all gulp down their shot of vodka at the same time and immediately follow it with eating the pickled thing in their other hand. The entire ritual was always done with the most solemn expressions on their faces. It reminded her of the three girls at the VIP lounge.

Gwendolyn would just take sips from her wine glass. She knew that if she wanted to discuss anything serious, her limit was no more than two glasses of wine. Having woken up around noon, this was like lunch to her. She still had enough energy to last through the strange dinner she found herself enjoying.

After about an hour, when everyone was sitting back from the table and the bottle of vodka was empty, Dimitri suggested they all move to the "drawing room." This was not the living room that the elevator opened on to but another smaller room, even better furnished, that looked out over the city. They sat in deep leather chairs with antique side tables. The dark hard wood floors were covered by large beautiful silk Persian carpets.

The three men settled into their comfortable seats, poured glasses of Armenian brandy, and lit up their Cohibas. After a sip and a few puffs, Dimitri leaned back and looked up at the ceiling, "All right, devotchka Margarita, what's on your mind? Why have you come to visit me?"

"What has Giles told you?"

"This is what I understand: He acquired my wonderful present, thanks to your help. But the operation met with a complication at the end. The previous caretakers of my painting were murdered, and the murderers have tried to pin the blame on you. There seems to be a Russian connection, as you met quite a few of my dishonorable compatriots during your work. Giles sent me links to all the news about it. I know the surface details.

"But what's strange is that I would expect this sort of violent Russian behavior while stealing a company or a mine, but over a painting? What is this world coming to? It was a gentleman's world of merely changing caretakers of great works of art.

"If the reproduction was perfect, no one noticed anything, and everyone was happy. The earlier caretakers have so many of these wonderful paintings on their walls that they walk past them many times a day and don't really see them anymore. When that happens, it is time for a change of ownership.

"But now? Now, it seems it has become the realm of robber barons fighting over railroads and aluminum mines. That's all I know. We must find these bastards and stop them, returning our activity to the peaceful and honorable one it must remain. We will be the policeman of this business. Your turn to speak."

"You understand most of it," Gwendolyn replied. "What I can add is what I saw that no one else did."

She proceeded to describe the Anglophile 'gentleman' and her encounter with him. She described those who had followed her through the market and how she had lost them, the burglary of her studio, the black Mercedes that tried to follow her from the museum parking garage.

She described the Robertsons, their home and staff. She went on for about half an hour with every detail she could remember, even her experience with the punks in the parking garage stairwell. She left nothing out. Then, she ended with some embarrassment by describing her meeting with the two professors and what she had said to them.

Dimitri did a Giles on her. He went silent for about five minutes, puffing on his Cubano cigar. She started wondering if he had even been listening. But he had been listening to her every word.

"Describe to me again the Robertson's house."

She did, though it was quite clear how the murderers had entered the house. Then, he really surprised her.

"I should look into buying something similar in Malibu. Many friends of mine have urged me to buy a place there for quite a few years. I wonder, now that the owners have died, if their only daughter would consider selling it to me. Do you know how to contact her?"

Gwendolyn nearly fell off her seat. "Dimitri Fomavich! Are you joking?"

"No, not at all. But you're correct in your reaction. First thing's first. Fine. Let's find this fake gaspodeen and make things right in the world again. So, what do you want me to do?"

"Want you to do?" she cried out in anger. "Find that bastard and make him admit to his crimes, so I can go home!"

Dimitri lost his temper with the sharped-tonged young woman. "Now, you listen to me," he growled with anger flashing in his eyes. "Listen clearly. I appreciate your artistic ability, and how well educated you are. I really do like you but understand this: I don't need to help you at all. I can change my hobby to collecting fine Arabian racehorses or vintage sports cars. It's all the same to me.

"Why should I risk my entire standing in the world and all that I have gained for my family to do this for you? No, I've changed my mind. I will not help you. It's just not worth the aggravation." He leaned back and took a sip of his drink.

Gwendolyn was in full panic now. It was the first time in her life that she truly desperately needed a stranger's help and she had blown it. Leaning back in her seat, staring blindly at the ceiling, she did something she had not done in an exceedingly long time. Tears started flowing down her cheeks. This turned out to be the best thing she could have done.

"Oh, for God's sake! Don't cry, my dear devotchka," he said with

117

genuine tenderness in his voice. He grabbed the box of tissues nearby and pulled a few out. Dimitri kneeled beside her and wiped her tears with the tissues. "Don't cry. We'll figure something out." He stroked her lightly on the back of her head.

Gwendolyn almost started laughing in her tears but had enough feminine sense to know she should let his manly guilt bite a bit more. She stopped crying, took the tissues he was using on her face, blew her nose into them, and returned the wet tissues back into his hands.

He continued, still kneeling beside her. "We'll fix everything. But we must do it together. I can't do it for you. As Giles has helped you so far, by getting you here into my home, I will also help you, but it has to be me helping you, not you helping me. You must take the lead on this."

"But how?" She almost started crying again. "I don't know anyone or anything here. I know nothing of the culture or how to talk to people. I'd have no idea how to do this, even in my hometown. I'm an artist, not a hunter-killer. Quite simply, I'm lost. I'm lost here without you!" Again, the exact correct thing to say.

"Yes, I know. But don't worry. I will help you. But what's key is that at the end, only you who can extract what evidence you need to clear your name. I would have no idea what would work with the LA police, or what would work in your courts."

"You will help me, then?" she asked in a plaintive voice.

"Yes, of course, I'll do whatever I can."

"What should we do now?" Gwendolyn gave him a desperate hug.

"Please don't think yourself foolish to have talked to the professors. You're completely right that they may find the culprit first and even carelessly warn him that you're here looking for him.

"First thing tomorrow morning, one of my associates will meet them and explain that you already found this Ilyich. We'll offer to pay them for their help with $6,000 each, which is more than they earn in a year. We'll also make it clear that they will be happy with it and forget the whole thing. And they will be. I hire associates who can be very persuasive.

"However, what you did gain was the location and time of a meeting where he might very well be. You need to go to that dinner meeting. If he is there, identify him. We will then follow him home. Once we know where he lives, the problem is practically solved.

"I remember my wife came to me once, saying she needed 100,000 Euros to buy an original Pushkin-signed *Yevgeny Onegin*, one of his few novels, written in verse. Now, you understand, Pushkin is the patron saint of all Russians. We memorize his poems when we're only five years old. Of course, I was interested.

"I met a man very similar to your description, except I remember he had a Corgi, not a Bulldog, with him. No matter. I asked to see the manuscript, supposedly an original with the signature of the magnificent man himself.

"He wouldn't let me touch it, but he showed us the signature and a few pages of the book. Every Russian knows this sad story of Yevgeny and Tatyana. Seeing this book so close was like having a splinter of wood from the True Cross lying in front of me. But my natural distrust and need to bargain stopped me from buying it right there.

"I offered him 60,000 Euros. He politely refused but gave me his contact information in case I changed my mind. My wife, who is much more literate than me, was enraged that I would not buy her this treasure right then. After a few days of her relentless imploring, I contacted him. He told me he had already sold it for 125,000 Euros. I'd have reached through the phone line and strangled him, if I could. Naturally, I tried to find him. I would have gladly bought it for 200,000 Euros and considered it a bargain.

"He disappeared. I personally tried everything, including waiting all night outside the address on his card. All his contact details, including his name, were not real. He changed his phone number and email.

"I even went to the company that owns the server from where his email originated. They had the same information I did. I never did find him. My wife damn nearly divorced me over it. That would have cost me many, many millions.

"After a few years and many expensive gifts, I think she has forgiven me. But I'm not sure. Anyway, the crisis has passed. But I promise you this: If you can find him again, get what you need, then give him to me.

"I will personally take from his hide every bit of pain and grief he gave me over this and even more, the pain and grief I have given myself for not being smart enough to buy it that exact instant.

"So, go to this meeting and identify him. We will locate where he really lives and set him up for you. After that, we'll take care of the rest. But by then, you will be on your way to the airport. How does that sound?"

"Sounds good. Let's do it."

"Fine. From what you said, you only have four days until this dinner. You will need to check into the hotel and decide how you will infiltrate that meeting without being recognized. We will wait outside. You will identify him to us in some way. We will follow him home.

"Once we know where he lives, we'll let you in. You find him, get the evidence you came for without killing him, and get out. We'll do the follow up, as you Americans like to say. You must be absolutely sure you have what you came for.

"You will not get a second chance. If you need to scour the place when he is not there, we can help you do that, too. Remember, just as with Giles, I cannot be connected to this in any way, at least directly.

"I'll give you a phone number that only you can use. I'll also give you a sim card that you must use when you call me. On our last phone call of this little project, you will press star-pound-star and the sim card will erase itself. There cannot be any evidence that directly ties us together. I trust you. I just don't want any complications if things don't work out as planned."

"Ah, a plan!" Gwendolyn exclaimed. "Now, I have something to wrap my mind around. Thank you so much, Dimitri Fomavich! If you want another painting, I'll do it for free. What else should I do in the meantime?"

"I doubt Giles would do anything for free. But that is a nice gesture. In the next day or two you'll check in to the Petroff Hotel. For my part, I will look for any other possible associations, if this one is not the right one. If he is not in Moscow, the only other place he could be would be St. Petersburg. My associates and I will continue tracking down other possibilities of his location.

"As for you, besides finding a different firing range to practice in and not talking to any more professors, there is only one other important thing for you to do."

"Only one? I can do that."

"Visit the Tretyakov with me tomorrow."

"With pleasure, my dear sir."

CHAPTER TWELVE

Captain Slarpniak was a great bull of a man in his early fifties, with a clean-shaven face and head with several rolls of muscle where his head met his neck. Though born and raised in Chicago, he had ended up in LA when he was discharged from the Marines. First, he did a stint as a bodyguard for a rapper.

He quit that after he took a bullet in the chest for his employer, who blamed him for not taking more bullets. Then, he tried a few jobs as a bouncer at various south LA night clubs, until one of his best buddies convinced him to try entering the LAPD. He found that was his true calling and rose quickly through the ranks.

Rugby was his great passion. He still played competitively on a Long Beach team. This is what kept him in excellent shape and not gone to fat like so many of his colleagues. He worked hard to keep his Stormtrooper figure. At 6' 4" and 245 pounds, he was a dominating force in any room he entered.

He delivered solutions to seemingly intractable problems, and he was a leader of men. Just as important, he could handle the media very well. He did good interviews and was quite photogenic on the evening news. Those were excellent reasons that kept his superiors happy. He was put in charge of the Robbery Homicide Division at age forty-three.

When the Robertsons were murdered, he took direct control of their homicide case. It was considered very high profile with intense media coverage. It was just the kind of case that a darling of the media like Slarpniak would naturally rise to.

How he handled this case would either open a path to the chief of the LAPD or leave him cast aside as something like a captain of a precinct station or even worse. He would lose so much face that his career would be finished. So, he made sure everything he did was at the top of his game.

Slarpniak addressed his lieutenants in the War Room, a large conference room with an oval table in the middle and boards hanging on all the walls where they would stick yellow Post-It notes and the evidence they had so far with any possible conclusions. The walls were still quite empty, even two days after the strange 911 call.

"All right. What do we know so far? Let's do a review. Antony. What do you have? Take me through the wall diagrams," Slarpniak asked his right-hand man, Lieutenant Antony Rodriguez.

"Well, sir, we do have a lot of evidence, but so far, except for the 911 call, there is nothing conclusive. But the 911 call is the primary evidence at present. So, let's start with that. I've emailed all of you the recording of the 911 call. The transcript is written here on the wall.

"The suspect called 911 at 4:12 on the morning of Saturday, describing events that allegedly happened sometime around midnight. Let's listen to it again."

"Hello. You have called the 911 dispatch line. What is your name, where are you, and what is the reason for your call?"

"Never mind where I am. My name is Gwendolyn and I want to report that I killed the Robertsons of 23418 Anacapa View Drive in Malibu earlier tonight. But I can explain."

"Please go on."

"I was a guest at the Robertsons for almost two weeks. Yesterday afternoon and evening, Mr. and Mrs. Robertson attended the BAFTA ceremonies and events. They came home just before

midnight. I was already in bed. About a half an hour later, Ferdinand, I mean Mr. Robertson, came into my room, and tried to rape me. He had been drinking quite a bit, judging from his breath.

"While he was trying to force himself on me, I was screaming and fighting back. But he was much stronger than me. I reached for my pistol in my handbag on the floor by the bed. Mr. Robertson saw this, and we struggled for control of it. Just when he almost got control of it, Mrs. Robertson came into the bedroom and became hysterical at the sight of her husband struggling with me in the bed. He pulled the pistol from me and toward her. It went off by accident, shooting her in the head. I think she was killed.

"When Mr. Robertson saw this, he let go of my hand that was still holding the pistol, and I shot him in the head. I wasn't even aiming. It just went off, and he fell to the floor. I think he's dead. I panicked, grabbed my things, and ran out of the house. I kept running until I couldn't. I thought about what I should do and decided to call you. Did I do the right thing? I just don't know."

Sobbing sounds.

"You absolutely did the right thing. Where are you now?"

Silence.

"Are you hurt?"

Silence.

"Let me call an ambulance for you and make sure you haven't been hurt."

Silence after a strong exhale.

"What is your last name?"

Heavy breathing.

"Hello? Please answer me. You need help. Ma'am, hello? Are you still on the phone? Ma'am?"

"The phone went dead. The suspect hung up. The call was made from a disposable foreign cell phone using a stored value system from Lycamobile. We tried but failed to trace the call to a common carrier with call records."

"Thank you, Antony. Now, let's move on to the next station on our wall: the physical evidence."

On the wall were photos and the floor plans of the house and surrounding property. "Now, Antony, take us through this section."

"Let's first look at the guest bedroom diagram and the location of the bodies. Just inside the bedroom door, you can see the outline of the position of Mrs. Robertson's body. Notice how she fell backward, laying face up with the bullet wound to the forehead. She was wearing a nightgown.

"Mr. Robertson's body is laying on his side to the right of the bed facing toward it with a bullet wound to his right temple. He is still wearing his dress clothes from the evening's events, as confirmed by witnesses. Notice how his pants and underwear are down around his ankles. The bedding has been pulled away and lies on the floor to the left of the bed. This photo of the bed shows the smear of menstrual blood, presumably from the suspect.

"These drawings show the floor plans of the house of the victims. You can see the bedroom where the shootings happened is on the first floor on the southwest corner. Mr. Robertson's office is on the southeast corner of the first floor. Mrs. Robertson's bedroom is on the second floor above the guest bedroom. Mr. Robertson's bedroom is also on the second floor above his study. They slept in separate bedrooms.

"We haven't been able to retrieve the murder weapon. The bullets were fired from a 10 mm low velocity handgun. Both bullets were lodged in the victims' brains. We have measured an estimated radius someone could have covered in about four hours of running and walking. We've also identified the paths she would most likely have followed. We are searching for the handgun in those areas.

"We've recovered the fingerprints of the suspect all over the room and the ground floor of the house. She made no attempt to hide them. We also have her DNA sample she left on the bed sheets. We are trying to identify her, but if she has no prior convictions or has never applied for public employment, we may not be able to make a match. So far, we haven't found one in any database across the country. That pretty much sums it up for physical evidence.

"Oh, there's another thing. The security system was not working the entire day. There are no records from 06:00 Friday morning. Previous days show that the house alarm system is turned off around 06:00 every morning, but the cameras always stay on, except for last Friday, when they were turned off, too. This might have been user error. Don't know."

"Thanks, Antony. Now, lead us through what we know from the people closest to this case."

"Sure, Captain. Let's move over to this wall. Here you will see their photos, their connection to the case, and what came out of our interviews with them. The first one is Lorenzo, the full-time driver of the Robertsons for sixteen years. He lives in an apartment over the garage. He also spent the most time with the suspect, taking her around LA looking for a place to live. Most of the useful information came from him. However, he's quite emotional about it and very protective of the suspect.

"When he first heard about the case, he fainted and had to be hospitalized. While recovering, he confessed that he was the one who did it. Fortunately for him, he has an ironclad alibi. He was an exotic dancer at a gay bar in Santa Barbara during the time of the crime. There are too many witnesses who can collaborate this, so we can dismiss his confession.

"What he did tell us that was useful are the places he took her during their days driving around LA. The first trip was to pick up her things at the Santa Monica Holiday Inn. They went to Venice Beach twice, once to the Getty Museum, and the rest of the time he would drop her off at LACMA.

"He also told us that the suspect told him that she needed to return to Philadelphia last Friday evening, where she has an ailing grandmother in the hospital. We are checking with all the area hospitals, but we just don't have enough facts to make any kind of connection. Another thing about Lorenzo is that he is adamant that she could never have done such violence, even if provoked. Even more significant, when he heard the recording of the 911 call, he was completely certain that it was not her voice.

"The chef only spoke a few words with her, and the rest of the staff never spoke with her. They all easily identified her photo. Of course, we have no record of what the Robertsons knew about her. Their daughter is flying in tonight, and when we meet with her tomorrow, she might give us more insight.

"Now, off to the side here is something strange. These two claim that the suspect attacked them in the stairwell of the LACMA parking garage. They claim that she attacked the one who came in a wheelchair, completely unprovoked. Seemed to them that she was lying in wait. He had a broken arm and knee. He needed his friend to push the wheelchair.

"Apparently, she is an expert in martial arts and is armed with a stiletto which she has attached to her inside left forearm. Those two together weigh four times her weight but were visibly frightened that she might find and attack them again. They were also extremely disappointed that there's no reward for what they had to say. We may want to consider offering one."

Slarpniak broke in: "Fine, but tell us something about Gabriella, their daughter."

"She has an art degree and for the past four years, she has been the head of a non-profit based in Thailand. This non-profit specializes in restoring the damaged Buddha statues in the destroyed temples across Asia. We know nothing about her relationship with her parents."

"Thanks, Antony. Now, let's all move back over to the first wall with the 911 transcript. We'll go through the current evidence again, but this time we'll make comments and share thoughts to help form an acceptable, plausible case. Try to push the envelope. Despite appearances, what else might have happened and what would be the motive?

"Let's start by comparing the details in the phone call and what we know. We've confirmed that the Robertsons indeed attended the

BAFTA ceremonies and left around 2300 from a party at the Beverly Hills Hotel. Mr. Robertson had indeed been drinking quite a bit. Witnesses heard Mrs. Robertson quarrelling with Mr. Robertson over him flirting with several of the young women actresses before 2300 and shortly after that, Mr. Robertson agreed to go home.

"So far, the timeline fits. It takes about thirty minutes to drive from the hotel to their home. They go to their rooms, probably not happy with each other. Mr. Robertson thinks his wife has gone to sleep and he decides to have his way with their guest around 0030. The suspect screamed, awaking Mrs. Robertson, who goes downstairs to find out what is happening.

"She hears a struggle in the suspect's room, enters and is shot dead in the doorway. Mr. Robertson realizes what he has done and stops struggling with the suspect. The suspect then takes advantage of him loosening his grip on the pistol and shoots him in the head. He falls dead to the floor by the side of the bed.

"Continuing from what the suspect says, she grabs her bag, probably has to pack it quickly, and in panic runs away. She runs or walks for about four hours and then decides to call 911 on her foreign cell phone to confess. But then toward the end of the call she gets cold feet and stops cooperating. It's been two days and we haven't heard anything more from her. Anyone have any ideas?"

Antony spoke for everyone else. "I think you've summed it up very well, Captain."

"Does anyone have anything more to add?"

Silence.

"Should we move on to the next bit of evidence?"

"Yes, sir," another lieutenant agreed.

"Well, I don't agree," Slarpniak impatiently snapped. "Come on! Is that all this recording has to offer?"

Someone asked, "Sir? Why would she have a foreign cell phone?"

"Excellent question, Jimmy. Why would she? Even better, how would she have one?"

"She travelled recently and brought it back with her, sir."

"But why would she have one in Los Angeles? Doesn't she have a US cell phone? Or if she does, why didn't she use it? Come on, guys. Run with it."

The officers in the room started to brainstorm.

"She returned from a trip overseas recently and had the phone on her. She didn't use the US cell phone because she did not want the call to be easily traced."

Another one added, "We can ask Homeland Security to scan their data base of photos of people entering the US over the past month and compare them to the photo we have of her. If we find a match, then we might have some answers, including her real name."

"If we have her real name, then we can find out a lot about her, including any rap sheets, bank transactions, etc." another one suggested.

"We can do a voice analysis on the recording. That might tell us something, too."

"What would that tell us, Bobby?"

"Captain, we could see if the FBI has any exact matches in their voice data base."

"All right, fine. You guys together have at least half a brain. Let's not get too carried away. We have other things to look at, too. To summarize, Antony, I hope you are taking good notes. The suspect might have been traveling recently to have a foreign cell phone and she didn't want to be identified when she called.

"But, if she decided to call 911, why wouldn't she want to be traced? That's strange. Or it could be as simple as she had credit on her foreign phone that she wanted to use up.

"Did anyone think that maybe she hadn't been traveling at all, but rather that someone gave her the foreign cell phone to make the call? Did anyone note a slight accent? According to the hired help at the Robertsons, she had grandparents on the east coast, around Philadelphia. That's where she told them she was from. But I don't hear a Philadelphian accent. What am I hearing? Let's listen to it again."

They all listened to the recording again. And yes, they agreed she had a slight accent and that it was not from Philadelphia. Slarpniak said that some of the vowels sounded like how his Polish grandfather spoke. But no one could be sure because her voice was nearly hysterical.

"Antony, send the recording not just to the FBI, but also to an accent specialist. Gwendolyn is not a Polish name. One of Lorenzo's notes is that her grandmother living near Philadelphia raised her for at least some part of her life. If this is even true, that means she is at least third generation American and that her English must be at a native level without any non-American accent.

"Before we go any further, let me remind you again. We should come at this from two angles. One is that everything is exactly as the evidence indicates. The other angle is to assume that everything that appears to be true, is not. In this case, we must determine what the motive was, until we can ask the suspect herself.

"The simple conclusion is the first angle. Gwendolyn was sexually assaulted. The Robertsons were killed during the struggle and the suspect ran away with a confession call to 911. There was no motive other than self-defense.

"The few minor details like using a foreign cell phone and having a slight accent could all have simple explanations that would not detract from the main premise. We could do a quick review of all the other evidence and if nothing contradicts it, we could say case closed.

"Before we do so, let's look at things from the other angle. Let's assume everything in that 911 call was a lie. Her name is not Gwendolyn. The Robertsons did come home from BAFTA, but there was no sexual assault. They were killed and placed in the positions we found them. Maybe she wasn't overseas recently and someone else gave her the foreign cell phone. That means she had accomplices and that it was planned."

"But sir? To what end? If she had accomplices and it was

planned, what was the motive? And why would they have her call 911 with that story?"

"Yes, James, you are completely correct. Those are hard questions to answer. Antony, you told me that their daughter is flying in from Thailand tonight. Go meet her and take her to her hotel. Try to get just one answer from her before letting her rest for the night: did her parents have any enemies?

"Bring her to their house tomorrow morning. We'll meet her there and try to find some answers with her help. Perhaps she'll notice something we haven't."

"Yes, sir."

"All right. Let's try to come up with alternative motives by tomorrow. Remember, nothing was stolen, despite all the expensive paintings and objects around the house. When we talk to the daughter tomorrow, we might find there are motives, or we might not.

"Because the victims died quite quickly, there are no blood traces that would indicate their being killed anywhere else but where their bodies were found. There are no strange dirt or mud shoe traces that indicate someone else entered the house. So far, it's hard not to accept things as they appear. But when we move over to the witness section, we have more food for thought."

"Sir, the driver's testimony and your comment earlier that the 911 caller had a slight accent might be enough to raise doubt that the suspect even made the call. If she didn't make the call, then the whole case falls apart. Seems to me, sir, that either the suspect did it or someone is trying to make it look like she did it."

"Riley, you just opened up a new can of worms. Following this line of reasoning, we would need to find a motive for someone to frame the suspect. Until we find one or the other, we will never get to the bottom of it. But you're right. The 911 call has its problems, not least is her hysterical voice that makes analysis difficult. I think we should hold that thought until we have more facts."

"What about the two who came in for the reward? Ray, you were present for their testimony. What can you add?"

"You know, sir? Though they wanted a reward for what they had to say, they were truly scared of the suspect. I believe she did do some serious damage to the one and would have done the same to the other.

"This action plus the murders of the Robertsons would definitely show she can be violent and that she might even be psychopathic if she was really waiting in the LACMA parking garage stairwell for two random men to walk by and beat the living sh*t out of them, as they claim."

Lieutenant Wang spoke up: "Unfortunately for that line of thought, those two are the ones with a rap sheet of muggings and violence, including violence against women. They both spent time in juvenile for these crimes. If you ask me, I think they were the ones who jumped her, but got more than they were expecting. Just my opinion, sir."

"Johnny, I do value your opinion. Thank you for that. Sounds like those two are useless. Does anyone else have something to add?

"No? All right then, let's end our little party now. We'll meet back tomorrow after we have more pieces to this puzzle, namely any FBI matches for voice prints, fingerprints and her DNA, Homeland Security's match of her photo, voice analysis for any foreign accents, the IT report on the security system, and the very important testimony of the Robertson's daughter. We'll be at the Robertson's house in the morning before 0800."

Everyone filed out, leaving Captain Slarpniak staring at the wall of evidence. It would be so tempting to run with the most obvious explanation. But what if he was wrong? That would be the end of his career.

Until he found the suspect, everything else was moot. Why does she not turn herself in and solve the whole thing in an instant? What was stopping her? It was clear to him that the most important thing was to find that girl.

"Where is she?" He asked out loud to the empty room.

CHAPTER THIRTEEN

At 3 AM, Gwendolyn was awake staring at the barely visible ceiling of her bedroom, dimly lit by a night light. She could hear the winter wind blowing with a low-pitched howl outside.

She was wondering if she should get up and take some more Valerian when her cell phone vibrated on the side table. She never turned it off, hoping to receive a call from Giles telling her they had found the perpetrators and that the nightmare was over. She reached over and opened the message. It read:

Returning to LA to take care of matters. Police want to talk to me about my parents. Don't worry. I know you didn't do it. I'll help you from any angle I can. I've got your back.

G.

"Gabriella?" Gwendolyn exclaimed out loud. "How does she even have my phone number?" Then, to herself, *Probably from some mutual friend or ex-boyfriend. We probably do travel in the same circles or did anyway. That's nice of her. I need all the help and friends I can get now. But why does she want to help me?*

***

Lieutenant Antony Rodriguez was standing outside the arrivals gate at Bradley Terminal at LAX holding a carefully printed sign with Gabriella's name on it. He was still on duty, but he had changed out of his uniform to put her at ease. Gabriella could just ignore him, take a taxi, and disappear into the LA traffic. Slarpniak would not be amused if she did that. Having arrived early, Antony reflected on his life.

Men of the extended Rodriguez family made only four career choices: military, police, fireman, and incarceration. The one thing they all had in common were their crew cuts. Antony did not follow any of those paths. He wanted to break out of the mold and stereotype.

He did something very startling to his family. He let his hair grow long, moved out at age eighteen, and enrolled in Cal State Long Beach for a few semesters, studying pre-law classes. He was the first in his family to go to college at all.

He sold used cars at a local dealership to pay his way through school, but then he dropped out of college at age twenty to marry his pregnant girlfriend. Besides, he could make a decent living selling cars. He was considered the family disgrace, though he made more money at twenty-five than his father did with thirty years in the California Highway Patrol.

After years of living in a kind of mental funk, something startling happened that jerked him awake at age thirty-four: his father was gunned down during a routine traffic stop on Interstate 5.

Fortunately, all his eight children were already adults. But it really effected Antony for months after. He could barely concentrate on anything. Then, only a few months later, when his favorite little brother, Jose, died fighting a warehouse fire in Long Beach, he nearly snapped.

After almost losing his wife and child to a year of alcoholism, with some serious introspection, he got his head screwed back on straight. This light at the end of the tunnel occurred when he happened to pass Cal State Long Beach one day and, in a rush, all of his past hopes and dreams came flooding back.

In short, he finished his degree in pre-law. But at thirty-five, he knew he was too old to have any kind of meaningful career in law. So, he made his mother proud and joined the LAPD.

He wanted to use his law education and bring some justice to the world; to help put the kind of bad people who had killed his father behind bars. After only a few years, he had become second in command of an important department and with any luck he would replace Slarpniak when he was promoted for cracking this case. *What a long strange trip it had been.* He thought to himself.

His introspection was interrupted by a slender young woman with intense green eyes, dressed in the Bohemian way that artists do. "Hello, I'm Gabriella. Are you expecting me?"

"Why, yes, I am. Sorry, I was lost in thought. Let me take your bags for you."

"You should be glad you were holding that sign. I would have never found you otherwise. Are you my driver? Then take me home. Didn't know someone ordered a limo for me. Wonder who it was?"

"Turns out that the City of LA ordered me to pick you up. It's a side job I do to make a little extra on my time off. Just joking. My name is Lieutenant Antony Rodriguez of the LAPD, Homicide Special Section. I am the main detective on the case of your parents' tragic demise. The entire city mourns the loss of two of its leading citizens."

"You're the main detective on the case of my parents' tragic demise? Really? We can talk on the way to my home." They started walking toward the parking garage.

"Well, I'm sorry, but you can't go home just yet. It's the center of a crime scene. I've been instructed to take you as a guest of the City of Los Angeles to the Santa Monica Holiday Inn. Tomorrow morning, I will take you to your home where hopefully you can shed some light on this case. Captain Slarpniak, the head of our department, will be there. We are very interested in any perspective you may have."

Gabriella stopped in her tracks. "The Santa Monica Holiday Inn?

You're joking right? Oh, I see you're not joking. Is that the best the city can do? Take me to Shutters on the Beach. Do you know where that is? You do? Good. I don't need the city's hospitality.

"I don't mind sleeping with the bugs and snakes in a tent in the middle of a Cambodian jungle, but the Santa Monica Holiday Inn? You want my cooperation, don't you? Oh, never mind. Just take me to Shutters. I need a long walk along the 3rd Street Promenade to distract me."

They walked in silence to the parking garage. Antony did not liked how things started out. He was thinking about what he could say to get things back on track.

"Let me guess, Lieutenant. Your car is that black Crown Victoria over there. I was right? Now, how did I know that? What was it, old police surplus?"

"Did you have a tough flight, Gabriella?"

"No, on the contrary. It was very smooth. Why would you ask that?"

"Just seems that we're not exactly hitting it off very well," he replied while putting her luggage in the trunk.

"That has nothing to do with my flight and everything to do with you being a cop." She was about to open the back door to get in.

"I'd rather you sat up front with me, so we can talk while I drive." She never liked being told what to do, but she got in the front seat just the same.

He pointed out, "As you can see, I'm not wearing my uniform. Let's just pretend I'm not a cop."

"All right. Let's pretend you're my limo driver. So, how's life in LA these days? Traffic getting any better?"

Antony stopped the car in the middle of the exit lane of the parking garage. "Gabriella. Please. I'm just trying to do my job solving your parents' murder."

"Oh, are you? I think you and your entire department have no interest in solving the murders, but in capturing Gwendolyn and closing the case as soon as you can. I have nothing more to say right now. Just drop me off at the hotel and pick me up at 8:00 tomorrow morning. You can find me in the lobby."

"Gabriella. Come on. It's not right to say that. We are looking into all the evidence from every angle."

"Let's review the facts tomorrow at my home with the whole gang."

"May I ask you one question tonight about your parents?"

"No, you may not. We'll do all the Q and A bit tomorrow."

After fifteen minutes, she broke the silence.

"Oh, I see you know your way around LA. Thank you for taking PCH in the back way to Santa Monica and avoiding the zoo on the freeways."

"What kind of limo driver would I be to not know something so basic?"

He thought he saw a slight smile break her frown. There might be hope after all.

After he dropped her off at the hotel, he called Slarpniak.

"Just dropped her off, Captain."

"Did you find out anything, Antony?"

"No. She has a bit of an attitude. I don't think she likes cops and it seems she doesn't respect what we've done so far on the case."

"What does she know?"

"Just what the media says, I'm guessing. She seems to be full of her own ideas."

"Well, let's see if the Enlightened One will show us the true path tomorrow morning. We should cut her some slack. Her parents were brutally murdered in her bedroom, after all. What time are you picking her up?"

"0800."

"Right, the team will meet you at the house. Call if anything changes. Wear your uniform tomorrow."

"Fine, Captain. See you tomorrow."

***

Gabriella walked over to the check-in counter. A young twenty-something man asked her with chipper arrogance. "Hello, Miss. Do you have a reservation?"

"No."

"Well, I'm so sorry. We are all booked up until April 10th."

"Let me talk to the manager."

"So sorry, he's terribly busy now. Perhaps you can try the Holiday Inn? I can call over to see if they have any rooms. They usually do."

"The Holiday Inn? Are you fricking joking? What is it with the Holiday Inn? I see him right over there. Hey, Jonathan! Guess who is trying to check in to your wonderful hotel?"

"Gabriella? Is that you? It is! I'm so sorry about what happened! It must be simply devastating. Just awful," he said hurrying up to her. They exchanged air kisses.

"I haven't seen you since you had your eighteenth birthday party here, almost ten years ago. Now, that was a party."

"Yes, good times were had by all."

"Heard you're living in Thailand now. Running a non-profit."

"Yes, we're restoring destroyed religious sites in Asia."

"You must be exhausted. We have your favorite room ready for you. The one with the best view of the sunset.

"Arthur, let me have the key to the Sunset Room. Thank you. Check her in as Gabriella Robertson. We don't need her credit card. She has all the credit she needs to stay at our humble abode.

"Let me take your luggage, Ms. Robertson. Oh-h-h that sounds so grown up, doesn't it?"

Arthur looked at her with the most pleading eyes, hoping she would forgive his mistake of not recognizing the Robertson's daughter. Her eyes replied with a hope-you-learned-a-lesson look.

It was impossible not to like Jonathan. He had been the Events Manager when her parents organized her eighteenth birthday at the hotel. He had been the perfect host. He always made people share in his jolliness.

Gabriella dropped some of her annoyance with the LAPD and decided to give them a chance. She looked forward to meeting the detectives the next day. In the meantime, she wanted to see what craziness the 3rd Street Promenade would offer that evening.

She particularly liked the street musicians. When she lived with her parents, they always made sure her wallet was full of cash. She used to walk down the street with a small stack of $100 notes and drop one into an up-turned hat or an open guitar case sitting on the ground. It would cause the musicians to skip a beat or two.

Gabriella never gave money to anyone else. To her, street musicians were offering a public good with their music and should be paid accordingly.

She missed the old black guy, famous for his version of *Stand By Me*. But there were plenty of others singing for their dinner. Some were better than others. But no matter, it took a lot of bravery to sing on the streets.

Before returning to her room, she took off her shoes and stepped into the lapping waves of the Santa Monica Beach near the pier. The sound of the waves always calmed her. She let the waves have their effect on her as she tried to decide how to accept her parents' deaths. It was something she had been trying to do since she had received the phone call two days before.

It was not an issue of any suppressed sorrow. Gabriella had no problem in letting her inner feelings surface. She guessed the biggest point was that it was not her 'parents' deaths', but the death of two individuals, one her mother and the other her father. She had different even conflicting feelings about each of them. She never really stopped to think how she felt about each of them in a distant dispassionate sort of way. Now she could do that. It would take her the coming weeks and months to grapple with it and bring closure.

She admitted to herself that she had not been an easy child to manage. But if she had been, she would not be the kind of person she was now. While growing up, she always felt like she was being smothered. She had to find other ways to cause a stir without publicly humiliating her parents. Gabriella loved them too much to do that.

Things like dancing nude in the moonlit garden must have really caused a stir, but it was the only time she could feel free. She danced like the young maiden chosen to dance with the Devil by the bonfire in a secret forest. Her mother pretended to be scandalized, but Gabriella guessed she secretly wished she could do the same.

She should have asked her mother to join her. That would have been considered nearly normal for LA but seeing both his women dancing nude in the pale moonlight might have been just too much for dear old dad.

Gabriella knew he always watched her. Sometimes she felt like Salome dancing for King Herod. But instead of asking for a Baptist's head, she asked her father to put her through the finest art schools, giving her the best MFA talent and money could buy. She had plenty of talent and he had plenty of money.

Her father always did the right thing for her. But she blamed herself for perhaps inspiring him, if that is the right word, to pursue his interests with the B and C list starlets that would so plague his relationship with her mother. In that regard, Gabriella felt so sorry for her poor mother.

Clearly, her father was a rogue in many ways, especially in how he treated his wife. But Gabriella also knew that her father was not a rapist. He always showed the greatest respect to women, which was one of the things that was charming about him.

As for drinking, he became increasingly jolly with every sip. The more he drank the gentler he would become. No, she could not accept that her father was sexually violent. She would make it her crusade to clear his reputation.

As for mother dearest, she always played the Mother Mary role. Thanks to her Catholic upbringing, including time in a convent in her early teen years, she knew how to play that role very well. There was even a painting hanging on her mother's bedroom wall of her as a baby being held by her mother, done in the style of an old Medieval Italian icon of the Holy Mother.

Unfortunately, Gabriella's father had no idea how to play the Joseph role. How could he lay with his wife with that looking down on them? So, there was that, too, that came between her parents. If she could not be a Mother, would she have reverted to a Mary Magdalene character, the role she was playing when she met her future husband?

Roman Catholicism is full of architypes for a young woman's fertile mind to follow: women who bricked themselves into church walls and slowly starved to death, women who caressed Jesus's head with expensive oil, virgin girls who would rather be martyred than be touched by the dirty hands of a heathen king. Her father must have been happy to marry her off to what was considered a 'good catch' in those days.

Gabriella pondered all that while walking back to the hotel. She ensconced herself at the hotel bar overlooking the sparkling moonlight shimmering on the waves. She ordered a California red and took a handful of Valerian. In about an hour she had to go asleep. The next day would be challenging.

But for the next hour, she just wanted her mind to wander where it must. As the powerful taste of the herb faded away, she tried to remember where she had learnt about its wonderful relaxing properties. Ah, she remembered. It was from Yuri Yanakovich, the pretty Ukrainian boy with whom she had something going for a while. She wondered what had happened to him. The last she knew he was working near Santa Cruz as a professional hacker in an Internet security company.

Yuri was also a talented sculptor. He did a sculpture of her as Psyche. It was so moving; it would have even persuaded Cupid to stay with her into the morning light. She always wanted to do a sculpture of him. He was a perfect Slavic example of Adonis.

No wonder Gwendolyn had fallen for him, but that was before Gabriella had. He was the one who had given her Gwendolyn's phone number and email. He always wanted her and Gwendolyn to get in bed with him together. She was supposed to persuade Gwendolyn to do it. That is what broke them up.

While that thought was running through her mind, she noticed she was starting to draw the interest of an out-of-town bore. He moved three seats down the bar and sat down next to her. He tried to start some small talk with her, but he only demonstrated that he was a half-wit with nothing to say. Even worse, he had not even taken a shower yet.

When he leaned over and put his arm on her back, she paid her bill, pushing away his arm and his pathetic attempt to pay. As she passed him. He rose to follow her.

"Look, a-hole, if I wanted your attention, I'd ask for it. And if you try following me to my room, I'll break your neck. Are we clear?"

He sat back down, embarrassed.

"Good boy." She patted him on his head as she passed.

CHAPTER FOURTEEN

Never met Gabriella, but from what I'm understanding, she is like a mirror image of me, peering at me through a looking glass from a parallel universe. Gwendolyn reflected, now wide awake. *Never answered her texts. Maybe I should. My guardian angel, Giles, has gone into hiding. Maybe it's time to find a new one.*

She picked up her cell phone to text back but held it with its pale light illuminating the space in front of her. *But just who is she and why is she taking such an interest in me? I'm the main suspect in her parent's death. How can she be so sure I didn't do it?* she asked herself. *Ah, screw it! I need all the help I can get from anyone anywhere. There is no certainty at all I'll succeed here. In fact, most likely I'll fail and die trying.*

Gwendolyn texted back: **Thanks! When this is all over, would love to meet you. Your mother told me all about you. Seems we have a lot in common**.

She went back to sleep thankful of the hope that Gabriella's text gave her. Maybe Gabriella could clear it all up at her end and Gwendolyn would not need to risk herself with Russian thugs in Moscow.

No, she had a plan and would stick to it, unless Gabriella told her differently within the next few days. Tomorrow she would meet

Dimitri and visit the Tretyakov Gallery, one of the great art museums of the world. Mental dueling with him would take a lot of energy. So, she purposely cleared her head of any thoughts and fell back to sleep.

Gwendolyn woke up just after 7 AM. The pitch-black outside was punctuated by the weak streetlights. She went to the Executive Lounge for breakfast. She was on her second crepe with black caviar when the lounge manager came over to her and said, "Your friend will be downstairs waiting for you at 9:00. He told me to tell you to leave your backpack in your room. You won't need it today."

Finishing breakfast just a few minutes before 9:00, she went back to her room and prepared herself. She left her backpack and its contents in the safe in her room, but she still took her trusty stiletto, attached inside her left forearm as usual. She still did not quite trust Dimitri. Checking herself in the mirror before leaving her room, she was pleased that everything was in place.

The elevator doors opened to the lobby and she walked to the door, not knowing how she would meet Dimitri exactly. Her cell phone vibrated with a new text message. **Dubri utra, my dear [good morning]. In the black Morgan just to the right of the front door.**

She stepped out into the freezing air and sure enough there was the black car parked with the engine running about ten yards from the front door. *Wait a minute!* she exclaimed to herself. *Is that a stretch Morgan limo? No, please don't let it be!*

The driver jumped out and opened the back door for her as she approached the car. "There you are! How is our dear devotchka this morning? Were you well fed and watered yesterday evening?" Dimitri greeted her from the backseat.

"Yes, indeed, Dimitri Fomavich, I was. Thank you, again. Now, please don't let this be a stretch Morgan limo. I think there are laws against that."

"Oh, I see you like it. There are two companies in Orange County, in southern California, who do the best job. First, I asked them for a Ferrari limo, but they said that was not available. I asked them for a full three meters' extension on a new model Morgan, but they would only give me one meter.

"They don't understand customer service very well. They told me something about their license with Morgan would not allow them. Of course, I don't believe a word of it, but the final product is wonderful. Don't you agree? I have to admit it's easier to park this way, than if it had the full three meters' extension."

"I can see why that would be important here."

"I'm guessing you had your full eight hours of sleep. Lights out at 2300 and back on at 0700."

"Are you spying on me, Dimitri Fomavich? If so, you can stop right now!"

"I'm not spying on you at all, my dear. No, I am only having one of my employees make sure everything is good with you. If I ever hope to have one of the great Russian Masters, we'll see shortly this morning hanging in my dacha, I must make sure you stay safe. I hope you don't mind.

"Remember, you have enemies here. Enemies that would love, and I mean love, to snuff your sweet breath of youth out. As you Americans say, you're not in Kansas anymore, Toto, or as we would say, Totoshka." He motioned to the driver to start driving.

"All right, all right; never mind. What's the plan today?"

"The plan is to see some great art. But we can do anything you'd like. We can visit my dacha outside the ring roads, about an hour way. I have the local peasants looking after it, so I can use it all year round."

"Peasants?"

"Yes. When one buys large dachas in certain parts of the countryside, the property comes with those who live on it. Mine happens to also include a village of about eighty people. They come with the land."

"Serfs? Are you talking about serfs? Has the current Tsar brought back serfdom?"

"No. no, my dear. You truly are very funny sometimes. Of course, not. They are free to move away whenever they want. But if they live on my land, then they fall into my care. If I am not good to them, the entire village could up and move to my neighbor's village.

"They farm their own lots and I share with them whatever they grow on my fields. It all works out. I don't have to pay them wages for any work they do for me, but I take care of them in other ways.

"If Svetlana's family can't pay for her college tuition, I'll take care of it. If they need to find a suitable husband for her, I can take care of that, too. If Babushka Smitrova needs expensive medical care, I'll take care of that. Of course, they can apply for positions in my company and then I would pay them a nice salary. I give them preference in hiring.

"My driver here comes from my village. Russians are much more collective and cooperative than you Americans."

"Sounds very bizzaro to me. Let's just stick with the Tretyakov Gallery, if you don't mind."

"We were going there first anyway. If you want to do something else afterwards, let me know."

"While we're driving along, do you have any fresh ideas to help solve my predicament?"

"Predicament?"

"Yes, predicament. The trouble I find myself in."

"Oh, predicament. Yes, I do. This is what I want you to do. Tomorrow morning check in to the Petroff. We have only three days left, tomorrow only two. Since Giles set you up nicely in your current hotel, you should not check out. I must assume your current passport is not your real one or your real name. If that's not the case, I can easily prepare another for you by tomorrow."

"I guess one can't have too many passports."

"Fine. Would you like to be French, Spanish, Irish, or what? We can take a photo of you at the museum. We just need a white wall."

"Oh, Irish sounds good to me."

"What should your name be?"

"Surprise me."

"Fine." He made a phone call. "Done."

"How does Katy Murphy sound?"

"No Murphies, please. Make it Kate Murray."

"Oh! I get it. You don't like the Murphy's Law. Yes, I can understand that. Let me change it." He made another phone call.

"Kate Murray it is. My driver here will come by around 0800 to pick you up and take you to the Petroff. He'll give you your new passport then. If I show up at the Petroff, people will start talking and that is the last thing we need.

"The hotel manager is an old classmate of mine from secondary school. If he saw me, it would be all day of eating and drinking before I could get out of there. We don't want our quarry to take notice of anything that may disturb him."

"Great! Another plan. I like plans. Saves me from doing any thinking."

"I'll do the strategic thinking and you'll do the tactical thinking."

"For now, let's just pass a few pleasant hours viewing some of the greatest art ever to flow from a brush."

After about ten minutes of driving, the driver spoke to Dimitri in a worried voice. Dimitri looked out the back window and grunted an order. Dimitri made a few calls on his cell. When finished, he leaned back, looking more relaxed.

"When are you going to tell me what's going on?"

"Seems we are being followed by one of my business rivals. So sorry about this inconvenience, but we'll have to delay our museum visit for a few hours. Fortunately, this has nothing to do with you. He is just trying to embarrass me in front of my new mistress. That must be what he thinks you are. He tries to do it every time. Of course, I do the same to him. But I am always better prepared.

"Meanwhile, you'll have a chance to see different parts of Moscow and the countryside outside. I know it will not look like much under a meter of snow, but with some imagination you can see green meadows with cows chewing their cud and broad fields with golden wheat swaying in the summer breeze."

"No! Really?" Gwendolyn raised her voice, looking out the back window. But she could not tell which car was following theirs. "Which one is it?" She nearly yelled.

"If you want to follow along, it's the black Mercedes."

Gwendolyn could not hide her fear.

"Look at me, Margarita. Look at me. I'm not stressed out. Not at all. Why? Because I'm prepared. Most importantly, I'm prepared mentally for anything. If it will help, this is a bullet proof car. Just keep the doors locked and we'll be fine. As for them? I have a well-prepared surprise for them. By lunch time, they'll wish they hadn't gotten out of bed this morning.

"As for you, you must stay calm. I know this is not what you're used to and is probably stressful. Just remember it's nothing compared to when you will enter the home of your new friend in a few days and have your special conversation with him. If you are not calm, cool, and collected then, you may pay with your life. Am I clear, Margarita?"

"Yes, very clear. But you told me not to bring my gun today."

"Indeed. I wouldn't want to be near you when you start firing it. You'll probably shoot me or yourself just pulling it out of your backpack," he said with a big smile. "That reminds me. We should stop by my shooting range afterwards and practice. They have the exact same model as yours. You can use it."

"So glad you're not taking this so seriously."

"Oh, but I am. I'm taking this deadly serious. That doesn't mean I have to go to pieces and start crying, does it? I'm pretty sure how this will play out. But if something unexpected happens, I want you to do exactly what I say, when I say it. OK?"

"OK, I guess."

"Today, don't guess. Leave the guessing to me."

"Fine. But where are we going?"

"We're driving toward my dacha. I told my driver to be careful, but to drive like we haven't noticed anything."

"What point are they trying to make? What would they do if they caught up to us? Are they trying to kill us?"

"No. no. They're not brutes. They may shoot up the dacha from the outside with us in it. You know, shoot out all the windows. That kind of thing. They may shoot my driver, which would force me to have the embarrassment of driving you back to Moscow on my own.

"But I wouldn't be embarrassed anyway because you're not a Moscow girl. You wouldn't think anything less of me for driving my own car. Things like that. But don't worry. We're not actually going all the way to my dacha. If we were, I would be forced to show it to you anyway."

"Wait a minute! Are you telling me …?"

"No, no, again no. I am not joking. We really are being followed. I assure you, as a man of honor, that this is not being staged in some way to get you to my dacha."

"Well, I'm glad of that. Otherwise, I would have to stay in Moscow longer and have two men to kill."

"Now, you see? That's the spirit! You need to get your fighting spirit on. Something good is coming out of this already."

"My fighting spirit is alive and well, thank you very much!"

He looked over at her. She was biting her lower lip, trying to stay calm.

"Look at you. Now you're making me upset. Trust me. This is far worse than if I was with a new mistress. You're my guest. Vasily Vladovich must be punished for this." His voice was showing his anger. He picked up his cell phone and made another call.

"All right, it's done. Vasily Vladovich will think twice before he tries this again."

"What will you do? Have him killed?"

"No, this is not the Yeltsin era. We don't do that much anymore. It must be serious before we use such extreme measures. Fortunately, we have a government that works for us, unlike where you come from.

"I called my friends in the Tax Bureau. They will send a SWAT team to raid the offices of his shipping company in Saint Petersburg. It's nothing more than a smuggling operation anyway. That will cause him a few years of headache trying to avoid charges of all kinds.

"Anyway, once I explain to him that you're a foreign guest dear to my heart and not some floozy ballerina looking for some new diamonds, he'll understand and even apologize for being so rude. But in the meantime, I shall take delight in watching him squirm awhile. Are you OK over there?"

"Yes, fine. How did I get myself into all of this? All I wanted to do was paint."

"All right, all right. Let's try to hurry this up." He said something to the driver and the car sped up.

She looked out the back window again and noticed only one car sped up with them. It was the black Mercedes. They drove east into the sun, passing office blocks, factories, and apartment complexes with laundry hanging above the balconies, frozen solid and flapping like boards in the wind. She marveled at that.

"Yes, believe it or not, it works." Dimitri noticed her interest in the frozen laundry and explained. "Just takes longer. No one has dryers here and it sure is better than having a lot of wet clothes hanging around the small apartments, making the air damp and easier to catch colds."

About thirty minutes later, they passed the last bit of Moscow and were on a two-lane highway on the way to Nizhny Novgorod. They drove about another fifteen minutes. Except for a large delivery truck about a mile ahead of them, there were no cars on the highway that far out. The Mercedes had allowed about a quarter mile to open some space between them. Gwendolyn could barely see another two trucks about another quarter mile behind the lone car following them.

Dmitri said something to the driver and they sped up to pass the truck in front of them. But instead of continuing past the truck, they moved right in front of the truck and slowed down. Instead of putting the fear of God into them by honking his loud air horn, the truck driver behind them slowed down, too. At this point, they were invisible to the dark Mercedes.

"Now, pay attention. Things will happen very quickly. I think you will enjoy this."

Dimitri yelled "Cechac! [Now!]" to the driver and they quickly pulled over to the narrow shoulder. They continued driving but slower, letting the truck slowly pass them. As it did, Gwendolyn was shocked to see that the truck's rear door was open, and the roll-on roll-off ramp was down banging along the surface of the road, kicking up sparks.

The Mercedes was boxed in by them on the shoulder, a truck in the passing lane, and another one behind it that was closing the gap quickly with the truck in front and the Mercedes in between. The Mercedes had nowhere to go but up the ramp and into the truck ahead.

As they passed, Dimitri rolled down his window and gave them the Bronx salute as they disappeared into the back of the truck. The ramp was pulled up and the door closed behind them. As the three trucks disappeared into the distance, their car returned to the highway, did a U-turn, and headed back to Moscow. "And that is that, my dear."

"Oh ... my...God! That was awesome! I mean really awesome! Wow! How did you manage to pull that off?"

"Believe it or not, we had to practice that about twenty times before we could get it right. We destroyed a few cars and sent a few drivers to the hospital, but in the end, we got it right. Unfortunately, we won't be able to use that one anymore. But no problem. I have many escape plans. I have an entire team of people who do nothing all day but think up such things."

"What will happen to those in the car?"

"I counted four of them. My team in the truck will take care of them. If they don't surrender right away, my guys will use metal cutting torches and take the doors off their hinges. They will be outnumbered and outgunned. They will surrender. No prank is worth losing their life over and that is all this was supposed to be. They know it and they know that I know it.

"But they must learn their mistake of working with the wrong organization. So, after we beat the sh*t out of them and take everything they have, we'll throw them in a ditch by the side of the road somewhere halfway between Moscow and Nizhny Novgorod.

"Hopefully, sometime before night fall, someone will pick them up and take them to a hospital. There are enough cars and trucks passing this way that one of them should stop. If not, they won't survive the night. If we were assholes, we would have the truck drive down some country lane far from the main road and drop them to their certain doom. But we're not. I'll have a van drive by around 1800 to make sure someone has picked them up.

"It's a terrible way to go by freezing to death. The sleep comes on, but you know it isn't sleep but death itself hugging you ever more tightly. And there is nothing that you can do about it. You try to keep your eyes open, but they become slowly too heavy. Little by little you give in and then give up. As for the car itself, we'll sell it to the Chinese to pay for our troubles, including a pleasant lunch at the museum. Are you ready for some lunch now?"

"Dimitri Fomavich, you are just too much. Too much. Yes, I'm ready."

It took about an hour to drive to the museum. Dimitri was busy making phone calls - doing deals and setting up meetings. It was business as usual with him. Gwendolyn decided that she had to become even tougher inside to get through this terrible adventure. As the adrenaline slipped out of her blood, sleepiness came over her. She napped off and on all the way back to the city.

The driver dropped them off in front of the museum. They were greeted by two men who opened the car doors for them. Gwendolyn wondered if there was a VIP entrance to the museum like they have at airports. But no, the men turned out to be two of Dimitri's bodyguards, who would make sure there were no surprises in the museum.

Once they entered the museum. Dimitri told Gwendolyn to stand by a white wall for her passport photo. One of the bodyguards took her hat and coat. He would hold them the whole time they were in the museum. "Why don't we just check our coats in the cloak room like normal people?" She asked him when the other guard took Dimitri's coat and held it, too.

"And let someone put a tracking device or a snake in my coat pocket?" He asked. "No thanks. That's why I have these guys with me, to carry my coat."

"Life's tough when you can't trust the cloak room girl."

"Hey, why do you think they call it cloak and daggers?"

"Oh, never mind. Let's look at the 19th century Masters."

Dimitri stopped and was admiring Surikov's *Boyarynya Morozova*, when he exclaimed, "Now, do you think you could do that one, Devotchka?"

"Are you crazy? That's a 3 by 6 meter painting! I could do a 1 by 2 meter version."

"All right, let's keep looking."

"How about one of these Shishkin's? I just love him."

"Yes, they are beautiful, but I already have that wonderful landscape of yours. No more landscapes."

"Well, then what about one of these great Repin's, like this one, *The Unexpected Return*?"

"The one about the son who shows up at home unexpectedly after being released from a Siberian prison camp? That's cutting a little too close for me. I could be put into one of those Siberian work camp prisons at any time. It is one of the hazards of my job. That's why I get paid so well, I guess."

"Fine. I get it. How about a Kandinsky? I could do one of his in an afternoon."

"Nothing that I can't immediately understand what I'm looking at."

"All right, since this is only a mental exercise and nothing serious, you choose, and I'll decide if I can do it or not."

"Oh, this is profoundly serious. I already mentioned it to Giles. I have his full support."

"As far as I'm concerned, until my problem is cleared up and soon, you can both go to hell." The anger of her predicament suddenly welled up.

"Oh, come now, my dear. What kind of attitude is that? It's all just business. Whoever killed the Robertsons to hurt you only did it for business reasons. You just don't have those kinds of personal enemies. You might have artistic rivals, but no real enemies.

"You can't take any of this personally. If you still want to take it personally, then I'll lose interest in helping you. Besides people who take things personally will always make mistakes. And I don't want to have any part of someone who will make mistakes. I know I have a strong Russian accent, but am I making myself clear?"

"Yes, crystal clear. Sorry. Now, what will it be?"

"Let's walk. I am looking for something manly. No landscapes unless it's a storm at sea and a ship is sinking. No still life's, flowers, food, or small dead animals strung up. No portraits of people I don't know. No domestic scenes. It has to be something dramatic - dramatic and manly."

"Hmm, dramatic and manly.... I can only think of wars, hunting, or boxing."

"Yes! That's it, exactly. There can only be one such painter and he is in this museum somewhere. I will tell you the painter and you choose the painting. Sound fair?"

"Sounds fair. Let me guess. Vereshchagin. You want me to paint a Vereshchagin, right?"

"You are simply amazing! That's exactly what I want. Let's go for a browse. Oh, this is fun! I feel like Father Frost has introduced me to the Snow Maiden, Snegurochka! That is my new nickname for you. Lead the way."

"According to the floor plan, his gallery is down two and three to the right. This is a huge museum! They must have tens of thousands of paintings."

"Over 100,000, actually."

"Incredible! Afterwards, we must come back and look at these Petrov's and Ge's that we're passing. Not to mention the Repin's and the Shishkin's."

"We'll choose my painting first, and then we can go see or do whatever you want, as long as one of those things involves food."

"I'm surprised you like Vereshchagin. He usually painted battle fields in Central Asia. You told me you don't like still life's?"

"Ah, still life's. I get it. Now, that's funny. That's a real Russian sense of humor. I like that."

"I like Russian humor. It's very similar to mine. I had a Ukrainian friend once who told me this joke: "What's the difference between a pessimist and an optimist in Ukraine?""

"Ukrainians and Russians are basically the same people and culture. My answer as a Russian would be the same, I'm sure. A pessimist can't believe things can get any worse. An optimist believes they can. How's that for an answer?"

"Damn! That's right! See, that's my idea of humor."

"I wish you could speak Russian. It's such a rich language for humor and profanity, in equal parts."

"I tried learning it when I had a Ukrainian boyfriend. But he never encouraged me or helped me. I guess because he didn't want me to understand what he was saying on the phone to his Ukrainian and Russian girlfriends."

"Now, you see, that is a perfect example of how we men think over here."

"Hate to say it, but I think it's not just the men here and I don't think it applies only to men either."

"Well, I wouldn't know about that. Enough of silly subjects. Let's think Vereshchagin now. Pick one out for me."

"For the record, my choice would be Repin's *Barge Haulers*. Those faces and those muscles straining at the rope."

"I don't want anything that is too strenuous to look at."

155

"I thought you said you wanted 'manly'?"

"I did, but what's manly about pulling a barge? Manly is being the barge owner.

"Never mind," She said, rolling her eyes. "Back to Vereshchagin. How about *The Vanquished*?"

"Too morose."

"I suppose *The Apotheosis of War* and *Mortally Wounded* are the same?"

"Nothing to do with death in such obvious ways."

"I guess we'll have to be only very subtly 'manly'?"

Then they both stopped and studied *A Surprise Attack*.

"How about this one?" She asked. "But it has at least one dead soldier in it."

"I like it. I like it a lot. The dead soldier? Oh, him. He might be just a drunkard passed out. What I also like about it is that it's right by a window which faces the back side of the museum. What a great location for us to switch yours for theirs. Yes, thank you. I accept your kind offer."

"Remember, Dimitri Fomavich, I only take my work orders from Giles."

"No problem. Now that I know what my reward will be, I can concentrate better on what I need to do to have it. Let's get something to eat and practice firing at moving targets."

CHAPTER FIFTEEN

"Good morning, Gabriella. Did you sleep well?"

"Yes, Lieutenant, simply fine. I was awake hours ago and took a long walk on the beach. I'm ready. Hope you are. Did you bring the whole team? I want all your experts there."

"We'll all be there, eager to hear what you have to say."

"Let's go." Gabriella let herself in to the back seat. On the way, she looked out the window at all the familiar places in the town that was hers growing up. She used to ride her motor scooter to Malibu and Santa Monica. She bought it when she turned sixteen using daddy's birthday money.

Respecting her mother's fears, she never went farther than Santa Monica after the time she ventured to Venice Beach. Her mother had blown a gasket over that bit of teenage rebellion.

Her father always had Lorenzo follow her ("just in case her scooter broke down"). Lorenzo was instructed to call back to the house if anything unusual happened. Going to Venice Beach must have fit into that category.

As soon as she parked the Vespa, her mother had immediately called her on her cell phone, completely hysterical. Gabriella rode straight back home when she heard the phone drop as her mother collapsed, fainting to the floor. After that, Gabriella respected her physical boundaries.

Whenever she hung out with the beach dudes and babes, Lorenzo was always nearby. It was only later when she made a deal with him that she would stay somewhat tame and not break any laws if he would leave her alone. He had some professor lover at UCLA whom he could visit for a few hours.

It was only by doing this that Gabriella could satisfy her own curiosity of the opposite sex. She never had interest in the normal school places like broom closets and on the grass behind the bleachers like animals. No, she wanted to learn from older men, experts in the subject. The idea of needing to teach the boys how it is done always made her laugh and sex was no laughing matter.

Now that she was the same age as those 'older men', she realized that they were still boys but with men's bodies. She decided that it took a boy until after thirty to become a man. But they were not a bad way to start out.

If her father ever found out that his only daughter lost her holy virginity before her seventeenth birthday, he would have had a heart attack. The poor boy-man would have been arrested under the statuary laws that protect minors from being preyed upon. But the truth was, she was more the hunter than the prey.

She was curious about the shops, bars, and restaurants that did not make it and were replaced by something else. Trends come and go. She noticed that there were fewer piercings and tattoo parlors than ten years before. She had never done that.

It was her way of rebelling against her peers. She never cared about fitting in with them: never felt the attraction of looking like an Indian bride with a nose ring or looking like a Japanese gangster with tattoos. She sometimes wondered what would happen if someone got their fork stuck under their tongue stud while eating. How would that feel?

When they pulled up to the front of her childhood home, she could almost feel the stifling, smothering pillow on her face that she had always felt while growing up there in the lap of luxury. Maybe if she had had a sibling, things would have been better. She really did not want to go in.

The first thing she noticed when entering was the crime scene yellow tape everywhere and tags on everything. There were about a dozen people busy examining everything with various tools of the trade and more voices coming from her room, which had the most attention. *Damn it! Why did it have to happen in my room?* she whispered to herself.

As she walked in, everyone stopped what they were doing and looked up. What they saw was a tall, slender woman who looked just a bit past twenty with natural golden hair and the beauty of her Italian ancestors. She wore vermillion red silk, loose-fitting Gong Fu style top and pants. Above all that was her signature accessory: a large always flamboyant silk scarf draped around her neck and shoulders. The one she wore that day was dark jade green covered with black panthers in various poses of stalking and pouncing.

"Good morning, everyone. Who's in charge here?" she asked while entering the living room.

"You must be Gabriella. So good of you to come. Sorry about what happened to your parents. I'm Captain Stanislaw Slarpniak, head of the Homicide Division at the LAPD. Just call me Stan," he said as he walked over from the other side of the room. "We have some questions for you. Maybe you can shed some light on anything we might be missing."

"Um-m, well, sure, ... Captain Stan. What can I do for you?" The 'Captain Stan' remark caused some in the room to quickly turn away stifling a laugh.

"Just 'Stan' is fine. It seems that we have all the pieces for a powerful case here. The case is almost open and shut. We have a suspect, a lot of evidence, and a motive. There are plenty of successfully tried cases with much less than we already have now. But we would like to at least explore some avenues before we make our conclusions. Let's go into the dining room and sit down at that wonderful dining table. Antony, take notes."

Despite herself, Gabriella could not help but follow Stan the Man's command. "And what avenues might those be?" she asked.

"For one, did your parents have any enemies?"

"You should ask the family lawyer about that. The only enemies my parents had that I know of were themselves."

"We did ask him, and he refuses to cooperate. We can't force him either. As for your parents being their own worst enemies, that probably describes most long married couples. But that would not explain this case, really. There is a third person in the equation, a Ms. Gwendolyn. No one seems to know her last name. Do you know her? Know anything about her?"

"Never met her. I don't know anything about her." Not actually true. They had met without being introduced at an art opening in Chelsea on Manhattan's lower west side. Gwendolyn was with her Adonis boyfriend, Yuri. Besides being the hostess of the event, Gwendolyn also had a few paintings at the opening. Her paintings took the loneliness of Edward Hopper to a higher level.

They were what he would have painted in the 21st century, capturing the loneliness of the digital ennui, the false substitute for the company of another person. Rather than staring at a cup of coffee alone at a diner, her subjects were staring at little electronic screens in groups where instead of talking with each other, they would text to each other just a few feet away.

But it was her one sculpture in the show that had blown Gabriella's mind and made her a secret admirer ever since. It was a twisted tormented woman's version of the Vexed Man. Anyone who saw it would have struggled not to cry out in solidarity to all the inner anguish women have felt since Eve. Gabriella almost gave up being a sculptor after seeing that.

The rest of the evening she could not get close enough to Gwendolyn to talk, but Yuri found Gabriella, impressing her enough that she took his card. But she never used it until hearing from a mutual acquaintance that Gwendolyn had broken up with him.

She and Gwendolyn did travel in the same circles of the

international art world, but somehow the spheres never aligned to allow them to become friends. Gabriella knew all about her, but Gwendolyn would not have known her from Eve.

Gabriella always since nurtured the hope of enlisting her to go to Thailand and do something good with her art. She marveled at how Gwendolyn had ended up in her home. If she had known, she would have flown back immediately. Perhaps none of this would have happened if she had.

Why did Gwendolyn even stay with her parents? Her parents' guest was a highly successful artist already. All four of her paintings had sold at that art opening for a total of $128,000. The sculpture was not for sale, but a museum would have bought it for that same amount.

It probably had something to do between her parents' outstanding art collection and how her father was always very charming with the young women - actually with any woman. Maybe she had just needed a place to stay while settling in LA. Whatever the reason, Gabriella was sure it was a good one. But now it was time to get back on task.

"Gabriella, let's take a walk through your house and see if you notice anything peculiar."

"Before I do that, tell me what you know or think you know so far. I only know simple logic and what the media has told the world. What's your version? Maybe I can help you that way."

"All right. Normally, I wouldn't discuss an active case like this, but I believe you want to help and even can help us. Antony, fill her in with what we know so far."

Antony went through all the evidence they had.

"Play for me the 911 recording," she asked.

Antony played it. As soon as Gabriella heard the recording, her slightest doubts were dispelled.

"All right, Stanisloff, [pronouncing his Polish name the Russian way, sure to anger the overconfident captain] let's take a stroll through the house. I'll try to help you explore the 'other avenues' you told me of. Quite frankly, I want to help you save your career by not making a huge mistake in this investigation.

"First thing, did you notice anything odd about the recording? Did you pick up on, say, a slight Polish or Russian accent? When you get a chance, listen carefully to how she pronounced the 'o' vowels. You said she was from Philadelphia, didn't you?"

"Thank you for your kind offer to help my career development. I'll assume that means you have good intentions. Good. As for her accent, I did notice it and we are doing a voice analysis. But without a verified recording of her voice for comparison, that is only an unsubstantiated opinion."

"Let's go to my bedroom, the scene of the crime. Now, before we go in, I will tell you now that I have no interest in putting down the excellent police work of Captain Slarpniak and his very professional team of detectives. However, I'll tell you now that you are wrong. Gwendolyn did not kill my parents. She is being framed by someone else."

"Oh really? You have my full attention."

"So, there's my bed with the covers tossed aside with the famous telltale red mark, not much but enough to make the point. The chalk lines support the story. But let me ask you this, Stan: did anyone do an autopsy of my parents?"

"No. The cause of death is very clear."

"Then, let me ask you in another way: have you ever gone balls deep with a woman having her period?"

"God no!"

"Then, let me explain, my dear sir. Balls that go deep with a woman having her period would be covered in her menstrual blood. Did anyone care to check that? Because if the man's cojones aren't, which I'm sure they're not, then there goes the entire basis of the story."

"But where did the blood come from?"

"God knows. Maybe they stole her sanitary pads and rubbed it on the sheets. How do you even know if the blood belongs to her?"

"You're right. We don't know whose blood it is. We are assuming here. Antony, call down to the morgue and ask them to check out Mr. Robertson's willy for any signs of blood. Please continue."

"So far, I have cast doubt on the identity of the 911 caller. I have probably removed the foundation of the whole story, too. My father never raped her. Another thing, you probably should pull out the bullets and determine where they were made? If they were not made in the US, that means most likely the murderer is from the same place the bullets were made.

"Of course, if they are made in the US, he could have picked up the weapon here. US-made bullets would prove nothing. But if they come from someplace like Russia or China, that would tell you something about the real murderer. You can be sure that a young artist would not have the underworld criminal contacts to buy a gun where it's a crime to have one. Where were the bullet casings found?"

"We haven't found them. The suspect probably took them. Antony, call back to the morgue about that, too. All right, you're finding some holes in the case. Ah... Sorry about the pun. I didn't mean it. But there was no robbery. What would the motive be? That goes back to my first question: who would want to harm your parents?"

"Stan, I think you are asking the wrong question. How about we look at it from the opposite direction. How about this for a scenario? Who would want to harm Gwendolyn? Framing her for murder is the goal. My poor parents just got in the way."

"Oh, now there is a fresh angle. I would not even know how to answer that question. Only Gwendolyn can answer that, and she is keeping herself well-hidden. Jesus, Gabriella! If what the morgue comes back with supports your idea, you have just blown the whole case wide open. If you're looking for a job, I have one for you as one of my senior detectives. I'm serious about that."

"I'm happily employed now. Besides, the only job I could do for you would be suspect sketches."

"Funny, but seriously we have to get back to work. Thank you so much for your time."

"Stan, don't brush off the missing bullet casings. Why would a panicking and hysterical girl grabbing her things and running out the door to escape the horror of what happened, take the time to search for and pick up bullet casings? It's simply not making any sense. Did you look upstairs in my parents' bedrooms?

"I noticed coming in that there were some heavy shoe impressions on the carpet steps coming down from upstairs. Perhaps the murderer or murderers who killed my mother made them when they carried her body down the stairs to place at the so-called scene. Maybe they carried my father down, too, and did the same."

"Oh those? Yes, I saw them. Probably made by one of our fat detectives looking around the house. We have your cell phone number. Will you be staying at the Shutters and how long will you be in town? I suppose you must have a lot to take care of, including the estate and funeral preparations. I must say you are holding up surprisingly well. We will not be bothering you any longer unless something else comes up. Antony will take you back."

"When can I move back in here?"

"Not until we close the case. Anything else?"

"Yes, Captain. I know it is in your power to ignore everything I have told you. You can cancel anything the morgue might do. Stick to your story and run with it. You can put a price on Gwendolyn's head, put her on the FBI's most wanted list and the Interpol list, too. You may find her, or you may not. Either way, her life would be destroyed. You would get your promotion and life would go its merry way. Or you could do the right thing. Whatever you do, just know that I'll be watching."

"Nice to know you'll be watching. Rest assured that I'll do the right thing."

"I meant not the right thing for you, but the right thing period."

"Understood, sweety," Slarpniak's bulldog face and gruff voice showed no reaction. "Antony, here's twenty dollars. Bring us back some coffee after you drop off our guest. But make that call to the morgue first."

"No problem. Let's go, Gabriella." Antony tried to be cheerful. While walking to his car, he called the morgue to order an autopsy of Mr. Robertson's private parts and investigate the origins of the bullets.

***

Driving back to Shutters, it looked like Gabriella, sitting in the front seat, would start crying, so Antony left her in silence. He called the morgue as instructed while he drove her back. By the time they reached the hotel, she was crying. This was something Antony was not expecting. He then realized that Gabriella's tough girl act was just an act. It totally disarmed him.

He did not know what to say or do and she was not getting out of the car right away. Slowly, he felt a sadness come over him, as he thought about his own father's death. All he could think to say was, *I know how you feel. I lost my father to a violent premature death, too. It makes no sense. How can it?* He wanted to reach over and hug her, but that might get him in trouble.

However, Gabriella did something unexpected. She reached over and hugged *him*. She sobbed into his ear, "Please, dear Antony, please find out what happened, what really happened. I don't want the world to falsely remember my father as a rapist. Here's my card. Let me know. Can you promise that to me? Can you?"

"Yes, Gabriella. Yes, I promise. Please don't cry. I'll let you know."

"Oh, thank you so much." And she kissed him on the cheek. While getting out of the car, she managed to smile at him through her tears. "I hope to hear from you soon."

She turned to enter the hotel lobby. Once inside, she brushed away her tears and went to her room. She stared for a time at the ocean outside her window.

As for Antony, all he could do was say that she would hear from him soon and watch her gently sway and disappear into the hotel. He sat there for a few minutes quite moved by her fragility hiding under the tough facade she showed at her house.

He remembered the coffee errand and drove off. Between the traffic and the line at Starbucks, it was nearly two hours before Antony returned.

"Hey, everyone! Antony brought us coffee. Put the coffee down there and follow me." Slarpniak led him into the kitchen.

"Antony, I've been thinking about what Gabriella said. I don't want to complicate things. This case is about the Robertsons, scions of LA and not at all about a bohemian artist girl, who happened to be their guest. We will find her and bring her to justice. Are we clear? Good.

"Now I want you to call over to the morgue and cancel everything we asked them to do. When we get back to the office, we'll fill out all the paperwork with the FBI and Interpol. I'll discuss with the Chief about what kind of reward we can offer for our one and only suspect."

"Sir, are you sure that's what you want to do? It wouldn't hurt to put all doubts to rest. Don't you remember you said this exact thing in the War Room?"

"No doubts, Antony. None at all. The War Room is for mental exercising, for mental gymnastics. But out here, at the scene, we must be practical with the city's resources. We must be practical with ourselves, too. With this case solved and closed, I may be moving up and I'm grooming you to take over this department.

"You will have real power and a finger on the pulse of all the major crimes of this city. I don't need to remind you of the nice bump in pay you'll get, too. So, let's all just stay focused on what's important. Now, go ahead and call back the morgue."

"Um, sure, sir, sure. Right away, sir."

With that, Slarpniak patted him on his back and returned to the living room. Antony pulled out his cell phone and stared at it for a few minutes. Then, he dialed.

"Hey, Ralph, it's me again. You know what I asked you to do?"

"Yes, Antony, I do. What you asked for was inspired. I did it right after you called. You know something? You were right. There was no sign of blood anywhere in the groin area of Mr. Robertson. His shlong was as clean as a communion wafer on Sunday. Didn't even have any signs of pre-cum or anything else. He didn't use it that evening.

"Also, we pulled the bullets out and they appear to be foreign made. I would say Russian-made if I had to guess. But I won't know for sure until I see the results from the lab tomorrow. I'll let you know as soon as I do. Excellent police work there, you guys!"

"Oh, wow, Ralph! Ok, now listen to me. Email me your final report when you have it. File all the supporting evidence where it would be hard to find until needed. Slarpniak asked me to call and cancel all of this. He has his eyes on the prize. But you were too fast. This will be our little secret."

"Just tell him the results. This should change everything."

"You don't know him, Ralph. Once his mind is made up, he gets stubborn. I mean dangerously stubborn. So, if he asks you about it, just tell him I called and cancelled it like he asked."

"But that's suppressing evidence, Antony! I can't do that!"

"If you don't do as I ask, he will find the reports and eliminate them completely. I've seen him do it many times already. Just think about it. What does this new evidence say, exactly? It just says that he didn't rape her and that the bullets were foreign made. It doesn't prove the suspect was innocent of the murders. To do that, we need more evidence, a lot more. In fact, we need either the suspect to have an incredibly good alibi or, if it wasn't her, for the actual perps to show up and confess."

"I guess that makes sense. But why the sudden change?"

"Slarpniak changed everything. He's impatient for that promotion. He has thought it through and decided that justice can take many forms, as he tells me often. So, just keep this evidence under your hat and we'll see how things transpire. OK?"

"OK, but I'm not happy about it. What are you going to do?"

"I don't know what I can do. I just don't know. Slarpniak's in the driver's seat. Let's see what he does."

"Or doesn't do."

"When I'm in the driver's seat, I'll do things differently."

"Did you say 'when'?"

"Did I say that? I meant 'if', if I was in the driver's seat. Still let me know where the bullets were made. All right, Ralph. Gotta go." And he hung up when he saw Slarpniak approaching the kitchen.

Slarpniak came in with a cup of coffee. "Here's your coffee. Did you call over to the morgue?"

"Yes. I cancelled the requests."

"Good. Why don't you drink your coffee and then walk the grounds looking for any new evidence? Maybe you'll find the murder weapon tossed in the bushes." Slarpniak sensed that Antony needed a little time alone to align his mind with what was required. He had seen this many times before and Antony always came around.

"Sure, Captain," Antony replied, a bit colder than he wanted. But he could not help but think, *What's the point of looking for evidence if you already made up your mind?*

Slarpniak left the kitchen. Antony had a few sips of coffee, then threw it away. He went outside. He was glad for the opportunity to walk alone for a while. He walked aimlessly for some time. Then, he knew what he had to do. He entered the garage, but with thoughts so heavy he did not even notice the cars he would have marveled at normally. He took out his cell phone and Gabriella's card. He stared at the two for a few minutes and then he dialed her number.

"Yes?" Came her weak voice through the line, absent of all the confidence it had before.

"Hey, Gabriella? It's me, Antony."

"That was quick. Do you have any good news for me?"

"Yes, I do. Turns out your father did not rape her. He's as clean as a whistle." He regretted saying something so silly as soon as it came out of his mouth.

"Did you say 'whistle'?"

"Yes, but never mind. There's more. The bullets are foreign made. Won't know until tomorrow where exactly."

"Thank you for that, Antony. Thank you for saving my memory of my father." Then, in a harder voice, she asked, "Now, what will you do with this information?"

Her sudden change of voice startled him. All he could do was repeat what he had told Ralph, "What does this new evidence say, exactly? It just says that your father didn't rape her and the bullets were foreign made. It doesn't prove the suspect was innocent of the murders. To do that, we need more evidence, a lot more. In fact, we need either the suspect to have an exceptionally good alibi or, if it wasn't her for the actual perps to show up and confess."

"Antony, I'll just pretend I didn't hear that. I'll ask you again. What will you do with this information? You must find my parents' true murderer. You must. Don't let them get away with it!" Her voice broke into sobs.

"Yes, yes, dear Gabriella. Don't cry. We'll find them. I'll find them. I promise." He regretted having said that, too. Because in his heart, he knew there was not much he could do, or even would do. Slarpniak was well connected and powerful beyond his department. After Antony finally found his true calling and had his life in order, he did not want to lose it all over this strange sobbing woman.

"Please, Antony! I beg you, please find my parents' true murderer. Be that shining knight for justice that every girl dreams of," her voice breaking back into sobs.

"Yes, my dear Gabriella. I will be that knight of justice. I will make everything right." He replied with some emotion.

"Thank you, dear Antony. I know you will." And then she hung up.

CHAPTER SIXTEEN

Having had a much better day at the shooting range after lunch, Gwendolyn was starting to get the hang of it. She was still terrified about shooting anyone. But as Dimitri explained to her: "As long as your reflexes work like clockwork, it doesn't matter how you feel about it. Clockwork reflexes come from practice. You can deal with your feelings on Sunday at church, but at least you'll still be alive."

By the end of the day, Gwendolyn decided to be alone. She returned to the hotel and wound down by swimming in the indoor pool (she could only have ice-skated on the outdoor pool). She had a light meal in the Executive Lounge and later curled up in front of the fireplace in her room with a book.

Trying to adapt to Moscow time as soon as possible, she went to sleep early. Almost as soon as she turned the lights off a little after 10 PM, her cell phone vibrated with another text message from Gabriella: **Have an insider in the investigation. Have proof Dad didn't rape you. Will let you know things as I learn them**.

Gwendolyn fell asleep wondering how that could change anything, and decided it changed nothing in the end. Or might even make things worse by removing the self-defense motive mentioned in the 911 call. Around 3 AM, another text woke her up. This one read: **We know the bullets are from Russia. Where are you now? Never mind. Don't want to know. There's a Russian connection.**

Yes, dear Gabriella, there is indeed a Russian connection.

Gwendolyn agreed and went back to sleep. Around 5 AM she woke up feeling rather optimistic that with Dimitri's plan she could pull it off. She dreaded the showdown and still was not sure how she would get a full ironclad confession out of him. She would figure it out when the time came. Being creative was one of her strong points.

She considered that for a while until another thought suddenly broke into her mind: a thought that made her sit up in bed panicked. *Wait a minute! I know what their motive was. They want to force me out of the art forging business. Even if I get him to confess, I'm still screwed, and they still won. Oh, no! Can't have that! What to do? What to do? Damn it! I must make him confess a different motive altogether. But what?*

Gwendolyn texted Giles her dilemma and waited for his reply until 6 AM. There was no answer. She got up and prepared to meet Dimitri. *I must explain this to him. Maybe he would have a better answer.* She thought to herself as she packed a weekend bag and her backpack. A twinge of fear gripped her heart. Her strange vacation was coming to an end, one way or the other.

While finishing her breakfast, the lounge manager informed her that her ride was waiting in the lobby. *In the lobby?* she thought. *Dimitri told me he would not be able to take me to the Petroff and that I would have to take a taxi there. Great! I can tell him my new worries.*

She returned to her room, gathered her things, and took the elevator to the lobby. Walking to the front door, she did not see Dimitri. *Maybe he's outside.* As she walked to the lobby doors, a young man she did not recognize standing by the bell boy station motioned her over. She did, with concern.

"Dubri Deen, Margarita. I am an associate of Dimitri Fomavich. Here is the address written in Russian for the taxi driver, but everyone knows where it is. He wants me to give you this envelope."

"But I need to talk with Dimitri!" Gwendolyn could not hide her disappointment. "Something has come up. Something that complicates everything. I need to meet with him today before we go any further."

"All right, fine. Stay calm. I'm sure he can clear up whatever it is. I'll let him know. If he has time today, I'm sure he'll meet you."

"I must speak with him today."

"I understand. Now, I must get going. Good day." And he walked out the door.

Gwendolyn sat in one of the lobby's thick leather easy chairs in a near panic. Her mind went blank for a while. Then, after some minutes, she slowly regained control of her mind. *Well, all I can do is get to the Petroff and check in*. So, without thinking any more about it, she took a taxi to the Petroff.

On the ride to the hotel, she thought of all sorts of plausible scenarios, each more complicated than the last. She was a bit befuddled by it all. She reached into the envelop and found her new Irish passport. She opened it and saw her face looking back at her with a forced smile and worried eyes.

Kate Murray. That's my third name now. Wonder when I will ever get my old name back? Or worse, how many more new names will I have before it's all over?

Gwendolyn tried to make sense of the Irish written alongside the English but gave up. *How did they get Dublin out of Baile Átha Cliath?* she asked herself.

The taxi dropped her off at the grand entrance of the hotel. As Gwendolyn entered the even grander lobby, the young woman behind the counter greeted her. "Hello, Miss. Welcome to the Hotel Petrovsky Palace. Do you have a reservation with us?"

"Ah, no."

"Let's see what we have available. Your passport please. Thank you. Oh, Ireland! Would love to visit there. Let's see, Miss Murray. Kate Murray? Yes, you do have a reservation. You made it by phone yesterday."

"I did? Oh, yes, I did. Totally forgot. Yes, that's right. Do you have a non-smoking room with a view of the gardens?"

And so, she checked in and settled into her room, which was very spacious, looking out over the parks behind the palace. And it was certainly a palace, originally built in the late 1700's. She decided to walk around the hotel to familiarize herself with it.

The main building looked like a crown with two long wings opening at wide angles and a large domed ballroom in the back. This was where the Literary Society would meet. The exterior was painted a salmon color with white trim. The park grounds around the hotel were nice, and a high iron fence with a proper gate separated the hotel from the rather bleak surrounding neighborhood. It also seemed to Gwendolyn that compared to the Ritz, the hotel could have raised its maintenance standards higher. But it was a place with a history, and that was good enough for her.

She was particularly interested in the domed ballroom. She hoped there would be a balcony, or somewhere she could look down upon the event, or curtains she could hide behind, but there was no such thing. What it did have was a three-story high dome ceiling painted a cheery yellow gold with windows all around it letting the sun light the entire room.

The hotel staff were setting up tables and chairs for the Society's dinner. There were nine tables with nine chairs around each one. At the far end of the room was a raised platform, where the worthies would sit behind a long table facing the round tables below, and the speeches would be done behind the speaker's lectern set up in the center.

Gwendolyn decided that the only thing she could do to be certain whether her target was there was to pretend she was a waitress and simply walk up and have a good look. But to do that, she would have to dress like one.

There was another smaller dinner event at one of the other ballrooms that evening. She would see how they dressed and the next day would buy something that could pass a not very close inspection, and a wig. She did not want him to recognize her.

It was already late morning and she had not heard from either Giles or Dimitri. She decided to go to her room and wait.

When Gwendolyn opened her door, she saw an envelope that someone had slid under it. She quickly opened it. It read: **Meet at the southwestern entrance to the Dinamo metro stop at 1300. We'll have lunch.** She looked that up and it was only one block away. She could handle that.

"Oh, thank God! Dimitri to the rescue again!" she exclaimed out loud. She decided to spend the next two hours writing down various possible motives that might work if she ever found and forced the culprit to confess.

At the appointed time, she took her notes and backpack, bundled up for the cold, and walked down the cold grey street to the metro stop. She stood in front of the entrance facing the street, waiting for the familiar stretch Morgan to show up. After about five minutes, a middle-aged square-shaped man bumped into her, putting a subway card into her hand, and motioned her to follow him. She followed him down the stairs, deep underground.

At first, Gwendolyn was irritated that Dimitri made her take the subway. But when she saw just how out-of-this-world the Moscow subway stops were, she thanked him. Each station was a work of art, each with its own style. She promised herself that when it was all over that she would spend a day just visiting all the subway stops of the system.

Gwendolyn followed about three feet behind him. When he stepped onto a southbound car, she did the same. As they approached the second stop, he pointed with his eyes to the door. She followed him off and up the long escalators. The stations were built to double as bomb shelters, deep underground.

Out into the cold they went, crossed the street, and entered a traditional Russian restaurant. They walked to the back and entered a closed door where Dimitri with a few others were sitting around a table in a private dining room.

"Ah, there she is! You must try the pelmeni here. The lamb ones with sour cream are outstanding. Come sit here next to me. How's the Petroff?"

"Dimitri Fomavich! Why did you make me take the subway?"

"Two reasons: First, I've been followed more than normal these past few days. Nothing to do with you. It's like the weather. Sometimes it's sunny and sometimes not. Now, it's a bit foggy. Second, I couldn't let you leave Moscow without seeing our wonderful metro. I remind you that you may be leaving Moscow tomorrow night if all goes well."

"Well, I'm thankful for the brief experience with your metro. Would love to spend a day visiting all the stops. But the reason I had to see you today is…"

"Not another word," he interrupted. "We must eat first. I took the liberty to order a nice Russian meal for us. A traditional Russian meal usually has enough dishes to cover the table three high. Relax. Giles told me your concerns. I've already thought about it. I have to say, good catch on your part."

"All right, but please no vodka. We need our minds clear for this."

"What? You still don't understand how Russians think? I will do nothing serious without some vodka to put everything in perspective. Every serious conversation first needs some vodka to clear the brain."

"Well, if you must, but none for me."

"I will order you a bottle of our fine Moldovan wine and you can do with it as you wish. By the way, these are some of my associates. They all will help in one way or another. As you Americans would say, they are on your team."

Having some experience at Dimitri's place before, Gwendolyn knew to only take a teaspoon from each dish until they all arrived. Then, she could decide which one she would have more of. On this occasion, when the last dish came, the total number of dishes on the table was thirty-three. She could eat no more, but she did have a glass of the Moldovan wine.

After an hour of lunch, Dimitri signaled to the waiter to clear the table and bring everyone a cup of coffee and a glass of cognac. After the drinks came and the waiter left, Dimitri leaned back from the table and lit up a cigar. "Now, my dear Margarita, what seems to be bothering you?"

She took out the pages with all the various possible motives. "Here's the problem. We need a motive for what happened. It's clear to me that the motive was to stop me from what I do for a living or to blackmail Giles.

"So, even if we get a full confession from him tomorrow night, the motive will have to come out, too. I may be cleared from murder charges, which is great, of course. But then I'd be wanted for art forgery and robbery.

"I wrote up several possible motives that, if I could force him to say, might work. I'd like to read them to you. Let me know which one you think is best."

"Don't worry about that, Margarita. When Giles informed me of your problem, I thought about it. After we find him, we will need him to confess the real details of the murders. We must only change his motive to keep you and Giles out of it completely. Getting him to confess a motive without supporting evidence would make no sense. If I can create that supporting evidence, then problem solved.

"My thought is this: you simply were framed for their murders. Mr. Robertson was killed because he took a sizeable sum of money from a certain Russian gangster to make a Hollywood movie, but then he didn't make the movie. He just kept the $1.5 million, thinking that being in LA, he was too far from the reach of the Russian oligarch.

"Oh, how wrong he was. As for poor Mrs. Robertson, well, she just got in the way. I can easily create whatever money trail we need. Our Russian hackers are the best in the world and know no shame."

"Fine, I guess," Gwendolyn said. "But you would have to lose $1.5 million to pull that off. I suppose you would actually have to transfer that money into Mr. Robertson's account and back-date the transaction somehow."

"No problem. Giles agreed with me that $1.5 million is the price of one of those original paintings we discussed in the museum, provided I take care of exchanging the genuine one for yours.

"The only thing is, you'd be doing a painting for me without being paid for your time. On the other hand, you will be paid with your freedom. So, my dear, it looks like you will be spending a lot more time in Moscow.

"Now, we have not agreed to the 'when' yet. I think he has some commitments that he needs you for. But soon after those are taken care of, we'll bring you back here. But I promise you, it will be in the summer and you can stay at my dacha."

"Um, I see. I guess I'll have to agree to the terms, except that I'll be staying at a pleasant apartment in the center of Moscow on my own. Thanks for your generosity, but your life is just too exciting for me. I need peace and quiet to work. No distractions. As for the $1.5 million, the Robertson's estate just got a bit bigger. Excellent news for the daughter. What's next?"

"Have you explored the hotel? If he does go to the event, how will you be sure that you have the right man?"

"I think the only way I can be sure is to pretend I'm one of the servers when they have dinner. That way, I can get close enough to everyone to see their faces. But I will need a uniform like the servers wear there. Where can we get one? I know what they look like."

"And I know exactly where the hotel gets them. We'll go by there and pick one up that fits you. I'll also have Sergei here get one, too, and accompany you to the event tomorrow night." She nodded to the young man whom she met at the hotel that morning.

"We'll pretend you're in training and he's your trainer. That way we won't have any complications if anyone speaks Russian to you. You would only need about ten minutes to identify him. We don't want to spend all evening at this. The hotel management will start wondering who you two are."

"Great. We have that taken care of. If I identify him, then what?"

"Here's the plan: Tomorrow afternoon, one of my cars will drive by and pick up your things but do not check out. Keep your backpack with you. Do whatever you want throughout the day. When the time comes, change into your server's uniform.

"Once dinner starts, you'll meet Sergei near the kitchen door. You'll find out where that is between now and then. You two will help serve the dinner. As soon as you have positively identified our man, tell Sergei. He'll keep an eye on him while you go back to your room, pick up your things, and check out. Then, you'll wait in the lobby until the event is over. The whole thing should not last more than two hours.

"Meanwhile, I'll have a car waiting outside. Now, one of two things could happen. He could drive away in his car. Or, he could walk to the metro and take that. Once you and Sergei determine which one it is, you two will either get in the car and follow him, if he's driving, or you two will follow him to the metro and all the way to where he's going. Let's hope he goes straight home and nowhere else. Otherwise, it will be a late evening."

"OK, fine so far. Sounds rather easy. But what happens next is what worries me."

"No problem. We are professionals here. Once we determine where he lives, we'll wait outside until he settles in for the night and the lights go out. Then, Sergei will pick the locks for you to enter his place. From this point, you'll need to handle whatever comes your way. I can only give you suggestions because I won't know what you'll face once you're inside.

"You'll have to find him and subdue him. You'll need to do whatever is necessary to get him under control and still be conscious. Sergei will give you some long plastic ties to tie his hands down, either to chair arms or whatever else is available. Assuming you've gone that far, you'll then have to record him with your cell phone video admitting to the crime.

"First, I want him to show his ID card next to his face to prove who he is. It would be best that he holds up his ID himself. So, he will need one of his hands free to do that. But right after he does that tie up his free hand. Once he agrees to cooperate, we should make

178

sure that no one thinks this was coerced in any way.

"Of course, everything he says must be in English. If he says anything in Russian during the recording, stop it and start again. I want you to make him repeat as naturally as he can his motive. I have it written here. Then have him admit to the crime and describe how he did it from beginning to end with details. The more details, the better. Once you have what you need, and you're satisfied, get out of there.

"Now, remember the hard part will be subduing him without killing him and getting him to cooperate. You'll have to threaten him credibly. He is a murderer and will not go easily. You can try reasoning with him. He is safely in Russia, so he is in no danger himself.

"Whomever he is working for will just have to find another way to compete with you. If he has more at stake than just being paid for a job, then you'll have to threaten him to the point that whatever he has at stake cannot compare to what you are prepared to do to him.

"Some obvious things, but when you subdue him, make sure he has no weapons or a cell phone anywhere near him. Before dealing with him, move silently through his place to make sure there is no one else there. If there is, you'll have to subdue and tie them up, too. I have no idea about his personal life, though I think we agree that he has a dog. You'll just have to shoot the dog. Your pistol has a silencer. Giles always thinks ahead."

"Shoot the dog?" Gwendolyn exclaimed.

"Yes, of course. It would be better to shoot the dog than for the dog to alert him and you two get into a fire fight or he calls the police."

"Oh damn! Yes, yes, of course you're right. Oh, why can't you guys do all this for me?" she nearly whined.

"We've been through that before. I'm doing way too much already getting you into the place. All of that can be explained, but if I or one of my associates are found inside his place, that cannot be explained away. Once inside you're on your own. Sorry."

"It's just that now we are talking about this in detail, I can see a hundred things that could go wrong."

"I always like to put things into perspective. What's the worst that could happen? You end up killing him and there goes your alibi. Then, you'd just have to come work for me as my artistic advisor. Most of Giles' clients are Russian anyway. I'll become your agent and keep you busy at what you do best right here. I'll sponsor you to become a permanent resident in Russia. You'll learn Russian and live a good comfortable life here in Moscow. That wouldn't be so bad, would it?"

"Now you're being a pessimist, Dimitri Fomavich. As an optimist, I think things could get worse. He could kill me."

"See? You're already starting to think like us. If that happens, then all your problems are solved. Do you want to stop by a church this afternoon?"

"No. I would rather stop by the shooting range."

"Oh, now you're thinking like an American. A Russian would go to church and pray for success. But I like your thinking better. Taking responsibility for your own success by being better prepared is the better idea. In my country, the Orthodox priests bless our artillery, tanks, and machine guns by praying over them, blessing them with holy water. That way, being blessed, God will make them better at killing the enemy. Even I think that's absurd. Never mind. Let's keep God out of this."

"What else?"

"What else? All right, so you get what you came for. Leave and the car will be outside waiting for you. We'll take you straight to the airport with your things in the boot, I mean, in the trunk, the trunk. We'll put you on the next plane out of here. Where we send you will depend on what happens inside. If you get your alibi, we'll send you back to the US.

"If you don't get what you want and 'the poor dear was killed by a burglar', we'll have to send you somewhere else, like Iran or Algeria. You might have noticed that we thought ahead and put an

Iranian and an Algerian visa in your passport. Then, when things quiet down, we'll bring you back and continue with my plan for you here."

"Sounds like you have it all covered." She sat glumly in silence for a few moments.

"What would you like to do now?"

After some more silence, Gwendolyn looked up and said firmly: "Let's get that uniform and go to the shooting range. I brought my backpack."

"See? That's what I like about you American women. You can take the bull by the balls when you need to. A Russian woman would have given up long ago."

"Thanks, but I think you meant take the bull by the horns."

"No, I meant what I said. Have you ever seen the women tourists having their photos taken while rubbing the only shiny part of that bull statue on Wall Street?"

"Oh, please!"

They picked up uniforms for Sergei and Gwendolyn. Dimitri also found a wig for her. "I hope you like being blond. Normally, we would have you wear a beard, but that would draw more attention than we want."

Then they all went to the shooting range and practiced firing their weapons for almost two hours. When Gwendolyn saw Dimitri standing next to her preparing to practice with her, she asked: "I thought you're not supposed to practice shooting after you've been drinking?"

"Wherever did you hear that? Besides, do you call that drinking? I only had three glasses and must be able to shoot well after drinking some alcohol, since that describes me most of the day. I must be prepared to shoot well at any time. Don't worry. I won't shoot you."

She practiced until she felt ready for whatever happened the next day. Concentrating on the targets helped her mind to relax.

Dimitri took her back to the Petroff in the Morgan. "Now, are we clear about tomorrow? This is the time to ask. No questions? All right, fine. I'll see you at the airport, no matter what happens. My associates will keep me informed. Meanwhile, relax this evening.

"The car will come by tomorrow at 1400 to pick up your things. Sergei will be at the hotel at 1800 when dinner starts. Everything else will be as we say it will be and you will be on your way back to the US tomorrow night." He gave her a smile and a pat on the shoulder. "Don't worry. You'll do fine."

"Thank you, Dimitri Fomavich, for everything. I wouldn't have been able to do this without you."

"Thank me tomorrow at the airport. I'm not doing this because I am kind. I want that Vereshchagin. Maybe I'll have a Shishkin for my second one."

"No, you *are* doing it because you have a kind heart deep down inside."

"It's true that my Russian sense of honor makes me want to help a damsel in distress. You should be thankful you're a damsel and not a dude. Dude, right? That's a word, isn't it?"

"Yes, it's a word. Whatever your reason is, thank you again." And she got out of the car.

CHAPTER SEVENTEEN

It was nearly 6 PM when Gwendolyn returned to her room. Wondering how she would get a good night's sleep for the next day's stress, she decided that a long swim in the baroque swimming pool in the basement, followed by a light supper in the hotel's grand dining room, then finally a chapter of *Finnegan's Wake* would do it. She banished the thought that this was the last night of the condemned before dawn and managed to fall asleep.

The next morning, Gwendolyn laid in bed going over all the details of Dimitri's plan. She memorized the motive she had to force him to say. She wrapped her mind around the fact that, at a minimum, she would have to shoot the dog.

She said to herself in exasperation, *why couldn't he have a cat like any normal city dweller living in a small apartment? Wouldn't have to shoot a cat.*

Then, she recalled all the details of the man she met for just those few minutes in LA what seemed like a lifetime ago. Satisfied that she had it all straight in her head, she got out of bed.

Her day would start with nothing to do and end with a few hours of intense activity. Gwendolyn had to think over her breakfast coffee what could distract her until the car came for her bag in the afternoon.

She decided to explore the Moscow Metro. She went online and chose a route that would be a good representation. Wrapped up in her winter clothes, she walked back to Dinamo Station on the Zamoskvoretskaya Line where her afternoon started the day before.

Her plan was to get off at every stop on her route and only see the underground area of the station. She figured it would take about five minutes to travel to every stop. Then, she would have about five minutes to see the station before getting on the next train. The total trip should take her about three and a half hours, just enough to distract her for most of the morning.

When Gwendolyn returned, she had a good-sized lunch, knowing that she would not be able to eat dinner. She returned to her room, set the alarm for 1:45 PM, and took a nap. She woke up and took her bag to the waiting car outside. Sergei greeted her and put her things into the trunk.

He patted her on the back and said cheerfully with a smile, "The fun starts at 1800. See you in the hall by the kitchen at 1745. Everything will be fine."

Somehow his breezy cheeriness worked on Gwendolyn. It was also helpful that this young 'associate' of Dimitri was quite easy on her eyes, reminding her of her crazy Ukrainian Yuri from some years before. She decided to take the rest of the day one step at a time. After the car left, she walked around the Petrovsky Palace gardens for about an hour. The brisk air on her face helped keep her mind calm and focused.

When she returned to her room, she took a long bath and otherwise distracted herself until the allotted hour. She put on her server's uniform, her wig, and went down to meet Sergei. He was there as promised, dressed in his server's uniform, too. The hallway was busy with servers already walking back and forth to the conference room from the kitchen. The attendees were also filing into the ballroom, looking for their place names on the tables. It was so chaotic that no one noticed two servers not doing anything yet.

Sergei motioned her over to him. "Here put this on." He gave her a little name plate to pin on her uniform. He told her it read "Trainee." His read "Manager." Being a manager would prevent anyone from questioning him and showing a trainee around would not be suspicious. Since there were about thirty people running around dressed like them, they had some space to operate.

"Let's wait away from all this. Let's go down the hall a bit. I don't want anyone overhearing us."

She followed him.

"This is what we'll do. In about five minutes, they'll start serving the starters and pouring the wine. The attendees should all be seated by then, certainly the honored speakers in the front will be. I will make sure we are tasked with pouring them their wine. I will take the white, and give you the red. I'll ask each one which wine they want. Now remember, when I say "Krasnoe Vino" that means red wine and for you to pour a glass. Don't be nervous and spill it. Only pour about two thirds of a glass. Not all the way to the top."

"I know how to pour a glass of wine, thank you."

"Ready? Let's go. No speaking English until we're finished here. Let's make it as quick as we can."

They walked back to the busy hallway. Sergei took the two bottles of wine from a young woman who was walking toward the ballroom. He handed the red one to Gwendolyn, saying "Horosho. Poydem. [All right. Let's go.]"

They walked into the busy ballroom. There was someone standing at the podium reading something to the gathered. They walked up to the end of the long table at the front and started pouring wine. She looked at each face closely. She did not see him, but there was still a chair empty.

Gwendolyn was becoming seriously disappointed when she did not see him. But just as they approached the empty chair, the hunted gaspodeen himself hurriedly came to his place and sat down, muttering "Kraznoe, pasholsta. [Red, please]." Gwendolyn nearly dropped her bottle of wine. With great concentration, she poured out his glass carefully so as not to do anything to cause notice. He glanced at her and took the glass with him to the podium.

He addressed the Society members loudly with his slightly accented English. "Dear colleagues, comrades in the study of English literature, we'll continue our monthly meeting in English, as usual. We will start with a quote to think about while we eat dinner. These are the words of Benjamin Franklin: 'Justice will not be served until those who are unaffected are as outraged as those who are.' I like that, but I prefer this one with a slight change of mine: Wine is proof that there is a God who loves us and wants us to be happy.'" He raised his glass to the room.

Gwendolyn and Sergei continued down the table, pouring wine as instructed. Gwendolyn could barely concentrate. When they came to the end of the table, the ordeal was over. She hurried out into the hall, giving the wine bottle to Sergei. He handed them off to a server on his way to the kitchen and followed her down the hall.

"That's him! That's him! No doubt at all. His face, his voice. All right, now what?"

"Go back to your room. Check out in about an hour and wait in the lobby. When you see me following him out, come over to me and we'll follow him together. If he walks, we'll ..."

"Yes, I remember all that. All right, I'll be there."

"I doubt it will end on time and judging by how good the free-flowing wine they chose is, he won't be leaving early. See you in a bit. I'll stay here, watching his every move."

Back in her room, Gwendolyn had to pace up and down for about ten minutes before being calm enough to sit down and think about what to do next. She busied herself by making sure her firearm was ready with its silencer on properly and the holster put on correctly. She practiced pulling it out of the holster smoothly. After being satisfied with that, she checked that her stiletto was also easily retrievable.

Confident with both, Gwendolyn put on her winter clothes, grabbed her backpack, and took the stairs to the lobby. She steeled her mind to the real possibility of shooting a dog and maybe even a man. She knew she would do whatever was necessary when the time came. She could feel the anger well up in her for what he did to the Robertsons and for trying to destroy her life. *It's just art, for God's sake!*

Gwendolyn checked out and sat as close to the front door as she could. She tried to read her book, but her mind was elsewhere and after five minutes rereading the same page without understanding a word, she gave up. She looked at her cell phone. She still had at least forty-five minutes to wait.

She watched people for a while and then went outside to clear her head with some bitter cold air. As soon as she stepped outside, she saw the black Mercedes parked with the engine running. She pretended not to notice and walked around the front of the hotel and out to the main street, never letting the front door of the hotel out of her sight.

Gwendolyn went back in to warm up. She walked to the ballroom, but Sergei motioned her away. She returned to her seat. Finally, some of the attendees who wanted to leave early started trickling past her, causing her to really perk up. She grabbed a Russian newspaper to cover her face and pretended to read it. She knew enough of the Russian language to hold it with the words the right side up. But how long does it take to read a *Moscow Daily*?

Gwendolyn remembered what one of her uncles had told her about his three tours of combat as a Marine in Vietnam, a truth for all wars from all times. He told her that infantry life in wartime was interminable periods of total boredom followed by brief periods of intense terror. Now she knew what he meant.

It was nearly a half an hour after the official ending of the event when Gwendolyn's heart leapt. She saw him walking to the lobby door, deep in conversation with two others. There was Sergei following about ten feet behind. Quickly pulling up the newspaper, she peeked out from the side as they slowly passed. As soon as her target stepped outside, she jumped up, and followed them out with Sergei next to her.

Their quarry stood in the middle of the courtyard, finishing his animated conversation with the other two. The cold fortunately kept it brief. The conversationalists walked out the front gate, stopped, and said good-bye to the one who turned and walked north. The remaining two turned south.

"He's walking back. Probably taking the metro." Sergei indicated to the car that he would call them about where to meet. "Look, we will pretend we are lovers. If he turns back to look at us, I will hug and kiss you, until he turns away. I hope that's fine with you. It certainly is with me."

"Just be careful with your hands or you'll be next, and no tongue in mouth. I'm not catching any Russian flu," she said taking his arm in hers. They followed the two men to Dinamo Station, which she was starting to know well.

The metro was still very crowded at 8:30 PM, so their job of trailing was easier. They took the metro going south. After three stops, the other one exited the subway car. Their man of interest continued for another two stops, getting off at Novokuznetskaya, south of the Moscow River.

They followed him for about fifteen minutes to a row of walk-up apartments. He entered one of them. After a few minutes, a light went on at the front room on the fourth floor.

"All right. Now we know where he lives. I'll call for the car to come here. Meanwhile, we will wait in the shelter of that bus stop, until the light goes out. We want him nicely settled in for the night."

"What if he gets drunk and passes out with the lights on?"

"That's all right. Now that we know where he lives, there's no rush." They sat down on the bus stop bench. He put his arm around her and a hand on her thigh. That was fine, but when he pressed his cold nose against her neck, that was not fine.

She elbowed him hard in the ribs. "You're going too far."

"Just trying to keep you warm."

"Then give me your coat like Jesus said."

"He never experienced winter in Moscow." But he kept his nose to himself.

After about twenty-five minutes, their car showed up and parked about twenty feet from the front door. As it passed, the front passenger window rolled down and Dimitri waved to them. Just about then, the light went out in the apartment above.

"Good. We're getting close. Now, let's wait about ten minutes for him to settle in and I'll let you in."

Oh, God! Here we go. Gwendolyn murmured to herself, forcing down the panic brewing again in her heart.

"Now listen. I know these old Soviet apartments well. When you enter the front door, there will be a foyer where people take off their winter coats and boots. From there, you will walk straight into the living room. There will be a hallway to the right which goes to the kitchen and a hallway to the left that will go to the bathroom and two bedrooms with the main one at the end of the hall. He'll either be in the bathroom or the bedroom, unless he likes sitting in the dark having a cigar in the living room.

"It'll be completely dark. Take this little flashlight. It'll help you not to bump into things and make a noise. Have your pistol out when I open the door. The dog will have heard us walking up the stairs and may be at the door when I open it. If so, shoot it right away before it can start barking." After a bit, Sergei motioned to the door. "Let's go."

He picked the front door lock. She followed him quietly up to the fourth floor. There was no elevator. He easily picked the apartment's door lock. She carefully opened the door, saying silently to herself, *Showtime!* She was ready, so when a small dark figure growled at her, she quickly shot it in the head. It went silent. She shut the door with Sergei outside, keeping it unlocked. She took off her coat, gloves, and hat, dropping them near the door.

Gwendolyn crouched down and inched into the living room. Her eyes were adjusting to the darkness. She looked around the living room. No one there. She looked right into the kitchen. No one there, either. She turned left and snuck down the hall. There was a bathroom on the left, a closed door on the right, and another closed door at the end of the hall.

The bathroom door was open. No one. She approached the closed bedroom door across from the bathroom. Slowly turning the doorknob, she opened it. It was an empty guest bedroom. There was only one more door left. She crept up close and listened. There was a pale light showing under the door. She heard some heavy lovemaking with a very vocal woman enjoying herself.

Damn! she thought. *There's someone else here. Will just have to deal with her, too. Didn't think the gaspodeen had it in him. Hate to spoil the fun.* She silently opened the door a crack to look in. *Ah, that's pathetic!* she thought when she saw the back of a middle-aged man sitting in front of a computer by the far wall with his pants down around his ankles, masturbating. She paused a moment, thinking what to do.

Gwendolyn decided that she would just walk up to him in his moment of self-love and embarrass him. After seeing his reaction, she would know what the next steps would be. She had her pistol out and walked quietly over to him. There was no weapon to be seen anywhere. So far so good. What happened next completely surprised her.

"Kto eta? [Who's that?]" He said, turning toward her. "A, eto ti. Pochemu ti zedes? [Oh, it's you. Why are you here?] Ya skazal vas boss zaftra vecherom. [I told your boss tomorrow evening.]"

"In English! I know you speak it well."

"Yes, yes, thank you, of course. I like it better that way, too. I told your boss tomorrow evening, not tonight. Oh, you're blonde! Vlad knows I like the dark-haired beauties, like Jezebel. I have a wig. Do you mind putting it on? Wait a minute. I remember you as the trainee who poured the wine at dinner tonight. Oh, you give a good pour."

"Oh, sorry, wrong client. I can fix that now." She had forgotten to take off her wig and change her clothes. She pulled off the wig. It was too dark for him to notice her pistol. She put it back in the holster. She considered how to pull it off without having to hurt anyone, except for the poor dog.

"O-o-o! That's a pleasant surprise! Now, come closer."

Gwendolyn walked up to him with his willy still in his hands. She took out the plastic ties and started tying down one of his wrists to the chair arms. She left the other one untied until after he held up his ID card.

"Wait. Vlad knows we use silk ribbons."

"Sorry. Silk ribbons are out of stock. All I have are these. Just pretend."

"If you say so, sweety. This is when you start doing your slow strip-tease for me."

"No, this is the part when you start giving me answers."

"What do you mean?"

"Take a good look at me. Do you remember me from some other place and time?"

He looked at her with fear growing in his eyes. "Yes, I do know you. You're the artist in LA. We met and talked. Yes, we were supposed to meet for tea and Armenian brandy. You found me. Oh, this is becoming more interesting by the minute. But why did you pretend to be a waitress at the Petroff?"

"I'll ask the questions. You'll do the answering. You see what I brought?" She pulled out her pistol and shoved it in his face.

"N-n-no! You don't need to use violence. I'll tell you whatever you want to know."

"Then start answering my questions. I'll just put a small video camera here. Just pretend it's not there. Answer well and I'll leave quickly. Don't answer and you'll be sorry."

"If I answer will you play with me?"

"Um-m, that depends on how I feel at the end, OK? Shall we begin?"

"Yes, please."

"Before we start, I want you to hold your ID card up by your face with your free hand and state your full name and your current location. Where is it?"

"It's in my pants pocket."

"The ones down around your ankles?"

"Yes."

Pointing her pistol at his shlong, she reached into his pants pocket and pulled out his wallet.

"If you try to kick me, I will fire, and you will bleed to death, as I watch."

"Oh no, don't worry. I want a happy ending to all of this."

Then, she tied the belt as tightly around his ankles as possible.

"This looks like your ID. All right, now I want you to hold it by your face and tell me your full name." She turned on her video.

He held it by his face and did as she told him. She turned off the video and secured his left arm, too.

"Now that we have that little formality done, let's start. But before I turn the video back on, I want to know why you were in LA the past two weeks?"

"That's a simple question. I was there because one of my patrons told me you would be there doing a painting, a forgery of something. He would pay me to steal your painting and then black-mail you to buy it back for some negotiated amount of money."

"That's stupid! Why would I buy back my own painting that you stole? I could always do another one."

"Because my client would threaten to reveal everything to the owner of the original."

"But that's stupid, too. So, you stole my painting and know who the owner of the original is. Since the owner still has the original, there was no crime committed. I am just an amateur painter painting a famous painting."

"Look. I don't know what he was thinking, but he promised to pay me if I did it. I failed in the end. I could never figure out which apartment was yours and there was only an insufficient time between when you finished it and when you would use it. I hired two local gangbangers to force you to tell where your studio was.

"They accepted the job, but then something happened. They ran off and wouldn't even return my phone calls. We tried to follow you but failed. By the time, the apartment manager told me - it's amazing how far a few kind words in a foreign accent can get you in the US – you'd already left. The whole thing was a failure."

"What are you talking about? You did find my apartment and you did break in. But that's not why I'm here. I want you to tell the camera here all the details about how you killed the Robertsons, and I mean all the details. Then, at the end, you will explain your motive, which I will tell you now --"

"Killed who? What are you talking about? I didn't kill anyone!" He interrupted.

"Liar! Don't make me get violent."

"But really! I have no idea what you're talking about. I told you why I was there. That's it."

She had to think a minute. He was proving more difficult than she had hoped. How could she beat the truth out of him without it showing on the video? A screaming man with a broken face would not help her case.

"I will ask you again. If you refuse to tell me the truth, I will cut off either a toe or a finger. Which would you prefer to lose: small toe or small finger?"

"No, no, neither! I am telling you the truth!"

"Oh, so small finger it is. These are nice scissors you have here. You could cut raw chicken with them. Let's see how they work. If not, I'll just blow it off with my pistol." She grabbed his little finger, and put the base into the scissors, and slowly started to squeeze."

"No, no, OK, OK, I'll tell you. Ah, you mean the Robertsons who were murdered in Malibu?"

"Now we're getting somewhere. I thought you wanted to put me in the mood for some play. I understand. You have killed so many people between last week and now that you can't keep them all straight. I'll turn on the camera now. Start talking."

"Oh, those Robertsons. I went to their apartment, pretending I was delivering flowers. It was around 8 PM, on Friday. The doorman let me in the apartment building when I gave him a twenty. I took the elevator to the penthouse floor where they live.

"When Mr. Robertson opened the door, I shot him. Then, I saw Mrs. Robertson going for the phone, so I shot her, too. I stole one of their small paintings from the kitchen. It was a Frans Hals. I had a customer who would pay me well for it. Do you want more details?"

She stopped the camera. "Damn it! You're lying again! You don't even know where Malibu is, do you?"

"Yes, yes, I do. It's, it's in Beverly Hills. H-how do you know I'm lying? Why are you asking me about it anyway?"

Gwendolyn readied the scissors to cut off his small finger. Her prisoner was sobbing his innocence.

"If you want to cut off his finger, you should point the scissors away from the rest of his fingers. You'll get a cleaner snip that way," Dimitri said from the shadows of the other side of the room.

"What? Di... What are you doing here?"

"Just was curious how you would handle things. Seems to be at an impasse. Now, I must say, I have never seen such an impressive book collection. I mean look at this." He held up a book in the dim light of his lit lighter. "Would you believe it? A copy of *Yevgeniy Onegin*, signed by the great Pushkin himself. Never thought I would see this ag..." He stopped himself before he said the word 'again,' tipping off who he was. "Carry on, M."

"Look, you ass-hole," she said, turning back to Ivan, "I'm sick of your little girl antics." She put down the scissors. "Now, you tell me the truth. This is the last chance I'm giving you."

She pulled out her pistol and placed the muzzle on his forehead. "No, I'm not going to kill you instantly. I'll shoot your balls instead."

Gwendolyn pointed it at his groin. "You'll slowly bleed out, and sometime between twelve and fifteen minutes you'll die a most painful death. Have you ever been kicked in the balls? I mean really kicked? Imagine that but a hundred times worse. Damn it! I'm sick of listening to that stupid bint faking it." She fired a shot into the computer screen, splintering it, and then aimed again at his groin.

He emptied his bowels in the chair, his eyes tightly shut with tears rolling down his face, ready for the bullet to end his life.

Dimitri stopped her. "Hey, why did you have to shoot out the computer screen? I was watching that. Just joking. But I believe him. He didn't do it. We have the wrong man."

Gwendolyn's mind went blank after she heard the words, 'he didn't do it.' The idea that he was not the murderer had never occurred to her. It just had never entered her world of possibility.

"Well, let's just say we have the right man, but he's not the murderer. But I bet you he can find the real one for us. Can't you, chuvak [dude], you pathetic piece of sh*t? What is the name of the one who hired you?"

The question was only answered by whimpering and silence.

"Not to change the subject, but can you believe it? Here's Chekov's *The Seagull*, complete with hand-written stage notes by our nation's greatest playwright. This must be the only copy in existence. Now look, you bastard. I'm going to count to three, and if you don't tell us the name of the one who hired you, this goes up in flames."

"Are you crazy? No! It is the only copy in the world!"

"Ah, he can speak after all. All right, here goes: One. Two. Three."

"Oh God! What have I done to deserve this? I didn't kill anyone!" He then broke down into uncontrollable sobbing, like a baby.

Dimitri lit the book on fire with his lighter. It immediately caught fire. He rushed to the bathroom so as not to start a fire in the bedroom.

He came back holding the remainder of the book, with charred pages burnt all the way to the binding. "Would you look at that? These old books really burn fast!"

"You monster!" The pathetic old fool gasped between sobs. "What is wrong with you people? I didn't have anything to do with any murder. I told you what I was doing in LA."

"Oh, dear. I think we need some more warmth in here. Let's see. Oh, here's one in English. The author is … let's see, I can't quite make it out." He lit his lighter. "That's better. Let's see. It begins with a D, David, I think. The last name looks like... Thoreau. Must be French, but why would he write in English? No matter, looks like it will burn nicely." He lit his lighter. "You have a lot of books. We have all night. You decide how many you want burned up."

"He'll kill me if I tell you, but those books are worth more than all our lives. His name is Alexander Mikhailovich Popov."

"Now we're getting somewhere. You see this nice big suitcase you have here? I will fill it with all these old books. I can fit almost these three shelves in it. Let's see who'll fit. We have two Dostoyevsky's, three Tolstoy's, wow old Ben Franklin himself. Now this is an old one, John Milton. Better be careful with that one. Screw it. I'll just dump them all in."

"Why are you taking my books? Those are very precious and should not be moved. I told you what you wanted to know. Don't take my books!"

"It's real simple. You like your books, right? Right. You don't want anything to happen to them, right? Right. So, this is how it will work: We will leave you here. My friend will cut off your plastic ties. You will be free without any more harm."

"But what about my books?"

"Ah, yes. I was coming to that. Tomorrow you will find this Popov of yours. Tell us where we can find him. After that we'll have more instructions for you and will tell you the time when you must do them. For every day you're late, I will randomly select one of these books, turn it into ash, and mail you its remains. Don't worry. I'll always keep the binding unburned, so at least you will have that to remember it by. Understand?"

"Yes! Yes, completely. Just don't hurt those books!"

"Good. Tell this us your cell phone number. I will text you tomorrow morning. I want you to text me back where we can find

Popov. You will have until 1800 to answer me. If we find out that you have told anyone about what happened here tonight and who this woman here is, I will let her shoot you in the balls, because you will have proven yourself useless to us and therefore, useless to the world.

"We just have a minor mystery to solve. Once it's solved, you'll never see us again. In the meantime, you'll be watched every hour of every day. If you try to run away, we will find you. Then, you'll wish you had never been born. Trust me on this. You really do want to cooperate. Besides, I know you want to make a good impression on this beautiful devochka. This is the best way to do it."

When they exited the building, Dimitri turned to her and said: "Very impressive, young lady! You did great in there! Look, its late. Let's meet tomorrow and compare notes. I'll be taking this car. The other one will take you back to the Ritz."

"All right, but I'm way too wired to go to sleep anytime soon. Besides still being alive, I did terrible. I almost killed the only lead we had to find the real killers. Thanks to you, we still have a path to follow. Let me buy you a drink at the hotel."

"We'll review everything tomorrow. Hey, I thought you didn't approve of me drinking so much?" he said with a laugh. "Besides, I have something else to take care of now anyway. I quote from one of my favorite American movies: 'My advice to you is to start drinking heavily.' No, don't do that. Just joking."

"I think that's great advice. Thanks. I'll be at the hotel bar upstairs if you change your mind."

"Oh, you Jezebel temptress! You femme fatale! Another time." And he walked away, laughing.

"Why do you men always have a one-track mind?" She asked, but he did not hear her.

CHAPTER EIGHTEEN

Back in the Ritz-Carlton, Gwendolyn dropped off her bags in her room and went to the bar. Being as wound up as a top, she had to find a place to unwind and be distracted at the same time. A classy bar in a luxury hotel full of strangers from all over the world was the exact place.

It was 9:45 PM, when she ensconced herself at the bar and, being in Moscow, she ordered a Moscow Mule. The bar tender replied, "You impress me, my dear customer, by coming this far to Moscow and ordering a hundred-year-old American drink. I'll have to check if we have the bitters." He disappeared for a while. "Yes, we have. Turns out you're not the first American to order a Moscow Mule in Moscow. Hah-hah!"

"If by American, you mean someone from the Americas, then you're correct. I'm from Mexico, but I'm not in the mood for you to practice your Spanish with me."

"Fine. I don't speak it anyway... Here it is. A Muscovite Moscow Mule."

"And in a copper cup, too! So far, so good. Oh-h, and it tastes good, too. Just needs more vodka for the next one."

"Got it. I thought you Mexicans only drank Tequila?"

"Do Russians only drink vodka?"

"Yes."

"Well, I guess I'm not drinking Tequila because Moscow Mules are made with vodka."

"Good answer." And he went off to take care of other customers.

"Do I hear an American accent?" a man sitting a few bar seats down asked.

"I'm from Mexico, though I have spent many years growing up in the USA."

"In defense of the bartender, when most of the world says 'American,' they mean the US."

"Now, you see, you made another mistake. Mexico is also the US – the United States of Mexico is our official name."

"I think this is about the right time to change the subject. Shouldn't you not be drinking something with ice in it when its freezing outside?"

"What? Are you a Chinese doctor? What drink doesn't come with ice, except a rum toddy or Christmas eggnog?"

He raised his cup, "Bingo! A rum toddy."

"Oh, give me a break! Look, I'm in Moscow, so I'm having a Moscow Mule, if that's all right with you."

"So, what brings you to Moscow at this time of year?" And he moved down to sit next to her.

"Business. And if this is the most entertaining you get, I'm moving."

"Oh, entertainment is what you want. All right, here's a joke for you. Stop me if you've heard it:

"Old farmer Jones had a hen house in the back of his house with a rooster. But the rooster was getting old and he wanted to replace him with a younger one. So, he bought one. Put it down next to the old rooster and went back inside.

"The old rooster says to the young one: 'Now, I guess this is when we're supposed to fight it out over the hen house. You'll probably win, but not after I do some serious damage to you. So, this is what I propose instead: I'll race you around the henhouse. Whoever wins will get the hens and the loser gives in. But you have to give me a five-foot head start.'

'Five feet? Hell, I'll give you 10 feet and I'll still beat you', said the cocky young cock.

'No, no, I only need five feet,' came the older rooster's reply.

'So, he paced out five (human) feet and called back to the younger one. All right, ready? Go!'

"About thirty seconds later, a shot gun blast rang out and the young rooster dropped dead on the ground.

"Farmer Jones was on his back porch and seething. 'Damn it! That's the fifth gay rooster I bought this month!'"

"Oh! That was good. All right, my entertainment meter just rose. Now, I have one for you." In that way, a bit over an hour and a mule train of Moscow Mules passed. Turns out the man was harmless, just a bit lonely and looking for some friendly conversation. With her mission accomplished, she returned to her room and fell asleep. She had entered the stage when tightly wound up turned into total exhaustion.

The next morning, she was having a breakfast of eggs benedict on smoked salmon with her usual caviar-filled crepes. She noted that she would greatly miss the caviar when she left Russia. So far, it was the only thing she would miss.

The lounge manager came over and told her that her ride would be in the lobby at 9:00 AM. Gwendolyn thanked him and decided that Dimitri knowing her sleep and breakfast habits was not an inappropriate thing after all. Returning to her room, she put her holster on the way Dimitri taught her with her winter coat over it. Down in the lobby, Gwendolyn looked for any familiar faces and identified Sergei smiling at her beside the concierge desk like he did the day before.

"Good morning! Dimitri told us all about last night. It still makes me laugh. You two will make a great team!" He was still chuckling as he led her to the stretch Morgan outside. "Top of the morning to you, my brave Irish trooper!" Dimitri greeted her. He and Sergei burst into laughter.

"What's so damn funny?" Gwendolyn hissed in irritation.

"Oh, come now, my dear devotchka. Everything about it was funny, starting with you forgetting to change out of your waitress clothes and wig. Then, you found the wanker on some stupid porn site with his pants down, literally. He thinks you're one of the servers sent over by the manager to make some extra money. Once he knows who you are, he still hopes to get your interest. I mean, that's just plain crazy. You played it well.

"Threatening to blow his balls off is pure class. Where did you learn about the kick to the balls and the twelve to fifteen minutes to bleed out and die? They don't teach that in art school, do they?"

"I must have seen that in a movie - or something," she replied, starting to see the humor in it.

"Well, it worked, whatever it was. If the art thing doesn't work out, I'll bring you in to my organization as a full partner. I can only imagine the heights we could achieve together. We just have to get you speaking Russian," Dimitri continued, only half joking.

"The 'art thing' is the only thing I do. Tell me, did you really burn that Chekov play?"

"No, I burned a copy of a Soviet-era science fiction book I found in the living room which you can find in any used bookstore in Russia. I have one myself. I took the burned book with me, so he won't know that I would never burn such precious books. Well, I would if I had to, but if my wife ever found out ..."

"But you found your precious *Yevgeniy Onegin.*"

"Yes, but that is my secret. It will be the greatest get-out-of-jail card I'll have with my wife. I'll save it for when I really screw up with her."

"You mean like her finding out about your mistresses?"

"For that? No. We've been through that so many times, she has learned to accept it as the price of having her lifestyle. No, I mean for something serious like shooting her brother. And oh, how I would love to do that! So, here's what we will do now: We'll go back to my flat and discuss strategy and the next steps."

"I must say that your move with the books was what got him talking. Why were you even there when you told me very clearly that you didn't want to be directly involved?"

"When dealing with foes, we have to understand what is really important to them. For some, it's their life. Others would rather give up their life than their balls. For some, it would be the safety of their loved ones. He falls into the last category. His loved ones are his books.

"As for me being there, I was curious about how you would do and I didn't want you to come to harm. I wouldn't be able to forgive myself if something happened to you. As for getting him to talk, yes, his books are his life, but you shooting out his computer screen showed him that you weren't joking about giving him a great kick in the balls. That was a professional touch."

"You liked that, huh? I did that just because I was sick of listening to it. Didn't even think about it, just did it. As for you being there, I think it was to find that copy of *Yevgeny Onegin*."

"Now, that hurts. I had no idea he would still have it. After all, he told me he sold it."

"All right, fine. Thanks anyway."

Back in his flat, they sat around the living room with her "team", as Dimitri called them, drinking heavy black tea from a large samovar, except for Gwendolyn, who asked for coffee. Her idea of tea was light spring-time Wulong from the mountains of Taiwan.

Dimitri started, "All right, what do we know? Let's review the facts. We found… what's his name? Does anyone know?"

Sergei answered, "Ivan Ivanovich Ilyich."

"Thank you. We also know that this Ivan is chicken sh*t, incapable of even choking his chicken, let alone murdering anyone. Is that how you say it, Margarita? Choking the chicken?"

"For God's sake, Dimitri Fomavich, how the hell would I know? I don't have a chicken to choke. Where did you learn your English anyway?"

"Oh, never mind. I never did know if I was with the right crowd when I spent some years in the US in the 1980's. I was studying computer engineering, to bring all of your technology secrets back to the Soviet Union. The US has always been extremely generous teaching its foes the technology that could be used against it. Just like our beloved Lenin said: 'The Capitalists would sell us the rope to hang them with.' Anyway, what else?"

Gwendolyn answered: "I think we can safely assume he did not kill the Robertsons and moreover, he didn't even know about it. He was working with Popov to break in and steal my painting. We don't know much about Popov yet. Ivan's story just doesn't make any sense to me. But maybe Ivan and Popov are a bunch of fools and we're wasting our time with them."

"Oh, you're wrong about that, my dear. I have done some research on Popov. He is no fool. In fact, if I were to bet on this, I would say he was using little Ivanchka [using the feminine diminutive of Ivan] as a decoy, while keeping his true plan a secret.

"He wanted you to know about Ivanchka, and if you ever did strap on a pair of cojones, as you 'Mexicans' say, and come looking for him, you wouldn't find anything useful. He wasn't planning on you not only finding him but getting him to talk.

"Oh, Popov doesn't know how far an American woman in her fury would go. You're a very different breed than the Ruskayas he's used to. He ought to get out more, or at least watch more Hollywood movies."

"Give me a break! What do you think Popov was up to?"

"He was doing just as you suspect. He was trying to get you out of the picture, out of the underground art market. Why? I guess because he wants to blackmail Giles out of some of the millions he has made over the years. Thanks to you.

"Maybe the deal would be something like this: Give us $10 million and we will inform the authorities about what really happened, and you can have your sweet Margarita back and working again. In addition, we want 50% of whatever you make in the future, or we'll do it again. Well, that last part is what I would add, if it were me."

"Has he contacted Giles already for the money?"

"I think he'll wait until the police investigation is completed and they've decided you did do it. Then his threat would be more believable. That is where we come in. We must find him and get whatever evidence we can out of him before he contacts Giles. I'm sure Giles would gladly pay whatever to gain your freedom."

"Fine. Now what?"

"I already texted Ivanchka. He has until 1800 today to text me back where Popov is."

"Once we know his location, what do we do then?"

"That depends on where he is. I guess you'll pay him a visit and ask him to record his confession. I hope he speaks English."

"Just like that?"

"No, it may take more to get Popov to cooperate. From what I've heard, he's not chicken sh*t. He clearly is a sh*t, but what kind, I'm not sure yet. It will be almost impossible to get him alone, to spend some quality time with him. He's like me, always surrounded by associates and every one of them a proven killer.

"So, let's just wait to see what little Ivanchka texts me back with. Meanwhile, I suggest we hang out here until then, eating and drinking a fine Russian lunch the way it should be."

"I think I'd rather not do that. Sounds like I better go to the shooting range for a few hours and get ready to deal with Popov and his 'associates'. Sounds like you guys with your 'associates' work at Walmart. You know that is what everyone working at Walmart is called."

"What else should I call them? They are my associates. They associate with me. I associate with them. We associate together."

"Oh Lord, call them whatever you want. I brought what I need. Now, if you'd please write down the address of the shooting range, I can let myself out and get a taxi."

"Oh, now you're being absurd. All right, paishli rebyata [let's go, guys], let's go shooting. We'll go together."

They spent a few hours at the shooting range and then returned to Dimitri's flat for lunch, which went boringly enough with Dimitri mainly speaking to the others around the table in Russian. The young woman whom Dimitri addressed as Svetlanichka, was always close by, pouring or serving as the situation required. Gwendolyn could not decide what to make of this woman servant, who clearly was much more than that. Dimitri clearly trusted her by discussing his business openly. For some reason, she made Gwendolyn nervous.

The whole thing had become much more complicated. From what Dimitri had told her about Popov, he was in a whole different league than Ivan. Popov was a real gangster and thug - just like Dimitri, Gwendolyn had to remind herself. She was glad that Dimitri was that way and not some effete American real estate agent.

Gwendolyn glanced at Dimitri, who sat at the end of the table, laughing at some joke one of the others had told, probably something about women or bears. Or maybe women and bears. They were ignoring her for the moment. They were all speaking Russian, eating, and drinking vodka. Dimitri probably drank an entire bottle of vodka himself throughout a typical day. Yet, Gwendolyn never saw him drunk, or even tipsy for that matter.

Then, her thoughts traveled back to Ivan. Ivan was easy - too easy. Yet, Gwendolyn shocked herself by how violent she had become so very quickly. If Dimitri had not been there, she probably would have shot and killed an innocent man with a very painful death. If she had done that, then her entire mission would have been lost. Gwendolyn was about to do some serious introspection when Dimitri decided that they would all retire to the drawing room.

It was around 2 PM when they all sat down facing the very wide picture window overlooking Red Square in the distance. Dimitri passed around Cohibas to everyone but her (women do not smoke cigars in Dimitri's world). Fortunately, he had an excellent air recirculation system that sucked all the smoke out.

Just as everyone was lighting up, the cell phone that Dimitri had placed on a table in the middle of the room started to vibrate.

Dimitri quickly picked it up and noticed it was the text message they were waiting for. He first read it out loud in Russian, then in English to Gwendolyn. **Found Popov. He's staying at his dacha in Krim** (Crimea). **It's eighteen kilometers on the coast to the west of the Massandra winery. Won't be back to Moscow until May. May I please have my books now?**

Dimitri typed out a response, but before he hit 'Send,' he read it to Gwendolyn. **Meet a young woman friend of mine at the Chorniy Prints Café very near to where you live at 1500. She'll be the one holding an old book that you probably will recognize. She'll return one for your good work. But we are not finished with you yet. You will not receive the rest of your books until our friend is safely back in the US.**

He called for Svetlanichka, who was standing in the doorway behind them. He gave her instructions while he walked over to the suitcase full of books and randomly pulled one out. Dimitri looked at it and said out loud in English, "Oh, a signed copy of short stories by O. Henry. How does he get these books anyway?" He handed it to her, and she left.

"What now?" asked Gwendolyn.

"What now? We pack our bags and go to Krim. But since it has been reunited with its motherland, you'll need a Russian ID card. Meddling foreigners will not be let in. We'll get you one of those and fly down there tomorrow morning. You'll be my imbecilic deaf dumb daughter.

"That damn Popov. He was smart to buy his Black Sea dacha in Krim. I bought mine on the Georgian coast, which had the best climate in all the old Soviet Union. How was I to know that we would go to war with the descendants of Dear Comrade Stalin about ten years later? And there Popov is with the best climate of modern Russia. And when he bought it, it was part of Ukraine. How did he guess that it would be a domestic flight again?"

"Did you say, 'reunited with its motherland'?"

"Yes, of course I said that. It's true. It was torn off from Russia and given to Ukraine by Khrushchev in 1954 as a gift. A gift!" Dimitri pronounced Khrushchev the Russian way with the 'K' silent.

He continued, "Imagine breaking off a large part of a state and giving it to another or simply making it into its own state. Wait a minute. You did do that. It's called West Virginia. Not to mention that almost everyone living in Krim considers themselves to be Russian and not Ukrainian," Dimitri droned on.

"Oh, come on, Dimitri Fomavich. Fine. We go to Krim, as you call it, and then what? Do we just invite ourselves to dinner? Or does Sergei pick the lock and we sneak in again?"

"No, too dangerous. We'll get our wanker friend to find out when and where Popov is going for the day. We must catch him outside the comfort of his dacha. We need to even the odds, as you Americans say. You people have such great expressions! 'Even the odds,' I love it! You don't have to speak any Russian, you'll pretend to be an imbecile."

"By the way, I don't do imbecilic"

"Well, slightly imbecilic. You don't have to drool. Just look about with empty eyes."

"I'll just pretend I don't know what's going on. Wait a minute, that'll be easy, because I won't know what's going on."

"Great, now that we have that cleared up, we can think about our trip. You know, it's been decades since I visited that area. That's where Yalta is. The Big Three leaders of the Second World War met at one of the palaces there to decide the future of Europe.

"One of our great wineries, Massandra, is there, too. They were the primary supplier of Russian wines to the Tsars. The Tsar himself only drank the absolute best that France had to offer, but the flunky nobility that always were present at their formal dinners drank the Massandra wine. Maybe we'll have time to visit some of these places. You'll have to try their heavenly Muscat wine."

"Sure, I'd give it a whirl."

"Give it a whirl? What does that mean?"

"I'll give it a try. Never mind. So, now what?"

"Give it a whirl? You mean to whirl it around the glass?" Dimitri, puzzled by her expression, gave up and continued. "Oh, now? We'll wait until my messenger returns. I asked her to meet and talk with Ivanchka to try to understand more of what we are dealing with. I, for one, am very curious about his relationship with Popov. I don't want Popov to get suspicious, wondering why one of his lackeys is asking about his whereabouts."

"So, now we'll just wait here until she returns?"

"Yes. But in the meantime, we can watch a movie." He picked up a remote control and started searching through the large flat screen hanging on the wall. "Ah, we'll watch this one. It's based on a novel written in the 1920's by Ilf and Petrov. Your Mel Brooks made a film of it. Not a bad one, either. It's called *The 12 Chairs*."

He clicked 'Start.' They settled in to pass the time being distracted by the movie. At least Gwendolyn understood the plot, having seen Mel Brooks' version.

About thirty minutes after the movie ended, Svetlanichka returned and reported back to Dimitri.

"Apparently, Ivanchka's nephew is one of Popov's bodyguards and knows his plans a day in advance. He can just ask his nephew what we need to know without Popov even being aware of it. Great news for us.

"So, now we fly to Yalta. I'll call my pilot to get ready. I'll throw some things into a weekend bag and call my wife to let her know a sudden business trip has come up. Then, we'll drive by your hotel and wait while you get your things. I hope we'll be back here in no more than three days. You should pack all your things and leave them in your room in case you have to leave Russia quickly."

"Great! We're springing into action."

"Don't forget your backpack. You may really need it this time. All right, wait for me here." He stood up.

"Who else is going with us? It's not just us two, is it?"

"Oh, God no! I would never bring a knife to a gun fight. I'll bring along another fourteen associates to help."

"I guess I'd be the knife in your analogy. That's fine. I agree with the more the merrier principle, except after the first date."

"This is no date, my sweet. If you want that, it'll have to wait another time."

"No. It's not a date I want. I was just being silly. God!"

"Hey! You're the one who said the word, 'date.'"

"Yes, but did I mention you anywhere in that sentence?"

He turned and walked away laughing.

After about ten minutes, the four of them gathered in front of the elevator.

"Where's the rest of them?"

"They'll meet us at the plane. All right, let's go."

About an hour later, after stopping by the hotel, they arrived at the Ostafyevo Airport, where Dimitri kept his small business jet. Gazprom owned the airport and opened it only for private business flights. They drove into the hanger and parked by Dimitri's jet. They climbed up the stairs into the plane. The rest of the team was already seated. Gwendolyn kept her backpack with her. Apparently, security was not a concern with Dimitri's airline. Every passenger was well-armed.

Dimitri took Gwendolyn to the back where it was partitioned off from the rest of the plane and told her: "We'll be there in a little over an hour in time for dinner."

"Sounds good."

She sat back with closed eyes. She tried to take a nap, while thinking about Popov and why they needed to bring a small army with them. She decided not to worry, taking comfort in numbers.

CHAPTER NINETEEN

They landed in Belbek Airport and taxied directly to a hangar where the plane would stay until they flew back to Moscow. The pilot and the flight attendant would stay with the plane. A minibus was waiting for the rest. It took longer to drive to Yalta than to fly from Moscow.

The minibus pulled up to a high metal gate that punctuated an equally high stone wall that hid an elegant old mansion from the 19th century. The minivan drove up to the front door and they all filed out. The door opened, and warm light poured out into the cold bleak winter's evening. The master of the house greeted them at the door. When he saw Dimitri, they gave each other three hugs and a kiss on the cheek. Dimitri introduced Gwendolyn to their host, who could not speak English.

Alexander Anatolyovich Smirnov was an old friend of Dimitri's in a similar but non-competing line of business. Turns out they had a common foe in Popov and had decided to cooperate. Dimitri would explain the rest at dinner. He directed his associates to the bedrooms upstairs. Since the house 'only' had 12 bedrooms, they would have to all share, two to a room, except for Dimitri and Gwendolyn, who each had their own room. Dimitri showed her to her room on the second floor.

"Now, listen, my dear. Do not open the door for anyone tonight, except for me."

"Except for you? Why would you be coming around?"

"Oh, I don't know, maybe to discuss strategy," he said with a smile.

"My ass, we will!"

"We can discuss your ass, if you prefer."

"Dimitri Fomavich! Are you fricking out of your mind? Tomorrow we may die. How can you even think such things?"

"That is the best time to do so, don't you think? I mean, we should enjoy what God gave us one more time before we meet Him."

"You can enjoy what God gave you by yourself. My door will be locked until the sun rises in the morning."

"I thought you American girls were all supposed to be easy-going and fun-loving."

"You've watched too much porn. We also get to choose our mates, and I haven't chosen you."

"Fine, but it's your loss."

"Why do you men always have to say stupid things like that? How is it my 'loss'? You know what? I don't care. I think I'll skip dinner. I'll see you at breakfast."

"Never mind what I said. I'm sorry for being out of line. Meet us for dinner in about half an hour."

"No, really. I'm still very full from lunch. I don't want to lose my girlish figure," she turned to him and squeezed his forearm. "Thanks for everything. I'm grateful for your help. I really am. But with fear and loathing in my heart, I'm in no mood for anything else, OK?"

"All right, then let's remove the fear and loathing from your heart. We will not meet our doom tomorrow or any time soon. We will succeed and put this all behind us." He smiled, patted her on her shoulder, and added: "By the way, I'll be in that room down the hall, if --"

"If what? If I change my mind? I won't, so don't lose any sleep waiting in expectation. You'll need to be well rested for tomorrow."

She turned and entered her room.

Gwendolyn flipped the wall switch, which only lit a small chandelier hanging above the center of the room. The low wattage bulbs were enough to see that there were two double beds, an armoire, side tables, and a divan next to a makeup table. Everything in the room would be considered an expensive antique. There was also a bathroom connected to the room. She locked the door. She had seen enough old movies to make sure the key was left in the keyhole to prevent anyone from peeping through at her.

She was tired from all the events and travels, so she fell asleep early and awoke early. Getting up, she noticed that someone had poked the key out onto the floor and tried to peep at her anyway. She was sure they saw nothing and with about twenty men staying there, she was not at all sure who would do such a junior high school thing.

It had been a late night for the boys. Their drunken singing of Russian folk songs did not keep her awake for long. She awoke at 6 AM, but the world was still pitch dark with just a sliver of a moon slinking off toward the horizon. The sun would not be up for over two more hours. Multiple sources of snoring echoed down the hallway.

After dressing, she realized how hungry she was for skipping dinner. She decided to explore the house and see if there was anything in the kitchen to eat for breakfast. She walked quietly through the halls down to the ground floor. The dining table was completely cleaned up. Gwendolyn entered the kitchen and noticed two middle-aged women washing pots and pans. She greeted them, "Dubri utra [Good morning]."

They stared at her in disbelief, wondering why one of the call girls was walking around so early. They were the morning staff and had not been there to notice that it was an all-male party the night before. Once they started talking to her and Gwendolyn could only look blankly back, they understood how wrong first impressions can be.

Gwendolyn tried some Russian and said, "Ya Vengriya [I am Hungary]."

They looked at her, completely puzzled.

Then, she corrected herself, "Prosti. Ya golodnaya. Ne govoryu Po-Russki. [Sorry. I am hungry. I don't speak Russian.]"

Then, they laughed and busied themselves making her coffee and a decent breakfast. All Gwendolyn could say was "Spasibo [Thank you]." That was about the extent of her Russian. Gwendolyn was quite the oddity to them. They sat at the kitchen table and watched her eat.

If they thought she was Hungarian, all the better. The way people gossip, word would get out that an 'American' was staying here and she did not want to raise any suspicions.

She abruptly stopped eating when the thought hit her: "What if Ivanchka tells Popov we're coming after him and he sets a trap for us?"

But she quickly reassured herself that he would not do that for fear of losing his beloved books. She finished her breakfast, thanked the kitchen staff, and decided to walk around the old mansion. Her feeling of dread was still strong. She had to find some distraction.

Deciding to start with the basement, Gwendolyn opened the door and descended to find a firing range and a movie theater, the two things it seemed that every gangster needs. But feeling how it was as cold as a tomb down there, she quickly ran back upstairs. The house itself was probably around 65 F. The second and third floors were bedrooms. Snores were coming through all the doors. Back on the ground floor, she wandered through rooms that were all furnished like in a Chekov play.

In the living room, she turned on the big screen TV and for about twenty minutes flipped through the stations, looking for at least a cooking show. The most entertaining program she could find was a soft-porn show of two women joggers having a shower together after their flirtatious run.

Gwendolyn turned it off and decided to bundle up and take a walk around the grounds. As she opened the front door to go out, a terrible alarm went off. She frantically searched how to turn off the alarm. Not finding it, she told herself, *Screw it!* and walked out. *That will get the morning started for sure.* She felt like a cat trying to get her humans out of bed.

As soon as she stepped into the snow-covered walkway, two guards ran into the house to shut off the alarm. It was too late for the late partiers to continue their sleep. Slowly lights illuminated all the windows above her. As she followed the path around the house, she remembered a jingle her father would yell loudly to wake up her brothers, *Up and at 'em, feet on the flo'. Come on, boys, you can't sleep no mo.'*

Gwendolyn walked behind the house. There were frozen ponds and icicled gazebos with fields of snow and barren ice-covered trees all about. The grey dawn was starting to cast its dreary light on the dormant land. It was well below freezing and the wind was making the frozen air worse. After about twenty minutes, she had to go back inside. *And this is the best climate in Russia?* She asked herself.

Entering the house, Gwendolyn heard voices stirring above, as the place awakened. She returned to her room and removed her winter clothes. She sat on the bed, checking her email on her cell phone, knowing she would soon be interrupted by someone.

Sure enough, about ten minutes later, Dimitri knocked on the door. She told him to enter. He sat down on one of the old chairs. He looked like he had not slept well.

"It was a late night. I hadn't seen my friend for about ten years. We had a lot to talk about. Well, you certainly woke up early and let everyone know about it."

"Sorry. I was up since six and was getting bored, so I went for a walk. Didn't know about the alarm. What's the plan for the day?"

"The plan is to wait until we receive news from Moscow about Popov's schedule for the next few days. We want to catch him outside his dacha, but not in a large public place either. Somewhere we can discuss things in private."

"What if it's more than a few days?"

"Then we'll be here for more than a few days."

"I'll lose my mind with boredom."

"Oh. We'll find things to do. Watch movies, practice at the firing range, eat, sleep, etc."

"I was thinking. What if Ivanchka tells Popov what we're doing? Popov could set a trap and gun us down in the street?"

"Well, then I guess my judgement of character would be proven wrong. I'm quite sure he won't, because that would be the end of his beloved books. I have instructions to destroy them if anything happens to us and he knows that. I haven't been proven wrong yet."

"Yet. God, I hope you're right."

"Just be mentally and physically prepared for anything," he said as he got up to leave. "Breakfast will be in fifteen minutes."

"Already had it with the kitchen help."

"No, you must join us, even if to just have coffee. You can't be rude to my friend twice in a row. He's our ally."

"I wasn't rude even once."

"Oh, but you were! I covered for you yesterday by explaining that you were not feeling well. You know, women and their time of the month and all that. But I can't do it for breakfast, too."

"Is that what you told him? How would you even know? You better not have told him we're more than just fellow travelers who have found ourselves on the same journey."

"No, I didn't tell him anything of the sort. We wouldn't be in separate rooms if we were more than that."

"You know, someone tried to peep through the keyhole at me last night. Was that you?"

"What? What kind of man do you think I am? Believe me, I have seen enough women in my time to know how they look. Just because I may have a passing fancy in you, doesn't mean that I would waste my time pursuing a woman who wasn't interested. That's all I'll say on the matter. If it happens again tonight, catch the bastard, and let me know who it was. I'll fire him right away."

"And then he tells Popov what we're doing here."

"You're right. I'll just have to pop him in the head and drop his body in the pond out back."

"Oh, give me a damn break. The pond is frozen solid. You'll have to bury him in the basement until the spring. It's not that important anyway."

"No, it is, and I need to know that I have honorable people working for me. People I can trust."

"Look, just forget it. It was just my American indignation taking over. I'll see you downstairs in fifteen."

As he approached the door, he stopped and grabbed the key in the lock. "All you have to do is simply put the key in the keyhole and turn it 45 degrees. That way no one can push it out. Problem solved, and you won't put my men in harm's way, being the great temptress you are." He smiled and left.

She picked up a shoe and threw it at the closing door and yelled, "Maybe I should wear a burqa, too!"

They all met for breakfast at a huge dining table that could sit twenty. Gwendolyn sat on one side of the host and Dimitri on the other side. She was still seething at the male chauvinist idea that whatever stupid thing a man thinks is blamed on the woman for somehow tempting him.

Since it is understood that a man cannot control his actions, a woman must somehow prevent him from even thinking bad thoughts by making herself unattractive and unavailable, absent from view. That is the mentality of the burqa and hajib.

The host started speaking to her in Russian. Dimitri translated.

"Welcome, my dear, to my humble home. Please feel like it's your own home. I deeply apologize for the embarrassment of the door alarm this morning. I forgot to turn it off last night. It goes on automatically. I also apologize for the weather; otherwise, I would love to show you all the beauty of Krim and, especially, Yalta.

"Dimitri has explained the trouble you find yourself in. You can trust that I will do anything in the little power I have to help you. I have never been to your famous country and I surely wish I could speak English so I could converse directly with you. Luckily, we have Dimitri here, who is far smarter than me. Please eat and be merry now, for tomorrow we may never do so again."

Gwendolyn thanked him and dismissed his apologies with her own: for the alarm, for not speaking Russian, and for coming at the wrong time of year. Then, they all started eating, while Gwendolyn sipped her coffee, still not able to let go of what Dimitri had said.

Against her best judgement, she interrupted Dimitri and told him a story.

"You know, Dimitri Fomavich, what you told me earlier this morning reminded me of an old Soviet joke that my Ukrainian friend told me once.

"A woman from Kiev married a Muslim man from Uzbekistan. The day after they moved into their new house, he told her: 'Now that we are married, dear wife, I must tell you a rule we will have. You see my hat? If you see me returning home with my hat pointed to the left like this, then everything is fine; you can relax. If I have my hat pointed to the right like this, things are not fine, and you better be careful of what you say or do. You'll need to do something to make my mood better.'

"She replied, 'Fine, dear husband, I accept your rule. But you will also accept mine. If you return home and you see me standing in the doorway with my arms at my side like this, everything is fine, and you can relax. If, instead, you see my arms crossed and I'm holding a rolling pin, then things are not fine, and you better be careful of what you say or do. You'll need to do something to make my mood better.' And they lived happily ever after."

Dimitri laughed and translated for the table of men to understand. They all laughed at the well-known joke. Their laughter made things all right again for Gwendolyn.

"Point taken, my dear, point taken."

"Now that we have that taken care of, what news do we have?"

"Right before breakfast one of my associates in Moscow called me and relayed a message from Ivanchka. Tomorrow afternoon, Popov is taking his mistress, who will arrive today from Moscow, on a tour of the Massandra winery. The winery is closed that afternoon for a "special occasion." We will, as you say in the States, 'crash the party.' So, we have all day today and half the day tomorrow to relax here. We can watch movies, mostly Russian I'm afraid, and practice our shooting. We may need it this time."

"Oh, Lord. Well, I guess tomorrow is better than next week. I want to get this over with, one way or another."

"Oh, no, you don't. There is only one way to end this, so we can all live happily ever after, as you put it. By the way, a Soviet joke would never end with 'And they lived happily ever after.' We laughed at the joke, but mainly at your American addition, which we always think very silly.

"What does it even mean to be 'happy'? What it means for us ex-Soviets is a full stomach and an empty mind. So, tomorrow we'll empty your mind of worry and trouble, not by putting a hole in it, but by getting what you're after and putting this all behind us."

"OK." Gwendolyn said as she leaned back in her chair and tried to empty her mind of the stress and turmoil it constantly wanted to slip into. She wished she had the kind of iron nerves that people like Dimitri had. They would never have made it to where they stood in the world without it. Of course, many more like poor Ivanchka do not have it either.

True, life was never easy for her, but she chose a world where all she had to do was a great job painting and others took care of the rest. She was never supposed to know how to use a pistol, let alone be able to put a bullet in a man's brain. True, she could defend herself if someone attacked her. But now she was the one doing the attacking.

Self-doubts came pouring in. What would happen if they did find themselves in a gunfight? Would she hide behind a wine barrel and cry? Would she be able to even fire back, let alone hit anything? Would she watch Dimitri die in front of her for nothing because she could not hold up her side? What would they do to her if they captured her? Would she find the resolve to at least put a bullet into her own brain? Breakfast started out fine, but it was not ending well at all.

Gwendolyn had a choice: either run to her room, hide under the blankets, assume the fetal position, and cry all day, or take action. Of all the questions in her series of doubts, the worst one would be watching Dimitri die trying to help her. This was not his fight but her own. He was helping her because he could not bear to see her cry. That was the truth of it. Another painting did not matter to him. So, action was her only choice.

"I think I will spend the day at your firing range in the basement, dear Alexander Anatolyovich. Would you please show me where to turn on the heat downstairs and where you keep your bullets?"

After Dimitri translated, he replied, "A fine choice of action, my dear. I think it would be a grand idea if we all did that today. We'll finish our breakfast first and all meet down there in, say, thirty minutes?"

Wearing two sweaters, she met them in the basement. She was glad they turned on the heat. It would have been impossible to pull the trigger wearing gloves. She was given her own target range with a large stack of clips for her pistol. Everyone else had to take turns with the other four.

"You have 3000 rounds there," Dimitri explained. "Hope that's enough. Make sure you keep at least thirty clips for yourself. In fact, take as many as you can comfortably carry in your backpack. Once the firing starts, you won't be able to restock."

"What! Do you think I'll be firing hundreds of times? I thought we would escape if we found ourselves in a real firefight."

"Yes, but what if our escape is cut off? There is no surrendering. We are dealing with people who don't take prisoners. I wouldn't either. Where would I put them? I'm not in the jailhouse business. And if I let them go, they'll just come looking for me later.

"At least I can negotiate, because ultimately, it's not my fight.

But you? If you surrender, you will be badly treated by men who don't know how to treat a woman any other way. After they're finished with you, they'll either kill you or sell you as a sex slave to the Afghan jihadists. No, my dear, you must win or die trying.

"I'm not afraid of dying. I've been living on borrowed time for decades. Most of us in our kind of business have. Popov is no timid book collector like Ivanchka. He was a captain in the Soviet Special Forces in Afghanistan in the 1980's. In Afghanistan, I was just a truck driver, never being more than an efreitor, a little corporal. I just did whatever was necessary to survive. People like Popov actively – no, eagerly - sought combat on the most personal level. They enjoyed killing and hated to see the war end. You had the same kind of people in your Vietnam war."

Gwendolyn lost some color in her face with that bit of positive news. "I see," she said with barely a whisper.

"Oh, come now. What's with the face? You must know this before we go into action. You see, this is what I deal with all the time. Sometimes, I have nothing to negotiate with either. Sometimes, enemies just want to kill me. In those cases, I shoot to kill and rely on my wits and skill. You have neither. That's why we're here to help. We'll talk again later. For now, just start blowing away those moving targets."

"Sure, I get it. Where is the nearest toilet?"

"Just down the hall."

"Thanks, I'll be right back," she said meekly and hurried down the hall. Once there, she locked the door and vomited her breakfast into the toilet. After bowing to the porcelain goddess, Gwendolyn was angry with herself. She knew all the things Dimitri had told her were true. Panic would kill her.

Gwendolyn leaned against the bathroom wall, trying to get a hold of herself. She had been hoping that somehow Dimitri would take care of everything and save her from screwing up, like he did in Ivanachka's apartment. She was extremely grateful that Dimitri had decided to help her. She would have been totally lost without him.

Again, she thought that he was risking his own life for something that was not his fight, his life as well as all those who had come down to Yalta with him. A painting was not worth any of that. She started to doubt that he was out of line for suggesting they sleep together. It was really the only way she could thank him properly.

No, Gwendolyn decided, she wanted no complications until everything was over. After she had what she needed, she resolved that if he still had interest, she would thank him in any way he liked. If she had to leave Russia quickly, then she would repay him when she returned to do the painting he wanted. Thinking of the future made her feel better. She splashed icy water on her face, looked at herself in the mirror for a good five minutes, and returned to the firing range.

She walked resolutely to the counter, picked up her pistol, and inside thirty seconds put two bullets in the center of six of the eight targets. The other two were within inches of the center.

Dimitri looked at her with surprise. "Now, that's how you do it. Let's move the targets out another ten meters and try again." She did even better with bullseye's in seven of the eight.

"Will you look at that! I don't want you to get bored. Let's change to moving targets. We'll do random movement, up and down, sideways, back and forward. Try that for a while and then I want you to empty your clip within fifteen seconds." And that is what she did until lunch.

Gwendolyn smiled at his approval. Ordinarily, she could care less for a man's approval, except for Giles opinion of her art, of course. She decided to stop analyzing and just enjoy his words of encouragement.

She continued practicing after lunch at the firing range and practiced with her knife in her room for the rest of the afternoon. They all had an early and light dinner with very minimal drinking. Even Dimitri was quieter than usual. After dinner, he and Alexander sat by themselves in the den by a warm fireplace discussing important things in indistinct voices. Everyone else distracted themselves by watching old Soviet movies.

Gwendolyn retired to her room and took a hot bath. Getting into bed, she distracted herself by reading and answering some emails. She thought how sad it would be if she could never finish *Finnegan's Wake*. Sometime after 10 PM, she turned out the lights and tried to sleep. She left her door unlocked and the key not turned 45 degrees.

CHAPTER TWENTY

After many hours of tossing and turning, Gwendolyn managed to fall asleep. When she woke up, she glanced at the door. She was a little disappointed that no one had tried to enter. Even the key was still in its place. "Ah, the boys decided to behave last night," she remarked as she got up and prepared for perhaps her last day.

This time when she opened the door to venture forth, everyone else was already up and about. She saw Sergei in the hallway.

"Good morning! Breakfast in fifteen minutes," he said cheerily to her.

"Dubri utra [Good morning]. Will see you down there." She replied with much less cheer.

"Great! Hope you have some more jokes for us."

They went their separate ways. She could not help but like Sergei. He was younger by a few years, still a boy really. But he had his Slavic good looks and was always full of charm. His English was excellent.

Gwendolyn spent her fifteen minutes staring at the fire in the living room fireplace. The dancing flames and crackling of the burning wood was soothing to her anxious mind as she wondered what the day would bring. She remembered the lines from a poet friend about a young Indian soldier fighting in the British Army against Rommel in North Africa before the battle of El Alamein:

"Tomorrow we are to advance across this mine-laden field of sand.
Most likely I will find the eternal sleep our Scottish officer tells us,
 But no matter. For me, in my heart, I died the minute I left India."

Gwendolyn took comfort in those words. She figured she had died the minute she left California. Any time she had after that was a gift that could be taken away at any moment. Once her mind that idea, she felt at peace with the world. She smiled, saying to herself, "Where would we be without poetry? She decided to have a good day, no matter its outcome.

Breakfast time had arrived. She gathered at the dining table with everyone else. Dimitri got everyone's attention and spoke for about five minutes, giving them instructions. There were a few questions and some discussion. After breakfast, Dimitri said to Gwendolyn, "I saw that you were enjoying the fire in the living room. Let's chat there over our cups of coffee, shall we?"

"Let's." She replied, and they moved to the living room. She settled into a comfortable leather chair near the fireplace, facing the bright whiteness of the snow-covered trees in front of the house.

"Tell me. What's the good news? Popov surrendered over night?"

"Glad to see you are in such good spirits. The word is they will be at Massandra by 1330. The winery is only about five kilometers from here. My plan is this. We will all leave here at 1145 to arrive there for a 1200 tour. That will be the last public tour and will get us up to when Popov will be there.

"The eighteen of us will be too many for the tour guide to keep track of. As the tour continues, you, four others, and I will stay back and hide behind the barrels. We will hide at the place they always take the tour to, where they keep the Tsar's wine.

"Then, we'll surprise Popov and have our little conversation. Remember whatever happens, we can't pop off Popov until you have whatever evidence you need from him. I like how 'pop off' and 'Popov' sound the same. Are you sure your video works? Good. Any questions?"

"How will we make Popov talk?"

"There is an escalation process. First, we'll start with reason. After all, he has enough wealth and good connections here that it would mean truly little to be a wanted man in the West. If he really is interested in the art world, you could offer to do some projects for him."

"Sounds very reasonable to me. But what if he doesn't go for it?"

"Then he's not a reasonable man. Most, if not all of us, deep down, are reasonable. But let's say he doesn't get it. We'll escalate to level two. Since we can't appeal to his mind, then we'll appeal to his heart."

"Appeal to his heart? I'm not going on a date with him."

"A sense of humor always. That is an outstanding thing about you."

"I wasn't joking."

"No, we'll see how much he really cares for his mistress. I'm told they're very close. If it were his wife, it wouldn't work. Quite simply, we'll threaten to put a bullet in her brain."

"What? We can't do that! She has nothing to do with any of this!"

"We're not going on a picnic here. We're not even going on a winery tour. But if you want to stop at the reason to his mind stage, you're taking a big risk that he won't go for it. Then, what? We shake hands, apologize for the interruption, and walk away amicably?

"As soon as we step outside the winery, his thugs will be waiting for us. You can bet that the local police will not get involved. They never do. And besides aren't you a funny one? A few days ago, you were about to blow an innocent man's balls off."

"Oh, damn it. You're right. You're right. Just don't ask me to do it, because I know I couldn't."

"Fine. I'll do it myself. And if that doesn't work, we'll appeal to the comfort of his body, since his mind and heart are clearly dead. That's where my four associates will come in handy. If his body is too numb to see reason, then we reach the last step. We will appeal to his soul and see if it is ready to face eternal damnation or not.

"Because that is where we will all end up. Well, OK, maybe not you. But people like Popov, our kind host, and me will all certainly go there. At least, we'll have a lot to talk about when we all meet. Quite simply, he'll cooperate, or he dies. That is the final stage. After that, you will learn Russian and become a successful local artist. And live happily ever after, as you put it. See? I have it all worked out."

"What happens after all that?"

"If we stop after the first stage, we all fly to Moscow today and you'll fly to LAX on the next flight with your evidence. If we stop at the second stage and you get the evidence you would be satisfied with, I kill Popov anyway and we proceed to Moscow tonight."

"You'd kill him anyway?"

"Of course, I'm getting too old to fight a long gang war with him. Because you can bet your life he would come after me with everything he has, which might be more than I can put together. Then, all of us Russian businessmen would see who has the best relationship with our dear feudal lord papa.

"He would divide up either mine or Popov's feudal estates to his favorites just like Henry the Second or our Peter the Great would have. Who knows which way it would go? Trust me. It will be best for us all if he goes. Anyway, that's how things are done here."

"My God! What kind of country is this?"

"It's part feudalist, part Stalinist, and part Las Vegas."

"Is this some place I want to live?"

"Oh. You'll have choices. We're not the only country that doesn't have an extradition treaty with the US. China might be nice. You would have to marry a Chinese man, which can be easily arranged. But you can't trust them. If they want to get their hands on one of their own who ran off to the US with the Chinese People's

Children's Welfare Fund, they would gladly cut a deal and hand you over.

"Let's see, where else? Iran would be an option. You'd just have to marry an Iranian man and wear a hajib all the time. But if you don't want to get married, you'd have to find a country where you could fit in as a native. I guess Cuba could be a choice, but there again, if they want the US to hand over a hijacker who took a plane to Miami, they would gladly hand you over.

"Ah, I know! You could live in Belarus, but that's much worse than here. Oh well, looks like Mother Russia is your only real choice. At least you've made friends here already."

"I get it. I get it. You made your point. God help me!"

"Praying would not be a waste of time."

"Do you really think God would take a personal interest in me over Popov's girlfriend?"

"It depends on who has burned the most candles in church and who has attended the most Masses in the past year. I guess she'll have you beat there."

"You're right. Let's leave God out of this. What other words of encouragement might you have?"

"I have more where that came from if you want. But you brought up God."

"Fine, whatever. We only have a few hours left. What more can we do?"

"I remember the effect I had when I told you yesterday about Popov's and my Afghanistan experiences. If you want someone to sneak into a village at night and slit the throat of a tribal elder while he sleeps, then Popov's your choice. If you want someone to enter a conventional gunfight, like any good foot soldier has done, then I'm not a bad choice. God only knows how many firefights I've had in the barren hills of Afghanistan.

"What I will do now in the little time we have is to give you some advice on tactics. You can handle your SIG very well. That's great, but not enough. Now, you will listen and take everything I tell you to heart. Don't take notes. You need to engrave what I will tell you on your mind. Are you ready? Are you listening? Yes? Good."

He then explained basic tactics to survive a fire fight in close quarters and finished with: "If it all goes to hell, save a bullet for yourself, if you can do it. If not, prepare yourself for the worst as I explained earlier. Any questions?"

"Um... Damn! Do you have any cyanide pills I could hide in my mouth?"

"No, don't have any of those. A bullet in the temple or the roof of the mouth is a lot simpler and quicker. By the way, I'm not joking about any of this."

"Unfortunately, I know you're not."

Dimitri saw Sergei walking by and called him into the living room. "Sergei, I have to discuss some things with Alexander Anatolyovich. Sit here and talk to Margarita. Answer any questions she might have."

"Sure, boss," he said as he took Dimitri's place in the easy chair. "So, we meet again."

"Yes, Sergei. What's your patronym? How shall I call you?"

"We don't need to use patronyms with our close friends."

"Close friends? Is that what we are?"

"We're all brothers here. Well, and a sister, too. We'll be going into combat soon together. When we'll be under fire, we won't have time for patronyms."

"That's fine with me. How did you end up working for your boss?"

"I answered an advertisement on one of our job boards for a position in internal security. I thought it meant Internet security. I have an MIS from Stanford. Yes, that Stanford. By the time I graduated, the relations between our countries became quite bad and no one trusted a Russian enough to sponsor him for a work visa, especially not for Internet security. So, when my visa expired, I had to return here.

"I interviewed with Dimitri Fomavich. He does all the interviews himself, even for the cooks and cleaning women. Once I understood what he wanted, I apologized for my misunderstanding. But he took a liking to me as we had similar experiences in the US. One of my skills I picked up in my teen years was lock picking. He decided to hire me and trained me in what I do now: internal security of his organization. I also do his Internet security as a side responsibility."

"What a marvelous story. So, what will you do during our little adventure?"

"I'll be with the others, waiting for you to come out. I don't do beating people to a pulp very well. There are others here far more qualified.

"I have to tell you something about Dimitri Fomavich. He didn't exactly tell you the truth about his military experience. He never was a truck driver in Afghanistan. What a joke!"

"Oh, really? I didn't expect him to lie about something like that. With all he has now, why would he be so insecure as to invent war stories. I'll never understand men's egos."

"What are you talking about, silly girl? He has a small ego, especially for a man in his position. You totally misunderstood me. He was a member of the 345th Independent Guards Airborne Regiment. He was the commander at the battle of Hill 3234. He was given the medals of the Order of the Red Banner, the Order of the Red Star, and Hero of the Soviet Union. They even made a movie about his unit in 2005, called *Ninth Company*."

"Really! Tell me more."

"Sure. There were thirty-nine of them fighting 400 Mujahedeen and Paki Army soldiers. They were defending the hill and killed over 200 of the enemy. They lost six, including a dear friend of our brave boss, and nearly everyone else was seriously wounded. Dimitri Fomavich was shot seven times and it took over six months before he could leave the hospital.

"At the firing range, he's busy watching and helping you. You've never bothered to watch him. He will shoot the center of every target with every bullet. A hundred targets with a hundred bullets in one hundred seconds. When you're surrounded by hundreds of religious fanatics with no hope of resupply or reinforcements, you need to make every bullet count. No. There is no one else I'd rather be in a firefight with. You will be with the best. Popov doesn't have a chance."

"I am so sorry for being so wrong. Where I come from, I'm used to men lying about their abilities and backgrounds by exaggerating or even inventing them. I called them 'men', but they're mostly boys. God, I'm so embarrassed!"

"I found that to be true for the years I was living in your country. Americans are funny. I can sit next to a complete stranger in a bar or a plane and within twenty minutes, I'll know everything about him, and I mean everything. But he'll know next to nothing about me.

"Not because I won't talk about myself, but because he never asks about me. I think that's because Americans' favorite subject to talk about is themselves. To me, that is extremely self-centered. You won't find that kind of narcissism anywhere else in the world."

"You know, you're absolutely right about that. One of the first things I learned from living in Asia was to be reserved. I've had the same experience as you. It always makes me laugh after one of those one-sided conversations. The fact is, they don't care at all about you.

"I think it might be insecurity. They need to lay themselves bare to a stranger with the idea that the stranger will reassure them that they are interesting and important people. As in: 'This is who I am. Am I not interesting?' And of course, by listening to them, you reassure them. Yeah, it's a national character flaw. I agree."

"Don't worry about it. God knows we've enough of our own national character flaws. Now, that we have that out of the way, do you feel better?"

"Oh, I do. I'm much more confident now. Thanks for that. But I have a question for you. Why is he doing all of this for me?"

"I don't know. I guess he likes you."

"But why would he risk his life for my minor problem?"

"If I had to guess an exact reason, I would say he feels it is an honor to help a damsel in distress."

"Are you joking?"

"No, I'm not. In traditional societies like ours, a sense of honor is far more important than life itself. Our people toast the memories of those who have done an honorable thing hundreds of years ago. Our boss would like to be one of those, as we all would. Well, all men would anyway. Women don't think the same way."

"Well, you won't find that where I come from. Helping a damsel in distress was maybe important in my grandfather's time. I guess when women won the fight to be the equals of men that all went away. But women are not men and never will be. We are, as they say in Indonesia: 'Same same, but different.'"

"Same-same, but different. I like that! You're certainly full of amazing facts."

"Yes, I call them factoids. Interesting useless facts."

"Funny. Look, we must start getting ready. See you on the bus." He rose and went back to his room.

Gwendolyn agreed and went to her room, too. She met Dimitri in the hall. He had managed to find a flak jacket that would help protect her from any bullets to her torso. She put it on, and he adjusted it to fit her.

She Googled the latest about her 'case' on the off chance that she had been cleared and they could cancel the wine tour. It was only worse for her.

The LA Times reported that Captain Stanislaw Slarpniak of the LAPD had announced that the investigation was mostly complete and that everything pointed to the suspect, known as Gwendolyn, having indeed killed the Robertsons just as the 911 transcript said. He had contacted the FBI and Interpol to track her down and bring her to LA to be taken into custody for questioning.

Ah, damn it! Well, that's that. There is nothing else I can do but to get Popov to confess, Gwendolyn said to herself. She tested her video on her cell phone. It worked fine. It was charged to 100%. She checked her pistol and knife. Both were in their holsters and ready for use. She put on her winter coat over the flak jacket and stepped into the bathroom.

Gwendolyn looked at herself in the mirror for a moment and said out loud, "Locked and loaded." She turned and went downstairs. It was time to get on the minibus for the quick ride to the Massandra winery.

The bus slowly worked its way around the narrow streets of Yalta. It was the first time Gwendolyn could see the town in daylight. The town gave way to countryside and the minibus climbed its way to the winery. They arrived in about ten minutes. Everyone was quiet on the way there.

They all filed out and made their way to the winery's front doors. They were the only guests there. The surprised staff were only three, as they received almost no guests in the winter. But on this strange day, they would have two sets of visitors. The tour guide greeted them and led them into the depths of the winery's caves.

She showed them the dust-and-cobweb-covered bottles from the time of Catheryn the Great. The guide mentioned that the current winery was founded by Prince Lev Golitsyn in 1894, but wine had been made there for at least two hundred years before.

The guide demonstrated how they changed out the old deteriorated corks for hundred-year-old wine. Their dessert wines could last hundreds of years. Sometimes, they would sell a bottle or two at Sotheby's for about $25,000 each to pay the utility bills and taxes. Reportedly, Putin and Italy's Berlusconi drank a $90,000 bottle of wine there on a visit. It was an excellent tour and distraction.

They proceeded deeper into the depths of the winery, where the caves with rows of barrels on both sides would disappear into the mountain side so far that the small lights gave out before one could see the end. Their guide told them the eight caves which stretched out from the center like spokes on a wheel were all over a half a mile long.

The oak barrels were laid on their sides with the tops facing out, each about six feet in diameter. As the group followed her down deeper into the bowels of the earth, they became more boisterous and even rowdy. Everyone started asking her questions and making comments. She was clearly overwhelmed.

The guide led the group about a quarter of the way down one of the caves. She showed them where several of the barrels had the double eagle head of the Royal Romanov coat of arms brazened on. She explained that when the Bolshevik government took control of Russia and confiscated all the property of the royal family, they forgot about their wine barrels at Massandra. So now, only a living member of the Romanov family could claim the wine of these barrels. No one had appeared to claim the wine.

This legend was met with all sorts of comments and expressions. As she led the group back to the guest center, Dimitri motioned to Gwendolyn to hide behind the space between the racks, about another fifteen yards further into the caves. Another four of his associates hid across from them.

After the group left, the guide turned off the lights, leaving the six of them in pitch darkness. Gwendolyn started to shiver, more from nervousness than the cold. Dimitri put his arm around her and held her close to him. She did not complain. She wanted to cry but knew she could not do that. She resolved to do her best to keep this real decorated hero alive.

Dimitri whispered in her ear, "You remember everything I taught you?" She nodded against his chest. "Good. Now, remember above all else, the most important thing is to stay calm. Your mind must be calm and clear. Can you do that?" Again, she nodded. "Good. Now, don't worry. We'll get out of this successfully. You're going to do great." He held her even tighter and kissed her on her winter hat.

She whispered back, "Please forgive me for being such a smart ass and a jerk. I am extremely thankful for your help. If we get out of this, I really don't know how to thank you."

"Don't mention it. What kind of man would I be to not aid a

helpless young woman in a foreign land? You being alive and your name cleared would be thanks enough."

Gwendolyn smiled thinking how she would love to find a man like Dimitri, if he was not as infuriating and bigoted as Dimitri. It would also help if he was not a gangster. She knew in life she could only rely on herself, but she thought it would it be nice to have a man to help her.

Unfortunately, in her world, she had to take care of the man-boys her age. That was probably why she was always attracted to older men. She pondered that for a while until the lights came on.

CHAPTER TWENTY-ONE

Approaching voices were heard in the distance. Gwendolyn had her pistol out, safety on, and was holding it close to her side. She murmured to herself, "Showtime!" Dimitri pulled out his own sidearm, but he clicked off his safety.

The guide led Popov and his beautiful girlfriend about a third his age to the same imperial wine barrels. When she finished her explanation and turned to lead them back, Dimitri gave Gwendolyn's arm a good squeeze then stepped out into the passageway, followed by Dimitri's other four men.

Dimitri called out Popov's name, while closing the distance to about six feet. The three of them stopped and turned to see who was calling out. Dimitri told the guide to leave, which she gladly did, running away as fast as she could. [Since Popov could not speak English, the author has translated what they said to the best of his poor Russian language ability.]

"Major Popov, a word with you please."

"What? Who are you? Wait a minute, I know you from somewhere. Ah, yes, Captain Kandinski! Captain Kandinski of the 345th Independent Guards Airborne Regiment, a veteran of the famous battle of Hill 3234. Who was it who played you in the movie? Can't remember. No matter. I heard you speak about ten years ago at a veteran's gathering in Moscow honoring the fine work you and your men did for the Motherland. I would love to talk to you about it in more detail over some vodka to bring your memories back alive."

"It would be great to share old memories from those years fighting the enemies of Socialism," Dimitri replied. "I would also like to hear about how many old men you killed in their sleep. But first, we have a little matter here to clear up.

"You see, Major, your goons have caused this young woman here quite a bit of trouble in Los Angeles. She is like a daughter to me, and so I've taken a personal interest in her problem. That's why we're talking."

"What did my "goons," as you call them, do in Los Angeles, exactly?"

"You know exactly what I'm talking about. But to remind you, she is just a young struggling artist who was the guest of a respected couple in LA. They were art collectors. The moment my friend left their home, your thugs murdered them and pinned the blame on our friend here. Now she is a refugee from her homeland."

"Ahhh, so this is the famous artiste I've heard so much about. That's quite a large heavy paintbrush your struggling artist is holding there."

"Now here is the thing about it: I know you have next to no interest in the US. It would cost you nearly nothing to admit that you were the one who ordered the murders done and clear our young friend's good name, so she can return home. You would not be able to travel to the US and some other countries, but you don't go there much anyway. What do you say?"

"Let's just assume for a minute that what you say is true. Why would I do that?"

"Because it is the right thing to do."

"Since when do people like you and me ever do the "right thing" for anyone but ourselves?"

"All right, fine. I will buy out whatever your business is in the

US. We can make this a business deal so that it fits into "doing the right thing" for you. Just tell me what it is I would be buying and what it's worth."

"The business I'm developing in the US is not worth much now, but it will be in a few years. No, sorry. It's not for sale. Now, if you'll excuse us, Captain. I would like to continue with my day."

"No, Major. I'm sorry, but I can't excuse you just yet." Dimitri raised his firearm.

Popov nodded into the distance behind them. The sound of automatic rifles cocking behind them echoed, causing Dimitri's group to look behind them. Popov had six of his henchmen hide even deeper into the wine cave than Dimitri's group. They were now standing behind them about ten yards away pointing their AK-15's at Dimitri's group.

"You see, Captain, I knew you would want to discuss something with me. I just didn't know what. Now, that I know what it is, my curiosity is satisfied."

"How did you know?"

"Captain, you should give your mistresses more generous allowances."

"Ah sh*t! Her?"

"It's an excellent tactic. You should use it, too. That's some free advice. Well, I should now say, you should have used it. I have no more interest in our meeting."

Dimitri pointed his pistol straight at Popov's head. "Now, we have a bit of a dilemma, Major. If your goons start shooting from behind us, you and your devotchka here will be hit, too. So, you can't order that."

"Yes, true. True words spoken by a famous combat veteran. But really now, Captain? Is this silly thing worth dying for? Besides, my friend and I are wearing our flak jackets, whereas I see you have forgotten yours."

Dimitri made some quick calculations. If he surrendered, they may all be killed by Popov anyway. If he started shooting, they would most certainly end up dead - perhaps Popov, too. Just as he was weighing the options, in walked another eight similarly armed Popov 'associates' from the entrance to the cave behind their boss.

"Now, Captain, I could see you were weighing your options. Now what do you think? With these guys behind me, they can shoot and kill everyone in this wine cave. I don't mind if my flak-vested colleagues behind you receive a few injuries. That's one of the hazards of the job."

"If we surrender, will you let us return to Moscow?"

"Captain, you are not in a position to negotiate with me. You'll just have to rely on my mercy," Popov said as he and his woman friend slipped behind the newly arrived line of eight.

Dimitri turned to Gwendolyn, "Sorry, my dear. I was betrayed and never expected this. I'm so sorry. I failed you."

"No, Dimitri Fomavich, you did your best and it's not over yet."

Dimitri ordered his men to drop their weapons.

"Wise choice, Captain. You men in the back, take care of those four."

The six behind Dimitri's group pulled Dimitri's four men to the side and one of Popov's men pulled out his side arm and fired a shot into the back of their right hands and another shot into their right kneecaps, making them useless as hired guns forevermore. They were left squirming in pain on the ground. Another two of Popov's men picked up all the weapons that were dropped, including Gwendolyn's backpack, and took all their cell phones.

Popov said to his men, "The captain will come with us. We do indeed have business matters to discuss, but not like he originally thought. As for the girl, do with her as you like, then kill her. You see, Captain, at least I may be merciful to you, if we can come to an agreement."

Suddenly, Popov's girl yelled out. "Alexander Mikhailovich! You will not harm that girl in any way! You will not! Have you no sense of decency?" She glowered at him with anger.

He looked at her for a few moments, also in anger. Then, his face softened. "Oh, for God's sake, you meddling woman! All right, bring her with us." He ordered. This show of international women's solidarity both fascinated and angered him.

Leaving Dimitri's shattered men behind, the rest of them walked back up to the ground level. As they approached the visitor's center, they could hear a firefight. Popov ordered them out a back entrance, avoiding Dimitri's men pinned down by heavy machine gun fire from Popov's group outside. Dimitri could not find an opportunity to take advantage of the situation and had to bide his time until an opening occurred.

There was a minibus waiting near the back of the winery. Gwendolyn and Dimitri were patted down, then had their hands tied behind them with the familiar plastic ties. Popov's men led them into the bus and shoved them into different seats. Popov entered the bus with the rest of his men from the group and the bus left. About five minutes later, Popov called off the attack on Dimitri's men, leaving them to care for the killed and wounded.

***

As they drove away, Gwendolyn looked out the window at the barren frozen countryside of Crimea, wondering what just happened. Of course, she did not understand anything spoken, but she understood fully well that things were not going to plan. At least she and Dimitri were alive and not hurt.

But what was next? She had to trust that Dimitri would think of something. She had no other choice. Thoughts came slowly to her as she was still in shock, bewildered by the turn of events. They had missed her hidden special knife, but what good would that be against many heavily armed men?

The minibus drove in the opposite direction from Alexander Anatolyovich's house, along the coast going eastward. The Black Sea looked foreboding, as the winter winds whipped up the waves, black as its name suggests. Within less than twenty minutes, they turned toward the sea and stopped in front of an enormous iron gate. The gate haltingly opened, revealing a small stone castle, hugging the cliffs thirty feet above the churning waves below.

The castle appeared to be something a rich nobleman in the late 1800's would have built on a whim of fantasy, in the manner of a long-lost time of medieval France or England. It managed to include all the stereotypes a castle should have from a thousand years before. It had crenellated towers and an iron portcullis that blocked the wooden doors to the courtyard within. There was a drawbridge to allow passage over the heaving sea below.

The minibuses passed through the modern outer gates, drove up to where the end of the drawbridge would rest, and parked. They all got out and stood looking toward the raised drawbridge. Then, with a great creaking sound of unoiled gears, the drawbridge slowly came down and they walked over it into the small courtyard of the castle. Popov was clearly enjoying himself. After all, he had a wonderful fantastic plaything with his castle, and he had just won a significant victory by being smarter and better prepared than Dimitri. He simply had outfoxed his foes.

As they walked across the courtyard in the middle of the castle, Gwendolyn looked over to the source of the smells that assailed her nose. A small stone building with a low wooden roof housed a horse stable. Popov even had to recreate the smells of his fantasy era. All but two of Popov's men veered off to a different side of the courtyard, where their barracks were. The six of them went through a different door, decorated with pre-Raphaelite stained glass, showing a medieval hunting scene: a poor stag surrounded by baying hounds in a forest.

As they entered the foyer, Gwendolyn could smell the smoke of a fireplace. The walls were all paneled with dark walnut. Wrought iron candle holders jutted from the walls with dim flames. The hallway of the foyer opened to a grand hall with a ceiling twenty-five feet high. The stone walls had narrow slits for windows randomly placed. At least Popov had put glass in all the windows, something his fantasy castle would not have had. A magnificent brass chandelier with about fifty candles hung down, providing a twenty-foot circle of light that faded into the surrounding gloom.

A ten-foot wide fireplace had a large fire that warmed the cold air to only about fifteen feet away. A large bear skin rug filled the space between the fire and the wide leather sofas facing the fireplace. Popov told Dimitri that it would be probably better to not take off their coats as the place was ridiculously hard to heat. He apologized that their lodgings for the night would be quite cold, but the rooms had many blankets. In fact, the place was really designed as a summer retreat, rather than a winter escape from Moscow, Popov cheerfully added.

They sat around the fire. Popov was glibly pleased with himself and ordered tea for everyone. A large brass samovar was brought out and placed on a side table by two servants. Tea was poured into antique gold enameled teacups and saucers. Sweets were brought out and placed within easy reach of the three of them. Their host had already dismissed his mistress. Guards with assault rifles were standing nearby.

Gwendolyn took her cup and just stared into the dark black tea. She decided that she thoroughly detested Popov. Besides being physically ugly, he had a manner about him that expected obedience from all he met. His eyes were dark and full of spite. He was vastly different from Dimitri. Both should have been cut from the same cloth, being successful middle-aged oligarchs with military connections, but they were not.

Not understanding Russian, Gwendolyn could only listen to the tone of voices and watch facial reactions. Her understanding was quite limited, but it seemed Popov's girlfriend had helped her in some way and her situation had taken a radical change for the worse. All she could do was rely on Dimitri keeping a cool head and figuring how to get them out of their predicament. Instead of being dead on the icy floor of the winery caves, she was holding a hot cup of tea in a fairyland castle. She had to live every minute as it came.

Dimitri knew what kind of sadistic person they were sitting with. He had to play it cool, just like when he and his men had been surrounded on the hill in Afghanistan. He needed to buy time, humoring Popov, until something opportune happened. What that would be, he was still wondering as he stirred sugar into his cup of tea.

Would his office in Moscow organize a relief force to come down and save them? Did he even have enough men to pull it off? Were they really prepared to take by storm such a fortified place? What about Alexander Anatolyovich? Would he risk everything to offend one of his powerful neighbors? Dimitri decided that he had to rely on himself to get them out of danger. He had to bide his time, waiting for an opening to not only save themselves, but to turn the tables and get a confession out of Popov.

As for Popov, he chattered gaily, like a little boy in a toy store. He invited Dimitri to discuss their common experiences fighting in Afghanistan. Dimitri played along, thinking that topic was at least one thing they had in common. Dimitri wanted to avoid talking about anything else. Popov asked him to describe the famous battle of Hill 3234. Dimitri dragged it out as long as he could, but he was no Scheherazade from the *1001 Nights*.

During Dimitri's retelling of the famous battle, Popov would interrupt with shorter stories of the combat he had seen. At the end, Popov related one of his in more detail.

"Yes, Captain, that reminds me of when we had to teach the Taliban a lesson in revenge. They had ambushed one of our battalion commanders who was returning with a squad of soldiers to base after a meeting at a nearby Afghan Army camp. They executed all twelve of our boys after they clearly had surrendered.

"We knew who led the attack but could never find him. The Afghan Army intelligence told us where his parents lived. They were nothing but elderly goat farmers in a small village about 150 miles northwest of Kabul. We were given photos of his parents.

"We landed at 2300, about a kilometer from the village so they couldn't hear us. When we reached the village all the lights were dark. All we could hear was the soft braying of the farm animals and a few dogs barking. We surrounded the village and closed around it like a noose tightens around a neck. There were sixteen mud compounds huddled together on top of a small hill.

"I had a Spetsnaz platoon. Half my men kept guard at the perimeter with orders to shoot to kill anyone who tried to break through. The other half split up and surrounded each house, having slipped over the mud walls. Dogs were shot with silenced pistols. You know, Captain, I hate barking dogs even to this day.

"When we were in place, we broke into their homes and pulled everyone out to the central space between the houses. There was much crying by the children, oh the little lambs." Popov paused for a moment, savoring his memories.

"Once we had everything under control, all in under thirty minutes, I ordered the helicopters to land nearby. I had brought with us bundles of three and two-meter-long wooden stakes tied under the helicopters. I ordered them laid out two by two in a row on the edge of the hill. Next, I had all the villagers stripped naked - I mean completely naked. The women and girls were raped, maybe even some of the boys, too.

"Then, my men built crosses, nailed the good villagers to them, and set the crosses into the holes to crucify them. The crosses were no more than 15 centimeters (6 inches) above the ground, so the wild animals could reach them. It took us most of the night to do all that."

"A fascinating story, Popov," Dimitri said, successfully hiding his horror. "But what happened to the Taliban commander's parents?"

"Oh, them? We took them to a clearing, both completely nude. We made each of them stand on an anti-tank mine. They were close enough to be able to cling to each other. But as you know, if either one faltered and lifted the pressure off the mine trigger, they would

243

both be blown so far apart that only the birds and the worms would find bits to feed upon.

"His parents lasted until about noon the next day before we heard the mighty explosion. I videotaped the whole thing and left it behind, so their son would know where they went. As for their neighbors, some were eaten by wolves before they were even dead. We kept a respectful distance, so as not to disturb the wild animals, who came to tear off parts of the bodies to fill their hunger. The carrion birds took care of the upper parts.

"I've always believed we should treat wild animals with the utmost respect. It took three days until the last one expired. Right before we left, we burned the entire village and the fields. Slaughtered all the farm animals.

"One more thing: we brought a pig with us. Before we left, we beheaded it and placed it above the door to the burned-out shell of his parents' house. And we wrote with the pig's blood on the side of one of the walls still standing the words, 'Vengeance is Mine, sayeth the Lord' in Balochi, the local language.

"My only orders were to teach them a lesson. My commanding officer never wanted to know the details. He just wanted to know if we were successful. I guess we were, because Afghan Army Intelligence told us that the Taliban commander went mad and roamed through the hills near his old village until winter came.

"The next spring, his frozen body was found in a cave nearby. I was promoted to major for that bit of service to world Socialism. Now, Captain, doesn't that sound so much more fun than defending pathetic ultimately useless barren hills?"

Dimitri was so horrified, he was speechless.

"Now, Captain, answer me. Would that be or not be a fun adventure?"

"I suppose given the circumstances, what else could you do?"

"Let me tell you something, Captain. I deeply miss those days. I could have done that for the rest of my life. I mean, when else can one get away with such fun other than in war?"

"They defintely were interesting times."

"Now, Captain, you probably are wondering why we are chatting so amicably in my Yalta home. It's quite simple. I have a business proposal to make to you. I have a list here that my forensic accountants have made in two days. The list has been corroborated with your mistress. So, I'm sure it's complete. If something has been left off, that'll just be a bonus for you. Here, take a look.

"According to our best estimates, your business, property, and other assets are worth about 127 million Euros. Now, here is another list of roughly half those assets worth about 60 million Euros. Of course, we can discuss what the final list will be. What I'm proposing is quite simple. I will let you go with no hard feelings in exchange for less than half your assets. If that's agreeable to you, we can work up a contract and you can go as soon as it's signed."

Dimitri was so angry that he looked at the list without seeing it. He was seething with impotent fury. He had to hide it. "No, I could not agree to that, Major. I came here not to harm you, but to convince you to do the right thing for this girl here. But you have turned this into robbery. My counter-proposal to you is to let us both go peaceably and admit your involvement in the murder of the Robertsons, so she can go home."

"Now, I knew, Captain, you would not agree right away. Let's first have dinner. You two must be very hungry, having missed lunch. I have ordered all your favorite foods, drinks, and cigars, according to your dear mistress. You never guessed she was so ambitious. We men never really do understand our women. I must say, I don't try to either. Come let's sit and enjoy the bounty of my generosity.

"Captain, I really am surprised you don't see the generosity of my offer. I am still leaving you with over half your assets. I could demand all of it. You can still live very comfortably and even with time build it back up. As for the girl, I still haven't made up my mind. I can't feed her to my men, though they deserve some fun. It's not easy working for me. But my dear Tatyana would hate me if I did that and I've grown rather fond of her. I'll think about it overnight."

Dimitri was silent. They sat around the long solid pine table with Popov and two of his top lieutenants. They were also veterans of the war in Afghanistan. Yes, the table was full of all of Dimitri's favorite dishes, but he did not have any appetite to eat or drink. Neither did Gwendolyn.

Popov noticed and called out, "Oh, come now, Captain! Eat, drink, be merry! You should enjoy life as it presents itself. Besides, you never know when a meal could be your last. Am I right? That's how we both lived in the Afghan hills."

Dimitri refused to answer. He knew that signing Popov's offer would be an easy way out for him. But without Gwendolyn, he could not consider it. Popov's story of what he had done in Afghanistan was appalling. That Taliban leader had acted as any war leader would locked in a vicious guerilla war. What Popov did in response was simply an atrocity, like what the Nazis did to their own Soviet people during World War II.

Popov and his associates would toast to various actions that happened in the war, but Dimitri refused to join them. Popov noticed and became angry. He pulled out his sidearm and pointed it at Gwendolyn's forehead. "Damn it, Captain, you will eat and drink with us and enjoy it! I don't need this girl to finish our business transaction." He then fired his pistol to a point just to the right of Gwendolyn's ear. She cried out.

Dimitri shouted, "All right, fine, fine! I'll eat and drink with you. Just leave her alone!"

Gwendolyn ate nothing after the bullet whistled past her ear. Dimitri reluctantly participated in eating and drinking with the loathsome monster. Dinner slowly came to an end.

"Well, Captain. I think you must admit that I tried to be a friendly host by preparing the finest dishes that you like so much. Shall we discuss the business details by the fire over a fine cigar?"

"There's nothing to discuss, Major."

"Well, I didn't expect you would not see the reasonableness of my offer. But no matter, I'm a patient man. Why don't you sleep on it? Give it some serious thought. Let me know your answer tomorrow morning. We have your rooms prepared. I'll take you there now."

Six of his guards took them down a spiraling stone staircase with Popov behind them. The way was lit by pitch torches stuck in wrought iron holders attached to the walls. They descended four flights of stairs. What warmth the main room had dissipated with every step downward.

"Be careful! The steps can get icy," Popov considerately warned.

After another flight of stairs, the guards stopped on a floor with a hallway of eight dark wooden doors facing each other. One of the guards produced a ring of old iron keys. He unlocked and opened the closest door. Inside was a simple bed with a straw mattress. There was a stack of blankets on the end. A hole in the corner served as a toilet and a trough of ice for a sink. There was no window, as the rooms were carved into the rock base the castle stood on.

Popov indicated with his flashlight that this was Dimitri's room. "Captain, this will be your room for tonight. Unfortunately, all my other rooms are occupied this week. I never got around to putting electricity and bathrooms down here. Sorry about that," he said with a sarcastic smile.

Then he added, rather cryptically, "Did you notice last night how close the moon was to being full? It was absolutely beautiful! We should see a great high tide by the end of the day tomorrow. Hopefully, you'll think clearly about my proposal while you dream of your nice warm bed and soft beautiful young mistress. Sorry, I'm sure it won't be your present one, but you can easily find a new one. You'll just have to be more careful who you pick next time."

***

The guards pushed him in, slammed the heavy door shut, and

locked it. They took Gwendolyn down to the last room in the hall and did the same to her. The door slammed shut leaving her freezing cold in complete darkness. This state perfectly described Gwendolyn's mind, as she quickly covered herself in all the blankets stacked at the end of the bed. Even with her coat and clothes on, she could not get warm enough.

In despair, she thought of the knife she still had strapped to her arm and started thinking to end her life in the dungeon of the strange psychopath's fantasy castle. She did not want to think what he had planned for her the next day. She could feel the tears welling up in her eyes. She got a grip on herself, deciding that her story was not yet over.

Gwendolyn tried to think of when and how she would make her move to escape. Of course, she would need to save Dimitri, too. She just could not believe that he still stuck by her. She could discern that Popov was trying to negotiate something with him and Dimitri was not agreeing. He still was not betraying her. Thinking of this, she fell asleep. The stress and turmoil of the day had taken their toll.

***

Meanwhile, Dimitri laid under his blankets, mulling it over. A small voice asked him why he was doing all of this for Giles' girl. Was she worth it? He was indeed surprised by Popov's generous offer - generous for their world. Losing half his assets would not affect his life, really. By living he could make it all back. What would losing his life here in this horrid place mean and for the strange American girl whom he knew less than a week?

He banished such thoughts. He had given his word to that talented and lively young woman. Everyone who knew him would know he broke his word, and much more importantly, he would never forget it himself. He would live but live with such a sense of shame. What kind of living would that be?

When he had faced almost certain death on the Afghan hilltop, rather than staying ducked behind a rock, he had risked his life to save his fellow men, some of whom he personally disliked. He took quite a few bullets for them. But he had given his word when he entered military service to always act honorably, especially when under fire. Now he was under fire again.

He spent the rest of the time before sinking into slumber thinking of how and when he would move to save them both. He reminded himself that honor is more important than life, just as all warriors have believed since the beginning of time.

At 6 AM the next morning, Dimitri heard the old iron key jangle in the door's lock. The door creaked open and in walked Popov. "Good morning, Dimitri. I let you sleep an extra hour. Hope you had a good night's rest." He sat down at the foot of the bed and leaned on Dimitri's knee. "Now, old soldier, what have you decided? To live to fight another day, or to die alone in an old dungeon?"

"You can go to hell, Popov! I'd rather die with honor than live like you do, as a vile insect on this earth. We are not the same at all. You, who take pleasure in raping and torturing innocent civilians, are a disgrace to your country, your people, and all humanity."

"Oh, well, if that's how you feel. Hey, you there, bring the girl!"

Gwendolyn was yanked out of bed and hauled down the hall. Dimitri spoke, "Let the girl go. This is just between you and me."

Popov replied, "No, I can't do that. She's an unknown risk left alive." He pulled out his pistol and put the barrel in the middle of her forehead. "Well, since you don't want to see reason, Captain, I guess it doesn't matter what happens to her, right?" He paused waiting for Dimitri's answer.

Dimitri lunged at Popov, but he was knocked down by two guards, standing between them.

"Well, Captain, I guess that's your answer." He pulled the trigger, but the pistol only clicked against its empty chamber. "Oh, damn! I guess I should check my pistol before I threaten people. I'm joking. I didn't have a clip in my sidearm. Captain, you are just too much, you really are. No, I have a much better end in mind. Take them and follow me." He smiled as he led them down the stairs.

One of the guards asked, "Sir, should we take off their clothes?"

"No, we don't want them to freeze to death. What are you thinking, soldier?" came his reply.

Four guards held them firmly and roughly walked them down another two flights of stairs. Popov turned an iron wheel that opened a door that looked like the kind found deep inside a ship that would seal one section off from another.

The door opened. They had reached the very bottom. The space with rock for walls and pebbles for a floor, opened to a cave where the sea lapped at the water's edge about twenty feet from the bottom of the stairs. About fifty feet away, they could see from the mouth of the cave the dark black sea stretching into the distance. Above them was a ledge cut into the rocks that could be reached from the floor above them. But what caught Gwendolyn's eye were two wooden posts about ten feet tall, rising from the shallow water.

They were each taken to a post and placed with their faces looking out to sea. Their hands were tied behind their backs with thick black ties around the post and through an iron ring, so they could not slide up over the top of the post as the rising tide lifted them. The water was numbingly cold around their shins.

"Now, you see, Major. This is more fun than simply putting a bullet in your brain. I think you'll agree. Do you remember what I told you about the moon being almost full last night? Well, now you will experience fully what that dreadful fact means. You see those marks on the cave wall to your left? They show the water level at each hour until high tide is reached. You see that the water is already at the first level. We lost an hour, letting you sleep late.

"But not to worry, we have plenty more levels to reach today. Now, I'm afraid you'll have to raise your heads a bit to see the last level mark, since it's about a meter above you. We'll reach that in about ten hours. You can roughly track the time of day by the tide's progress. You must agree with me that this is very clever.

"I'll drop by periodically throughout the day to see if your thinking has become clearer. Now, if you'll excuse me, it's too cold here and I haven't had breakfast yet. It'll be fig jam and crepes with fine Guatemalan coffee. Your favorite, I understand. All you need to do is say the word and you can join me. All would be forgiven."

His words were met by Dimitri shouting expletives that should not be translated here, in case young people might be reading this.

"Fine. Have it your way. In about eight hours, we'll have a party up on that ledge in your honor and memory. We'll be toasting you as you start to gasp for air when the water passes your mouths and reaches your noses. I hope your coats will keep you from freezing until then.

"I'll leave you two there until the fish have picked you clean. You might notice some rib cages green with algae sticking up from the water around you. As your American friend would say, 'Have a nice day!'"

They turned and left. The clanging of the metal door behind them sounded to Gwendolyn like the gates of Hell shutting her in.

CHAPTER TWENTY-TWO

The icy water of the rising Black Sea lapped just below Gwendolyn's knees. Her boots had been full of water before they had tied her to the post. The lower part of her coat swayed back and forth gently by the rising tide. Except for the biting cold, there was a certain sense of peace in the silent dark desolation of a rocky cave by the sea. But Gwendolyn's mind was churning like rough white-water hurtling down a roaring mountain waterfall.

Gwendolyn was the first to break the silence. With a wavering voice, she asked, "I've been very patient so far, Dimitri Fomavich. I think it's time to tell me the plan. What's the plan?"

Her question was met with silence. "Hello? Talk to me, Dimitri Fomavich. What now?"

In a voice, choking with emotion, he replied, "I'm so sorry, Margarita! It wasn't supposed to end this way. We had a great plan. I was betrayed by someone close to me. I wasn't expecting that."

"Understood. Well, here we are. Now what?"

"I've run out of ideas, my dear. I'm open to suggestions."

"I don't have any, either. I guess we can while away our remaining hours with a pleasant chat. Why don't we start by you telling me what you were talking about this whole time? I didn't understand anything."

Dimitri took her mind off the cold for a while as he described all the conversations that had happened, including Popov's proposal to him.

"What the hell is wrong with you, man? Why are you here, then? Forget about me. After all, this whole thing is my problem, not yours."

"You still don't understand. I could never live with myself for buying my freedom and leaving you behind. If I could buy our freedom, that would be different. But Popov considers you some kind of threat. You would have been dead already, except that his mistress stopped him when we were in the winery cave. At least going this way won't be nearly as terrible as what Popov originally had in mind."

"I guess I can be thankful of that."

"You should be. We can cheer the international solidarity of women."

"I've always heard about it, but never experienced it until now."

They went silent for a while. Dimitri broke the silence. "I can say I'm not unhappy about my life. I lived a full life. I earned the respect and honor of my countrymen from the field of battle. I have risen far in my career in business. I have an extended family that I have provided well for."

Gwendolyn thought about that for some time. Then she added to the conversation, "I suppose I must be satisfied with my life, too. I mean, I rose from a working-class family and have established myself. My works of art hang in the homes of some of the wealthiest families around the world. But I am not as old as you are. Life could have had a lot more for me. I guess in times like this we have to be philosophical."

"Yes, poor girl, you had so much more living to do."

They shared stories of their early lives, intimate secrets that only the condemned feel free to share. They fell back into silence for some time.

Gwendolyn became quite agitated when the water reached her

waist and said, "What really makes me angry is that they left me with my knife, but I never used it. I should have lunged it into Popov's heart as he sat smugly by the fireplace."

"What? Wait a minute! You have a knife? Where? They didn't find it?"

"No, they never found it. I always have a knife strapped on my inner arm. It's still there."

"Why didn't you tell me earlier? Now we have something to work with. Hope has raised her sweet head again!" Dimitri said excitedly.

"Good, good, but what can I do with my hands tied like this?"

"What can you do? Why, cut our plastic straps, that's what!"

"But how?"

"Only you can answer that, but it is our only hope. But be careful. If you drop it in the water, then we really are finished."

"Let me think about it." There were two releases: one that opened the straps, so the knife could slide down her sleeve into her left hand; the other one released the knife entirely if she wanted to use her right hand. She had designed it after watching old *Wild Wild West* reruns where Adam West had the same set up for his small pistol. She had trained herself to be ambidextrous when she was a young teenager.

Gwendolyn explained to Dimitri how it worked and asked him how he would do it without dropping the knife. They discussed it for some time. She was terrified about dropping into the dark water their only remaining key for escaping. It was her turn to do something significant for her cause.

She decided to try to loosen only the top strap, so she could push the knife down toward her wrist while the knife was still attached to her arm. She told Dimitri every step she tried to do. He made some suggestions, which she followed, but her coat sleeve was too thick and was always getting in the way.

"So, how are our two wet friends unto death doing?" Popov's voice boomed from the ledge above and behind them.

Suddenly stopping her fidgeting with the knife, Gwendolyn

gasped in surprise.

"Oh, I see the sea has not stopped rising. Why don't you command it to stop, Captain, like King Canute did? The sea didn't listen to him, but maybe it'll listen to you. Try it."

"Why don't you just leave us alone?"

"The water is already at your waist. Just wanted to see if you've changed your mind. I may not return until it's too late. Well, have you?"

"I'd rather die than hear your voice again. Go away and don't come back unless it's to release us without any conditions."

"Don't count on that. You're not in any position to negotiate anything. Maybe as the water is approaching your chin, you may think otherwise. Meanwhile, enjoy your cold bath. Some enjoy their winter swims. But they usually are much shorter than yours." Popov was laughing as he left his rocky perch.

Dimitri waited until he was sure no one was watching. Then, he told Gwendolyn to try again with the knife.

"I can't! The coat sleeve is always getting in the way." she replied even after trying to lift up her coat sleeve with her teeth pulling at the shoulder.

"Don't panic. Let's wait until the tide gets higher. It will probably lift your coat with it." Her coat was already spread out in a radius around her.

"Oh, God, Dimitri Fomavich! I'm freezing! I can't feel my feet. What good will it be to survive if they have to amputate half of me for being frost bitten?"

Dimitri could not help but laugh, despite their condition. "My dear Margarita, that's just what we needed now, a good laugh."

"Glad you find the idea of me shuffling about on a wooden board with little wheels for the rest of my life funny."

"Shuffling about on a wooden board?" He laughed again. "A wooden board? That is real Russian absurdist black humor."

"Yes, and I'll have a metal cup to ask for money on a chain hanging from my neck."

"Oh, yes, even better!" He laughed again. "Would you have a little dog on a leash, too?"

"No, I'd have a lynx resting on my shoulders with his long-pointed ears and his legs dangling down. No one would dare try to steal the coins from my metal cup."

"Will you have a cardboard sign saying, 'Need help to feed my lynx' like the students do sitting on sidewalks with their dogs in the college towns of California?"

"Yes. You'd have to help me write that in Russian."

"Oh, are you doing this in Russia? In that case, we would have to reserve a place by the Orthodox Cathedral's entrance on Sundays. The churches in Russia don't do much for the needy, but they at least let them stand for alms outside the church door."

"Yes, excellent idea. Let's make it St. Basil's in Red Square. Maybe I can get something from the tourists. In return, I can offer the world a public good by reciting limericks."

"Fine. But don't forget you'll have to give the church a cut of your earnings."

"What's fair? 25%?"

"St. Basil's would accept nothing less than 50%. A little country chapel would expect 25%."

"50%? Ouch, that's a bit greedy. But I guess it would still be better than spending all day at the outdoor food market or by the Metro entrance. I'd be closer to God there."

They bantered about that absurdity for a while, until Gwendolyn's coat was pushing up to her chin.

"All right, now try again. Having already been through a lot together, you can just call me Dimitri."

"Sure, Dimitri. Saves me a second and the seconds left are limited."

This time, the sleeve was out of the way. After about twenty minutes of trying, she managed to push the knife down her inner arm by pressing her other arm against it. She lowered herself, putting her face into the frigid water, so her arms were parallel to the water.

After about another twenty minutes she managed to press the release for the knife to spring open in a way that would not send the blade into her wrist.

"OK, the knife is open. I need to stick my head under the water to get the angle right. Here goes."

"Remember to rub the ties against the knife and not the other way. This is no time to slit your wrists."

Gwendolyn did as he suggested, and to her shock she cut them off after about ten minutes.

"Oh, my God! I cut them off! I cut them off, Dimitri! Now, let me cut yours off."

She waded over with the water up to her armpits and freed him. "Now, let's get out of here! Let's swim out of the cave and away."

"No, not a good idea. The currents are extremely dangerous here and we are weighed down too much by our clothes. No, we did not come here just to get cold and wet. We have some business to attend to."

"Dimitri, are you crazy? Swimming away is the only thing we can do. Do you intend to fight our way out the front door? Forget it. I'll just stay in Russia. At least I'll be alive."

"No, Margarita. We're going to finish this, and you will not only be alive, but safe to return to the US."

"If you say so. What's your plan?"

"Popov will want to return right before the water reaches our chins and try one more time to get me to sign his bogus offer. We'll be waiting for him up there at his lookout point in the shadows. He won't see us in the water. He'll assume he came too late. As he turns to leave, we'll overpower him and force him to listen to the reasonableness of our terms."

"Why would he think we haven't escaped?"

"Because we'll leave our coats floating in the water. They're way too heavy and they'll do nothing to keep us warm. Here, give me your coat."

He tied their coats by the sleeves around the posts, so it indeed looked like they were still tied to the posts with their heads under water and dead.

"Let's climb up the rocks to the ledge where Popov will come, hopefully soon."

The Black Sea's tide had raised the water level well above the sealed metal door behind them. But it also allowed a swimmer to reach the rocky outcrop just below the second level where Popov spoke down to them earlier. From there, they could climb up to that open ledge and get out of the icy water.

They climbed up and hid in the small dark cave off to the side where Popov kept water sport equipment. "Look, Dimitri! There are two jet skis here. Let's just get the hell out of here."

"No, Margarita, we are going nowhere but out the front door with everything you came for. No one would keep petrol in their jet skis over the winter anyway. Give me your knife. I'll need that more than you shortly. Let's hide under that tarp. Stay close, so we can hug each other and not freeze to death."

"You never give up, do you Dimitri? But considering the circumstances, I'll agree this once," she said with a smile and gladly hugged him tightly, so thankful to be out of the water and again with a plan to follow.

After about half an hour, Gwendolyn managed to stop shivering, Suddenly, they heard voices coming down the stairs with Popov's cheery laughing voice louder than the others. She counted eight voices and wondered how they would ever take them all on.

Popov's group gathered around the ledge and were puzzled by what they saw.

Popov was the first to speak: "What the hell? Don't tell me we're too late! Did we miss the show of them gasping for their last breath? I was either going to get his wealth or, if I was denied that, at least have a jolly good show.

"But what I don't understand is that, according to the tide level marks on the wall, they should have had another hour. Strange! Well, at least we can pull up those chairs and have a few toasts to wasted lives."

They all sat down, poured out vodka shots and laid out pieces of bread with smoked fish pâté. "Now, each of us will make a toast, starting with you, Boris. Make it somewhat philosophical, but not too long like you Georgians love to do."

Boris made a toast to the two strangers drowned below them and everyone followed by draining their glasses then taking a bite from their fish pâté sandwiches. The cheerfulness ended, replaced by a more somber reflective mood. After all, what a way to go!

Popov waited until last: How sad that such a war hero had to meet his end in such a way. He had some idea of honor to the end. Now he would exist only in the memories of his countrymen until they, too, followed him to the next world.

After a few generations, his memory would disappear, and only then would he die to the world. As for the strange foreign girl, well, she came to Russia looking for something and finally found it in the winter waters of the Black Sea.

Their somber revelry was interrupted by a guard rushing in with a very agitated voice shouting, "Major! There are about fifty gendarmes and police with SWAT teams outside the gates. What should we do?"

"What? What do they want?"

"They want to question you about what happened at the Massandra Winery yesterday. They want to know where Dimitri Fomavich is. Witnesses at the winery said you took him with you."

"Question me? Why me? No one has ever questioned me about anything! Something is not right. Why would I know where he is? Did you invite the gendarme chief in for an informal chat?"

"We tried that, but he insists you come out and go with them to the Yalta precinct for questioning."

"Is Police Commander Ivan Petrovich among them?"

"Yes, he is the one doing the talking on their side."

"What? I have always taken care of him and his sickly son. How is this possible? Something else is going on. Look, delay them for as long as possible. I need to think about this. Tell them I'm not here. Use your cell phone and let me know how the conversation goes.

"The rest of you, go and man the walls. Boris! Bring me a container of petrol from the storage room." A lengthy series of Russian expletives followed from Popov for a few minutes after the rest of them had rushed out.

"God! We're in luck!" Dimitri whispered in her ear. "My wonderful friend, Alexander Anatolyovich, has come through for us and almost too late. We'll wait until after Boris returns with the petrol."

Whatever was happening was a stroke of good luck. Her heart started racing. Maybe they could pull this off after all.

After a few minutes, Boris returned with a large can of petrol.

"Thanks, Boris. Just leave it there and go join the others."

They could hear Boris running back up the stairs. Popov's cell phone rang.

"What's going on? -- They say they know I'm here because they have an informant inside working for the police? I don't believe it -- They only gave us an hour, you say? All right, let me think about what to do. Just have everyone sit tight at their defensive positions until you hear from me -- Fine. Good."

After he hung up, Popov was busy mumbling to himself, terribly upset. Dimitri told Gwendolyn to wait under the tarp until he called for her. He then started crawling along the wall behind Popov. He crouched behind his seated enemy and suddenly pressed the point of the knife on Popov's throat.

"Planning on going somewhere, Major?"

"What the hell? What? Who? How can it be you?"

"Let's just say, Lady Luck got me out of the jam you put me in. As you will soon see, she's not happy with you," Dimitri said as he pulled Popov's pistol out of his coat pocket and placed the muzzle against Popov's temple. "Her name is Margarita. Margarita, you can come out now."

Gwendolyn threw off the tarp and walked over to stand in front of Popov. "Dimitri, tell this asshole to take off his coat and give it to me." Dimitri did so, and Popov handed his coat to her. She put it on. Dimitri then handed her knife back to her.

Dimitri took Popov's sweater and put that on, while Gwendolyn held her knife to Popov's throat, just nicking it slightly. Once Dimitri was holding the pistol to Popov's temple again, Gwendolyn backed off. But then, she suddenly lunged at their prisoner with her face inches from his.

She pulled back a bit and stuck her knifepoint nearly into his eye. "Well, Popov, how shall we proceed?" Gwendolyn hissed in anger at him.

He shrunk back with his eyes closed tightly. "Good God, Captain! Hold her back! Is she crazy?"

"Well now, Major, looks like you angered Lady Luck. I'll try to control her, but you know how difficult that can be with an angry woman."

He told Gwendolyn she was doing fine. She was intimidating a major from the infamous Spetsnaz.

Dimitri continued, "I'll give you a situation briefing in a way you can understand. You have fallen into the hands of an enemy that has no reason to show you any mercy, considering what you tried to do to them. Imagine that Afghan leader captured you after what you did to his parents.

"Outside the gates, you have the Taliban army who could either imprison you for an awfully long time or just simply shoot you on sight. But there is an interesting twist. The enraged Afghan leader, thanks be to Allah, has a proposal that could save you and your men from annihilation. Would you like to hear it?"

"Yes, Captain! Get to the point!" Popov shouted back in anger.

Gwendolyn did not like his tone of voice and stuck her knife into one of his nostrils, slicing through to the outside.

"For the love of God, call her off me!" Popov cried holding his nose, trying to stop the bleeding.

"Oh dear, Major. No nose rings for you. Looks like she doesn't like your tone of voice. Better be polite from now on. Take your handkerchief out slowly. You're starting to make a big mess down the front of you."

"All right, all right! What is it you want from me?"

"First, we will go upstairs and find a bandage for your nose. I don't think it will stop bleeding on its own. Then we're going to get from you what we came for. If you only had agreed to be helpful at the winery, none of this would have happened. Your unreasonableness has hurt so many people, including you now. But I hope, for your sake and your men's, that this will be the end of it.

"We will go together to your office and you will type a full account of what happened to the Robertsons in California with every detail. You will sign and date it with your ID number. Then you will fingerprint it, using your blood if we must.

"Next while we are at your computer connected to the Internet, you will transfer to one of my accounts 60 million Euros, the same amount you tried to extort from me. Finally, you will return all our things to us. At that point, Lady Luck and I will walk through your front gate and confirm with the Taliban baying at your gates that all is fine, and you should be left alone.

"It was just teenage boys having a little tussle at the winery, who had too much wine for lunch. We promise we will never do it again, as we have become the best of friends and all that."

Popov was silent for some time. Then, he started yelling at them. "Goddamn you, both you, you devil, and your whore! You're just bluffing! I shall stay silent until my men start looking for me, wondering why I haven't answered my phone. You both will be shot down where you stand."

Gwendolyn replied to his rant, "I don't know what you said, but I don't like your tone again. How does this feel, asshole?" She pressed his forearm against the arm of the chair and stuck her knife through the back of his right hand and into the wood under it, pinning it down.

"Don't move your hand, Major. It will only make it worse,"

Dimitri advised.

Popov was suppressing a scream of pain. He grimaced as he forced himself to not pull his hand away. Dimitri told Gwendolyn to pull her knife out and try not to maim him, as he might cooperate after all.

She pulled her knife out and wiped the blood on Popov's sleeve, glaring at him. He yanked his hand back, nursing it in his other, letting his nose bleed down his shirt.

"Major, we have less than an hour and so much still to do. Stop wasting time. She'll probably cut your ear or nose off next. Let's get going." Dimitri locked his arm around Popov's neck and yanked him up out of the chair.

"All right, all right, Captain! I can walk on my own." And he led them from the ledge and up the dark cold stairs.

"Be careful, Major! These stairs can be slippery," Dimitri said in a mocking tone.

Popov led them up past the ground floor where they had had their dinner to the second floor and down a wood-paneled corridor. As they passed a bathroom, Dimitri shoved Popov in and opened the cabinet. There he found bandages and wound ointment. Gwendolyn took them to bandage Popov's hand.

"Oh, look at the poor baby. He must have been bitten by a wild cat. Little Popovka, what did I tell you about bothering the wild things?" Gwendolyn said in her best motherly voice.

She patched up his nose and gave him a pat on the head. "See, all fixed up. And you didn't cry once. What a big boy you've become."

Popov clearly understood her condescension, even if not her words. Mothers must talk to their hurt little boys the same way all over the world.

He led them down the hall to a large comfortable round room under the tower, overlooking the cold restless sea below. He pointed to their things sitting on a sofa against the wall and sat down at his desk in front of an open computer.

Gwendolyn picked up their things, handing Dimitri his pistol and cell phone. She also picked up one of Popov's sweaters laying on the bed and threw it to Popov who thankfully put it on. She did not do it for his comfort but rather to cover up his blood-stained shirt that would appear on the video.

Popov started to sit down at his desk, but Dimitri stopped him. He searched all the drawers of the desk and removed another pistol from within, even though Popov could not hold a pistol in his right hand, let alone fire it. Popov tried to operate his mouse, but his right hand was basically useless.

Gwendolyn pulled out a thumb drive from her backpack and told Dimitri, "At this rate, we'll be here all night. Let's record him on the computer's video and use this to save it."

Once Dimitri set everything up, he pulled Popov back in front of the screen. He pulled out Popov's wallet, found his ID card, and held it up by the side of Popov's face. Gwendolyn checked on the computer screen that the photo on the ID card and Popov's face were the same and that the name and numbers were clear. She then nodded for him to start.

"See, … what did she call you? Oh, yes, little Popovka. Mama Luck is thinking of you and your pain. All right, it's time for you to tell your story. I know your motive was to extort Giles into giving you a large part of his business profits. The motive is the only thing we will change. Everything else will be as it exactly happened. You are to be as detailed as possible. Are you clear?"

Popov nodded in agreement.

"Good. Now we'll start with your motive as follows: You lent Mr. Robertson $1.5 million to make a movie. He took the money but never made it nor repaid your money. He thought he was safe in Malibu from any Russian oligarch. But you proved him wrong.

"You took advantage of their poor artist guest and pinned the murders on her. You now feel guilty and want to set the record straight. After you explain the motive, tell the rest of the details exactly as they happened. I'm turning on the video now."

"My name is Alexander Mikhailovich Popov. This is my

National ID card. I organized the murders of the Robertson couple in Malibu. Let me explain: ..."

Gwendolyn looked out the window to the waning sun sinking toward the black churning sea from whose deadly icy clutches she had just recently escaped. She was thankful to be enjoying the warmth of Popov's office.

She could not believe the whipsaw she was going through. An hour before, she had been tied to a post in the sea, slowly freezing to death. Now Popov was preparing the evidence she had come to Russia for. If Dimitri had listened to her, they would be swimming away into the sea, perhaps only to be crushed on the rocks or drowned by their useless numb limbs.

As Popov was speaking in a dreary monotone into his computer microphone, Gwendolyn stood by the fire in the bedroom's fireplace to dry her clothes the best she could. When Popov finished, Dimitri had him set up the wiring of the money. Popov had about four or five times more wealth than Dimitri and so, could liquefy and transfer 60 million Euros easily.

As they were doing that, Gwendolyn wandered down the hall and into the main bedroom. There she went through the closets and found two good winter coats and hats. She brought them back and showed Dimitri, who nodded in agreement. She had no intention of escaping death by drowning, only to catch triple pneumonia.

They were halfway through the wire transferring process when Popov, pointing to the clock on the desk, exclaimed, "We've run out of time!"

"Don't worry about that." Dimitri replied as he pulled out his cell phone and made a call to his friend, Alexander, waiting outside with his new son-in-law, the police commander of Crimea, telling him to postpone the assault. "All right, fine. We have another thirty minutes."

Just as Dimitri was putting away his cell phone, Popov lunged out of the chair and knocked Dimitri down to the floor. Popov was on top, pressing his forearm against Dimitri's throat, slowly crushing his windpipe. Dimitri could not defend himself, having dropped his pistol too far to grab.

Just as Dimitri started to see darkness, Gwendolyn took her pistol and delivered a heavy blow to the back of Popov's head. Popov rolled over moaning onto the floor not quite unconscious. Dimitri laid on the floor gasping for air in long rasping breaths.

Slowly, Dimitri recovered. With a hoarse voice, he said, "Thank you, my dearest. This is the second time you saved my life today. And all I do is constantly put you in harm's way."

Gwendolyn helped him up. "No, my dear Dimitri, you have saved my life. By getting this evidence, I can live again. Should we revive him?"

"No, not yet. We need to let the computer and the Internet do their thing now. We're waiting for confirmation. Should be about another five minutes. Then we can get out of here, but we'll need that worm to escort us out. Better get another bandage for his head. Judging from that puddle of blood he's making, he'll need some stitches. He won't forget you soon."

She bandaged the back of Popov's head while he was groaning in half-conscious pain. Dimitri held the muzzle of his pistol against Popov's forehead. After she finished, Dimitri slapped him and pulled him up to sit on a chair. Popov came to, impotently cursing the world and everyone in it.

Dimitri checked to make sure the video recording was fine and saved correctly on Gwendolyn's thumb drive. He pulled it out and handed it to her. "Let's put our new coats on and get out of here. I'll call and have the plane ready to take us back to the safety of Moscow.

"All right, worm, on your feet. You're now going to escort us safely out your front gate, like you would any guest who enjoyed your very warm hospitality."

He pulled Popov to his feet, with one arm holding him up and with the other arm stuck the muzzle of his pistol into Popov's side. By the time, they reached the ground floor, Popov was able to walk better on his own, but Dimitri still held him tight.

Out into the cold of the late February afternoon, winter storm clouds were starting to gather. Two gendarme helicopters buzzed above. They walked to the closed drawbridge. Popov ordered the guards to lower it and raise the portcullis. Together they walked out to the center of the drawbridge and stopped.

Dimitri turned to face Popov, and in front of everyone, shook his hand. Popov grimaced in pain. "Now, there will be no hard feelings, right?"

Popov nodded his head in agreement. "You'll be fine in about a month. Just be glad she didn't hurt you any worse."

Popov let out a low groan-growl of pain and anger. "Major, we're now at peace and this matter is closed. Do you agree?"

"Yes, now get out of here! I need a doctor now. I hope to never see you or her again!"

"And you won't. Thanks for everything, Major. You are too kind and a wonderful host."

As they continued their walk to the waiting police and gendarmes, Dimitri turned to Popov, who was glowering after them in anger, and said in English with a smile, "Have a nice day!" Then they ran the short distance to safety before Popov could order his guards to shoot them in the back.

Sure enough, there was Dimitri's friend, Alexander, waiting for them, standing next to the Crimean police general. Dimitri hugged his friend in a tight bear hug. "Alexander! Thank you, my friend! You saved us!"

"No, my dear Dimitri, we only provided the pressure, it was you who walked out the front door! Before you tell me all about it, let's get you back to my house where you can get warmed up and change your clothes. Your men are all there waiting for you, except for the two who didn't make it out of the winery and four others who will be in the hospital for some time. This way. My car is warm and waiting for you two over there."

Before they drove away, Dimitri confirmed to the Police

Commander that he would drop all charges against Popov. The drive was less than twenty minutes. Alexander told them there was a snowstorm starting and that they would not be able to fly back to Moscow that evening, but that it should be clear the next day. Gwendolyn closed her eyes and did something she had almost forgotten how to do: she thanked God.

Back at Alexander's house, she took a hot bath to thoroughly warm up. Gwendolyn sank below the hot water in the large bathtub so only her nose stuck out. She stayed like that with her mind emptied until the water started to cool. She dressed and met everyone at the dining table for a fine Russian meal.

Having not eaten since breakfast the day before, Gwendolyn was ferociously hungry. She ate two full plates of food and three bowls of steamy borsch. She allowed herself a healthy dose of wine, too.

Dimitri told the story from when they had first arrived at Massandra to when they had walked across the drawbridge not two hours before. The whole time that elapsed was only about forty hours, but it seemed like a lifetime.

Every time Gwendolyn heard the name 'Margarita' everyone turned to look at her in astonishment. That amused her, since there was nearly nothing she had done that was not a sudden impulse.

After the long recounting of the story, Sergei walked over to her with his arm and shoulder heavily bandaged and gave her a brotherly hug with his uninjured arm. Everyone else rose from their chairs and cheered her.

Everyone decided to go to bed early and have an early start on their trip back to Moscow the next day. Gwendolyn burrowed into bed with two hot water bottles by her feet. She sent a quick text to Gabriella, who was ten hours behind her: **Thanks for offering to help. Have the evidence. Now you'll really know what happened to your parents. Need your email to send it.**

She again thanked God and, despite the high-pitched whistling wind outside, fell quickly into a deep sleep, her thumb drive held tightly in her hand.

CHAPTER TWENTY-THREE

Gwendolyn slowly awoke. Despite sleeping over ten hours, the light of a new dawn had still not dispelled the darkness of the night. At least the wind and snow had stopped. As wakefulness cleared her mind from the forgotten dreams of the dissipating night, she quickly grabbed her phone and saw that a message had arrived. Gabriella had replied.

Great news! Send it to <u>gabriella!!!@yahoo.th</u>. Better wait a few days to return. Slarpniak, the head of the investigation, is really trying to nail you. He'll try to have your evidence thrown out, saying maybe it was coerced or something.

Damn, he does have a seriously bloody nose. Gwendolyn thought. *Shouldn't have done that!*

I'm working on a few things on my end. Hopefully, between us both we can get you safely back.

Gwendolyn quickly sat up in bed and grabbed her laptop. Plugging in her thumb drive, she saved her precious file to her computer and then backed it up onto yet another thumb drive. She typed her reply to Gabriella.

Please find attached the recording of Alexander Mikhailovich Popov, one of Russia's many gangster oligarchs. He ordered the killing of your parents. The motive was over a

financial deal gone bad with your father. I think your poor mother just got in the way.

You will have to get an English translation done. Use the most reputable translation company in LA. We don't want any legal challenges to the translation. Please do this immediately and send me a transcript. He recorded it in front of me, but I have no idea what he said.

My God, what I had to do to get this! Will tell you all about it when we meet. But for now, get the translation done and send it back to me. Then we can discuss next steps. I'll be waiting in Moscow for your good news. And thanks again for helping me.

Gwendolyn

Gwendolyn decided to stay in bed and check emails while she waited for everyone else to get up. But not five minutes later, Dimitri knocked on her door, telling her breakfast was in twenty minutes and to be packed, ready to go before then. She did so and headed downstairs, ready to face the adventures of the new day. She was pleasantly surprised and thankful that she had managed to dodge catching a nasty cold from her freezing soak the day before.

Everyone was already sitting when she arrived in the dining room. They were waiting for her before starting to eat. Dimitri told her that they would leave for the airport in thirty minutes. He did not want to be trapped by another storm front moving through that afternoon. They would discuss things on the minibus. After breakfast, everyone got on the minibus. Dimitri sat down next to her. He, too, had managed to escape getting sick.

"I told our host everything that happened yesterday. I'll split Popov's money with him. We discussed it and he accepted only if he would use the money to donate to an organization that provides shelter for battered women with children across the country. I'll use my part to support private orphanages. The government-run orphanages are hopeless.

"When you go outside the cities of Moscow and St. Petersburg, life conditions are terrible! 60 million Euros will go a long way to make a difference in people's lives. We'll make a saint out of Popov, whether he likes it or not."

"The only saints in this story are you and our gracious host," Gwendolyn replied.

"Oh, no, my dear. People like us are merely lesser devils. The only saints we have here are those who dedicate their lives to these nearly hopeless causes, trying to keep their centers of haven in this mean world open and operating on practically no public and very little private support."

Dimitri spent the rest of the time chatting with his associates sitting around him. Just as the minibus was turning onto the airport access road, his cell phone rang. The caller spoke for less than a minute. Hanging up, Dimitri told the driver to pull over to the side of the road. He spoke to his men, then gave the bus driver new instructions.

"While we were having breakfast, our friend Alex, sent some of his men to search our plane. They found the pilot and the flight attendant missing, probably were given an offer they couldn't refuse, and worst yet, his men found a bomb hidden in the hold. They will need to spend all day thoroughly searching the plane for anymore. That means Popov hasn't learned to forgive yet.

"We have to get out of here and back to Moscow, where I can plan our next moves. Our only option is to take a commercial flight. A flight from Moscow has just arrived and will return in two hours. We'll take that flight and leave the rest of my men here to protect my plane and go to the hospital to protect their comrades recovering there."

"How do you know the commercial flight is safe?"

"Popov is insane, but he's not stupid. Doing something to a commercial flight would be declaring war on the Russian State, the state that he vowed to defend. The State would hunt him down and exterminate him with all its resources available. The authorities would ignore my private plane being blown up, considering it just a fight between gangsters."

The minibus dropped them off at the main terminal and took the rest of Dimitri's men back to Yalta with a few to be dropped off at the hanger. Dimitri bought their tickets and checked in all their bags, including their weapons. He did not have time to set up any VIP treatment for them.

The flight took off on time. All remaining flights for that day would be cancelled again from the next storm front moving through in a few hours.

They spoke little on the entire flight. Dimitri did not want any of the other passengers to overhear them speaking English. That would cause suspicion that a foreigner had just visited Crimea, a place off-limits to foreigners.

Except for some turbulence in the beginning, the flight went smoothly enough. They were picked up at the airport by one of Dimitri's drivers.

"Margarita, we'll go to my Moscow flat for lunch and discuss our next steps. We'll drop you off at your hotel later. Right now, I have to make some phone calls."

Gwendolyn had to content herself with looking out the car window at the bleak grey Moscow of February. Anxious to learn the details, she wondered how soon Gabriella could send her the transcript of the Popov video.

***

Dimitri went silent as they entered his parking garage. His face became quite grim on the way up to his flat. When the doors opened, he dashed forward, yelling to his assistants, "Where's that damned bitch?"

"We took her cell phone and locked her in the storage closet right after you called last night, boss," one of them replied, pointing down the hall.

"Bring her out!"

A moment later, they brought the blinking traitor out, her eyes adjusting to the light.

"Stand aside!" Dimitri said as he attached the silencer onto his sidearm.

She sunk to her knees, and pleaded in Russian: "Oh, please, my dear Dimitri! Please, spare me. I did wrong. I know! I'll do anything to make it up to you. Please …!" Her words were lost in the most heartrending sobs.

"I can forgive anything, but not treachery," Dimitri answered. "Now you shall die a quick death, not like the one Popov had planned for me and my friend here. What did I ever do to you to deserve this? You are nothing but the whore you've always been, jumping into bed with whomever will pay the most. God, I hate you! You two, get some towels to clean her vile blood off my floor." He lifted his pistol to her forehead.

Just then, Gwendolyn jumped between the woman and Dimitri's pistol. "Dimitri! No! You would be no better than Popov! Yes, I understand you must be terribly angry with her. But there must be a better way. She is clearly begging for her life. Make her do something good with it, instead of wasting it by being stamped out like a cockroach you found in your kitchen."

"Cockroach in my kitchen? Oh, you have a way with words. She is worse than a cockroach. Get out of the way, Margarita!"

"No, Dimitri! You are much better than Popov and his kind. Please don't destroy all the respect and esteem you have built in my heart. You were glad when Popov's woman saved me. Now I'm doing the same for this poor wretch."

Dimitri lowered his pistol and stormed around the room, steaming and cursing. His mistress looked up at Gwendolyn in amazement. She had not understood anything Gwendolyn said, but the effect was clear. This strange woman from the other side of the world just saved her life.

While she was pondering that, Dimitri dropped onto the sofa, muttering to himself, "Chort desho! [Damn it to hell!]"

After about five minutes, he yelled at the wretch to sit down in the chair across from him. She slowly rose to her feet and very furtively walked to the chair. "Hurry up, you damned bitch, before I change my mind!" At that, she rushed to the chair, sat down, and stared at the floor with the most contrite expression possible. Tears were streaming down her face.

"All right, this is how it's going to be. I'm sending you back to your grandmother in the deep Siberian country village from where you came. There you will stay the rest of your life. The local police will keep an eye on your every move. Furthermore, you will work at the private orphanage there, doing something useful with your pathetic prostitute life.

"You will return as you left there: penniless and without any of the nice things you had by sleeping with various men, including me. I emptied your bank account this morning and took everything from the apartment I gave you.

"I would have kept you in luxury the rest of your life. But starting from now, you will live in poverty, but at least you will be doing some good for the world. You will live like a nun. I will make sure that no man dares have anything to do with you. You will dedicate the rest of your life to the poor forgotten and unloved children of your hometown. Is that clear? ... I can't hear you! Is that clear?" He yelled.

She cried out, "Yes!" nodding her head vigorously.

"Margarita, take her to the bathroom at the end of the hall. Let her wash up. We'll find a set of clean clothes for her. Don't let her out of your sight, even while she uses the toilet. If she wants to kill herself, fine, but not in my home. She can do that back in her village." Dimitri explained the fate he had for her.

"You did the right thing. Now, Dimitri, listen to me! While I'm taking care of her, do not make any decisions or plans about Popov. You're very upset and need to calm down. Do something useful in the meantime and make us some lunch."

***

When the two young women were in the bathroom, Dimitri's ex-mistress turned on the shower and undressed. She then hugged Gwendolyn closely and cried in her ear, "Spacibo, Spacibo! [Thank you!]" Then, she started to kiss Gwendolyn passionately on her neck and moved her hands slowly down Gwendolyn's back and under her sweater.

When Gwendolyn realized what was happening, she pushed her back. "Sorry, girlfriend, you're a fine-looking woman, but I don't swing that way. Just take your damn shower and finish up." Gwendolyn said while pointing to the shower.

She looked at Gwendolyn with surprise and stepped into the shower. The dejected pathetic woman sat down on the shower floor, letting the water pour over her, and started to sob uncontrollably. Gwendolyn sat down on the closed toilet seat, thinking how strange it must be for a woman who could only use sex or crying to express herself.

Yet she could raise no feelings from Gwendolyn. There were limits to her sympathy; after all, this was the woman who had nearly caused her death. So, Gwendolyn just took out her cell phone and checked her email, ignoring the sobbing.

After about fifteen minutes, Dimitri knocked on the door and asked in English, "I have her clothes outside the door. What are you two doing in there that is taking so long? Should I come in and watch?"

"If you step foot in here, I'll break your neck, asshole!"

"Hey, I thought you wanted me to calm down."

"I do, but you can keep your idiotic comments to yourself. She's just sitting in the shower crying. I don't care; I'm checking my email."

He shouted through the door, "Listen, you damned whoring bitch, I'll give you ten minutes to come out or I'll pull you out by your hair!"

At this, the sobbing immediately stopped. She rose and quickly finished her shower. She motioned for Gwendolyn to get off the toilet, so she could use it. She brushed her teeth and then dried her hair. Gwendolyn brought her clothes in and she dressed herself. She started to put on her make-up, but when Dimitri violently banged on the door, she dropped her lipstick down the sink drain. Gwendolyn opened the door and nudged her out.

Dimitri stood in the hallway with a small knapsack and two no-nonsense middle-aged women beside him. "Here, take this. There are two sets of clothes in there. And that's it; no money, no cell phone, nothing else. These two will take you back to the hole you should never have climbed out of. There you will report to work at the Malenki Totoshki Orphanage on Monday at 0700. You will be paid 20,000 rubles a month [about $350].

"I know you used to make that in half an hour in your previous work, but living with your grandmother on her pension, it will be plenty in a small Siberian town. You will be picked up by the local police and a tracking collar will be put around your neck, so everyone will know the criminal you are. In ancient times, we would have cut your nose off. Now, get out of my sight!"

She took the knapsack and the two other women roughly grabbed her by her arms, took her to the open elevator and away.

"Margarita, you can't imagine how terrible it is in the deep Russian countryside. It has returned to the times of the Tsar. There is nothing but mud, blood, and booze everywhere and the children don't have shoes for their feet. But enough of these unpleasantries. Let's have some lunch."

After eating lunch, Dimitri sat back and told her it was time for him to plan a response to Popov's attempt to blow them up. He thanked her for forcing him to calm down first, so that he could think of a better, more diabolical plan.

"No, Dimitri, you don't have to start a war. A simple one-minute phone call to Popov is all you need."

"Oh? And what should I say, apologize for inconveniencing him?"

"No, silly, this special thumb drive is all you need. You see, it has a terabyte of memory and while my thumb drive was recording Popov's confession, a little program from my Ukrainian friend was busy copying all of Popov's files, including passwords, emails, contacts, business links - everything. You'll have enough information to hurt him badly.

"You'll have evidence for all sorts of crimes he's committed, access to nearly all of his assets, and contact information for everyone he knows. You can keep it. I already have copied everything onto my computer. By the way, don't try to reverse engineer it. It will self-destruct at the first attempt."

Dimitri grabbed it and hastened to a computer set up on a desk in the next room. He sat down and plugged it in. He went through the file directory and whistled when he saw what was there.

"My God, Margarita! Oh, we have him by the short hairs, as you Americans like to say. How I love that expression! Oh, we have him all right! You're a godsend, my dear. Give me your friend's contact information. I'll hire him right now. He's a genius!"

Dimitri found Popov's personal cell phone number from his copied phone bill and called him. After about a minute, Dimitri hung up.

"Done! Peace will reign across the land. The inconvenience he put us through this morning cost him ten gold bars. There is so much information here that even after he's managed to change all his passwords and accounts, he'll be living in fear that I'll start releasing certain evidence to the appropriate authorities."

"Glad I could be of help."

"Oh, you have, my dear, you have! Now, what's next?"

"What's next is I want a hot cup of tea with lemon and honey over there by the fireplace and listen as you tell me what Popov said on the video."

"Let's do that," Dimitri said. "I think some fine cognac and a Cubano would be more to my liking. Are you sure about your tea?"

"Yes, you're right, bring me some of your fine port."

Dimitri ordered one of the two young men standing around to

bring the drinks. He picked out a Churchill from his humidor, sat back in his favorite easy chair, rolled the cigar under his nose, then lit it up.

"First, I'll tell you the real motive. He wanted to blackmail Giles into giving up half of his business. I guess Giles makes between 5 and 10 million Euros, depending on what kind of year he had. It was exactly as I guessed. Popov wanted to frame you for the murders and extort half of Giles income into the future. Too bad about the Robertsons. They were innocent pawns in Popov's chess game.

"People like Popov think all rich people, no matter what country they're in, are criminals, like they are here in Russia. Popov and his type see nothing wrong with killing another oligarch, even American ones.

"The idea that families could be rich for many generations is inconceivable here. Russia's oligarchs only became rich under Yeltsin in the 1990's. Before then, there were no rich Russians, none. We were all more or less equally poor back then. Our oligarchs' second generation are only now becoming young adults.

"From what I learned about the Robertsons, they were from large landholding noble families from around Naples. Probably Roman in origin, which makes their wealth over 2000 years old. More recently, they made an immense fortune as highly successful cattle barons in Argentina back in the late 1880's.

"They anglicized their name when a branch of the family moved to the US and made even more money in real estate in the Los Angeles area. Of course, they always married well, like their kind always do. We Russians are just relearning that ancient skill."

"Got it. What about Popov's video? What did he say?"

"After he repeated the motive we gave him, for which I've already started creating the paper trail - ironically, using Popov's money instead of mine - he described the actual events. He made the trip to the US with his family. They visited Disneyland and all the other sights in the LA area. That was their cover.

"He took with him two of his associates who were the trigger men. He also hired Ivanachka to do the easy part of tracking you down. As for the Robertsons, one of Popov's thugs engaged their driver in conversation and the driver told them everything they needed to know. Why wouldn't he? He had no reason to be suspicious. From the driver, they knew not only where they lived, but also their BAFTA plans on that fateful night and that the staff were all given that long weekend off.

"Ivanachka did correctly guess which studio was yours. Popov and his two thugs broke into your studio. They were confused by the painting you were doing. It was not finished enough for them to guess what it was. They knew you were an artist and figured you were doing what you do best in your free time. But they did get what they needed to create their fictional scenario. They found your used sanitary pads in the bathroom trash. They kept it in a humidifier for the few days they still needed to wait.

"They correctly guessed the night you would leave. It was their only chance to pin the murders on you. They couldn't do it with you there. So, they just waited outside until they saw you leave by taxi. They broke in and erased the security cameras' recordings. They still had to wait a few hours, enough time to organize their scenario.

"The Robertsons returned. She went to her bedroom upstairs and he went to his study on the ground floor. One of the thugs was upstairs waiting. Popov and the other one were in your bedroom. They made some noise that attracted Mr. Robertson's attention. He entered the bedroom and they shot him.

"They then smeared your blood onto the bed sheets and set the crime scene to look like it was a rape. Meanwhile, Popov's thug upstairs killed Mrs. Robertson. He brought her body down and placed it in the doorway to your bedroom. Popov was quite angry with that one, because he raped her before killing her. Apparently, that wasn't part of the plan."

"Wait! He did what? Did you say he raped her?"

"That's what Popov said."

"That's the proof I need! I can do many things, but I can't rape a woman. The police just need to do an autopsy to know that I could not possibly have done the murders. A man must have done it."

"You have no proof without Popov's video. Maybe her husband was the one who had sex with her."

"And then supposedly raped me less than an hour later? This was a drunken man in his sixties. He couldn't even do it once."

"They have pills for problems like that. He might have taken half a dozen."

"But assuming that the bastard consummated his rape, they could do a DNA test to show that it wasn't Mr. Robertson."

"Sounds like you know more about crime solving than I do, and I'm the one who actually does it. But of course, our police don't have the sophisticated crime labs your Hollywood police have.

"Anyway, to continue the story: after they were sure the crime scene was set exactly right, they took the next flight back to Russia. Meanwhile, Ivanachka had hired a Russian woman he trusted living in LA to make the 911 call, the call that would tie you to the murders.

"Popov told me after I turned off the recording that he was sure you would turn yourself in and fight the charges, like any self-righteous American would do. He would negotiate with Giles and when Giles agreed to his terms, Popov would provide the evidence that you were innocent. But to everyone's surprise, you fled, and not only did you flee, you came to Russia to hunt him down. And that, my dear, is basically all he said."

"I have a friend in the US who is having the video translated. I'll discuss it with her and decide how to proceed. Thank you, Dimitri. Thank you for everything. I could never have done it without you. In fact, you were the one who did all the work. And you risked your life for me. I'll never forget it."

"Well, I feel honored. The fact is I absolutely cannot say no to a woman who needs my help. I truly can't. This time almost was the end of me, but I would do it again, if asked. I'll never learn my lesson."

"So now what are you going to do with that pathetic Ivanachka and his beloved books?"

"First, I wanted to kill him and keep the books. But then I learned it wasn't him who told Popov about us. Since he did play a role in your difficulties, I should give all the books to you. Altogether, there are thirty-seven and they're probably worth at least 2 million Euros. I should also give you some of Popov's money for what he put you through."

"No, the battered women and orphans need the money more than I do. However, I think I will take the books, except for the Russian ones. Those I'll give to your long-suffering wife, who would appreciate them. You could even tell her they're from you and see about the possibility of you two getting back together again."

"What makes you think we're not together now? Why, just because I have mistresses? I hold my wife in the deepest respect, but there is a vast difference between a wife and a mistress. That should be obvious."

"Oh, really? I don't see how it's obvious at all. Maybe you can explain it to me."

"Well, you wouldn't understand, because --"

"I'm a woman? Ordinarily this would be the time a fight would start, but I'm in a good mood, so I'll give you a free pass for today only."

Dimitri went silent for some time, then changed the subject. They tried to chat for a while, but Gwendolyn could not think of anything else. The fact that Gabriella's poor mother had been raped before being killed furnished conclusive proof she was not the killer. They just needed to do an autopsy.

But what if she was too late? What if the bodies were already cremated? After buzzing with excitement, she turned back to despair. She flipped back and forth a few times, then decided she was being useless as a conversationalist. She asked Dimitri to send her back to the hotel.

As the sun was sinking in the west, the time to call Gabriella in California was nearing. Back at the hotel, Gwendolyn returned to her room and set her alarm for 5 AM to call Gabriella. That would be 7 PM in LA, which would give Gabriella another full day to get the translation done. Between the events of the previous days, a hot bath, and reading in bed, Gwendolyn was asleep by 9 PM.

After the alarm woke her up, she called Gabriella.

Gabriella's chipper voice answered. "Is that you, my dear friend? We have so much to talk about, but first let's get you back here."

CHAPTER TWENTY-FOUR

Before Gabriella had received Gwendolyn's email with the Popov confession, she was about to give up. It had been over a week since she returned, and she made no progress with the LAPD. In five more days, she would have to do something with her parents' bodies.

She had strong evidence that her father had never raped Gwendolyn, but not enough to clear Gwendolyn's name. But now she was sitting next to her computer with the transcript of the translated Popov video open before her. This changed everything. She impatiently waited for Gwendolyn's call. In her excitement, she nearly dropped her cell phone when it rang.

"Is that you, my dear friend? We have so much to talk about, but first let's get you back here."

"I have to start by thanking you profusely for helping me. You and the wonderful Russian friend I met here are the only two who have actively helped me prove my innocence. The experiences I have from this past week and a half are unbelievable. I mean way far out there. But I'll tell you all about that when we meet. So, did you read the translation of the video I sent you?"

"Yes! I mean, wow! No one ever thought to examine my mother's body. What a way to go! She hadn't had sex in maybe ten years. I hope he was gentle with her before he killed her. My evidence is nothing compared to what you managed to find.

"I have a good contact with the second in command of the investigation. He is the one who persuaded them to do the autopsy on my father. I'll tell him to do one on my mother, too. Let me do that first. Hopefully, I can get that done by the end of today. I'll call my contact now and not waste another minute! Who knows? Maybe I'll have the good news by the time you wake up tomorrow."

"Sounds great. Bye for now."

***

As soon as the call ended, Gabriella called Antony. They had not talked since he dropped her back at the hotel. Antony felt bad about the doubts that Gabriella brought up. He felt bad, because with a full understanding of how the US justice system worked, he knew that doubts usually meant innocence. But doubts would mean nothing, as the great gears of justice ground on, set in motion by a determined police detective.

These blind cold gears were built on American society's belief that someone had to pay, hopefully with their life, for such heinous crimes. The hard truth of the matter was that in the end, it did not even matter if that someone was even guilty. Someone had to be sacrificed to the gods of vengeance and retribution to bring "closure" to society's dark conscious.

It also irritated him greatly how Slarpniak carried on. It was not just his speed of declaring the case closed when there were serious questions. Nor was it his attitude that if a case could be proven in court, it was as good as solved, despite the existence of evidence that the court would never see. No, it was more personal than that.

Antony hated Slarpniak's patronizing treatment of everyone on his path of blind ambition. It was all about Slarpniak and that was not what Antony had signed up for. He knew he could do very well for himself if he got with Slarpniak's program, but the thought physically disgusted him.

Even so, Antony could have swallowed it all one more time if it were not for that intriguing Robertson's daughter. He fully acknowledged that she had some kind of special power to make him do things he would never do on his own. It was not really a sexual thing, as attractive as she was. No, it was not that. It was more that she was just so different from any woman or even person he had ever known. The attraction was more total than that of a man for a woman. He was attracted to her as a person; he wanted to be her friend. So, when her number flashed on his cell phone, his heart nearly leapt out of his chest.

"Hello, Gabriella? How are you?"

"Listen, Antony, I'd like to meet as soon as you can."

"Um, fine, I can meet you now. Where? Would you like to go for a walk or have a drink, or what do you have in mind?"

"Meet me in my hotel's lobby and we can take a walk on the pier."

"All right, I'll be there in half an hour."

During her wait, Gabriella burned a copy of the Popov video onto a CD and made copies of the certified translation at the hotel's business center. She placed both in a manila envelope, put them into her knapsack, and waited in the lobby. Antony entered the lobby twenty minutes after they spoke.

He must have gone through red lights to get here that fast, Gabriella thought. She hurried over and gave him the southern California cheek to cheek greeting. "So good to see you again, Gabriella. How have you been?"

"Been doing fine. Let's go for a walk." She hooked up his arm with hers and guided him toward the pier. They engaged in small talk until they reached the end of the pier.

"It's nice that you called, Gabriella, and I really enjoy your company. But if you wanted a date, it would be best to do that when I'm not on duty."

"I wouldn't mind a date with you, Antony, as long as you don't wear your uniform and are single. Not at all, but I see you are still honorable enough to not take off your wedding ring and you are wearing your uniform, so I guess this is not a date.

"Maybe under different circumstances we could be friends, but my poor dear parents are recently deceased and I'm still in mourning. I should be dressed in black with a veil. Regarding that, has there been any progress on your end?"

"No, I'm sorry to say. The suspect is now wanted around the world. It is only a matter of time before she turns up. The captain considers the case closed and until persuaded otherwise, I must follow his lead on this. He is my boss after all. Anything new with you?"

"I'm glad you asked. We've found the true culprit. You'll find the details in here. It's a CD with a video of him confessing to the crime. It's in Russian, so I had it translated and certified. That's in there, too." She handed him the envelope.

"Well, this IS something. How did you ever get such a thing?"

"Let's just say I have excellent connections all around the world."

"But now here is the problem: How do we know the confession was not forced?"

"We don't. However, he does mention some details that only he would know. But I've saved the best for last. Antony, I need your help." She looked into his eyes with innocent earnestness.

"In his confession, he mentioned that my mother was raped before they killed her. This is the proof we need. Your suspect can produce great art, but she cannot produce semen."

"Now THAT is very interesting."

"Yes. We know that my father did not rape the suspect despite what the 911 call described. In fact, he hadn't had sex of any kind. Now, I have to ask you to please contact your friend at the morgue and check my mother's … you know and get the physical proof that will support the confession."

They sat down on a bench. Antony took out the translation and read it. When he came to the end, he let out a long low whistle. He stared out across the Pacific with thoughts racing through his head. If he did as Gabriella asked, he would be going against Slarpniak, who was riding high in the department. If he did not play it right, he would be fired.

If he ignored her new evidence, however, there was no telling what she would do on her own. Being the Robertson's daughter, she could go public with what she knew, and the media would gladly listen. That could be all their downfalls. He was weighing the pros and cons of each.

Sensing his uncertainty, she put her hand on his thigh and looked into his eyes. "For God's sake, Antony! Please, do the right thing!"

"All right, all right. I'll call the morgue first thing in the morning." Her hand felt like an electric jolt on his leg.

"Thank you, Antony! You are my knight in shining blue armor."

He liked that analogy. But he had to sleep on it. He walked her back to the hotel and with a hug they parted ways.

He tossed and turned all night, racking his brains about what to do. When he awoke the next day, he asked himself a simple question: *what's the right thing to do?* The answer was obvious. He took out his phone and called his friend at the morgue. While the phone was ringing, he thought that either they would find nothing, in which case nothing further would happen. Or, if it were true, he still would have time to consider all the angles and ultimately decide what to do.

His friend, Ralph, answered, and Antony explained his new request. Ralph agreed that he would do it first thing when he arrived at work and that he should have some preliminary results before noon. Antony thanked him and called Gabriella.

"OK, Gabriella, it's done. We should know something sometime today. I'll do a background check on this Popov to see what kind of person we're dealing with. You know, I'm really putting myself out on a limb for you. This could all blow up and I'll be out of a job."

"Antony, you are not going out on a limb for me. It's for justice. And if you lose your job for doing your job, then it would be time to find another one anyway."

She let that logic sink in, then continued with emotion, "Let me know the results as soon as you can. Thank you, Antony! Thank you for being my friend."

"I'll call you later. Have to get to work."

He had to really struggle to stay focused on his drive to work. By the time he arrived, doubts and fears crowded into his mind. The easiest path would be to do nothing. That is what Slarpniak wanted him to do anyway. As he was passing Slarpniak's office, his boss called him in.

"Where did you go last night, Lieutenant? Don't lie to me. Dispatch told me you went to Santa Monica. You went to see that Robertson girl, didn't you? How dare you go around my back! That investigation is closed! Close the door!" Slarpniak then proceeded to give Antony a thorough chewing out that the entire floor could hear with words that cannot be repeated here.

"What do you have to say for yourself? Give me one good reason why I shouldn't fire you right now. I have the paperwork right here on my desk!" He lifted several pages from his desk and shook them at Antony.

"Sir, if you would let me speak," Antony mumbled in reply, quite shaken up.

"Well? What do you have to say for yourself? Speak!"

"Yes, I did meet with her. As you know, she has her doubts. I thought it was a good idea that we keep a dialogue open with her. If she gets frustrated with us, she could become our enemy and make trouble for us in the media. But if you think that's not a good idea and are willing to risk her turning the media against us, I promise to never communicate with her again."

Slarpniak thought that over and then grunted, "All right, Lieutenant, fine, but do not contact her again without coming to me first. Do you understand? You can go now."

Antony turned to go. Slarpniak reminded him, "Lieutenant, you are my second in command now, but that can easily be changed. Be careful! You could have a distinguished career here, or not. That decision is up to you."

By the time Antony reached for the door, he had made up his mind about what to do with any new evidence. He would take Slarpniak down. He would plot his revenge while waiting to hear the results from the morgue.

Antony sat at his desk steaming. Then, about fifteen minutes later, he had an idea. He put his cell phone in his pocket with the voice recorder on and returned to Slarpniak's office.

"Excuse me, sir. I have some things I would like to clarify with you," he said as he closed the door.

"What now?"

"Gabriella Robertson told me she has some new evidence that might cast doubt on the suspect's guilt. How do you want me to handle it?"

"Damn it, Tony! We have an ironclad case already. That damn Robertson girl can go to hell! In fact, I want you to do nothing else but placate her and stonewall her. Do whatever you need to do to keep her quiet."

"What if her father has no trace of menstrual blood on his member? What if her mother's body had some other proof that would cast more doubt on the case? Maybe we should do autopsies on both of the Robertson's bodies?"

"You're not listening to me. We have an ironclad case already. No need to confuse things with conjecture. We just need to capture the perp and go on to the next case. Look, Tony, you know we've done this many times before. We create a case based only on what we need to prove that the main suspect did a crime beyond any reasonable doubt to a jury."

"But that has always bothered me. What's wrong with spending the extra time doing true detective work and finding the real guilty ones?"

"Look, Antony, we've been through this before. The chief will retire in the next few years. I aim to run this entire LAPD one day and one day soon. And when I do, I want to put into important positions like-minded people who are loyal to me, like yourself. These are high-profile cases, you know, like the rape-murder of the Marriot daughter, the murders of that actress Velvet Flynn and her dinner party in Chatsworth, or that Danish prince case, and all the others.

"As we quickly solve them, we rise in the estimation of the entire city, and most importantly, the LAPD and the mayor's office. What we do here just doesn't make the chief look good, but the mayor, too. As for those found guilty, well, they were just at the wrong place at the wrong time. Bad luck, but they probably deserved their punishment anyway.

"Now, Antony, I'm sorry for blowing my top a little while ago. It's just a sensitive time now. You are my second in command and always will be. Let's make our jobs simpler and tell the city morgue to pressure that Robertson girl into removing her parents' bodies by the end of the week, or else the city will cremate and dispose of them as if they were unclaimed. Keep her calm but distracted until she gets bored and goes back to Thailand or wherever she whiles away her rich girl time. Are we back on track?"

"Sure, sir, anything you say."

"Great. Now go talk to the morgue and remember to tell me anything new that the Robertson girl comes up with. You can leave the door open."

Antony smiled as he walked away and turned off his recorder. Back at his desk, he called Ralph at the city morgue to invite him to lunch and to hurry his examination.

"Sure, sounds good, Antony. We'll meet at the sushi place on the corner at 1 PM. I'll bring the results of my examination. You'll find them very interesting. See you later."

Antony had over two hours to wait, so he decided to drive out to the Robertson's house to while away the time. It was a beautiful place and it might clear his head. He listened to the recording he had made of Slarpniak earlier. It was crystal clear. Antony could already guess the "interesting" results his friend had found. He smiled as he walked back to his car.

Antony arrived early to the sushi restaurant. He found a booth by the window and waited five minutes for his friend Ralph to show up.

"Sit down, my friend. It's been awhile since we last saw each other. How's the family?"

"Fine, fine. You haven't changed much. Have you ordered? I must be quick. You know we office workers don't have all day for lunch like you detectives do." He called a waiter over and they ordered.

"Well, what is this interesting news you have?"

"Here's the report. What it says is that there was indeed semen found in Mrs. Robertson's vagina and the DNA does not match Mr. Robertson's. She had sex that night with a man who was not her husband less than an hour before sustaining a shot to her head. Unless she had a deeply passionate quickie with a waiter in the restaurant restroom, I would say she was raped in her home before she was killed. There was also evidence of a forced entry."

"So, she was right all along!"

"I don't know who 'she' is, Antony. I'm just a techie. I examine dead bodies and make my reports. Now I suppose what I just told you flies in the face of Slarpniak's well-crafted case. I'll let you handle that any way you want. Just please be careful and don't make me lose my job. That's all I ask."

"Don't worry, Ralph. I'll take care of it. Don't tell anyone else."

Ralph finished his lunch, while Antony hardly touched his. He was busy reading the details of the reports. The file also had Ralph's first report about Mr. Robertson 'being as clean as a whistle'. There was a chemical analysis of the bullets that matched typical Russian-made bullets. It was all there.

Ralph stood up. "Hey, Antony, I have to go."

He looked up and thanked Ralph for all his help, then went back to reading the reports. When he finished, he stared at the ceiling for a while, let out a long slow whistle, and then dialed his cell phone.

"Hello, Beatty. This is Antony from the special homicides office. Does the commissioner have some time to meet me this afternoon? I only need about twenty minutes. ... Yes, it's urgent, but no one else should know about it. .... Sure, I'll wait. ... He will? At 1630? .... Oh, thank you, Beatty! ... Yes, I know. Cream-filled eclairs. ... Yes, with real cream. I'll stop by the French bakery on my way. Thanks again!"

Antony had a few hours to kill before his meeting with the commissioner. He returned to his office and busied himself with paperwork. At 4:28, he placed a box of six fresh eclairs on Beatty's desk. Smiling, she quickly placed them in her desk drawer. "Yes, I have no shame. Thanks, Antony. He'll see you now."

Antony entered the largest office room in the building, tastefully decorated with a great view of the city below. "Come in, Antony, come in. How are you? We haven't talked in a long time. What brings you to my humble abode?" the commissioner said as he rose and met his colleague halfway across the room with an outstretched hand.

He shook it and sat where the commissioner indicated at a meeting table. It was a nice gesture. Rather than making Antony sit on the other side of his enormous desk, the commissioner could pretend it was a meeting of equals. He was quite popular in the LAPD for small but meaningful gestures.

"Well, sir, first I must thank you for seeing me on such short notice. To not waste your time, I'll get straight to the point. It's about Captain Slarpniak and how he's handling the Robertson case."

"The Robertson case? Really? Tell me all about it."

Antony shared with the commissioner everything he knew about the case and all the evidence that Slarpniak had chosen to ignore. He played his recording of his earlier conversation with Slarpniak about the old cases where the evidence was wrongfully handled, hidden, or otherwise ignored, putting innocent people behind bars.

All the commissioner would say were comments like, "Oh, really? Is that so? Interesting."

Antony continued by showing the commissioner Gabriella's manila envelope with the Popov confession and translation.

The commissioner stopped him. "Leave everything you have with Beatty when you leave. I have an important meeting tomorrow with the mayor and the Police Oversight Committee, regarding a wrongful death suit being brought against the Department. If I have time, I'll get to it sometime this week.

"Now one more thing, I hope this is purely a professional concern and nothing personal. Though I must say, he's an over-preening little prick.

"I've told him to stop those media stunts he likes to stage. He pretends he's some kind of celebrity. And it's his open little secret that he's trying to replace me. He's even dappling in politics with the sycophantic way he strokes the mayor's ego, as if that needs anymore encouragement.

"But if I sense this is a personal thing between you two, I'll not do anything about any of this. I hate police departments where everyone is trying to stab each other in the back. Do you understand me?"

"Yes, sir, perfectly. As you know, this is a high-profile case and the Robertson's daughter doesn't seem like she'll just walk away. And you know as well as I do, the Robertsons were very generous with their support of the mayor's campaign. His door would be open to their daughter, don't you think?"

"Now, Antony, you are starting to irritate me with obvious facts like that. Look, I'll give it some serious consideration. Reopening closed cases where a jury found guilt is not in the best interests of the LAPD and the city. In situations like this, sometimes it's best to let sleeping dogs lie. There are many angles to this. Do you know where the suspect is?"

"No. sir, but I'm pretty sure Gabriella Robertson knows how to contact her."

"Tell Ms. Robertson to tell the suspect that it's safe to return to LA and that I would like to personally meet her as soon as she returns. Then tell me her flight details. If Ms. Robertson won't tell you, then try to get at least the day the suspect left and the city she'll be leaving from. That would narrow down the possible flights for you to figure out which one she'll be on."

"Sure, sir, I'll try, but Ms. Robertson hardly trusts me as it is, and she doesn't trust the LAPD at all. If we double-cross her on this and just use this as a ruse to take the suspect into custody, all hell may break loose with her."

"You'll have to trust that I'll do the best thing for the department and the city. Meanwhile, if that suspect is not walking through the arrivals gate at LAX within the next three days, that means you've let me down and I'll not take that lightly. Understood?"

"Yes, sir!"

"You may go now. Thanks for stopping by. Give my regards to your mother, a widow of a fine police officer. The kind I hope you'll be one day." The commissioner rose from his chair, signaling the meeting was over.

"Thank you for your time, sir." They shook hands and Antony left the office in a perplexed state of mind.

As he passed Beatty's desk, he handed over to her all the evidence he had gathered and said to her, "Hello, Beatty. Please make sure that the commissioner reads these files as soon as possible. It's important!"

Beatty smiled, took the files, and placed them on a high pile behind her, labelled "Inbox". "Sure, Antony. I'm sure he'll get to it when he can. Everything on that pile is important. Good to see you again. Have a great rest of your day." She turned back to what she was working on at her computer.

This did not help his state of mind. He decided to go for a walk around the block to gather his thoughts. He could not decide if meeting with the commissioner had been a huge mistake. He was sick of the entire Robertson case.

He wished it was simply over and that they could get on with the next one. His mind then centered on one idea: He had to get the suspect back to LAX, as the commissioner had made clear. If that resulted in him being completely shamed in the eyes of Gabriella, then so be it. She was not his type anyway and he certainly was not hers. He took out his cell phone and called her.

"Well, hello, Lieutenant! What's the good news?"

"Yes, I do have some news. The lab report shows that the video was right. Your mother was raped by someone other than your father that night. I talked with the commissioner. He told me the suspect is free to come back to LA. He wants to personally apologize to her. There may even be some compensation for her troubles." As he lied his face was turning red. He was glad he was not doing this in person.

"Oh, this is great news! I'll tell her right away. And thank you so much, Antony! You're my hero, truly my hero. Thank you, thank you so much!"

"No problem, Gabriella. It was the right thing to do. Can you do me a small favor for the commissioner? His schedule is quite busy, so he'd like to know when she returns. He wants to meet her personally."

"Well... I haven't told her the good news yet. I could let you know, I suppose."

"Thanks. By the way, were you ever able to figure out where she is anyway? I mean, it's clear she's in Russia, but do you think it's Moscow?"

"I don't know, and why is that important?"

"Oh, no, no, it's not. Just curious."

"Antony, I'm trusting you on this."

"No, no, Gabriella, don't worry! Everything's fine. Just let her know she's free to return, thanks to your efforts."

"Yes, fine." She thought out loud to herself. "Let's see, we're ten hours behind. That means its 3 AM there. I'll try calling her in a few hours. I'll let you know what I find out. She has to book her flight and all that. I know they have direct flights from there. Thanks again, Antony. We'll talk again soon."

"Looking forward to it." And he hung up.

He almost panicked that he had blown it with her. He still was not sure if Gabriella would tell him anything. He knew he had not come across very well in the call with her. She seemed to have sensed something was not right with his request. "Just curious" is never a good reply to someone who is suspicious. There was nothing else for him to do but go home.

At his home computer, he checked to see which cities in Russia were ten hours ahead of them with international airports. The answer was either St. Petersburg or Moscow. Then he checked on flights to LAX. There were no non-stops from St. Petersburg and half the flights went through Moscow anyway. *Aha, I found it!* He smiled.

There was one non-stop from Moscow to LAX. He decided that there was the highest chance that she would take this flight. All he needed to do was to get the passenger lists from Interpol for all the Moscow to Los Angeles flights for the coming week and be ready to meet her when her name came up. Before he tried to get some elusive sleep, he made an official request to Interpol for the information.

***

As for Gabriella, she was giddy with joy that the two young artists had managed to clear up what had first appeared to be a hopeless mess. It was too early to wake up Gwendolyn with the good news. So, how would she spend the next three hours? Like any artist would, she visited LACMA.

By the time she returned and walked out to the end of the Santa Monica Pier, it was already 6 AM in Moscow. The southern California winter sun was creating a glorious panoramic sunset on the calm waters of the Pacific. But it went unnoticed. Gabriella's mind was only registering the good news she wanted to share with Gwendolyn. Not able to wait any longer, she dialed her number.

CHAPTER TWENTY-FIVE

"Is that you, Gabriella?" Gwendolyn's excited voice came through the line.

"Yes. I have some great news! You're free to come home now. With my contact in the LAPD, we have confirmed the details in the Popov video. The LAPD Commissioner has confirmed that you are cleared. He wants to meet you and personally apologize as soon as you arrive. We did it! I checked and there is a direct flight from Moscow to LA leaving just before noon today. Do you think you can make it?"

"Let's see, it's 6 AM now, I can make it if I leave the hotel in the next two or three hours. I'll book the ticket right now. Let me confirm for you, so hold a bit. … Done. I'm confirmed. I'll arrive in LAX around 2:30 PM today your time."

"Great! I'll meet you there."

"Fine. I need to get going to catch that flight. See you then."

"Looking forward to it! Have a safe flight." And they hung up.

Then Gwendolyn called Giles. Her call went to voicemail. "Giles! It's me. Call me back right way. I'm flying back to LA today. I have all the evidence I need to clear my name."

About ten minutes later, Giles called her back. "I just listened to your message. Are you sure about this?"

"Yes, I have an ally in LA who has confirmed it."

"You have a what? Who's that?"

"Her name is Gabriella, the Robertsons' daughter. She has been helping me work her end with a contact she has in the LAPD. Her contact confirmed the details of a video Dimitri and I made of the real murderer."

"Yes, Dimitri has told me about that marvelous video you two made. What an incredible story! But are you sure you can trust the Robertson girl, and even more importantly her so-called contact in the LAPD? It could be a trap. You could be arrested as soon as you arrive."

"Look, Giles, you can believe what you want. Considering what I just went through to get this chance to clear my name, I'm willing to take this risk. It's either leave now or stay in this strange quasi-medieval, quasi-Vegas country for the rest of my life. No, my friend, I'm literally on the next plane to LA."

"All right, fine, Gwendolyn. What time do you arrive? If something happens, I want to be there and perhaps help you escape a second time."

"It's a direct flight, arriving today at about 2:30 PM your time."

"That means you have to leave in a few hours. All right, I'll be there to pick you up."

"Great, thanks. See you soon. Got to go."

"See you soon and good luck!" They hung up. She finished breakfast and was enjoying her coffee when she decided to call Dimitri. She had never called the special number he had given her, but she thought it best to say goodbye rather than text it.

Dimitri was like an LA drug lord in that he always carried at least eight cell phones with him. He found the correct one and answered. "Allo?"

"Dubri utra! It's me. I just got off the phone with my friend in the US. It's done! Popov's details have been confirmed. I'm free to go home all thanks to you! I'm catching the next flight to LA, which leaves at 11:55 this morning."

"Oh, my dear Margarita, so glad to hear that, but are you sure it's not a trap by the LA police?"

"I'm not sure but I'll take my chances."

"Fine. You must be at the airport by 1000. I'll pick you up in about ninety minutes, at, say, 0845?"

"You don't need to do that."

"What? Of course, I do. Not another word. See you in the lobby in ninety minutes." And he hung up.

Gwendolyn casually finished what she hoped would be her last wonderful Russian breakfast for some time. She had not unpacked from her bizarre trip to Crimea. So, she was checked out and in the lobby, well on time.

The gilded hotel lobby clock hit 8:45 and in walked Dimitri. She ran up to him and gave him a hug. He smiled, grabbed her luggage, and led her to his car. A little over an hour later they arrived at the airport. They did not speak much on the way. They were sad to part ways after all the adventures they had had together.

The driver parked at the curb of the departure lounge and Dimitri carried her luggage into the terminal. Gwendolyn put her bags on the scale at the check in counter with her backpack zipped up in her large suitcase.

She turned to Dimitri, "You know what's funny? I never fired in anger that heavy thing I've been carrying around with me. Well, at least not at a person. Thank God for that."

"Yes, that is something, isn't it?"

They walked in silence to the security line. They stopped and turned to each other. "You know, Dimitri, the Chinese have a saying: there is sound in silence. It's hard to put into words what my heart is trying to say. Anyway, thanks for everything. You're an extraordinary man and a wonderful person. I don't care what anyone says," she said with a smile and tears rolling down her cheeks.

He gave her a tight hug and a kiss on her forehead. "As they say in your south, 'Y'all come back soon, hear!'" he said in his best Russian attempt at a southern accent.

Gwendolyn laughed out loud: "Oh, no! That's too absurd for words. Yes, of course. I owe you a painting." She smiled sadly and proceeded to go through security. After finding the airline lounge near her gate, she settled in to wait the forty-five minutes until boarding.

She noticed with a chuckle how different the lounge was to the VIP one where the silly hotel girls had taken her what seemed years ago. She stared blankly into the distance, as her mind went over the whirlwind events of the past ten days. Her mind just arrived at the point she snuck into Ivanachka's apartment, when the loudspeaker broke in reminding her it was time to board.

Her seat was alone by the window. The champagne flowed freely as she was in a celebratory mood. There was just the minor matter of getting out of LAX without any surprises. She trusted Gabriella that everything would be fine. The airline fed and watered her well. She settled in for the twelve-hour flight. With her eye shades on and the seat all the way back, she slept well.

***

About 3 AM, a text message arrived, waking Antony from his fitful sleep. It was from Interpol, informing him that he had an email with the passenger list of the Moscow to LA flight that would arrive that afternoon. Antony leapt to his open laptop. There was the Interpol email. He opened the attachment and skimmed through the names. There was only one Gwendolyn on the plane. They had their girl.

He texted the Commissioner that she was on her way, arriving on the 1435 flight from Moscow. He looked at the email again and his heart froze when he noticed that it was copied to his superior, Slarpniak, too. It was normal protocol to make sure there was no rogue police activity.

How was he going to explain this to his boss? He gave up trying to devise an excuse and was prepared to be fired first thing the next morning. Once he resigned himself to that, he fell fast asleep, until his alarm clock rang three hours later.

Antony walked into his office at 8 AM much more cheerfully than usual, having thought on the drive in that he was sick of all the nonsense of his work. As he passed Slarpniak's office, he slowed down to quicken the inevitable. Sure enough, his boss noticed him and called him into his office.

"Antony, good morning! I saw that message from Interpol they sent you last night. How did you do it? How did you find her?"

"Well, sir, it was late, and I didn't want to disturb you. Sorry about that," Antony replied, feeling rather confused.

"Oh, I don't care about that. You have given us the breakthrough we needed. You are to be commended for your great police work. But tell me, how did you find her?"

"It was late yesterday evening. And it just kind of struck me as I was piecing together all the hints that Gabriella Robertson unwittingly gave me."

"That's great, but how did you know that she was returning today?" Slarpniak seemed to have totally forgotten how he had treated Antony the day before.

"I took a gamble. I knew they were in communication. So, I told Gabriella Robertson that the suspect's name had been cleared in the case and that she was free to return. And just as I thought, the suspect took the next flight back."

"Wow, when we arrest her at LAX, that Robertson girl is going to really hate you for betraying her trust. But you know what? Sometimes we must do whatever is necessary in the service of justice. It will be good for me, too, as I will successfully close another case. I mean, it will be good for all of us. I'll make sure you get a raise and a promotion after this is all over."

Slarpniak's cell phone rang. He picked it up and looked at it. "Oh, it's CBS. Have to take this call. I'll talk to you later. Good job!

"Hey, George, thanks for getting back to me. Now listen. I want your TV news team at Bradley Terminal's arrival gate at 1400. The

Robertson's suspect is returning from Moscow and I want you to catch it on TV as we arrest her. ... Yes, as I promised, you'll have the exclusive for TV, but the newspapers will be there, too. Now this is how I would like it staged ..."

Antony walked out of the office much less cheerfully than when he had arrived. *Yes*, he thought to himself, *Gabriella will really hate me after this*. He still had his job, but he had lost all his self-respect. He sat down at his desk and stared at his blank computer screen, with his face red with shame.

A while later, one of his colleagues came up to him. "Hey, Antony, did you hear? We'll nail the suspect at LAX this afternoon. The captain wants us all present at Bradley's arrival gate at 1400 this afternoon. Hey, man, what's wrong? You don't look so good. Why is your face so red?"

"Don't know. I think I need some air. I'll see you there," Antony said, as he got up and left the office.

He walked randomly, even blindly, around the city, almost being hit by cars as he crossed the streets without looking. His mind was in turmoil. He wanted so much to call Gabriella to tell her friend to not get on the plane, but it had already taken off. He even thought about jumping off the San Pedro Bridge, but he would probably have an accident trying to drive there.

Finally, he decided to go to a bar and get drunk, something he had not thought of for years. He would show up at the airport drunk, which would get him fired, but that was what he wanted anyway. He walked into a dark Irish corner bar, already with several patrons holding court at 10 AM. He ordered a double vodka tonic.

The bar tender looked at him very suspiciously. "Lieutenant, I don't think I should be serving you in your uniform. Is this a test?"

"No, this is not a damn test! I'm just thirsty and I need a drink. You got a problem with that?"

"But, sir, you're not allowed to bring a firearm into a bar in California. I simply can't serve you."

"Oh, damn it!" He got up and left. He walked a bit with a great black cloud around his head. Then he saw a liquor store. He walked in and bought a bottle of whiskey. He kept it in the paper bag and walked to a nearby park. Finding a quiet hidden corner of the park, he opened the bottle. As he raised it to his lips, his cell phone sounded indicating a text message arrived. He put the bottle down and read it. It was from the commissioner! All it read was **See you at the airport. Look smart.**

Antony stared at the bush in front of him for at least fifteen minutes, wondering what exactly the commissioner meant. Finally, he decided that he had no idea what it meant, but there was a possibility that the commissioner was putting forth a straw for him to clutch. If there was even a slight possibility that the situation might turn out fine, then he should give events a chance to play out.

As he walked out of the park, holding his untouched bottle, looking for somewhere to throw it away, he met a street man going through a trash bin. "Hey dude. Here. Have a party, but don't forget to invite three or four of your friends. You know excessive drinking is bad for your health and make sure you have your party down an alley, somewhere out of sight. Sorry, I don't have any glasses. You'll have to supply them and the ice yourself."

"Ah...., OK, thank you, officer. Wow, you cops are all right after all."

"Yeah, just consider it community outreach." Antony turned and walked back toward his office, relieved that he had narrowly escaped disgracing himself and his uniform in public. He decided that if things turned out like he expected, he would quit. Then he would have plenty of time to destroy himself in the privacy of his own home.

He went back to the office and busied himself with reports. He then went to lunch with a few of his colleagues that he liked and respected. They spent the time discussing sports and women, but Antony had no interest. He just wanted to pass the time as pleasantly as he could before the fiasco at the airport. When Antony approached the international arrival gate just before 1400 his heart sank.

There was a small stage with a podium on the right in front of the barrier that the arriving passengers had to go around. Lights and cameras were already set up. Antony's colleagues were starting to line up along the back of the stage. Slarpniak was busy talking with the CBS news reporter and the camera crew. Slarpniak noticed Antony.

"Hey, Antony, come over here."

Antony's blood ran cold. He almost panicked and ran away, but he held fast.

"Now, John, this is Lieutenant Antony Rodriguez, my right-hand man. It's thanks to his great police work that we know of the suspect's whereabouts. You have to make sure he gets some of the lime-light, too."

"OK, sure, Stan. How about at some point early on, you bring him onstage and he explains how he found the suspect?"

"No! No, I'd rather not explain that. I mean, we can't let bad guys know how we find them, right?" Antony almost stuttered.

"Fine, Lieutenant, then just explain briefly how thorough we were in our investigation. I'll give you a minute. Would that be long enough?"

"Thorough?" He coughed. "Yes sir, fine, I can do that. Um... I need to use the restroom."

As he walked away, he heard John say to Slarpniak, "Well, let's get you made up. You have to look good for the show."

Antony felt like he might vomit and headed to the closest men's room. He stood in front of the mirror and looked at himself. How he regretted giving away that bottle of whiskey! It was too late now. He wondered where the commissioner was and whether he approved of the show? Maybe he was too busy with other things. What a disappointment! He really thought that the commissioner had listened to him. He was obviously wrong. But what did that text message mean?

Antony kicked himself for reading more into it. If he had

Gwendolyn's phone number, he could text and warn her. He thought of other possibilities that were even more absurd. He gave up. Antony did all he could to fight the grinding wheel of "Justice" that would soon grind another innocent person to dust. He decided to play the day out and hand in his resignation the next morning.

After he splashed some water on his face, Antony returned and took his place on the stage. The plane had already landed. When he saw Gabriella smiling and waving to him from the crowd of friends and family meeting their loved ones, he gave a wan smile in return. She pointed at the stage and gave him a quizzical look, meaning, "What's going on with all of this?" Antony just shrugged, looked away, and wished he was dead.

***

As the plane crossed low over LA and landed, Gwendolyn felt both excitement about getting all of it behind her and dread that something might still go wrong. If so, she would be trapped. As the plane slowly approached the gate, her sense of dread grew. By the time she gathered her things and stepped off the plane, she was nearly in a panic. As she walked slowly toward Immigration Control, she considered following the signs to the international transfer area, where she could buy another ticket out of the country.

Before she knew it, her feet started walking toward the transfer area. As she turned a sharp right and took three steps in that direction, two airport security men who had been following her unnoticed, grabbed her shoulders and guided her back toward Immigration. "Sorry, ma'am, but Immigration is this way."

"But I have to transfer to another plane," she protested.

"Not today you don't. Our instructions are to make sure you don't get lost on your way to Arrivals. Consider it a special service we give to some VIP passengers," one of them said with a wry grin.

Now she really was panicking. What did this mean? It could only mean that someone was waiting for her, someone she did not want to meet. They escorted her to the front of the line for the Immigration check. The young man behind the glass looked at her quizzically, stamped her passport, and waved her through. "Welcome home," he said mechanically.

They walked to the carousel and waited for her luggage to come through. While they were waiting, Gwendolyn considered her rapidly diminishing options. She was already in the US. She could try and make a run for it, but where would she go? They would probably shoot and maybe kill her.

"Look, you two have done your job. Thanks for cutting me to the front of the line. But I can take it from here. There's Customs and the exit right beyond that."

"Yes, the door is right past Customs, but so is the domestic transfer hall. Our orders are to get you out the door. After that you're on your own. Until then, just relax."

At that point, Gwendolyn knew that all that she had gone through to prove her innocence was a waste of time. She knew Gabriella had tried her hardest and had clearly been tricked into getting her to return. Just then, her cell phone sounded twice, indicating text messages had arrived.

She opened her cell phone. The first was from Giles, **I'm just outside the doors. Turn right. There's a lot of commotion. A media frenzy with the police. If you get this in time, might be better to go to international transfers and take a flight out of here until we're clear on the situation. If I don't see you, I'll assume you received this in time. Either way, we'll talk soon. Too early to say 'Welcome back'.**

The other one was from Gabriella. It read **Waiting at the arrivals gate. Turn right when you emerge. I'm wearing a red hat. Some kind of police and media circus thing here. Don't know what it's all about. Welcome back. See you soon!**

Oh, the poor dear. That police and media circus is for me. Gwendolyn murmured to herself. *Damn cell phones! Wish these texts had arrived while the plane was still taxiing.* Before she could answer either text, one of her escorts tried to grab her cell phone. "You're not allowed to use your cell phone until you've exited the Customs area." Shoving her cell phone into her purse, she sharply pushed his hand away.

A few minutes later, her luggage arrived. She put it down on the ground and paused. She considered pulling out her firearm and shooting her way out of the airport. But in the end, she just picked up her luggage and meekly walked toward Customs. Again, they went to the front of the line. Customs took her declaration print-out and waved her through.

As they walked toward the sliding doors of the exit, she could hear someone speaking with a microphone. One of the men behind her spoke into his walkie-talkie, "We have her here at the exit door. She's all yours now." As the doors opened, the two behind her pushed her out and disappeared back into the airport's interior.

***

When it was confirmed that Gwendolyn's plane had landed, Slarpniak took the stage. Turning to make sure all his men were lined up behind him, he smiled at Antony and turned back to the cameras. He tested the microphone and asked the camera crews if the lighting was fine. They made a few adjustments, then indicated he was all set. Besides the media crowd, those waiting for friends and family also crowded around, wondering what was going on.

Antony's mind was spinning in a panic. He doubted he would be coherent when his turn came to speak. He tried to think of what words to say, but he could not get past the first few. Maybe he would tell the truth and expose Slarpniak. Maybe, but did he have the resolve to pull it off? He doubted it. He would mumble something to get through the charade.

When the special VIP escort informed Slarpniak that they had Gwendolyn and were escorting her through the arrival process,

Slarpniak motioned to the cameras that he would like to start. The CBS journalist first made a few introductory remarks before the cameras turned to the stage.

"Ladies and gentlemen, I would like to have a special news briefing regarding the Robertson's murder case. Thanks to my excellent police work, well ... and to my department behind me, we have come to learn that the main suspect has indeed arrived from Moscow just now. We will take her into custody as she walks through that door in just a few minutes.

"We have built an ironclad case supported by copious evidence. Now that we'll soon have the perpetrator in custody, we can call this 'case closed.' But before I go any further, I would like to extend a special thanks to Lieutenant Rodriguez, my right-hand man."

The crowd started cheering. Antony slowly walked to the microphone. He was never one for being in the limelight. The cheering confused him even more. As he stood in front of the microphone, trying to remember what he was supposed to say, he looked out to the crowd and saw the commissioner and six other policemen approaching the stage.

The commissioner stepped onto the stage and walked over to Antony standing in front of the crowd with his mouth open. "Yes, I want to personally thank Lieutenant Rodriguez for his great police work. Without him, we would have arrested a young woman in error and destroyed her life, all because the head of the department wanted to have another 'case closed' under his belt. Hey, you officers over by the arrival doors, come over here. There'll be no arresting of arriving passengers today."

There was a gasp from the crowd. The only one who did not gasp was Slarpniak. He was red in the face, having forgotten to breathe. He was surrounded by the officers who had arrived with the commissioner.

"Yes, dear viewers, and our friends in the media, it's all true. It is extremely embarrassing to the reputation of the LAPD, but our colleague Captain Slarpniak has invited all of you here to witness an example of the LAPD at its worst. Well, I want to show you your police department at its best.

"Ordinarily, I would never do such things in front of TV cameras and crowds, but I think since you're all here anyway, we'll do it Captain Slarpniak's way. I want to officially announce that Captain Slarpniak is relieved of his duties and will be placed into custody, pending investigation of his conduct in leading the investigation into this case and many others before it.

"Replacing him will be Lieutenant Rodriguez as acting head of the Special Crimes Unit. I say 'acting,' but as we go through our department procedures, I am completely confident he will remain as the permanent head. Wait! Did I say 'Lieutenant?' My apologies, I meant to say, 'Captain Rodriguez.' Let's all applaud one of the best examples the LAPD has of an investigator serving the cause of justice and the good people of Los Angeles."

Everyone started to cheer Antony, who was not quite sure if he was even awake. Slowly a smile appeared on his face as it sunk in that the commissioner had come through for him after all. The cameras kept rolling and flashing. He was the hero of the hour in a city full of heroes, both real and acting.

***

During the applause and attention given to the stage, the sliding doors opened, and Gwendolyn was shoved out. All she could do was turn right and walk away from the doors and the commotion at the stage. She saw the red hat and waved. Gabriella ran up and gave her a great big hug. "You made it! Now, let's find a taxi and get out of here."

Giles, this time with a shining bald head and large white moustache both well-waxed, walked up, too, and gave her an affectionate pat on her back. "Let's get out of here before they change their minds. I have a getaway car waiting outside.

"You must be Gabriella. Come with us. We all have a lot to talk about. Here, dearie, let me take your bags and that useless winter coat." And they all quickly walked out the airport door, crossed the street to the parking garage, and into an idling taxi, waiting for them.

The two women got into the back seat and Giles took the front seat. The driver turned and said to Gwendolyn, "I knew you'd do what had to be done. Welcome back!"

"Al! Oh, how I'm glad to see you again! I thought I never would. What a story I have to tell."

"I'm dying to hear it. Where to, boss?" He asked Giles.

"Looks like it'll be Plan B, Al."

"The best plan there is." And he drove out of the parking garage and onto the highway.

They drove south for about three hours, first on the highway and then along the coastal road to a bungalow overlooking the Pacific Ocean – one of Giles' 'safe houses' he owned near important art markets. Gwendolyn and Gabriella talked the whole time about their shared experiences studying for their MFA's, their mutual boyfriend and all his idiosyncrasies, and many other things besides. They were like long lost friends catching up.

Gabriella also explained about her NGO in Thailand and all its important restoration work they were doing in Asia. She invited Gwendolyn to join her. Gwendolyn demurred. She just did not feel ready for something like that yet. Besides, she had to do at least one more painting in Moscow and maybe another for a client in Mexicali.

As Al parked the car, Giles turned and invited Gabriella to stay the weekend with them. They got out and walked up to the wide veranda, overlooking the ocean. The waves were crashing on the beach just steps away.

Giles pushed a cart of various bottles and ice out to join them. After he made everyone's favorite drink, he offered a toast to their most brave and intrepid friend, who had managed to prevail against all odds.

"So, now, tell us all about it."

Gwendolyn spent the next few hours telling her story and answering questions about every detail until the sun set. She concluded, "And thanks to all of you, here I am."

"You two stay here. Gwendolyn, I want you to help me cook dinner."

Once in the kitchen and out of earshot of the others, Giles told her, "We will be much more careful in the future. It was getting too easy and we were getting too careless. Of course, we never expected that our business would take such a brutal turn. Anyway, you deserve a vacation. Here is the print-out of an itinerary for that trip to Peru and Machu Picchu that you've planned for so long.

"When you return, I'll have more work. Of course, you owe Dimitri a painting and maybe Señor Garcia one, too. Maybe that is what you'll do first. I already have another project in Lisbon lined up. I know doing another project may be the furthest thing from your mind and I would totally support that decision. With what you've just been through, I would have second thoughts myself."

"No need to worry, Giles. Thanks for the trip. First Class all the way. I'm surprised you didn't hire a team to carry me up the mountain on a silk divan. After about two weeks of adventure in the Andes I'll be ready for some quiet time painting. I guess it would be too late for La Jolla?"

"Glad to hear that. Gwendolyn, you're the best there is. It's your life's calling. The world would be a sadder place without your talent being put to excellent use. La Jolla can wait. Things may change while you're away, too. Who knows? Maybe Hong Kong or Tokyo will be inviting you.

"Now for more important matters: show me how you make your famous salmon steaks."

FINAL THOUGHTS

Gwendolyn and Gabriella thank you very much for reading their story and they trust you enjoyed it. This is the result of many years of work. They ask you, dear reader, to please leave a thoughtful and considerate review on Amazon. These are especially important to the author. The link is below. If you ctrl + click on the link below or copy and paste it into your browser, you will be taken directly to the book review page.

https://www.amazon.com/review/create-review?asin=1735260606

Also, please leave a review on www.goodreads.com:
https://www.goodreads.com/book/show/54626456

In addition, the author has written another 45,000 words to this story, but for whatever reason did not include them in the final cut. These are dream sequences, expanded conversations, back stories giving characters more depth, personal anecdotes of characters' life experiences, etc.

If you ctrl + click on the link below or copy and paste it into your browser, you will be taken to a landing page on the author's website. When you sign up for the writer's newsletter, you can download some of this content for free. You can always unsubscribe later.

https://adept-mover-8713.ck.page/cf24ec5f66

This is the first book in a series of Gwendolyn, our favorite art forger. Stayed tuned for her further adventures. If you have joined our newsletter email list, we will keep you informed of all things new.

ABOUT THE AUTHOR

Born in Philadelphia, Thomas Murray is foremost a storyteller and has been writing all his life. He was a published member of the San Francisco Poet's Union and winner of Bay Area poetry and short story awards. He currently lives in a palace in Portugal.

Having lived on 5 continents for over 25 years and traveled to 88 countries, he has trained his mind to be sensitive to the wide range of nuances that make up the personalities of everyone he meets. Appreciating global cultures is fundamental to everything he writes. He includes many details about the places and characters to make the readers feel they are part of the story.

He is currently writing the next in his series about Gwendolyn, the art forger. When he is not writing, he is travelling and learning foreign languages, currently Portuguese.

You can learn more about Thomas and his writing at
https://www.thomasmurraywriter.com/

Please like his Facebook page:
https://www.facebook.com/thmurraywriter

You can contact the writer at Bastet Publishing: info@bastet.ink

Made in the USA
Coppell, TX
19 July 2021